KT-394-139

the Milliner's Secret

NATALIE MEG EVANS

Quercus

First published in Great Britain in 2015 by

Quercus Publishing Ltd
Carmelite House
50 Victoria Embankment
London EC4Y 0DZ

An Hachette UK company

Copyright © 2015 Natalie Meg Evans

The moral right of Natalie Meg Evans to be
identified as the author of this work has been
asserted in accordance with the Copyright,
Designs and Patents Act, 1988.

All rights reserved. No part of this publication
may be reproduced or transmitted in any form
or by any means, electronic or mechanical,
including photocopy, recording, or any
information storage and retrieval system,
without permission in writing from the publisher.

A CIP catalogue record for this book is available
from the British Library

PB ISBN 978 1848669116
EBOOK ISBN 978 1 78429 106 8

This book is a work of fiction. Names, characters,
businesses, organizations, places and events are
either the product of the author's imagination
or used fictitiously. Any resemblance to
actual persons, living or dead, events or
locales is entirely coincidental.

10 9 8 7 6 5 4 3 2 1

Typeset by CC Book Production

Printed and bound in Great Britain by Clays Ltd, St Ives plc

Praise for Natalie Meg Evans

'Rich in detail, this is a pacy and engaging read, full of cloak and dagger intrigue, beautiful clothes and romance' *Sunday Mirror*

'Fresh and exuberant and full of authentic detail'
Rosanna Ley, author of *The Villa*

'This story is as glamorous as the gowns it describes' *The Lady*

'A truly accomplished and delicious debut novel'
Laurie Graham

'A delicious treat of a novel. I loved the setting in 1930s Paris and I was utterly charmed by the story's delectable heroine, as she struggled to make her mark in this seductive but perilous world'
Margaret Leroy, author of *The Collaborator*

'A fascinating evocation of a great fashion house and the knife-edge the designers live on. Natalie Meg Evans is a born storyteller'
Sara Craven, bestselling writer of romances

993491230 9

Also by Natalie Meg Evans

the
Dress
Thief

Winner of the 2014 Festival of Romantic Fiction's
Best Historical Read award

Winner of the 2015 Public Book Awards

Shortlisted for the 2015 Romance Writers
of America (RWA) RITA Awards

About the Author

In the late 1970s, Natalie Meg Evans ran away from art college in
the Midlands for a career in London's fringe theatre. She spent
five years acting, as well as writing her own plays and sketches
before giving it up to work in PR. She now writes full-time from
her house in rural north Suffolk.

Natalie Meg Evans has been awarded numerous other acco-
lades for her writing including the Harry Bowling Prize (2012).
She was also nominated for a coveted Daphne du Maurier award
and was named a finalist for a Romance Writers of America
Golden Heart and RITA © award.

This book is dedicated to my sister Anna

GLOUCESTERSHIRE COUNTY COUNCIL	
9934912309	
Bertrams	03/08/2015
AF	£7.99
GCD	

This book is dedicated to my sister Anna.

Paris: Saturday, 13 July 1940

They would have been a spectacular sight in any city at any time. Bare shoulders, impish hats and upswept hair. One, a blonde in her mid-thirties, crossed the dance floor on a zephyr of sex appeal. A younger blonde walked as if she suspected the room was infested with snakes. The third, a redhead, followed like a sleepwalker.

A band pumped out a hot jazz version of 'La Marseillaise' – so loud, bottles on the bar shimmered. 'They know it's illegal to play that, don't they?' The younger blonde, whose name was Coralie de Lirac, glanced uneasily at the stage. 'Nobody's dancing.'

'It's too damn early,' said the older one. 'I can't get used to being in a nightclub at teatime.'

A month before, hours after they had marched into Paris, the Germans had moved the clocks to Berlin time and imposed a curfew that effectively sealed people into their homes. Then, realising Paris would grind to a halt, they'd relaxed the curfew to midnight. If you stayed later, you were stuck wherever you happened to be until five the next morning. But, then, Coralie reminded herself, the Nazis hadn't invaded France for the convenience of its inhabitants. 'Let's get a table,' she said. 'Don't make eye contact with anything male under ninety. Una? Keep your mind on the job.'

'Of course. Though we may have to kiss a toad or two before we find what we're looking for. Oh, don't take fright, Tilly dear.' Una McBride threw an arm round their redheaded companion, who had stopped dead at the word 'toad'. 'Coralie and I will take care of such niceties. Or "un-pleasantries", which will be closer to the truth.' Una's drawl marked her out as American.

Coralie indicated a table. 'Over there. Come on, or we'll be mistaken for the floor show.' Before they got much further, though, the club's proprietor spotted them and ushered them to a table of his choosing, closer to the music and the bar. A young man with a boxer's physique, he wore a white tuxedo and a rose in his buttonhole. 'Mesdames, enchanted. Welcome to the Rose Noire.' He kissed their hands in turn, lingering over Coralie's. 'Mademoiselle de Lirac, you have been away too long.'

'I'm flattered you noticed.' As she sat down in the chair he pulled out for her, Coralie undid and refastened her bracelet, to avoid meeting his smile. When she'd first started coming here in the summer of '37, Serge Martel had been a glamorous figure, oozing charm, taking care of customers' every whim. She'd been poleaxed when she'd heard he'd later been arrested for violently assaulting one of his female singers and sent to prison for seven years. Eighteen months he'd served. Nobody knew how he'd got out so early – who had greased the prison doors – but there was something new and unnerving in his manner. Coralie tried to catch Una's eye, but her friend was busy sizing up the clientele.

Martel, meanwhile, clicked his fingers at an elderly waiter shuffling towards them with a tray of champagne. 'Quickly, quickly, man. We have thirsty ladies here.'

The waiter called back, 'If I was younger and faster, Monsieur, I'd be in the army!' but he hurried forward nonetheless.

Félix Peyron poured vintage Lanson into three glasses, and Coralie noticed how his hands shook. An institution on boulevard de Clichy, he'd aged as though the shock of defeat and invasion had knocked the life out of him. It looked as if he'd taken to rubbing talcum powder into his cuffs to whiten them, but tonight his collar looked distinctly yellow next to Martel's tuxedo. How did Martel keep his tux so white, she wondered? It was easier to get to Heaven than to find washing soda these days, and laundries gave priority to German linen. Paris had not been bombed, like Warsaw or Rotterdam, but everything was running low: food, fuel . . . hope. For ordinary citizens, anyway. Counting the field-grey uniforms in the club, the caps with their silver eagles laid down on the best tables, Coralie formed her own conclusions about Serge Martel's recent good fortune.

Having placed the bottle in its ice bucket, Félix stepped back and bowed. 'You are welcome at the Rose Noire, Mesdames, as beauty is always welcome.'

'Why, Félix, you wicked seducer.' Una picked up her glass. 'We'll have to keep an eye on you, I can see that.'

Here we go, Coralie thought. If it wore trousers, Una fluttered her eyelashes at it, though tonight her attention was really focused on the stage. Specifically on the Romany violinist, whose sweaty curls obscured half his face and whose shirt hung off one shoulder.

'The Vagabonds are on good form tonight.' Coralie spoke lightly, watching Una's reaction.

'Aren't they just? But I wish they'd stick to jazz standards. Changing the time signature of "La Marseillaise" doesn't fool anyone.' Una blew tumbleweed kisses towards the stage, and the violinist broke off long enough to return one. Gentle applause spread around the room. People were looking their way, women in particular. Coralie saw one pull a silk flower from her evening bag and pin it into her hair, as if she felt underdressed in comparison.

Félix, lighting their table candle, chuckled. 'People see a love affair flowering and it makes them happy, though we are at war.'

'No, sir, it's our hats that are stealing the show.' Una tapped the miniature Gainsborough confection pinned over her ear, ruffling its cascade of flowers and dyed feathers. She said to Coralie, 'I promised you these bijou babies would be a sensation.'

'*I* said they would be. I wish you'd stop pinching my ideas.'

'Oops.' Una took an indulgent gulp of champagne. 'I forget I'm only the muse and not the milliner. By next week, they'll be the rage. There'll be a queue from your shop to the river.'

Coralie waited for Félix to leave. 'Assuming we're still here next week. Tilly?' Their friend was staring into her glass as if she suspected prussic acid among the bubbles. 'Drink it or put it down. People will think you've got something to be scared of.'

'Have I not?' came the whisper.

'Well . . . try not to show it.' Then Coralie said, out of the side of her mouth, 'I don't think she can do this, Una.'

'What choice does she have? We can't risk taking her home because all our houses will be under surveillance. Her only chance is "over the line into the free zone and keep moving". And before you talk of putting her on a train to the border, imagine her negotiating timetables, not to mention police checks.'

Una was right. Ottilia had to escape Paris and a car ride was her only hope. They now had to acquire by charm what they couldn't get by queuing at a police station – her name on a road-travel permit. An *Ausweis*, to give it its official, German, title.

Una extracted a Chesterfield cigarette from an elegant case, her gaze never leaving the stage where the Vagabonds were polishing off the last bars of 'La Marseillaise'. 'Stand and clap when they're done,' she instructed Coralie.

'Why don't we wave the French flag while we're at it? Then we could all get arrested and carry on the party in jail. I've never seen so many German officers in one place. I thought they hated jazz.'

'*Your* German friend liked it.'

'He was different.' *Off limits*, Coralie's tone warned. 'We shouldn't be here. Any of the regulars might recognise us.'

'Sure, but not Tilly. And, hey, we have a saying where I come from – "If you want to hide in the mustard, wear yellow."'

'We're not in the mustard but we could be in the soup.'

Una rose to clap and, reluctantly, Coralie did too. The Vagabonds acknowledged the applause, then retreated into the shadows at the rear of the stage. Ottilia seemed to have slipped into a trance. Sitting down again, Una fitted her cigarette into a cream-coloured holder and accepted a light from a man at a neighbouring table. She blew a little smoke on him. '*Merci mille fois*. I guess we'll catch up later.'

Once he'd retreated, she whispered to Coralie, 'Don't look round, but see those conquering heroes at the bar?'

'How, without looking?'

'Take my word for it, they exist. I sense they would like to buy us our next bottle of champagne. Shall we strike up a conversation?'

Coralie rolled a look their way and her stomach rose in revolt. The men wore black uniforms and lightning-strike SS insignia on their collars and they must have noticed Una smiling because their features suddenly sharpened in anticipation. Putting her hand against her mouth so that nobody could lip-read her words, Coralie said, 'They could be Gestapo. I can't be sure, but something feels wrong.'

'Gestapo means "secret police", right?' Una lit a second cigarette. 'Not *that* secret, lolling around in uniform, giving us the glad-eye. Hold your nerve and give this to Tilly.'

Coralie put the cigarette into Ottilia's fingers, finding them ice cold. Una was right, of course, it was too late to alter their plan. A car was leaving here at dawn and all Ottilia had to do was sit in it. Provided with forged documents, a change of clothing and a couple of months' worth of francs and occupation currency, she had every chance of getting to the Spanish border and freedom. All they needed was a German policeman of sufficient rank to apply his signature to the permit in Una's handbag.

All they needed . . .

Plaintive notes announced the Vagabonds' second set. The boys had changed into crimson silk shirts with Magyar sleeves and tight sashes. Their leader, Arkady Erdös, was tuning his violin, his dark gaze raking the audience. So he'd swung the forbidden 'Marseillaise'? *What do I care?* he seemed to be saying.

Trouble was, they *would* care, those rule-obsessed Germans. Coralie whispered, 'Does Arkady know he's taking an extra passenger?'

'Sure he does, and the others will find out when they snuggle up in the car together.'

Ottilia had put her cigarette straight between her lips and was drawing on it with such urgency that its end glowed amber. Forgetting to be cautious, Coralie scolded, 'You look like a factory hand after a night-shift!' Digging into her friend's beaded evening purse, she searched for the twenty-two-carat cigarette holder she'd reluctantly allowed her to bring with her. She'd just located it when breath on her shoulder made her jump. The holder flipped out of the bag, carrying with it a small, fawn-coloured booklet.

Her blood ran cold.

Serge Martel smiled down. 'Ladies, some military gentlemen have asked permission to join you, if—'

'Tell them no.' Coralie covered the booklet with her palm. 'Girls only tonight.'

'You don't understand, Mademoiselle,' Martel said silkily. 'They "ask permission" but they are not expecting a refusal. What are you hiding under your hand?'

'Nothing.'

Martel lunged and, a moment later, was flourishing the booklet. It was an identity card. Nothing unusual in that. They all carried one, by law. But this was Ottilia's *true* identity, stating her real name and country of origin. She was meant to have burned it! Simply possessing it could mean lethal trouble. And not just for her, for all three of them. Coralie said slowly, 'Monsieur Martel, please give it back to me.'

A playful eyebrow answered her. Martel shared the same platinum-gold colouring as many of the officers at his tables, but not their spare professionalism. His stock-in-trade was his affable manner, his sexy familiarity with women. Liked a joke, did Martel. As he tilted his head, Coralie saw that his nose was crooked, as if someone had once swung a granite-forced punch at him. Perhaps that was why he kept the lights in his club so low. Because he was vain. Even back in the old days, when she'd liked him better, she'd sometimes caught him preening.

In the lightest voice she could muster, Coralie said, 'You know that technically ID cards belong to the state? And they are rather private.'

'Do hand it back, Serge honey.' Una exhaled smoke. 'Don't be a cad.'

'But I wish a little peep, Madame. Maybe I am curious.'

'Remember what curiosity did to the cat.' Una delicately
stubbed out her cigarette. 'There is above-top-secret information on that card that would oblige me to kill you should you
become acquainted with it.'

Coralie shot her an appalled look.

'Secret?' Martel echoed.

'Uh-huh.' Una paused so long, Coralie was tempted to push
her off her chair. 'It will reveal our friend's date of birth and thus
her age, which she's lied about for ten years solid. We would be
forced, one way or another, to silence you.'

'Have me arrested?' Martel's gaze travelled to the black-
uniformed men three tables away. Just as Coralie was sure she'd
forgotten how to breathe, he gave a belt of laughter. 'We're
playing charades, but you win, Madame. *Voilà!*' He tossed the
card on to the table and it fell open against the candlestick. They
all saw an unsmiling snapshot of Ottilia with side-parted hair,
curls clustering over her ears.

Line by line, the card revealed her. 'Ottilia Johanna von Silberstrom. Born Berlin, 19 December 1909. Auburn hair, light
brown eyes. Profession, none.' In the upper right corner, blood
red in the flare of the candle, was stamped –

'*Juif*,' Martel said softly. 'Or *juive*, I should say.'

Ottilia began to cry. Una pulled out a fresh cigarette. She was
shaking.

'You've brought a Jewess into my club, Mademoiselle de Lirac?
You are putting my licence, my reputation, *my life* at risk.'

Coralie heard real anger and another ingredient. She couldn't
identify it until Martel began goose-stepping his fingers towards
the card. He was imitating German boots. Even in his rage, he
couldn't resist a joke. She pressed her palm down on the identity
card, wishing she could melt it with her body heat.

'Ladies? May we intrude?'

Her startled gaze met a trio of jet-black uniforms. Una's 'conquering heroes' had made their move.

'Ladies?' the German officer seemed puzzled by their silence. He was the senior, to judge from his collar insignia of three diamonds. 'Earlier you seemed very friendly.'

'You're mistaken.' Coralie's voice was a fingernail rasp. 'If we gave that impression—'

'You wish to join us? How delicious!' Una sprang back to life, though she sounded as if she'd run upstairs fast. 'Serge, dear, drag up more chairs. Don't keep the gentlemen standing.'

Martel conceded an ironic bow. A minute later, the men were seated, delivering strained gallantries. All through it, the senior officer stared at Coralie's hand.

'What do you hide there, Fräulein?' As Coralie stared back mutely, he snapped something in German. A junior officer responded by holding out his hand in silent command.

But Serge Martel got there first, snatching the card up only to drop it into the neck of Coralie's gown. 'Gentlemen, I was reprimanding this young lady for letting her *carte d'identité* fall from her bag. "Is not your identity your most precious possession?" I asked her.' He spread his arms rhetorically and only Coralie caught his complicit wink. Still playing his games. 'In these oh-so-difficult times, you risk others misapprehending not only what you are –' a glance here for Ottilia '– but also exactly *what you were*. Is that not so, Mademoiselle de Lirac?'

Coralie swallowed. 'As you say.'

The senior officer shrugged. The danger had passed.

Reassuming his professional persona, Martel promised to send up the best champagne. 'A magnum – and, *meine Herren*, oysters from the west coast –' he kissed his fingers '– on ice, with a mignonette sauce that is famed throughout Paris. You will honour me by enjoying a platter with these beautiful ladies?'

They would, it seemed. Pre-war, oysters would never have been served in July, Coralie thought scornfully. But, then, the occupiers were greedy for Parisian luxury, without understanding its subtleties. People like Martel provided it and pocketed the profit. Martel sauntered off, and the officers named themselves and gave their ranks. After which Una did too, adding, 'As you already know, to my right is Mademoiselle de Lirac—'

Coralie forced a smile.

'And Mademoiselle Dupont.'

Had Ottilia heard? Dupont was her new surname. Coralie nudged her. Honey-coloured eyes opened wide. Comprehension stole in. 'Good evening,' Ottilia said. In German.

Una covered the moment. 'Shall we give our ranks too? We're all chiefs. See? We have feathers in our hats.' She gave her doll-hat a flirtatious flick, which made the men laugh. They seemed intrigued to meet a real live American. The United States remained neutral, making Una as safe in Paris as she'd ever been.

Coralie touched Ottilia's wrist. 'The Ladies. Follow me,' she whispered. The ID card lodging uncomfortably between her breasts needed to be torn up and flushed away. She needed, too, to put Ottilia in front of the mirror and make her repeat her new name fifty times. But she also wanted to dissect Martel's words. *Exactly what you were.* 'Were' not 'are'. How much did he know about her own secret?

She was not Coralie de Lirac. She was not well-born, or French. Or even the Belgian émigrée her own identity papers declared her to be. Her origins were buried layers deep, known only to herself and one other. Or so she'd thought.

One thing was sure: the men preparing to toast them in Martel's over-priced champagne would have a simple enough term for her.

Enemy.

PART ONE

PART ONE

Chapter One

Three years earlier, south London

It was a well-aimed fist and it spun its victim into the gutter.

'That's for hiding money from me.' Jac Masson laboured for breath as sweat ran into a moustache the same grey-gold as his hair. To his daughter, staring dazedly up into a smoke-tainted sky, he resembled a lion anticipating the taste of blood. Violence always came easy to Jac, but something had pushed him over a line today, borne out by the explosion of pain in her eye.

'On your feet, lazy *pute*, and go back to earning a living.' Jac raised a foot, but before he could deliver a kick, he was hit broadside by a young man pounding towards him in a blur of shirtsleeves. They both went down but the younger man recovered first. He stood over Masson, fists bunched.

'You want a fight, you rotten Frog? Then take me on and leave Cora alone.'

'Frog?' Masson lumbered to his feet. All six feet two inches of him cast a menacing shadow. 'I'm Belgian, not French. If you don't know the difference, shut your mouth.' He sneered at the fists raised against him. 'Put those away, you scrawny Irish beanpole. I do what I want with my own.'

'His own', meanwhile, was trying to crawl out of the gutter, using Masson's waistcoat as a handhold. Masson caught the hand

and twisted it. 'Girl, I want your full wage packet at the end of the week, and I'll count every sixpence in front of you. Get back to work.'

He stalked away down Shand Street towards Tooley Street, which was clogged with slow-moving traffic and pedestrians, pausing briefly to toss an object into the road.

The young man, Donal Flynn, ran to pick it up. It was a leather purse, which he shook into his palm. Clucking in disappointment, he walked back to the gutter and hauled Cora to her feet. 'Are you all right?'

'My face . . . I must look like Joe Louis on a bad day.'

'Even if you had two black eyes, you'd never look like a heavyweight boxer.'

She managed a pained grin. 'Flyweight?'

'Just about. Lucky I was around, though. I'd just delivered a crate to the infants' school.' Donal poked a thumb at nearby Magdalen Street. It was noon and shrill playground noises reached over the factory roofs. 'I heard him bellowing your name, so I knew you were in trouble.'

'That's one way of putting it. I went down like a plank, the air knocked out of me.' She looked over her shoulder. 'Let's go, case he comes back.'

'He won't – not if he's going where he usually goes at this time. How much was in the purse?'

'Five pounds. He chased me round half Bermondsey and only caught me when I tripped. When I wouldn't hand it over, he started in on me.'

'He's got no right.'

'He's got the right, Donal. He's got the hardest punch round here and that's all the permission he needs.'

Cora Masson made use of Donal's shoulder while her lungs

recovered. Blood dripped from a cut above her eye, mixing with the grit on her cheek. Fanning out the skirts of her summer dress, she groaned. The printed rayon was smeared down one side with grime, and since they were outside a leather-curing works, she knew what that grime might contain. 'None of the factory hands came out to help. If you heard me, they must have done.'

'They're scared. People say your dad once pulled apart a man with his hands.'

'He did. He tells me about it sometimes.' She brushed the horrible image away. 'I'm supposed to be on my way to the Derby.'

Donal laughed, incredulous. 'You didn't think he'd let you have a day at the races? You'd be thinking miracles happen.' He shot a glance down Shand Street. No sign of Jac Masson. The Spotted Cow on Tooley Street had reeled him in, it seemed.

'I never told him I was going and I'd love to know who did.' Cora took Donal's arm. 'Walk with me to Bermondsey Street, then I'll be all right.'

'Back to work?' Donal sounded relieved.

'Back to the factory. The buses might still be there. They might!' she insisted, as Donal shook his head. 'They'll make a roll-call and it'll be pretty obvious I'm not on board because I'm the one who always leads the singing.' She burst into a music hall number; '"He used to be all chuckles, now he'd rather use his knuckles. I'm the girl who gets a shiner from the old man every night."'

'Save your breath,' Donal interrupted. 'I'll help you walk, but you're too much to carry. And the buses won't have waited.'

He was right. The kerb outside Cora's workplace was littered with cigarette butts and sweet papers, and a single rose torn off somebody's Sunday best boater. The mess told of a crowd surging across the yard and cramming on to the buses. The hat factory was still going full-blast, its ducts belching out fully formed clouds, which turned yellow-brown as they met the smog that always hung above Bermondsey. Its unique smell, with keynotes of resin and wet dog, was less pungent than usual, thanks to a stiff breeze. It depressed Cora to think of the banks of machinery behind those brick walls, still turning, blowing, stamping, as if the only thing that mattered to the world was more blessed hats.

Donal helped Cora to a section of low wall, taking her weight more easily than his earlier comment had suggested. He carried no spare flesh, but he was fit from pushing laundry crates around the streets six days a week. And while Cora was tall – her height and fair colouring proclaimed whose daughter she was – she was lightly built. 'Underfed' was how schoolteachers had described her during her childhood. Having made sure Cora could sit unaided, Donal went to retrieve the barrow he'd abandoned earlier.

When he returned she asked for her purse.

He handed it to her. 'Empty as a kipper's socks.'

'Not quite.' She extracted a white ticket. Number 22, which happened also to be her birthdate and her age. 'My lucky number. I knew I was going to get chosen in the raffle this year.'

Donal nodded. 'My sisters were dead jealous.'

'Well, they don't have to be now. See, that's how luck works. Fate delivers a parcel, all shiny, and it turns out to be horse sh—'

'Don't swear, Cora.'

Today, 2 June, was Derby Day, the pinnacle of the English flat-racing season and a high point in the Londoner's calendar. Since early morning, buses, trains and private vehicles had been pouring out of London, heading for Epsom Downs. Pettrew & Lofthouse, Hat Makers of Distinction, where Cora worked, had a Methodist board of directors who disapproved of horse-racing and, indeed, any form of mixed-sex gallivanting. But even they were forced to concede an annual tradition that allowed a lucky group of workers to join the outflow. This year – 1937, Coronation Year and, by definition, exceptional – they'd agreed that a hundred workers should be chosen to go, rather than the usual fifty. Last Friday afternoon, ticket number 22, with Cora's name on it, had been pulled out of Old Mr Pettrew's big top hat.

'Wouldn't have killed one of those buses to wait.' Cora gave the ticket to the breeze. 'I nipped home to change and my dad ambushed me.'

'Where'd you get that five pounds from?'

'Where d'you think?' Since Christmas, she'd worked evening shifts at the laundry owned by Donal's grandmother. Finishing at Pettrew's at six, she'd make her way to the Flynn's building on the corner of Tooley and Barnham Street to put in a further two hours' work before going home to prepare tea for her dad. 'Ten hours a week scorching my knuckles for a few bob and that bloody man thinks I'm going to drop it in his pocket?' She hurled the purse into Pettrew's yard. 'D'you ever wonder if life's worth living?'

'Here.' Donal offered his cap. 'Wipe your face. I don't mind if you get blood on it.'

'Haven't you got a hanky?'

'It's at home.'

'So what's this?' Cora flourished a square of linen.

Donal shoved his hands into his jacket and groaned because he always fell for it when she pickpocketed him. 'If you'd been alive fifty years ago, they'd have hanged you, Cora.'

'No. I'd have got away and they'd have hanged *you*.'

Strangers often took Donal for Cora's younger brother, though he was actually three years older. While she was fair, he had the black hair of Galway but, for all that, they'd grown up to look a bit alike. 'Injured innocence,' as Cora explained it, 'and soupy blue eyes.' Donal had got into the Troc-Ette Cinema on Decima Street at child's rates until he turned seventeen.

Watching her dab her cheek, he said, 'I taught you how to throw a punch back at a bully.'

'Wouldn't dare.'

'My dad never hits my sisters, only us boys.'

'*My* dad is a gentleman – breeding is all in the fists, don't you know.'

Donal chewed over this ambiguous statement, before adding, 'Dad never laid a finger on my sister Sheila, not even before she became WPC Flynn, because she's halfway to being a saint. He threatens to wallop Marion and Doreen all the time, when they stay out late with their young men. Never does, though.'

A pair of motor charabancs were pulling out of a factory opposite, open backs crammed with women hanging on to their hats, men in flat caps and jaunty cravats. Another race-day convoy. Someone hoisted a banner bearing the legend 'Better stick with Bennett's Glue'.

Cora felt a wrenching jealousy. What must it be like to enjoy the moment, without having to store up excuses for daring to have a good time? She yelled above the growl of engines, 'I hope you stick to your seats.'

'We're the ones stuck,' Donal said glumly. 'Least you had the chance to go. My gran doesn't believe in holidays except on a saint's day, and only if it's an Irish saint called Patrick. Then she only gives us half a day and the halves get shorter every year. Same dirty streets, same dirty river. That's my life.'

Cora squinted into a sky that was blue with promise behind

the smoke. 'When the sun shines on the righteous, it rains on us.' She tugged his arm. 'Let's go anyway.'

But not in a torn rag of a dress. 'I'll have to borrow something off one of your sisters,' she informed Donal. They were walking by way of Tooley Street to Barnham Street, where they both lived, though at different ends. Donal needed to return his barrow to the laundry and put on a jacket. 'We'll sneak in and out,' she told him. 'By the time anybody realises we've gone, we'll be on the train to Epsom Downs.'

As they walked up the passageway to Flynn's Laundry, Donal pointed out that they were both broke. You couldn't go racing on less than ten shillings. As for borrowing a dress, Marion and Doreen were 'fearful protective' of their wardrobes. Sheila, he conceded, didn't care for clothes and dressed like a policewoman even when she was off duty. 'But you wouldn't want any of her battle-axe outfits.' He unlatched a gate, adding, 'If Gran sees us, I shall ask to go. I'm no good at lying.'

'Better make sure she doesn't see us, then.' Following Donal into a yard enclosed by low buildings, Cora ducked under a line laden with men's combinations, thirty pairs or more. Must be a new ship in. Many of Flynn's customers were seamen whose vessels came into Rotherhithe docks from Hong Kong, India and the South Seas. A contrary place, Bermondsey. A backwater on the doorstep of the world. Seeing movement in the window of one of the laundry houses, she told Donal to park his barrow quickly. Why did it have to squeak? Too late.

A woman in a green apron emerged from an outbuilding. Her sleeves were rolled, her white hair twisted up so tightly it stretched her eyes and the cords of her neck. Cora never saw Granny Flynn without thinking of a spring onion.

Granny glared at Donal. 'One hour to deliver one load?'

Taking in Cora, she mumbled something unintelligible. Shortage of teeth and an indelible Galway accent made Granny hard to follow even in these parts where a third of the population was immigrant Irish.

Donal translated: 'She's asking if you've come to help out.'

'Blast that,' Cora said. 'The heaviest thing I want to lift today is a race card.'

'I could use an extra pair of hands at an iron.' Granny eyed Cora's torn sleeve, her grazed arms. 'Even if they are both left hands.'

'Sorry, Granny.' Cora's first job had been here, when she was fourteen. Out of school on the Friday, arms deep in suds on the Monday. The best thing she could say for Pettrew & Lofthouse, it had got her away from endless washday. She'd never disliked Granny Flynn, and the other women had been friendly, but lifting sopping blankets out of boilers in fuggy steam all day had thickened her lungs. Her hands had peeled from the caustic, and the skin between her fingers had become so raw, it had bled.

She'd asked once, back then, 'Why should I be in agony so other buggers can have clean sheets?'

After clipping her ear for swearing, Granny had answered, 'Because you're working class, which means all work and no class.'

Cora had called at Pettrew's the day after and asked to see the hiring manager. Beavering on the production line at a hat-maker's wasn't much of a step up socially, but at least her hands had healed.

She said now to Granny, 'Any other time I'd be thrilled to wield a flat iron in your company.' *Be polite.* She might need more casual work the way things were going. 'But I'm off to hobnob with the upper crust.'

Granny gave a cackle. 'You won't have seen yourself in the mirror, then?'

Cora muttered to Donal, 'That green dress Sheila wore at the St Patrick's Day party here, has she still got it?'

Donal shrugged uneasily but Cora led the way to the main house, saying, 'It'll be back in her cupboard before she's finished her shift. She'll never know.'

Donal closed the kitchen door behind them. 'She'll know. Sheila always knows who ate the last biscuit or who gave the gas money to a bookies' runner. And, Cora, she'd say you ought to go back to work, like your dad ordered.'

'Donal, if you ever want to do more than push a barrow down dirty streets, you need to stop taking orders. There's a world out there and you've got a brain. You were the best at maths in school by a mile. You're good-looking, too, when you're not cocking your head and staring at your boots.'

'Let's see to that eye of yours.' Donal ushered her down into a scullery. At weekends, the Flynn household was as noisy as a zoo, but today the younger children were at school and everyone else was working. Donal's mother had died twelve years ago, in the same year Cora's mother had left home. Molly Flynn, it was said, had dropped dead from exhaustion, ten babies plus her wash-house work. Whereas Cora's mother, Florence Masson, had chucked her bloomers over a ship's mast. Which was a fancy way of saying she'd scarpered with a sailor.

Inaccurate, as it happened. Florence had left England with a man called Timothy Cartland. An actor, not a mariner. They'd gone to New York to make their fortune on Broadway.

'I've just realised,' Cora said, as Donal dipped a napkin into cold pump water and added a slosh of witch-hazel. 'It's twelve years to the day since my mum left. We went to the races, she stalked off after a row and we never saw her again.'

'Put this to your eye and I'll see if the range is hot. You could use a cup of tea.'

The pad stung, and she shouted after Donal, 'I reckon Mum had the right idea. Off to the Derby and vamoose. I'll do the same one day, jump aboard a ship and go.' She realised too late that Granny Flynn was standing halfway down the scullery steps.

'Go to sea, is it, Cora? I've heard you like the company of sailors.'

Donal's face appeared behind the old woman's shoulder. 'Gran, don't. That's how rumours start.'

'It's how other things start, too, and I'll say what I like in my own house.' Granny came all the way down and pulled the pad from Cora's eye, sucking a breath through her gums. 'Swelling like a bantam's egg. Give it an hour, you'll be seeing the world soft-boiled. Am I to take it you're off to the races?' When Cora confirmed it, she sniffed. 'Where does the money come from?'

Cora put a hand under her skirt. She fiddled with her stocking top before bringing her hand out triumphantly and waving notes at Donal, who was blushing and staring at the floor. 'Five quid, still warm. Count them, Donal.'

He did. 'Where'd you get it?'

'I stuck my hand in my dad's pocket.'

Granny looked scandalised. 'Stealing from your own father?'

'He was using me as a punch-bag at the time.'

Donal burst out, 'Had he seen, he'd have kicked the head right off you. And me.'

Cora grinned. 'He didn't, though, did he? We can have the day of our lives on a fiver. Give in, Donal.'

Granny folded her arms, the physical embodiment of the word

'no'. 'You'll hand it all back, Cora Masson. What's yours is legally your father's and you owe him your duty.'

Cora regarded the old woman thoughtfully. Granny liked to take a moral stand, but her sermons were generally strongest on Mondays, the day after she'd made her confession at church to Father O'Brien. This far into the week, the religious starch had usually been steamed out of her. 'Wrong on both counts. I'm over twenty-one. And if we're talking about conscience, yours should tell you to give Donal the rest of the day off.' She shoved a wispy curl behind her ear. She could go alone, but where was the fun in that? 'Derby Day is St Patrick's other holiday. There'll be more Irishmen on the Downs than you'd find in the Emerald Isle.'

Granny planted her fists. 'I need Donal here. We're flat out.'

'You're always flat out. And he needs a few rays of sunshine – look at his cheeks. What's one afternoon?' Cora sensed Granny was weakening. 'We might back a winner, bring home a fortune. Then you could retire to the primrose pastures of Penge or Catford and never have to look a pair of grubby combinations in the eye again.'

Granny leaned forward. 'Think you'll escape these streets, girl?'

'Why not? My mum did.'

'So they say, but you're like all the rest of us, stuck like a hobnail in a crack of the pavement.' She peered at Cora's ruined stockings, then at her shoes, with the little bit of heel that had stopped Cora outrunning her father. 'I'll say this for Florence Masson, she was always bandbox neat. Dainty, kept her figure. The consequence of being a retired actress, I suppose.' Granny pronounced 'actress' as if it were an indecent, foreign word.

'She wasn't retired, not in her mind. She was always saying, "when I return to the stage". But you're right. The day she left, she looked like a bunch of spring daffodils, for all the sky was raining its eyes out.'

Granny's reply got stuck behind her remaining good tooth. Stumping up the scullery steps, she jerked a thumb at Donal. 'Have your day out and I suppose you'd better take him. He'll be company for you on the walk home when you've lost every penny.'

As the eldest of the Flynn girls and a steady wage-earner, Sheila had her own bedroom. She was no beauty – people hinted that she'd joined the police force because the only way she could get a man was to arrest one. So it was with little expectation of finding anything worth wearing that Cora tried the wardrobe.

Locked, but the key was easily found on top of the wardrobe. 'Lack of imagination, WPC Flynn.'

Then again, Sheila wouldn't be expecting anyone as tall as herself to be searching. Prepared to find serge skirts and limp cardigans, Cora gasped at the rainbow hoard. There were lace stoles, real silk evening dresses, some embroidered with metal thread. A gown of magenta velvet took up a quarter of the space.

The labels were from leading London department stores: Harrods, Debenham & Freebody, Liberty. The emerald-green dress, pushed to one end of the rail, was very much the poor cousin.

When she slipped it over her head, Cora was instantly enveloped in exotic perfume. Well, well. If she'd been asked to guess Sheila's favourite scent, she'd have said lily-of-the-valley or carbolic soap, not hot-house flowers and spice.

The green dress had ruched sleeves wide at the shoulder, drawing attention to a belted waist and slim hips. Cora twirled in front of a dressing-table mirror. Not bad, bit dull. What about one of those bright artificial silks? But Donal was pacing the landing outside, terrified his sister might come home unexpectedly. So Cora helped herself to rayon stockings and a pair of cream crocheted gloves. Meeting her reflection, she searched for the guilt that should have been there. It wasn't. Sheila Flynn had enough dresses to clothe a chorus line. On a constable's wages? Cora thought of her own wardrobe: a couple of work outfits, a winter suit and the dress she'd just taken off. Could saintly Sheila be taking back-handers? Or maybe she stole from shops. 'Cora, get a move on!' Donal hissed through a crack in the door.

Hat. She'd lost hers, a cheap straw with artificial cherries, running away from her dad. She worked surrounded by hats, hat-makers and hat-trimmers, yet had never had a decent one of her own. Fact was, she couldn't afford Pettrew's prices and they wouldn't let you buy the rejects. Those got taken off to be pulped.

Another reason not to feel guilty, Cora told herself as she fetched a pink and grey hatbox off the top of the wardrobe. Ten to one it was Sheila Flynn who'd ratted on her. Sheila often called at Jac Masson's workshop after nightshifts at Dunton Road Police Station. They'd share a pot of tea in Jac's shed at the railway end of Shand Street, and Jac would pass on titbits of news. Who was stealing scrap iron around the place? Who'd just acquired a motor-van or a pair of shiny boots he couldn't rightly afford? As a foreigner, Jac didn't subscribe to the Londoner's code that said you'd rather cut out your own tongue than nark to the police. People hinted that Jac and Sheila were sweet on each other, but that couldn't be right . . . Jac must be thirty years older. No, it was a business deal. Tea and information.

Sheila doubtless dished out tales about Cora. How else had Jac known about the race-day ballot, and about her ironing money? Feeling quite justified in her theft, Cora lifted the lid off the hatbox and made a noise of disgust. The mound of black feathers inside looked more like a dead crow than a hat. Lifting it out, she found it had a label stitched into its sisal lining. La Passerinette, Paris.

Her eyes widened. Paris was where she went in her dreams. Her favourite films of all time were set there and sometimes, when life scraped like a rusty wheel, she'd imagine herself as Jeanette MacDonald being fitted for new clothes by Maurice Chevalier and singing 'Isn't It Romantic?' in harmony with him. Cora put on the hat in front of the mirror, tilting it forward until it obscured her injured eye. It had a fishnet veil that dropped down to her top lip. Suddenly, the hat made sense. Not a dead crow, but a fantasy of iridescent feathers. It wasn't Cora Masson staring back at her, but a stranger whose face was composed of striking planes. She sucked in her cheeks and murmured huskily, 'She boards a train, blind to other passengers who gasp at her beauty and shake their heads, recognising the sultry—'

'Have you gone nuts?' Donal demanded from the doorway.

'I'm being Marlene Dietrich in *Shanghai Express*.'

'You sound like my sister Doreen after she had her tonsils out. Please, let's go.'

Her last act was to grab a handbag off a hook on the door. Olive green, cheap leather, but she needed something to carry her winnings home in.

As the train pulled out of London Bridge station, she and Donal travelling third-class to save money, Cora studied her borrowed feathers in the window's reflection. There'd be a price to pay for this. There always was.

Ticket number 22 had been pulled from the hat in the company canteen last Friday, during the afternoon break. Pettrew

& Lofthouse was progressive, allowing staff twenty minutes off during the long second shift. Giant teapots would pour out strong tea, resembling a line of silver swans dipping their beaks to feed. You could choose either a currant bun or a slice of bread-and-butter with your tea. When her winning ticket was pulled out, Cora had pushed back her chair, her bun half eaten, and struck up a Charleston in the middle of the floor. It was a dance her mother had taught her, and it lived inside her feet, ready to burst out at the smallest provocation. Scuffing and kicking, flashing her hands towards the iron-vaulted ceiling, she'd played to her audience. Even the cool regard of Old Pettrew and his fellow directors had failed to quell her.

'Go on, Cora, give us a shimmy!' her friends had roared, the moment she began to flag, and she would have done, had she not been brought out of her trance by a loud 'Ahem, Miss Masson?' It was her section forelady, Miss McCullum, indicating Cora should precede her out of the door.

In her private office, Miss McCullum had said, 'Cora, that display was most improper.'

'I know, miss, but I'm celebrating.'

'Quite so, but Pettrew & Lofthouse holds to the values of its founders. Singing quietly while we work is one thing. Impressions of Josephine Baker over the teacups is not what I expect from you.'

Cora conceded, though she really wanted to say, *Then you don't know me very well, do you?*

There was a brief silence while Miss McCullum consulted some recess of her mind. 'You have won a place on the Derby Day outing, but are you certain you wish to take an afternoon's holiday?'

Cora blinked. What a stupid question.

'We've been keeping an eye on you, Miss Lofthouse and I.'

Miss Lofthouse was sister to the joint-chairman and a director. 'What sort of eye?' Cora demanded warily.

'We consider you a candidate for promotion, as demonstrated by the recent discretionary pay increase we awarded you.'

'Oh.' Cora didn't understand 'discretionary', but last month, four shillings extra had appeared in her pay packet. Kindly meant, no doubt, but not as welcome as the forelady might imagine. News of pay rises always leaked out and favouritism was poison in a close-knit environment. As for promotion, that meant walking up and down the aisles, checking her friends' work, carrying the can for their mistakes as well as her own. All for a bit of extra money she'd likely never see anyway.

Miss McCullum continued crisply, 'I tell you in confidence, Cora, that my position in ladies' soft felt may soon fall vacant.' A raised eyebrow invited response, but Cora couldn't think of one. Everyone knew that foremen and ladies had to have been millinery apprentices, schooled in the arts of blocking and fine finishing. Pettrew & Lofthouse hats adorned the heads of politicians, lords and ladies, even royalty. The directors were gentlemen, arriving for work in chauffeur-driven cars – except for Miss Lucilla Lofthouse, who came on a bicycle. But that, apparently, was because she'd been a suffragette and was still making a point. Supervisors spoke with rounded vowels and correctly applied aitches. And they dressed the part. Take Miss McCullum's cigar-brown costume and lace collar, the spectacles suspended from a thin gold chain. Whenever she walked into the makeroom, where Cora worked, everyone stopped talking.

'I've only ever worked on ladies' felt and woven straw,' Cora blurted out. 'And I never could block a hat, not one anybody would want on their head, because I'm cack-handed.' She waved her left hand. 'They forced me to be right-handed at school, so now I can't do anything properly, not even peel a spud. A potato, I mean. And I've never touched buckram nor sisal, nor plush. I'm just a trimmer. I couldn't be forelady.' *I'm not a lady*.

'Indeed, you are many years from such a position. I was about to say that Miss Lofthouse and I have considered creating a subordinate post, that of assistant forelady, and we consider you suitable for such a role. You would learn on the job.'

What had that got to do with her going to the Derby, Cora wondered? The question must have shown because Miss McCullum said, 'Absenting yourself in pursuit of rowdy pleasure ill befits a future supervisor. You will wish to withdraw from the party, I dare say.'

Seriously? In talking of future promotion, the forelady was dangling a very thin jam sandwich on the end of a very long fishing rod, whereas the Derby was six days off, and the best fun Cora was likely to have all year. She wouldn't say it to Miss McCullum, but the work here was stupefyingly boring. Always the same grosgrain ribbon to work with, always in navy, gravy or bottle green. Once in a while, a new line might demand a rosette or even a tiny feather, but Pettrew's hats were essentially dull. Oh, yes, smart and hard-wearing, but dull. That was the point of them.

'There's a world out there, Miss McCullum, with wonderful colours in it. I want a bit of time off, so I get to see them.'

The eyes beneath the level brows turned cool. All Cora knew of the very private Jean McCullum was that she'd followed the Lofthouse family from Scotland when they bought out the old firm of Pettrew's. Miss McCullum shared the family's unadorned Methodism, so would never raise her voice or resort to intemperate language, but she could convey a sermon just by looking at you. And the brown dress made Cora feel that her own red polka-dot and yellow cardigan was shouting something undignified.

'By "time off", Cora. I presume you mean "freedom"?'

'Nothing wrong with that.'

'No.' Miss McCullum clicked her tongue. 'Under firm regulation, freedom is a good thing. And this is my point. Name another respectable trade where a girl such as yourself can rise to a level where she may eventually draw a salary of two hundred pounds a year. As much as a well-paid man. Don't settle for a life of low-paid manual labour, Cora. Seize your chances.'

'I do seize them.'

'The *right* chances. I began at the milliner's bench too. And Miss Lofthouse is one of only a handful of female board directors in the whole of London, and she's a trained milliner. You could be a forelady by the age of thirty. You'd not run from that?'

Cora didn't know. Her thirties felt centuries off. But Derby Day was here now. Her gaze strayed to the window, to a vista of scudding clouds even factory smoke couldn't dim. Who liked rules, except the people who made them? Everyone had ideas about what she should do with her life and they all led her through the factory gate. She knew Miss McCullum was being kind and didn't want to seem ungrateful. So why not tell the truth? 'I fancy my chances in Paris, Miss McCullum.'

'Paris? Goodness, why?'

'*Love me Tonight.*'

'I beg your pardon?'

'It's a film. And you have to see *Roberta* with Irene Dunne. So glamorous. The dresses, the hats . . . I'd be in Heaven in Paris.'

'Films are not real life, Cora.'

'Oh, they are, Miss McCullum. They're other people's lives, that's all.'

'You really want to live somebody else's life?'

'Every minute of every day.'

Miss McCullum blinked. 'I don't think you can have thought it through, dear. Assuming you arrived in Paris, what would you do?'

'I can sing a bit, and you've seen me dance. I could go on the stage, like my mum.'

'No. You aren't small or pretty enough.'

Cora nearly opened her mouth to point out that that hadn't stopped Joan Crawford, but in the end, said nothing. Being an actress was a red herring. She didn't know what she wanted to do with her life, only that she couldn't bear the idea of growing old at a workbench, or marrying some bloke called Albert or Bill just to get away from her dad's fists and the factory whistle.

Now, as the Epsom-bound train chugged past the cramped backyards of New Cross, Forest Hill, Croydon, Cora reran that conversation and finished it: 'The thing is, I don't *want* to stay at Pettrew's. I want to go to Paris. Or Timbuktu or China. Anywhere, Miss McCullum. But I haven't got the courage. I'm a coward, see, like Granny Flynn says: stuck like a hobnail in a crack in the pavement.'

Donal and Cora bought passes for the public grandstand. Standing only, but you got a decent view of the racecourse. The other side of the white rails was The Hill, where the public roamed for free, a mosaic of spectators, cars and open-top red double-deckers. Sunlight bounced mercilessly off metal and Cora was glad of her shadowy veil. 'What race is next?' she asked Donal. A squadron of jockeys was cantering towards the backfield.

Donal checked his card. 'That'll be the two thirty going down to the start. Half an hour to the big one.' The betting rings were heaving, tic-tac men signalling coded messages. Odds were being bellowed, starting prices chalked up, rubbed out, rewritten. Each time the price of a horse changed, a roar went up. She'd given Donal two pounds. They'd each bought their fares and grand-stand passes and kept back a few shillings to feed themselves. Everything she had left was going on one horse, to win.

'Here's the plan,' she shouted, over the roar that heralded the start of the two thirty. 'You get us a drink and something to eat and I'll maggot into the crowd. I'm going to find out which horse is the best outsider for the Derby Stakes.'

'Outsider? Are you sure?'

'I like outsiders, Donal. I feel like one myself.'

As Cora got near the runners' and riders' board, the two-thirty thundered past. Deafening, and when the winners were declared, the crowds went wild. It was a quarter of an hour before the boards were wiped clean and the Derby runners were chalked up. She read the list.

Cash Book and Perifox were joint favourites at seven to one. After that, it was Le Ksar and Goya II at nine to one. Cora rolled their names on her tongue, waiting for the jolt that would tell her she'd pronounced the name of the winner. Her eye stopped at number ten: Mid-day Sun. She felt . . . not electricity, just an emotion, the roots of which she couldn't find.

Mid-day Sun was on at 100 to seven, as was a filly, Gainsbor-ough Lass. Those were mile-long odds. She looked for Donal, but all she could see were men and women scanning their race cards. She'd have to make her own choice. Her eye kept going back to Mid-day Sun. One hundred to seven, *if* he won. For a stake of two pounds ten, she'd win . . . she felt her brain grinding . . . between thirty and forty pounds. That would get her away from her father and keep her while she found herself a more pleasant job. *Cora, you can stop getting your hopes up*, she admonished herself. The chance of Mid-day Sun winning the Derby was about the same as her dad coming home with a fish-and-chip supper and a big bunch of flowers. Even so, she couldn't shift the fizzy-sick feeling in her stomach.

A man in a group in front of her was saying that his choice, Perifox, came from Kentucky and that he liked the going firm. Kentucky . . . was that a posh name for Kent? Cora dug her heels into the grass. It felt pretty firm. What about Mid-day Sun? Did he like firm going? She stamped and a yowl filled her ear. She turned to see a man in full morning dress hopping in apparent agony. She moved towards him, ready to catch his top hat if it fell off. He glared at her. 'Why the devil did you stamp on my foot?'

'To know if the ground was hard or not.'

'The heel of your shoe is, I promise you.'

She was desperate to apologise, but all she managed was an inappropriate grin. He was ridiculously good-looking. Light-haired, brown eyes, with a glint of green. Hazel, a colour she'd always craved for herself. His mouth was long and firm with the promise of humour, though she'd have to wait for proof as his teeth were clenched. It said volumes about her background that she was admiring a man for being well-shaven and clean, but so it was. How often did she look at a man's collar and find it pearly white, unless it had just come through Granny Flynn's laundry? How often did she see a suit that fitted, none of the seams gasping for breath? A dark grey morning coat, top hat with a black band – good enough to be from Pettrew's – and striped twill trousers advanced the impression of good breeding. The most striking thing about him was his beauty. *Beauty.* She'd never used that word about a man, ever. Suddenly, she had a feeling she'd seen him before.

'There is something amusing about me?' He spoke in the clipped way the Pettrew's directors did when they stood up in their silk plush hats to address their workers.

'Sorry, I was trying to pick a horse.' It came out as 'an 'orse'. You can take the girl out of Bermondsey . . . Her mother, whose finest hour had been playing Gwendolen Fairfax at the Prince of Wales Theatre, had taught her that to speak nicely, you must start by lifting your nose as if smelling a rose, and saying, 'an egg'. Saying 'an egg' now would make her sound barmy. *Just don't say anything beginning with H*, she told herself. 'I didn't realise anyone was behind me.'

'Did you not think in a crowd there would be someone behind you?'

'I was trying to picture the winning . . . er, runner. To feel a spark.' Her new, cultured voice seemed to do the trick. The man looked intrigued.

'Did you? Feel a spark, I mean?'

'Sort of.' She was feeling one now and it wasn't just this man's looks doing it: it was his smell, reminiscent of empty spice jars. 'I get it in my belly. I mean, stomach. I mean, in my middle.' She patted the place. 'I fancy Mid-day Sun.'

He glanced at her waist and, for the first time, smiled. She'd tucked her gloves into her belt, not wanting a barrier between her hand and her borrowed bag. Thieves were rife at race meetings. The gloves had curled over, like begging paws.

'Interesting. To say he's unfancied would be an understatement.'

'Stupid choice, probably,' she agreed.

'Not wholly. He won at Lingfield, at the Derby Trial Stakes, so he's proved himself over a mile and a half in good company.'

'Blimey, has he?' Lingfield wasn't Newmarket or Ascot. It wasn't even York . . . Actually, Cora couldn't have found Lingfield on a map if her life depended on it, but that didn't matter. Mid-day Sun had form, so her funny feeling wasn't so funny. 'I wouldn't be surprised if he turned out to be a bomber.'

'Now you've lost me – bomber?'

'Comes from behind.' As Cora spoke, an auburn-haired woman did just that, slipping a cream-kid hand under the man's arm. With a fleeting glance for Cora, she said something in a breathy voice. Not in English, in German.

Lots of foreigners came to Pettrew & Lofthouse, and because she'd learned French from her father, Cora was often asked to show them around the make-room. French was the language of the hat trade, but she'd picked up a smattering of German, too, because some of the best Berlin department stores regularly sent their buyers.

So she knew that the woman disliked being in a crowd and hated the smell of frying food. And when she gazed up at her companion and murmured, '*Nicht so, Dietrich?*' Cora sucked in her cheeks, assuming they were saying how much like Marlene Dietrich she looked. It was only when the man replied without looking at her that Cora realised *he* must be called Dietrich.

He hadn't sounded foreign. Though, now she thought of it, he did choose his words carefully, the way a stamp collector picks rare pieces from a box with tweezers. It explained why they were there, alongside the suburban matrons and stripy-suited commercial men, instead of swanning in the members' enclosure. Poor saps must have bought the wrong passes.

The man called Dietrich recalled Cora's presence. He said, in English, to his companion, 'This young lady thinks Mid-day Sun could be a bomber.'

Auburn brows lifted. 'Really?' She sounded bored. Like many women there today, she wore white from head to toe. A silver

fox collar made a sumptuous frame for her face and her clutch
coat revealed a dress of snowy chiffon. She wore silk stockings
and kid shoes that the grass hadn't yet marked. A triple row of
pearls closed the gap between glove and sleeve. As for her hat,
Cora couldn't take her eyes from it. White beaver belly, its crown
formed two V-shaped peaks, like yacht sails at different points on
the horizon. Or, if you were being fanciful, it was a trifle topping. It would have looked silly on virtually every woman in the
world, but on this one, it was almost perfect.

Almost. Impelled by an impulse she couldn't explain, Cora
spoke: 'Your hat's crying out for a brim. It's too narrow to balance
your collar. Either you need more hat, or less fur.'

Had they been anywhere else, deafening silence would have
greeted this remark, but as the Derby runners were now parading
past the stands, her impudence went no further than Dietrich
and the woman, who asked in heavily accented English, 'You
are a hat-maker?'

'Yes . . . I'm – I'm a milliner. Quite a famous one, actually.'

'Indeed?' The woman appraised Cora's black-feathered hat so
intently, she wondered if it had slipped back, revealing her bad
eye. She knew it when the woman said, 'You have had an accident, perhaps?'

'I tripped getting out of my automobile.'

'And you were in Paris recently?'

'I . . . um . . . not that recently.'

'Because your hat comes from La Passerinette, in boulevard
de la Madeleine.'

Cora felt the ground shift. How did the woman know? 'Boulevard . . . as you say. I don't always wear my own hats.'

'Why not? Surely, at the Epsom races, a good milliner wears
her own designs.'

'No.' Cora dug for a credible reason. 'I'm here incognito. That's why I'm not in the members' enclosure. Ladies are always wanting the hat off my head.' Only she said "at off my 'ead'. *An egg, a bloody egg*.

'If you are well known, I will have heard of you. What is your name?'

She could have said Cora Masson. But 'Cora' had always felt like a charwoman's name and 'Masson' was marred by her dad's knuckles and his drunken breath. A swift glance at the runners' board showed her Le Grand Duc at odds of 100 to nine. When he wanted to impress the butcher or the coalman, her father had his bills sent to 'Jacques Masson de Lirac', claiming descent from some ancient French dukedom. If he could pretend, so could she. 'My name is Coralie de Lirac.' 'Coralie' had been her mother's pet name for her.

'You have a card?' the woman asked.

'A race card?'

'Business card. I am curious about this La Passerinette hat. I have – I *had* – one very similar and would like to know if somebody is copying it.'

Anticipating questions she couldn't answer, Cora improvised, 'I dropped my cards when I fell out my motor-car but tell me your address and I'll send you one in the post.' The anticipated snub finally arrived.

'One presents cards only to social equals. Dietrich,' the woman touched her companion's arm, 'I am very bored now. Take me away.'

Donal chose that moment to return, clutching jars of ginger beer and two paper parcels reeking of fried onion.

'Extra mustard, Cora!' he shouted, over the heads of the crowd. 'By the way, some geezer in the queue reckoned the

Kentucky horse is a banker.' Reading her crushed expression, he stared hard at the departing man in immaculate morning dress, the lady in her silver fur, and blared, 'Ruddy hell, *they* didn't try to pickpocket you, did they?'

Cora took a long swig of ginger beer. Its sweet gassiness made her feel empty and sick at the same time. Too long since breakfast. Donal pointed at the runners' board. 'Perifox. He's the one.' When she sniffed, he said, 'He's an American champ, goes like a bullet.'

'If he's come over on an Atlantic liner, he'll be wanting a lie-down. Epsom's a rogue's course. Any horse can win if it's ridden well and has a bit of luck. I'm backing Mid-day Sun.'

Dropping fried onion in shock, Donal listed all the reasons why she was idiotic, ending with '*And* he's owned by a woman. Women don't win classic races.'

'She isn't running, is she? She's not riding either. She just owns him.'

Donal's face closed. 'Women don't own Derby winners.'

'Says who?'

'Everyone.' He cast his head from side to side, searching for a reason. 'Women can't buy the best horses – they never have enough money. And men won't sell them good horses because women pick horses like they pick hats. They want the chestnuts and the greys or the ones they feel sorry for. It's a man's game. Men ride, men train, men win.'

That sounded like life in a nutshell, but Cora flicked a speck of mustard into Donal's face. 'Times are changing.' *I could be a supervisor at Pettrew & Lofthouse, on two hundred pounds a year*. And a woman could be leading the winner into the ring in half an hour's time. Anything can happen. She belched delicately behind her hand, the ginger beer doing its usual trick. She still felt sick, and still hungry. 'I need to dash – Donal, you put my money on for me.' She handed him two pounds ten shillings. 'On the nose, to win. Don't go all soft and do an each-way.'

'You'd be mad not to back him each-way. He could come third, just, but he won't win. You'll lose the lot.'

'My money, my risk. You're going with Peri— What's his name?'

'I might. Or the one with the Russian name.'

'Le Ksar?'

'That's it. But probably Goya eye-eye.'

'What?' Cora checked her race card. 'Goya the Second, nitwit. You want to give the bookies a laugh?'

Donal gave a superior sniff. 'You never give the bookies the horse's name, Cora, only the number.'

'Yeah, well, get in that queue. I've got to run.'

Cora was violently sick in the ladies' lavatory. After she'd pulled the chain, she leaned against the cubicle wall. Her tumble in Shand Street had finally caught up with her. After washing her hands and rinsing her mouth at the basin, she went out into sunshine that seemed to have doubled in strength. By the time she found Donal, it was eight minutes past three, but the race had been delayed.

'Couldn't get the horses in a line.' Donal threw her an odd glance. 'You all right?'

'Did you put my money on?'

'I still think you're mad. To be honest—' Someone bumped into him and, as wary as Cora of thieves, he clamped his arms to his sides. A roar like a flock of invisible birds rose from the blind side of The Hill. The Derby Stakes was under way.

The first five and a half furlongs were run on the far side, so they couldn't see a thing. Then everyone was looking to the left. Those with binoculars raised them. An instant later, the field was peeling round Tattenham Corner. Someone adept at reading jockeys' colours cried out, 'It's Renardo, Fairford and Le Grand Duc.'

Cora and Donal stared at each other in dismay.

'Fairford's leading,' their informant shouted. Cora strained to catch the first sight of horses coming onto the straight, only Donal was jumping up and down because the cry had gone up that Goya II was challenging Fairford for the lead. 'Go on, my son!' he bellowed.

'Where's mine?' Cora wailed. 'Where's Mid-day Sun?'

'Fairford's lost it,' somebody shouted. 'It's going to be Goya the Second or Le Grand Duc.'

'It's Perifox!' somebody else countered.

'Goya!' Donal beat the air to drive his horse home. 'I backed him nine to one.'

Cora felt sick again. Donal was right: she was a sentimental sop who had no place on a racecourse. But she'd been so sure.

Horses swept past, two bays locked in a private challenge.

'Who's won? Donal, who's won?'

'It could have been Goya. Holy Mother, I'll buy myself a bicycle if he's done it.'

'Who was coming up on the outside?' But nobody could answer her, not even the know-all behind them. It was a painful wait, until a new roar went up and the winner's name appeared on the board.

Cora's shriek hurt even her own ears. 'He's done it! Mid-day Sun! I could kiss him. I'm going to kiss you!' Reaching for Donal, she was surprised to find herself grabbing a complete stranger. Donal was already heading away, through the crowd.

*

Mid-day Sun first, Sandsprite second, Le Grand Duc third. When Cora finally collared Donal, his face resembled cold suet pudding. 'Oh, God,' he said.

She gave him a hug. 'I'll share my winnings, then you can have another go. The way my luck's going, we'll win enough to get you two bicycles.' She'd have danced a jig had Donal not been a deadweight. So she jigged on her own. 'Miss McCullum can stick her promotion. I can give notice. I'll leave home tomorrow. What's that poor bookie going to say when I tell him he's got to hand over thirty-five quid or more?' She waited, waited longer than she liked. 'Donal? Give me the betting slip.'

At what point did she realise it wasn't disappointment crushing Donal? 'Where's my betting slip?'

'I—'

Looping her arms round his neck, she kicked his right leg from under him. He went down, herself on top, her knee on his chest. Never mind that people stared in shock. 'Where is it, you dimwit?'

'Cora, I didn't place the bet. I thought Mid-day Sun would lose and I could give you your money back and you'd be pleased. I didn't want you to be disappointed.'

Disappointed? She swung the olive green handbag, whacking him until somebody shouted, 'Lay off, love. Only a few shillings, eh? Your brother was only trying to help.'

She took her rage out on the stranger instead. 'It's not a few shillings, it's everything! Everything! And he's not my brother. He's a snotty-nosed git who pushes laundry because his own granny thinks he's too useless for anything else.'

She strode blindly away and within minutes was in a country lane, her shoes streaked with the white chalk that surfaced the road. If wrecked shoes was the price of solitude, so be it. She'd honestly wanted to break Donal's nose when he was on the ground — which frightened her. That was her father's temper coming out.

Up ahead, men were clustered around a pair of piebald horses. One horse was rearing while the other squealed and kicked. The men were Gypsies. On Sundays, back in the days when her parents had loved each other, they'd often taken a bus to the Sussex Downs. There'd be Gypsies there selling lucky heather and giving donkey rides. While her dad ran alongside Cora on a jogging donkey, her mother would step into a wagon for a crystal-ball reading. 'Superstitious tosh,' was how Jac Masson denounced it, but Florence had held firm.

'They see things, Jac, and you don't want a Romany curse on you. I don't, any rate.'

The last time they'd done that trip, Cora recalled her mother walking back to them, saying, 'I'm to have another baby, Jac. The old woman said I had two daughters in my palm. What d'you say to that?'

Her dad had groaned but he'd looked pleased. Maybe he should have popped into the wagon himself. Then he'd have discovered that his palm had just the one daughter in it and he could have worked out a thing or two. Cora wondered if the men up ahead were selling the piebalds, or preparing to race them. A few yards on, she realised she'd walked into one set of travellers buying the services of a stallion from another. The squealing horse was a mare. The rearing one was definitely a lad.

Cora turned. She'd never got on with horses. In Barnham Street, one long-ago summer, a tinker's stallion had tried to mount a rag-and-bone man's mare. Sparks flying from iron shoes, the rag-and-bone man fighting the stallion off with his whip.

Donal, no taller than the side of the cart, started trying to help. He'd been dragged twenty yards when the mare bolted.

Donal would be searching for her. Maybe she'd go and find him. She had to sooner or later as he had their return tickets . . . but instead she walked through a gateway into a field ringed with wagons. Barefoot children scampered around the remains of campfires. Women sat on wagon steps, smoking pipes, knitting. One called, 'Wait, lady!' but Cora turned away, only to be brought up short by an extraordinary vision.

It was an open-topped car parked between two wagons, its radiator grille, headlamps and wire wheels so highly polished that sunlight lanced off them. Paintwork as red as lipstick had lured a group of boys, who stared the way children do, wanting to touch, fearful that the man lounging against a scarlet wing would chase them off.

She recognised him by the Ascot hat on the car's bonnet, and the fair hair lifting like feathers in the breeze. Dietrich. First or last name? Did he have a taste for slumming it? And where was his stuck-up friend?

Just then, her left hand was taken in a business-like grip. Cora spun round to find a pickled-walnut face staring at her from under a hat resembling a dented stovepipe.

The woman turned Cora's hand palm up. 'Tell your future, lady.'

'I've got no money.'

The Romany woman chuckled. 'I know that. All you had has been taken.'

That took the wind out of Cora. If this woman had the gift, and was offering a palm-reading for free . . . Cora put her handbag on the grass and splayed her fingers. 'All right, Mother. Will I get out of the hat factory? Will I ever get a spark of fun in life?'

The woman stared down intently. 'You've a long life path. You will spend your life making.'

'Making what?'

'With your hands. Stitching. Shaping. For others.'

To Hell with that, Cora swore. Today had taught her something. She wanted to wear hats such as the one she had on, or like the German cow's trifle topping. *Wear*, not make. She wanted to swan about with nice-looking men. Wanted money in her purse and some in the bank.

The Romany said flatly, 'You will pursue love.'

'Pursue it how far?' Sheila Flynn must have a much bigger head than hers, Cora thought, because the feather hat was slipping backwards again. She couldn't straighten it without breaking the gypsy's grip. 'Take a look at my love-line.'

'It is unclear. It is severed.'

Cora blew a stream of air upwards. Feathers were tickling her brow.

'I see children.'

They always said that, these women. *I see a cradle, a blue one and a pink one*. It was all tosh.

'You will kill.' Eyes sharp as vinegar met Cora's.

'That's enough.'

The woman dropped Cora's hand and walked away. A second, even older, woman came forward, hand out. 'Shilling.'

'I said at the start, I've got no money.'

The crone pointed to the grass. One of Sheila Flynn's gloves lay beside the bag and Cora realised she was expected to hand it over. And its twin, obviously. 'They're not mine,' she said.

'A shilling for a palm reading,' the woman insisted.

This could go on all day. Cora gave up the gloves – they were the sort easily bought at a draper's, after all, but the crone thrust them back, rasping, 'Betrayal!'

Cora inspected them. They looked pretty innocent to her. 'Can I help?'

She greeted Dietrich like an old friend. 'I'm embarrassed, but you wouldn't have a shilling on you?'

He took a two-shilling piece from his pocket and the crone pocketed it, then stumped away. Obviously they didn't give change round here.

'She wouldn't take my gloves so it would have been my shoes.'

Dietrich considered her in silence. The sun burnished his hair and it burst on Cora that, yes, she *had* seen him before. In the Catholic cathedral of St George, Southwark, where her father had taken her as a child. There'd been a little side window she'd loved to stare at while the rituals of the mass went on over her head. A golden chalice had stood in the embrasure, bathed in light streaming through stained glass. The window depicted a knight entangled with a dragon. 'You're my St George,' she said.

'Riding to your rescue with a shilling? You were right about Mid-day Sun. I take it you did not back him in the end? Otherwise, you would not be short of cash.'

She groaned. 'It's a long story. What about you?'

'Each-way on Le Grand Duc. Only a few pounds, though.' *Only a few pounds. How the other half lives.* 'You believe that fortune-telling nonsense?'

'Just a bit of fun.' Cora shrugged.

'It did not seem so much fun a moment ago. You looked sick, like a wounded raven.' He lifted her feathers and she flinched.

'"Raven" isn't very complimentary. Ever seen one close up? Beady eyes and a bloody big beak.'

He laughed. 'They are majestic and intriguing birds. And

highly portentous. Don't they hold the survival of the Tower of
London under their wings? But, all right, not a raven, a blackbird.
Decidedly inferior. I'd rather be a raven.'

'Where's your lady-friend?'

He nodded towards a yellow wagon. 'Learning her fate. She
is consumed by a burning question and the only person who can
answer it is an illiterate stranger who spends her life moving pots
and pans from field to field. You women always want to know the
small detail of your future, when, really, it is all written clearly
enough.'

'In the stars?'

'In the newspapers. Politics forges destiny, not Fate or chance.'

Cora frowned. Politics hadn't drawn ticket number twenty-two out of the hat. It wasn't politics that had stopped Donal
putting her stake on Mid-day Sun, either.

'Why must women be passive? Cannot they steer their own
lives?' he pressed.

'Don't know.' 'Passive' was a new word, but she dug out its
meaning. 'I've never been behind a steering-wheel.' She looked
at his motor-car. 'Does that go fast?'

'It is a Mercedes Roadster and it goes very fast. You would
like to try?'

'I wouldn't dare. But—' Words were lining up on her tongue,
words that might earn her a snub. 'I'd like to sit next to you while
you drive it, the wind blowing the curls out of my hair and the
smog out of my lungs.'

'Smog?' He frowned at the word.

Fair exchange, Cora thought. *I'll keep 'passive' and you can have
'smog'*. 'Dirty London air,' she explained.

An idea seemed to root in his mind. 'Where would you like
to go?'

'Brighton for a pint of cockles on the beach.' Then she remembered she was supposed to be a fashionable London milliner. 'I mean, for champagne and crab, um, sandwiches. Then over to France, not stopping till we hit Paris.'

'You want to go to Paris?'

'Not half. See, I've decided to run away.'

'How extraordinarily apposite. Tomorrow I am going to Paris.'

'No! On holiday?'

'Holiday and business. I have work, but I also have tickets for the Expo.' He explained: 'Exposition Internationale, where the world comes to Paris to discover architecture, technology and exotic food. You've heard of the Expo, surely?'

'Of course.' Never.

'I have a reservation on the Pullman. The boat train? Two seats. You may have one, if you like.'

Cora stared. He must realise she couldn't pay her way. And what about Miss Snowdrop? 'Isn't your friend going with you?'

'Ottilia? No, no. She was in Paris all of April. She's making her home in London now. Her husband insists.'

Her husband? 'Who was the other seat for?'

'The other seat,' his gaze raked over her face, her wide cheekbones and pointed chin, 'is for my man. But he can get another train.'

'Your man?' Oh, Lord. There were chaps who went in for funny business with their own sex. Not in Bermondsey. God help them, they wouldn't survive half an hour there, but in the theatrical districts of London. Her mother, when she was still getting work, had brought one or two fruity-voiced types home until Jac had put a stop to it.

'My man, yes. My servant.'

'Servant. That's what I thought.'

'So, you wish to come?'

To Paris, with a total stranger? Tomorrow was . . . well, it was tomorrow. Which left no thinking time, no packing time. No time for goodbyes. Though who to . . . apart from Donal? A practical obstruction hit her. 'I don't have a passport.'

'I do, and mine allows my wife to accompany me.'

'You have a wife?' Had these people never heard of marriage vows?

'Certainly, and you could easily be her, as you match her colouring and build very closely. Though, I hasten to add, you are much younger. All you need do is give your name as—' He broke off as a figure in white stumbled out of the bow-top caravan. Cora braced herself for unpleasantness. Ottilia – was that her name? – would likely object to Cora being in the same field as her lovely self.

But Ottilia didn't see her. Or Dietrich. She stopped to pull on her gloves and her pearl bracelets were hampering her. Dropping a glove, she stared down as if she hadn't the resolve to pick it up. Suddenly, the invitation for the Pullman struck Cora as outrageous. Cruel, even. 'How can I come to Paris with you? I have moral standards, even if you don't.'

He smiled, as if her about-face amused him. 'Ottilia is a friend. As for my wife, she and I live separate lives. She remains at home in Germany.'

So he was definitely German. And that was another thing. Throw in her lot with him, and she'd never be able to set foot on home territory again. The war to end all wars had finished almost twenty years ago, but there wasn't a house on her street that hadn't lost a son, brother or father. Her dad, who had come to England as a refugee and joined an infantry regiment, still had nightmares about the trenches and the invasion of Belgium. He couldn't say the word 'German' without spitting.

Yet, German or not, this man was offering to grant a wish expressed not two hours earlier. 'I'd have to go home, leave a note. I can't just hot-foot it.'

'Sounds like good sense.'

Good sense that was to alter the course of her life more profoundly than any Gypsy seer could have imagined.

Chapter Two

Cora headed to the railway station. She'd given up trying to find Donal among the grandstand crowds. He'd find her as soon as he wanted to go home.

But when five thirty came, and Donal still hadn't arrived, she went in search of him. No sign of him among the home-going crowds, or in the grandstand. He wouldn't have left already? Not with her ticket in his pocket. Would he? Had she finally goaded him too far? Three hours later, she was sure of it.

Faced with the prospect of an eight-mile walk, Cora leaped on to the rear platform of a double-decker bus as it slowed to let a group of spectators pass in front of it. She shouted to those who craned round to look, 'Got a seat for a London gal who's lost everything except her faith in human nature?' The bus was going back to the city, a works' outing on board, and she squeezed between two girls of her own age and joined in the singing, though, actually, she felt like crying. They dropped her on the Walworth Road, giving her a two-mile hike home.

It was close on eleven when she reached Barnham Street and peeled off her shoes. While her blistered feet soaked up the cold of the kitchen floor, she listened for sounds of occupation. The house felt empty. So where was her dad? The pubs were long shut, so maybe he'd gone back to work. He worked for himself, and his hours were chaotic. Cora often thought that if he hadn't needed to eat, he'd spend his life shuttling between his workshop and the pub.

Cup of tea was what she needed. Reaching for the kettle, she found a note poking from its spout.

'C. Masson: report to your father's premises soon as you read this – WPC Flynn.' A police serial number was written alongside the name. God help me, Cora thought, she's turned official. She knows I took her clothes. How? Donal wouldn't have told, surely?

She sat over her tea, picturing Sheila writing her note, her clumpy lace-ups grinding dust into the quarry tiles. Nobody locked their doors round there, but she hoped Sheila hadn't been wearing uniform when she called because that really would get tongues wagging. She read the note again. No mention of Jac having been told anything. If she acted fast, she might be able to save the situation. What if she offered to pay Sheila for the loan of her clothes and maybe used her black eye as a bargaining chip?

'Thing is, Sheila, my dad always *seems* good-natured. Gentleman Jac when you meet him on the street. But when it comes to my mistakes – any excuse to give me a pasting. He can't punish Mum any more, see, so he takes it out on me. You wouldn't drop me in it, would you?'

But Sheila might. *Then I'd have to run away*, she told herself. Take up the German fellow's offer. But she knew she wouldn't. Imagine Dietrich What's-his-name's face if she actually turned up at Victoria Station with a suitcase.

Anyway, she didn't have a suitcase. What she had was a job and a life and she'd better make the best of it. She took off the Paris hat and replaced it with a headscarf. Headscarves always looked penitent, somehow. If you said 'sorry' in a headscarf, you were more likely to be believed.

What to do with the hat? If she walked up to Sheila holding it, it might just trigger the Flynn temper. Best hide the hat for now. From the kitchen cupboard, she took an old toffee tin and prised off the lid. Inside was a collection of buttons and belt buckles, and the heel torn off a lady's petite dress shoe.

Daffodil yellow, a fashionable colour twelve years ago, though a muddy tidemark wrote a sad ending to the story. On Derby Day 1925, they'd set out for Epsom Downs, Cora's mother in a new yellow and green outfit. Only it had rained without pause and The Hill had turned into a bog. Cora remembered her mum falling on her bottom in the filth and howling, 'I look like I've sloshed through a farmyard! Some bloody day out this is.'

'More fool you.' Jac had laughed. 'Boots next time. I can't carry you and the kid on my shoulders.'

Words had flown and Cora's last memory of Florence Masson was of her disappearing into the crowd, her coat darkened to the colour of mustard, her green hat dripping dye on to her shoulders. The heel of a shoe sucked off as she ploughed through the mud.

'How angry do you have to be to leave your heel behind?' Cora asked, as she pressed the toffee-tin lid gently down on Sheila's hat. *And how desperate do you have to be to leave your child?*

No answers offered themselves. Finding a torch and absentmindedly slipping the olive green handbag over her arm, she set off to answer WPC Flynn's summons.

Jac Masson's premises crouched in the shadow of railway arches. The one-storey shack had been mended with so much corrugated iron, it rattled like a set of rusty keys whenever a freight train passed. Cora aimed her torch at the double doors. A smudge of light behind a windowpane warned her that somebody was waiting.

Inside, she gagged as solvent fumes hit the back of her throat. She never went there without wondering if her dad's lungs were pickled, like those ancient leather shoes they sometimes pulled from the Thames foreshore. For all that, it always astonished her how Jac, with his meat-handler's hands, could turn plain wood and reeking materials into beautiful objects. Into replica Coromandel screens, glimmering with gold leaf and coloured enamels. She loved that word: 'Coromandel'. Exotic, sensuous. The only thing about Jac Masson that was.

After coming out of the army, he'd got work as a theatrical scenery painter, which was how he'd met Cora's mother. Soon, his drinking had started to lose him work, and after a few years, there wasn't a theatre in London that would employ him. Florence had been earning well at the time, and she'd bought him a business from a man who was retiring, which specialised in enamelled folding screens. The sort found in superior dress shops and in wealthy people's drawing rooms.

Jac had taken to the work. Being alone all day, nobody to answer to, suited him and a flair for graphic art had put him in step with the new art-deco style of the twenties. He had developed his own motifs, featuring hummingbirds and luscious flowers and his work had become quite sought after. *If he'd been anybody else*, Cora thought, *he'd be running a factory, perhaps from one of the new units on the Great West Road*. They'd be living in a smart semi with a garden. But, being Jac, he insulted his suppliers, painted what he wanted, not what his customers asked for, and drank any profit he made.

Even his shed radiated stubborn depression. No electricity, just hurricane lamps and a smelly paraffin stove.

The light she'd seen came from the area he called his 'paint-bay', which was separated from the main workshop by a cowhide curtain. Behind the curtain he applied his paints and gold leaf, or sprayed surfaces with Japan-black lacquer, layer upon layer, until cheap pine panels resembled inlaid ebony.

Cora heard a whisper and went to peer through a hole in the leather curtain. In the bluish light of the paraffin stove, she saw her father. He was sitting on the ancient club chair he'd bought from a junk shop. Side-saddle on Jac's knee, her ugly policewoman's hat tipped back, was Sheila Flynn. They had their arms around each other.

Kissing! Cora's mouth turned down in disgust. Her dad and Sheila Flynn gorging on each other's faces! Jac's hand was wedged inside Sheila's jacket, under her shirt. As for *her* hand, it was where it definitely ought not to be.

Cora closed her eyes and heard, 'So, shall we tell her in the morning, Jac?'

'Must we tell her at all?' Jac's voice was a rumble. Slurred but intelligible, which told Cora that he'd been drinking beer, not whisky. 'Won't it be obvious when we've gone?'

Gone where? Cora opened her eyes and found a bigger hole to peer through. There was a selection because Jac had once hurled paint stripper at the curtain and it had burned through it, forming what looked like bullet holes. Oh, God, they were kissing again. Cora saw tea things laid out on the seat of a chair. A teapot and a tin mug, a rose-patterned china cup and saucer. Her mum's teacup! A prized possession because it had been among the props used in *The Importance of Being Earnest*. How dare Sheila Flynn drink from it! Cora was about to wrench back the curtain when she heard Sheila say, 'I'm going to give her hell for taking my things.'

'Leave that to me,' muttered Jac.

'It's only a rag, that dress, but what a cheek, going into my room. My best hat, too. And she'll have seen all the other stuff.'

'What stuff?'

Sheila's voice turned girlish. 'I had a shopping spree. All the pocket money you give me gone on lovely things.' It became a baby's lisp. 'Oo like me looking pretty, don't oo, Jacky?'

Too much. Cora hauled back the curtain, breaking a fingernail in her hurry to shine her torch into the lovebirds' eyes. She was rewarded with a comical display of shock. Sheila got off Jac's knee so fast that he yelped. She demanded, 'How long have you been there?'

'How long have you been fornicating with my dad?' Cora shot back. 'He's still married to my mother, or had you forgotten?'

Jac got up, stiff joints making him ungainly. 'You'd better know, Cora, this woman is everything to me. Don't you misuse her good name, not in my hearing. '

Sheila preened. *See?* her little smile implied. *I'm the special one.*

Cora pointed the torch at her father. 'How much is everything?'

Sheila answered, 'We're getting married. We're going to set up house in Barnham Street, so you'd better start looking for new lodgings.'

'How can you marry him when Mum's still alive?'

'Divorce,' Sheila said triumphantly. 'The new law says three years' desertion is grounds and your mother's been gone a lot longer than that.'

'But you're Catholic,' Cora lobbed back. 'So's Dad, when he can be bothered. You can't believe in divorce?'

Jac found his voice. 'I believe in anything that will make me happy. Coming home to Sheila every night is all I want.'

'But what about me? I don't earn enough to take a place of my own.'

'You'll go into lodgings. Or,' Sheila threw Jac a playful look, 'she could rent my bedroom. Donal wouldn't mind.' Then, her gaze closing on the green silk dress, she bared her teeth. 'You can pay to have that washed, Cora Masson, and I shall want new stockings, too. And where's my hat?'

'Who blew the gaff on me?' Cora wasn't playing for time. It was suddenly more important than anything to know if Donal had betrayed her. If he had, she hadn't a true friend in the world.

'Somebody left the key in the wardrobe and I heard you'd been hanging about the place. Since Donal wasn't likely to be dressing up in my things, it had to be you. So? I'd say a fiver for a day's hire. It should be twice that, except I know you'll have lost all your money on one horse. You've no more sense than – what?' Anger flared in Sheila's eyes. 'What have you got to grin at?'

'You. I reckon that when it comes to being a self-righteous prig, you take the biscuit, Sheila Flynn.' Cora gestured to her father, and took a deep breath. 'When it comes to theft, he takes all the bloody biscuits. He's been living off my earnings since I left school. Marry him? You need your head examined. He might say he's in love and buy you a few fancy dresses, but give it a couple of years, you'll be stuck with your arms in the wash-tub, looking forward to a black eye every Saturday night. Men like him—'

They don't change. It sighed through her mind, above the screeching wheels of a passing locomotive. The building shook and the roof panels made the noise of a saw cutting bones. *He's taken your life and he won't change.*

The sound came not from within her head, but from the darkness in front of her feet. Obeying an impulse she didn't fully understand, she flashed her torch beam over the floor bricks. Laid in herringbone pattern, fifteen years of Jac in his work-boots had pressed them into the soft earth. Something odd . . . an area in the middle had sunk in the shape of a church window, narrow at the top, wide at the bottom. 'What's under there, Dad?'

'*Salope!*' Jac spat the horrible word at her. 'What right have you to question me? Sheila has told me everything about you, how you go with men – with sailors.'

'I darn well don't!' One sailor only, and she'd really liked him. He'd been gentle.

Jac hawked in her direction. 'Stumbling on to the dock, looking for a tart to stick it in, they find you!'

'That isn't nice, Jac.' Sheila crimped her lips, but her distaste was for Cora. 'But now we're speaking of it, you were seen on Coronation night, back in May, going with a boy off a ship—'

'A filthy foreigner!' Jac leaped in. 'At least your mother whored with her own kind.' Suddenly they were moving towards her. Had Jac seen something in her face to threaten him? Was he stoking his anger to justify an explosion of violence? Cora knew that her father meant to harm her and that Sheila wouldn't stop him. If anything, Sheila's coy smile was egging him on. *Go on, Jac*, she seemed to be saying. *You've done it before.*

Cora saw the game's end quite clearly. 'Get out!' a voice screamed in her head. She dropped her torch and ran. Outside, confused by the dark, she dithered, then let her feet do the thinking. She ran towards Bermondsey Street and Pettrew's. If necessary, she could scale the factory wall and hide in one of the outbuildings. At Pettrew's gates, she listened for the sounds of pursuit.

All she could hear was her own heart. She said farewell to the chimneys and the forbidding, black windows, knowing she'd sewn her last hatband – never would she be assistant forelady under Miss McCullum.

Chapter Three

Paris, 16 June 1937

Coralie de Lirac woke by degrees until the smell of laundered cotton reminded her that she was in her bedroom, in the Hôtel Duet. Banking her pillows behind her, she inhaled a waft of rose-attar. Thornless Zéphirine Drouhins in a vase on the dressing-table had transformed into organza crinolines as she slept.

The moments before the day asserted itself gave her time to believe in her new existence. To those left behind in London, it must seem that Cora Masson had simply vanished. It was true. Cora Masson no longer existed.

She mentally reassembled her surroundings, beginning with walls of watered silk, wedding-veil curtains and a Chinese carpet. A cream-painted armoire took up nearly a whole wall. There was a sitting room through an arch with deep-buttoned chairs and a sofa sprung like clouds. A pearly bathroom made her gasp each time she walked into it. When poor Cora Masson had wanted a good wash, she'd gone to the council swimming-baths.

Outside, boulevard de Courcelles hummed with light traffic, which paused now and then to allow birdsong through. An elegant road to the north-west of Paris, it straddled the 8th and 17th *arrondissements*. Parc Monceau lay just across the street, where Coralie loved to walk early in the morning when the grass sparkled. She was learning how to be alone for the first time in her life.

By mid-morning, impatient residents competed with tourists for pavement space. The Exposition Internationale was open for business, and according to the hotel porter – a man never without his copy of the newspaper *Le Petit Parisien* – up to 150,000 visitors swarmed through its pavilions each day.

Hearing a knock, she called, '*Entrez, s'il vous plaît.*' Speaking French was becoming second nature. Dietrich had accepted her story of being Coralie de Lirac, orphaned daughter of Belgian-French émigrés to London. On the train journey, he'd been curious about her millinery career, but hadn't pressed when she'd brushed him off with 'I make hats when I feel like it.' In his world, it seemed to be normal for young women to take jobs for fun and drop them when more exciting prospects offered themselves. As for her fluency in French, which had amazed everyone she'd ever met in London – he spoke three languages and seemed to think it perfectly reasonable that she should speak two.

He'd been unimpressed by her accent, however. 'You sound like a kitchen maid. I shall send you to a teacher I know.' So, twice a day now, Coralie crossed the Seine to converse with a Mademoiselle Deveau, whom Dietrich had met some years ago in Berlin. He'd been her pupil. 'Anyone who can get Germans sounding their *rs* at the back of the throat and pronouncing -*euille* like a native will buff you up in no time.'

Two two-hour lessons each day had brought Coralie's French on fast, but such concentrated mental effort tired her. To relax, she always walked to Mademoiselle Deveau's Left Bank flat, taking a different bridge each time so she could see Paris from new viewpoints. The hotel's commissionaire would have called a taxi for her, and Dietrich provided her with cash for such essentials, but she loved exploring. Paris stone was the colour of unbleached flour, or of golden pastry. Roofs were all of uniform pitch, with dormer windows peering through the slates. First and second-floor balconies were black-metal lace. She even found herself admiring trees, lampposts, Métro canopies . . .

'You are responding to the genius of Haussmann,' Dietrich had told her. 'He married stone with light to raise the eye from the pavement to the sky. For the trees lining the boulevards, thank Napoleon the Third. As for curly street furniture, you are admiring art nouveau.'

Dietrich enjoyed educating her, when he had time. He was busy for much of the day, catching up with his many contacts. On their arrival, though, he'd devoted a whole day to her, taking her to the department store Printemps. Handing her over to a saleswoman, a *vendeuse*, he'd said, 'Mademoiselle lost her luggage on the journey. Please ensure she has everything she needs.'

For three hours the *vendeuse* had held her captive. The over-sized armoire now held summer dresses, jackets and shoes. Her chest of drawers was full of gossamer lingerie so fine Coralie was reluctant to wear it.

Soon, Dietrich promised, he would take her to his favourite couturier for clothes that would change her for ever. She'd objected. There was only so much change a person could take in one go, and he shouldn't be spending money on her. Bringing her to Paris had been enough. But he seemed to take pleasure in it, and as for money, there didn't seem to be any shortage.

A maid set down a breakfast tray. '*Bonjour, Madame. Vous avez bien dormée?*'

'Like a whippet that chased a bus all the way to Brighton.'

She answered in English because . . . well, good luck saying it in French. She answered the question differently each morning and the girl always laughed, though Coralie doubted she understood a word. After sweeping back the curtains, letting in a tidal wave of sunshine, the maid left. Coralie gave a long sniff.

Good. No coffee. It had taken a week for the kitchen to cancel the coffee and send up tea. At first, they'd obliged with a pot of hot piddle. It had taken another week to get a brew that was the right shade of brown, with milk, not lemon. Lemon with pancakes, yes. A squeeze of lemon to rinse your hair or bring your windowpanes up sparkling . . . but in a cuppa? They had a lot to learn, the French. But they really knew how to make bread, and their croissants were beyond words. The hotel got those from a baker whose wares jumped from his oven on to your plate and were served with white butter and jam – called *confiture* – which bore no relation to the red paste she'd bought at the Barnham Street corner shop.

Stop thinking about Barnham Street.

She poured tea and piled her plate up, intending to slip back into bed before her nightgown grew cold. Only the telephone rang.

'Battersea Dogs' Home, Lady Basset speaking.' She knew who it was, since only one person in Paris ever rang her. Except he wasn't in Paris; he was in Germany on business. He'd left four days ago, saying that he was going first to Switzerland, then tracking back to Berlin. He wasn't due in Paris until the day after tomorrow.

'Good morning, Coralie. Did you get my roses?'

'They came with dinner. Know something? Nobody has ever sent me roses before.' Or any flowers, unless you counted a bunch of violets Donal had shoved at her one Easter-time—

Don't think about Donal.

'I am glad to hear it. I wish to be the first with you for everything.'

She bit her lip, wondering how he'd react if she told him that you can't unscramble an egg or put the stalk back on a cherry. If the merchant vessel *Antigone* hadn't sailed into Rotherhithe docks five weeks ago, she'd still be virgin-intact. But it had and, well, that was a conversation best left for later. 'I'm having breakfast in bed. How about you?'

'Lazy girl, I had mine hours ago. I get up with the sun. A habit from when I lived in the countryside and it amused me to walk to the nearest farm and shout in the cockerel's ear to wake the wretch up.'

She laughed. She liked the way Dietrich told her stories, even when he was talking about ordinary things. One of the nicest things he'd said in their first days together was that she made him think in pictures, not in straight lines.

She'd puzzled over it. 'Pictures – because I'm a dunce?'

'You express yourself through imagery, which tells me your mind is that of an artist. I find that stimulating.'

Shaken at being called an artist, she'd almost betrayed herself. 'I only ever painted one picture, when I was five. It was for our school victory – I mean peace – parade to celebrate the end of the war. We had to daub something to do with the armistice. I painted my dad in his armchair because that's what I thought armistice meant. Nobody was impressed.'

Dietrich had replied fiercely that schoolteachers had no business embroiling children in war or politics. The hazel eyes had iced over. 'Politics, like wine and strong cheese, is an adult taste that should not be forced on the young.'

She took a croissant and sat cross-legged on the bed. 'Where are you? Still in Berlin?' He had a flat there and a house in a town a little distance outside. His wife lived there, he'd told her, with their children, a boy and girl. She'd known Dietrich fifteen days now, if she counted Derby Day, and that was pretty much all she'd learned about him.

'I'm in a café, on Leningrad, with a taxi waiting outside.'

Leningrad? 'I thought you were in Berlin.'

'Rue de Leningrad. Less than ten minutes away. May I take breakfast with you?'

Her heart pattered. She'd thought the line sounded clear! 'I wasn't expecting you back yet.'

'I hoped you would be pleased. I wanted to see you. So?'

'You said you'd already had breakfast.'

'Hours ago, on the train. So?'

'Of course.' She could hardly keep him away. Didn't *want* to keep him away. She'd been alone for four days, unless you counted Mademoiselle Deveau and the maid, and the woman who'd come in and styled her hair. Four days without a chat was a long time for a factory girl.

Flicking crumbs off the bedspread, she wondered what to put on. One of her new dresses, or stay in her nightie? Pink slipper satin, it felt more like evening dress than nightwear. Only . . . she was completely naked underneath, which would scream invitation. On the other hand, she'd told him she was still in bed so it would look odd if she greeted him in a button-front dress and a cardigan.

Sort yourself out, girl. Dietrich had settled her here because he wanted her company at night as well as during the day. He had taken a suite one flight up and an unexpected business trip had not altered the undeclared contract.

Truth was, she was frightened of disappointing him and it all

ending. Dietrich wanted to be 'first' with her, but he was going
to find out sooner or later that he'd been pipped to the post. How
to tell him? In her world, girls didn't talk about such things. Not
to men, at any rate. Either they kept themselves virginal for their
wedding day, or they got their fellas drunk first time so they
didn't notice. She couldn't see herself getting Dietrich drunk,
not if he didn't want to be.

Did it even matter? She wasn't so stupid as to think there was
a future for the two of them. Even without a wife back in Germany, marriage was unimaginable. He wasn't just wealthy and
part of the international set, he was titled. Dietrich August Graf
von Elbing. 'Graf' meant 'Count', he had told her. It was why
the waiters and doormen at the Duet called him 'Monsieur le
Comte'. They were never going to call her 'Madame la Comtesse'.
In France, they called girls like her '*irrégulières*'.

'"Can't get away to marry you today, my wife won't let me!"'
she trilled, to cover her nerves, as she turned on the taps at the
bathroom basin. He'd said he was ten minutes away but she reckoned about fifteen, Paris traffic and all that. In front of the mirror,
she combed her curls into the sleek shape the stylist had designed
for her.

She was brushing her teeth when a finger-tap came at the door.
Surely not? Rushing out of the bathroom, she found herself face
to face with Dietrich. Through peppermint froth, she accused
him, 'That was never fifteen minutes.'

'Nine, I think.' Dietrich threw his jacket on to a chair, then
took off his tie and threw that too. Looking shockingly wide-
awake in shirtsleeves and a buttoned waistcoat, he indicated her
toothbrush. 'You look like the Statue of Liberty, if with a somewhat reduced torch. Good morning. Shall we go to bed?'

Unseated by the direct question, she seized the first excuse that came to mind – Dietrich must have spent hours on a train so didn't he want a proper, hot bath first? Not waiting for an answer, Coralie rushed back into the bathroom and turned on the taps. Then she rinsed her mouth and checked herself in the mirror, which was so steamy, she looked like a ripe peach. Returning to the bedroom, she asked, 'Cup of tea?'

'Tea? Good God. Coffee, if you must. I shall drink it in the bath.'

She called room service, then busied herself rearranging the china on her breakfast tray, because Dietrich looked as if he meant to take her in his arms. He looked edgier than usual, though that was probably because he'd travelled through the night. She wished she could act like women in films, slink and say 'dahling', but she'd had no practice. Nobody had ever tried to seduce her. Actually, she'd never made love inside a building. Southwark Park for her. 'You can't drink coffee in that bath. It's a monster tub. It sucks you down.'

'Then you must sit with me, keep me from danger.'

'Don't suppose you'd fit down the plughole.'

'Coralie?' His eyes were tolerant, his smile too, but she sensed his frustration. 'You're pelting me with nonsense.'

She dashed away to turn off the bath water and he followed her. She felt him absorbing her shape. Her first two days in Paris, she'd been unable to eat or sleep. Every time she'd closed her eyes, she'd seen her father advancing on her, Sheila smiling in collusion. Dietrich had acquired sleeping grains, which he'd given her with strict instructions not to overdo it.

'Something happened to you, to do with this.' He'd gently touched her black eye, which was going through its rainbow stage. 'As I know you have run away, can I presume that it was more like an escape?'

She'd nodded, chasing down the veronal with gulps of water.

'Whatever is in your mind, throw it behind you. Before you know it, you will have the habit of happiness again.'

She'd tried that, and since then at least the desire to eat had returned. As her choppy reflection in the bath water proved, three good meals a day had already erased traces of childhood hunger. Dietrich's shadow suddenly overlapped hers.

'They're a long time with that coffee. I'll phone again,' she rambled nervously.

Dietrich began to unbutton his shirt. 'Tell them strong and no milk. A quarter-teaspoon of sugar.'

She used the time to put a robe on over her nightdress. When the coffee arrived and she took his cup in to him, he was basking with his arms draped over the rim, his hair like a halo. The bath really was a monster – he could lie full-length. *How muscular he was*. The thought was out before she censored her gaze. She'd never properly seen an adult male body before. In Southwark Park, she'd made love under the stars. In films, only women took baths and they stepped into the water swathed in towels before disappearing under a snowdrift of bubbles. She'd never seen how water made a man's chest hair darken and straighten, or turned fair skin bronze. Damn, she was blushing. 'I'll leave you to your, um, washings.' *Washings?* Oh, God.

'But you haven't given me my coffee. Sit down and talk.'

She chose the bath's edge and fixed her eyes on the expanse of muscle between Dietrich's chin and navel.

He sat up, palming water from his face before taking his coffee. 'Why have you put on an outdoor coat?'

'It's my dressing-gown.'

'But the intention is the same. Did you think it would rain in here?' He flicked water. 'Or were you afraid you would get cold? It is easily eighty degrees Fahrenheit.'

'Only eighty?' And look how steam was moulding slipper-satin to her curves.

He *was* looking. 'Take it off. I want to see your arms. And your throat and shoulders. You have a heroic shape, Coralie, which I saw even before I noticed your poor eye the first time we met. Don't hide from me.'

'I'm not hiding.' She removed the dressing-gown.

'Closer.' Dietrich reached with the hand not holding his cup, and curled it around her waist, drawing her towards him. She could feel his sodden handprint as his eyes closed. When he cupped a breast through the satin, she gave a soft cry. Eyes opened lazily and she felt he was smiling, though his mouth didn't move. So grave, so perfect, she wanted to lean forward and trace his lips with hers.

'Take this cup.'

She reached for it, lowering her lashes because otherwise she would see his arousal. That was the sort of reality you dealt with by steps, first in the dark, then in demi-light. As she took the cup, the coffee aroma hit her. Blood rushed from her head and from far away she heard the shatter of china and tasted soap. Then, red-tinted nothingness.

When she came to, she was warm, naked and steady breathing filled her ears. So. Dried like a child then put to bed like a drunk, having landed head first in Dietrich's groin. If she was going to faint every time she smelt coffee, Paris would finish her off.

She couldn't resist checking that Dietrich was in one piece. Flying coffee might have scalded him, or broken china could have stuck in his eye. He seemed all right, his features almost boyish in repose. She fitted herself closer and his arm came around her, drawing her against him. The Hôtel Duet's soap smelt of spring hyacinths.

'Coralie.' He woke more with each syllable and then there were two arms around her and his lips were on hers, explorative, then urgent as desire took him over. Coralie let him lead, glad that he wanted nothing imaginative from her this first time. He was a man who would take the lead in everything, drawing her along . . . and why not? Letting go and trusting, her body cried out in delighted relief. If he noticed she wasn't a virgin, he didn't comment. Or seem to care. So that worry slipped away and love crept into the bed.

Sneaking in when her eyes were closed.

Chapter Four

She'd won a pot of honey once, in a charity raffle. The carpet in
Maison Javier's salon was the same colour. Its pile encroached
over the toes of her shoes. They were about to watch the afternoon parade and Coralie felt as frightened as an under-rehearsed
soloist.

Dietrich led the way to a cream leather banquette, and sat with
one arm along its back. Coralie tried to copy his posture, but it was
difficult in a dress and she ended up sitting like somebody waiting
for a job interview. He'd brought her here, to rue de la Trémoille,
after taking her for lunch on the nearby Champs-Élysées, explaining
that he'd selected this house because Roland Javier was Spanish. As a
Spaniard, Javier revered womanhood. He never sought to dress his
clients as little girls, or surreal sideshows or, indeed, as boys. 'Also,
most of his mannequins are very tall. There is no point showing
you *haute couture* worn by pocket Venuses.'

Wrapped in the afterglow of more lovemaking, Coralie had
smiled and nodded. In bed with him, she'd stepped into womanhood, learning to look without blushing, to touch and be
touched. Finding herself in the salon of an elite couturier sent
her back a few paces.

Dietrich raised her hand to his lips. 'You are allowed to enjoy
this, you know. Did you never go to Molyneux in London, or
Stiebel or Norman Hartnell?'

'Not really.' She presumed he was naming dress designers, but wasn't sure so she avoided his eye by searching in her handbag, a neat little rectangle of the softest leather, from Hermès. A gift from Dietrich. Just to say something, she scolded, 'You shouldn't be spending all this money on me.'

'And who *should* I spend it on?'

The name 'Ottilia' bounced into her mind, followed by 'Your wife?' but instead she answered, 'Yourself, of course.'

'There are only so many black, grey or French-navy suits one man can own, and since I'm always on the move, I cannot collect cars or horses.'

'Why are you always on the move?' In her experience, men who shifted around a lot were escaping from the police or from debt collectors.

'I have restless feet. But for all that, I take no pleasure in buying shoes. Would you admire a man who owned forty pairs?'

She got the feeling that he'd just shuffled off a difficult question but she let the subject drop, because Josette, the *vendeuse* assigned to her, was setting down glasses of chilled wine and wafer biscuits sprinkled with almonds. How indulgent – alcohol at three in the afternoon. No sooner had she released the thought than another took its place, that of her father heading down Shand Street for his lunchtime pint. She breathed deeply until the image went away. She might be her father's daughter in some respects, but not when it came to the demon drink.

Music filled the salon, waterfall strings seeping from a proscenium arch flanked with flowers. Shallow steps led down to a walkway ending in front of the banquette. 'Catwalk', Dietrich called it. Ten or so other ladies shared their banquette, which must have been thirty feet long. Some undoubtedly were mothers and daughters, and they all shared an effortless posture, legs sloping to the side. All wore suits or smart town dresses. Coralie felt that – without even shifting their profiles – they'd evaluated her flowered pink cotton, with its neck flounces and pussy-cat bow, and marked her down. She loved the dress she was in, insisting on it even when that first *vendeuse* at Printemps had tried to dissuade her: 'It is too fussy for Mademoiselle and rose does not flatter such fair skin.'

Too bad. Pink was her favourite colour. In fact, she liked it so much, she'd bought another dress in carnation, and one of dark madder. But, to judge from the glances she was getting, pink wasn't considered smart daywear at Javier. Why hadn't Dietrich said anything?

She was wondering if he'd let them leave, when a girl in black fastened back the proscenium curtains. A middle-aged woman, whom Josette whispered was the *directrice*, announced that the afternoon parade was about to begin.

Coralie settled down, intrigued in spite of herself. All she had to do was pick out a couple of dresses, and Dietrich would buy them. Everybody happy.

The first mannequin had golden hair. She sauntered past them while the *directrice*, whose name was Mademoiselle Liliane, described her ensemble.

'Heloïse wears number one, Esprit. Fashioned in lustrous cotton, this simple dress is perfect for afternoon tea, a visit to a museum, even a stroll in the woods. Mesdames, Monsieur, appreciate the narrow pleats, which flare as Heloïse moves. Esprit drapes when still, swings as she walks, a symphony of line and movement.'

After ten minutes' similar commentary, Coralie's head spun. How were you meant to remember so many different names? Esprit, Élan, Eldorado, Elderberry. Actually, there hadn't been an Elderberry, but all the same . . . and whoever made these clothes – Javier, was that his name? – was wedded to white. White everything, worn by long-necked girls with dancer's arms. It was like watching a flock of storks. No patterns, spots or stripes. It was all so drab.

So, instead of watching the clothes, she concentrated on the girls. Two were petite brunettes, Nelly and Zinaida. They laughed, and were what Mademoiselle Deveau would call '*animée*'. The tall ones shared a gravitas, as if extra inches meant they couldn't smile. Some were statuesque, others slender as reeds. Their complexions were flawless, and there must have been a resident hairdresser round the back somewhere. Coralie had been happy with her body an hour ago. Now all she could think of was the fat she'd put on her bottom, and the shoulder muscles that were a legacy of ironing at Granny Flynn's. As each girl wafted away through the arch, another took her place in tempo with Mademoiselle Liliane's commentary. There must be a mad paddle to get them into the next costume, the next hat. No sign of it, though, as they came out, calm and majestic as swans.

'Lovely, yes?' Dietrich asked.

'They could have come straight out of Hollywood.'

'I mean the clothes.'

'Oh, they're really nice too. It's just there's a lot of, you know, white.'

'This is a spring–summer collection. Ah.' Dietrich nodded at a girl in a raw silk tailor-made. 'Black. Happy now? Be sure to take the number of any items you like.' He gave her the pad and a pencil Josette had left on their table. Coralie had assumed it was for noting down the drinks' tab.

'To be honest, Dietrich, they aren't really me.'

Did his eye halt for an instant on her flounces, on the pussy-cat bow? 'Do you imagine I have brought you here by mistake? Javier is not for women who like their clothes to shout to the rafters. Ottilia wears Javier.'

Bugger. Ottilia. Obvious, really, when she recalled the woman's Derby Day outfit. Coralie sketched a jealous zigzag with her pencil then wrote 'Esprit' because that was the only name she could remember. When Mademoiselle Liliane named the black crêpe tailor-made 'Envie', she wrote that down too.

Sighing, Dietrich beckoned to a mannequin. 'Mademoiselle, if you please?' The girl assumed a languid pose beside them. 'Coralie, look properly. See? A plain dress, perhaps, but take your eyes for a walk. This sleeve?'

Obediently, she followed his pointing finger. Silk in a shade of blue that reminded her of prayer books left in a cupboard too long.

'Take in the detail.'

She peered, as if reading the label on a very small tin. The sleeve ended in a turned-back cuff with tiny mushroom buttons pushed through loops without a wrinkle. A pattern of rose briars had been worked in thread exactly the same shade as the dress. Every stitch was of identical length, and that she *could* appreciate. It had taken two years' training to reach the standard required for Pettrew & Lofthouse, every stitch precisely one sixteenth of an inch. 'I'd have made the embroidery jollier.'

'You are still missing the point.'

To her relief, out came azure blue day dresses, after which the mannequins appeared in beachwear, then in skimpy tennis dresses. At last, some jazzy fabrics. The evening gowns that finished the parade were muted but their shapes were sexy and the girls wore big costume jewellery. Coralie put down a couple more names and Dietrich smiled. He picked up her hand and his smile turned confidential.

'Have you had enough?' she asked, meaning, *Shall we go back to the hotel?*

'Coralie, we haven't even started.'

She strangled a groan.

As the final ripple of white disappeared through the arch, her *vendeuse* returned. 'You are a little overcome, Mademoiselle de Lirac? It is a long show. Monsieur Javier could not decide which of his models to choose and, in the end, allowed nearly sixty. But you are pleased?'

Coralie nodded, rather too vigorously. 'Lovely, Josette, thank you. Only I don't think I want to try anything on today.'

Josette returned a perplexed frown. 'Indeed, no, that would not be at all possible.'

Coralie knew she'd put her foot in it, but wasn't quite sure why.

The following day, climbing into a taxi the Duet's commissionaire had ordered for them, she heard Dietrich instruct, 'Boulevard de la Madeleine.' As they drove off, he said, 'We're going to our favourite hat shop.'

'And I thought we only had fair hair in common.'

He gave a piercing look. 'More than that, surely. If there was racing today, I would take you to Longchamps and let you bet on the winner. Then our affair would have come full circle.'

Our affair. As the cab sped down boulevard Malesherbes, Coralie turned the word over. 'Affair' meant adultery. Affairs were sordid, and usually short. Yet there was nothing sordid in the way she felt about Dietrich. His face in profile, his voice on the telephone, calling down to invite her to lunch or lovemaking. Or the hot knife that ran across her stomach when he put his hand to the small of her back or took her arm. That felt as pure as a church candle, though she supposed the world saw it differently. She wanted Dietrich to feel the same reverence for her.

As the taxi swung into place de la Madeleine, a cliff-face of sacred columns took her mind off her fears. She was still craning round for a last view of the church of St Mary Magdalene as the taxi pulled up behind a highly polished Talbot, with a chauffeur at the wheel. This was boulevard de la Madeleine, she supposed. The moment Dietrich opened her door, Coralie was out, rushing up to a window filled with hats on metal stalks.

They were all pink, from palest peach, intensifying to coral and flamingo before fading at the end of the line to the colour of unpainted plaster. Some were trimmed with goose feathers, others with dyed spotted guinea fowl, or cockerel, though the fashionable world referred to that as *coque*. One had a brim lined with downy ostrich, which would send you mad with tickling. Her eye kept coming back to the last in the line. Plaster-pink, or 'shrimp', to be a little more succulent, it was simplicity itself. A platter of dyed *coque* feather, it would curl diagonally across the face. Even though it carried reminiscences of Sheila Flynn, Coralie craved it. Then her glance slid upwards. Etched into the glass – La Passerinette. Above the letter *i* a small grey bird was pictured in the act of perching. A sparrow? A finch? Or a poor creature about to be caught on birdlime? She felt a bit the same.

Five minutes inside this shop would expose her. She looked for Dietrich, willing to turn her ankle – anything – to win back her seat in the taxi. But the cab was leaving and Dietrich was holding open the shop door for her.

'You're on the wrong side of the glass, *Liebchen*. Come on.'

*

La Passerinette's salon was just large enough to accommodate two tables, each with a triple mirror, and a sofa to which Dietrich headed with a familiarity that heightened Coralie's discomfort. A single assistant was attending to an ancient lady in black. That they'd interrupted a dispute became obvious when the customer barked that her head measured 'Fifty-six centimetres and always has. Don't tell me it's fifty-seven. Damn fool!'

The assistant was struggling to get her tape measure round the woman's hair. 'To be sure, Madame la Marquise, one must take account of your curls. Madame still has a remarkable number.'

'Counting, are you?'

'Not at all. Please sit still.'

Coralie saw the girl's difficulty. Because she had a curvature of the neck, the marquise was poking her chin forward to see herself in the mirror. Her coffee-brown curls were slipping backwards. Then they slipped right off and Coralie choked off a giggle. The assistant deftly replaced the hairpiece before turning to look at Coralie through spectacles as thick as jam-jars.

'I beg your pardon, but Mademoiselle Lorienne will come in a moment, if you would kindly take a seat.'

The girl failed to acknowledge Dietrich. Perching beside him on the sofa, Coralie whispered, 'Aren't men allowed in here or what?'

He replied quietly, 'The poor girl doesn't see me. To her, the world is a blur.'

'How can she be a milliner?'

'Perhaps by serving only ladies more shortsighted than she. Normally, she's hidden in a back room. As it is nice and quiet, we'll wait for Lorienne.'

Just 'Lorienne'. Why was Dietrich on first-name terms with a woman running a hat shop? He volunteered no more, so she studied the shop, liking its dusky pink walls and the overblown chandelier that cast reflections on the hats in the window. I'll have one of those pink ones, she promised herself. Assuming they didn't cost a fortune. Grey and pink hatboxes caught her eye and her gasp of recognition made Dietrich look up in concern.

'The hat I was wearing the day I met you,' she said, despite herself. 'Black feathers? It was from this shop and came out of a box the same as those over there. Your friend Ottilia said she had one like it.'

'It was made here, made specially. There was only ever one model.'

'That's unbelievable.'

'I don't see why.'

It *was* strange, but she couldn't blurt out the whole story. So she tried half the story. 'I borrowed it off a neighbour. Sort of . . . Sheila Flynn's her name. If it was Ottilia's hat, how did Sheila get hold of it?'

Dietrich stared upwards, as if surveying a selection of ideas. 'I can imagine what happened. Ottilia loved the idea of black feathers but disliked the reality. The hat made her look deathly – so she gave it to her maid. I'm guessing the maid took it to London when she accompanied Ottilia, and sold it. Dealers pay good money for cast-offs with Paris labels. The coincidence must be that your neighbour bought it. Or it may not even be such a coincidence, if somebody had many copies made with fake La Passerinette labels. That happens. We could find out, if you wanted to go back to London.'

'I don't want to.'

'Coralie, you look as if you're staring into your own grave. Is there something you wish to tell me?'

'Yes. I wish you hadn't brought me here.'

'But it is a wonderful shop.'

'Dietrich, why did Ottilia pretend to be interested when I said I was a milliner?' *When I said* – three small steps towards confession. Join up the clues. Get it over with.

'She *was* interested.'

Coralie shook her head. 'A woman like her? Don't be polite.'

'All right.' Again, Dietrich consulted the air above him. 'Ottilia floats through life like a flower-head cast upon the river. I dare say she minded seeing another woman wearing her hat but it is not her way to make a scene. She would think it vulgar.'

'She certainly thought me vulgar.'

'Did she? My memory is of you treading on the top of my foot – which hurts still, by the way. And of seeing your back, straight and slender, and hoping you would turn round so I could see your face. Which I hoped would be lovely. Finding it was, though complete with a black eye, I was intrigued.'

'What brought you to England?'

'To attend country-house sales and buy pictures. And to see Ottilia. She made me to take her to the Derby, not to see the racing – she doesn't like horses and hates crowds – but because she'd heard that at Epsom one finds Gypsy fortune-tellers. I told you that day, she had a question to which she needed an answer.'

Coralie's image of Ottilia was of her staring at the ground, her white clothes blowing like foam. 'She was crying when she came out of that wagon.'

'She learned that there is danger in asking for the truth because you may get it.' This was accompanied by such a particular look that Coralie reddened and changed the subject.

'I thought you were slumming it. People of your class usually swank around in the members' enclosure.'

'Neither Ottilia nor I relish being recognised. Now this you must observe . . .'

The shop assistant had placed a black felt disc on the marquise's head. As Coralie watched, she pinched it into a cone while her other hand described a shape in the mirror for the marquise's benefit. She then made a crown and a partial brim from the fabric, like a sculptress working with clay. She bent so close to her work that her glasses fell down her nose, and when she produced scissors, Coralie's eyes widened. They stayed wide as blades trimmed inches off the brim.

Coralie thought, *If I tried that, there'd be blood and bits of ear all over the place.* The girl pinned up the shallower side of the brim, then stood back, enabling Coralie to see the marquise's reflection. The old noblewoman had been restored to dignity. Her wrinkled butter-bean face had been given width at the temple, her beaky nose softened. Even her wig seemed less absurd now it was framed in black. To think that a pair of hands and a few snips could work such a change. The girl was a magician.

'I don't like it.' The marquise wrenched it off and threw it away.

'Perhaps Madame la Marquise will do me the honour of saying what she does like?' The girl's voice was soft. Weary.

'I'm sick of black!'

'But Madame always wishes for black.'

'Madame always wishes for black,' the old woman echoed, reminding Coralie of a mynah bird in the window of the barber's shop on the Old Kent Road. 'That one!' A twiggy finger pointed to the window. 'The one that's all feathers. The faded pink one.'

Coralie gasped. 'But that's the one I want!'

Dietrich tutted, amused. 'No more feathers, surely? Ah, too late, *Liebchen*.'

The assistant had lifted it from its stand like a sacrificial victim, sighing, 'Madame la Marquise has never asked for such a colour before.'

'How do you know? How old are you?'

'Twenty-nine, Madame.'

'Well, I'm eighty. My husband died before you were born. Who says widows have to live and die in black?'

The assistant placed the pink feathers on the marquise's head.

'She looks like an old broiler hen,' Coralie moaned quietly.

Her misery mixed with Dietrich's chuckles as the marquise pushed herself upright and commanded, 'Have the bill sent to my country place and box the hat up. I shall wear it to travel in.'

Opening the door carrying a La Passerinette hatbox proved difficult, and Dietrich got up to help. As the marquise stumped past, he said, 'Madame, permit me to say that you will look quite ravishing in pink.' To Coralie's amazement, the old woman graciously extended her hand for him to kiss.

As Dietrich sat down, Coralie hissed, 'Anyone would think you were auditioning for Prince Charming at the Finsbury Park Empire.' It was out before she could stop herself and the alteration in Dietrich's expression chilled her. 'I didn't mean to say that. Don't be angry.'

'Then don't mock me.'

'No. I'm sorry.'

'I do not understand why you say some of the things you do.'

'I'm jealous.'

'Of an old woman? You can be sure she will be ridiculed by everyone who sees her. Does she need your sneers as well?'

Tears welled with nowhere to go but down her cheeks. 'I was being rotten. Don't hate me, Dietrich.'

He handed over his handkerchief. Her bag was down by her

feet somewhere. 'Understand, Coralie, I will take a great deal of pain for those I care for but I have no tolerance for mockery.'

'So you do care for me?'

'Very much. Now, I shall go and find Lorienne. Perhaps she's napping. It is a hot day and hot weather ruffles the mind.'

She closed her eyes as he left. If anyone knew how men hated being teased, she should. How many times had she had a back-swipe at home for some flippant remark? Donal was the exception, taking her jibes in good humour. Or maybe he *had* minded – she'd never bothered to ask. Oh, Donal. Her last words to him had been so cruel and she'd probably never see him again. It was Dietrich she must concentrate on. He deserved her respect. He could have turned his back on her when she'd hurled herself at him at Victoria Station. She'd never forget the cocktail of disbelief, pity and . . . what? pleasure? with which he'd greeted her.

On 3 June, just a few minutes short of eleven o'clock, she'd sprinted into Victoria, eyes everywhere, as she tried to locate the Pullman train. No time to go to the Ladies and tidy herself, though she'd spent much of the previous night walking the streets. From Bermondsey Street, she'd crossed the Thames and had slunk around the wharves until the attentions of lone men warned her that she might not survive the night unmolested. She'd gone back south of the river and found sanctuary in the familiar surroundings of Southwark's Catholic cathedral. There, she'd slept surprisingly well on a hard pew, waking with just enough time to get to Victoria.

Grabbing a station porter's arm, she'd gasped, 'Boat train?'

The porter indicated the furthest end of the vast railway terminus. 'Platform eight. The queue's moving – you're cutting it fine.'

She'd hurtled towards the longest line. Was that tall figure at the barrier Dietrich? Belted summer coat, Homburg hat? It had better be. She forced a last effort from her legs. 'It's me, Coralie, wait!' At least she'd remembered to call herself 'Coralie'.

She'd thrown herself into his arms, hardly noticing the male attendant staring down a distinctly put-out nose. Dietrich had held her, panting, at arm's length.

'Like Mid-day Sun, forty miles an hour. Brownlow, give me your ticket. You're taking a later train.'

Dietrich hadn't rejected her, but he might after her performance just now. She'd seen it in his eyes.

Expecting him to return with a milliner in the style of Miss McCullum, Coralie was astonished when an elegant woman of about twenty-five preceded him into the salon.

'This is Mademoiselle Royer,' he told her. 'Privileged friends call her Lorienne.'

The woman's hands were alabaster-white against a black linen dress, nails long and polished. Not really milliner's hands at all. She wore three strands of black pearls around her left wrist, and Coralie saw an echo of Ottilia, but in the negative. Her most extraordinary feature was her platinum-blonde hair – *peroxide, buckets of it* – though there was nothing of the tart about her as the hair was twisted into an effortless pleat. Deep brown eyes, high cheekbones and a voluptuous mouth completed a beautiful woman. *Knows that pouting gets her further than smiling*, Coralie judged. *With men, anyway.*

Lorienne Royer placed her hip against Dietrich's leg, but even as she welcomed Coralie to La Passerinette, her words were aimed at him. 'We can do something with this. A lofty brow and Saxon colouring. Natural straws will suit Mademoiselle de Lirac perfectly.'

Coralie butted in, 'I'd rather have pink.' The brief desire to appease Dietrich had faded. That was half her problem in life. Her resolutions were not colour-fast. They ran in the wash, but damned if she was going to be topped off with a boring bit of straw. If the marquise could rebel at eighty, she could do it at twenty-two.

Lorienne shook her head. 'Those are special-occasion hats. Will Mademoiselle please come to a mirror?'

At the table previously occupied by the marquise, Coralie was confronted with her own face from three angles. She looked away, and saw the assistant with the thick glasses standing outside on the pavement, staring sadly towards her. Or perhaps just staring as she must be too shortsighted to make anything out. As the girl came back inside, a thought flashed through Coralie's mind: *She hates this place.*

'Would Mademoiselle de Lirac please look into the mirror?' A buffed nail brushed Coralie's chin. 'So I can take a long look?' Without breaking her study, Lorienne asked the assistant, 'Was the marquise in a tolerable mood?'

'No. I'm afraid she was in one of her queer tempers.'

'Did she decide upon her new hat?'

'Yes, Mademoiselle Lorienne. The biretta. The *coque* in wild-rose pink? Only she called it "calamine".'

'What?'

'Calamine.'

Coralie yelped as a fingernail dug into her jaw. After a hasty apology, Lorienne turned to the girl. 'You sold the rose pink biretta to the Marquise de Sainte-Vierge? What a triumph. You've excelled yourself. No – don't say anything, just fetch me straw shells for this customer.'

Coralie flashed a look of sympathy, but the girl's head stayed low as she edged past, flinching as Lorienne raised an arm – to shake down her bracelets, as it turned out, not to hit her. Coralie risked turning once more to see if Dietrich had witnessed the moment, but he was staring at the window, or through it, turning a silver key in his fingers. The key had a tag tied to it. She frowned. *Why did he have a house key on him when he lived in a hotel?*

'You are lucky,' Lorienne said, after studying Coralie's reflection for a good five minutes. 'Most shapes will suit you, so long as we stay away from narrow crowns.'

'No witch's hats, then?'

Had that stab at humour been a ball, it would have rolled into a corner.

'The crown of a hat should be as wide as, or wider than, your cheekbones. Yours are the broadest part of your face, and you have a small chin. Too much hat overshadows *gamine* features. Too narrow will make your face seem lozenge-shaped. You understand?'

'Perfectly. The sort of hat I like is—'

'Your complexion is fair, but there is colour to your cheeks, which is why Violaine will bring straw in shades tending towards grey, not yellow. Yes?'

No, actually. Coralie's irritation swelled until she realised that the 'Yes?' had been fired towards the doorway, at the assistant, who was waiting with a selection of unblocked straw bodies, known as *capelines*.

'Shells, I said!' Lorienne then explained for Coralie's benefit, 'She presumes we'll be blocking from scratch, but that's not possible as you need your new hats quickly. When your clothes arrive from Javier, you will perhaps come back for hats to complement them, blocked to your precise measurements.'

Coralie hid her surprise. At Pettrew's, hats had come in three or four standard sizes, with in-betweens created by varying the thickness of the inner band. This shop must serve wealthy women if bespoke blocks were in use. Lorienne turned to address Dietrich. 'Mademoiselle de Lirac has an air and style different from other ladies you have brought here, Herr von Elbing.'

The reply came back instantly. 'Mademoiselle de Lirac is entirely original. Comparing her to others is like comparing a graceful building to a fine painting. It would miss the point of both.'

Coralie left with three hats: a Panama, a broad-brimmed sisal and a gypsy bonnet that made her look like a blonde Vivien Leigh, all eyes. She adored them all but she wasn't going to say so. In La Passerinette, she'd felt like piggy-in-the-middle of a lovers' tiff. Something existed between Lorienne and Dietrich; this idyllic Paris existence had a serpent in it, after all. The Good Book said you should leave serpents in peace, but she didn't think she could.

'How do you feel?'

How did she feel? Enveloped, with Dietrich's legs wound around her. She had a double heartbeat, or perhaps it was his adding to hers. Where had it come from, their ferocious passion? On leaving La Passerinette, they'd lunched in a restaurant close by, and he'd been preoccupied. She'd worried she'd let him down again by having the wrong-shaped head, or asking for pink hats too often. Or perhaps her 'Prince Charming' reference rankled still. So, to return to the hotel and be flung on the bed, her clothes almost torn off, had been briefly stupefying. And then the clocks had stopped as she turned into the woman Dietrich seemed to want her to be – a creature of claws, teeth and uninhibited appetite. Sometimes dominant, sometimes yielding, discovering the power of mastery when it came to love. It was nothing to do with strength. It was in the mind, and that made it intoxicating. Best of all, there would be a next time, and a next time.

So, how *did* she feel? Nothing poetic offered itself, so she found images. She felt as light as beaten egg white, and weak as spinach dropped in boiling water. 'I couldn't walk from here to the window.'

'I will take that as a compliment. You know that between five and seven in the evening half of Paris is in bed together? It is the time set aside for love.'

'Is that why the chambermaids never come tapping at the door?'

'They may well be in bed themselves.'

'I hope the cook isn't. I'm starving again. That's why I keep imagining myself as food.'

Dietrich sank his teeth gently into her shoulder. 'You are ice-cream and honey, with a skim of salt.'

'That's nice . . . I was thinking of myself as some kind of ome-lette. Can we eat early?'

'You may order room service for yourself as I have to go out tonight.'

'Oh, Dietrich, why?'

'Business.'

'Can I come too?'

A little silence. 'Stay here and rest. Today you seemed tired.'

'I've got things on my mind. Things I have to tell you. See, I'm not exactly what you think I am.' There, she'd said it.

Another silence. The same? Colder? Longer? 'Go on.'

'I'm not really a milliner. I pretended I was, but I'm—'

'Playing at it.' He placed her hand on his belly so she felt the rise and fall of his breathing. 'Like Ottilia, who bought La Passerinette because she found herself in Paris, bored, and decided a hat shop would be the thing.'

'Wait, La Passerinette *belongs* to Ottilia?'

'Entirely. And listen to this: once she decided she would be a concert pianist so the most expensive piano in Berlin was delivered to her house. Three lessons later, she gave up. Why be a milliner, Coralie, when very ordinary girls can do it better?'

She let out an exasperated breath. Ottilia was like a bad dose of measles, all over her and up her nose. And if she never got a clear run at a confession, she'd never do it. She couldn't go on letting Dietrich think that she was a rich London girl, playing at a career, free of family ties, when the reality was so different. Sordid, even. 'Dietrich . . .' his breathing was growing shallower '. . . I want to tell you about . . .'

'Mm?'

She'd been going to say, 'Cora Masson,' but her courage ran out. She asked instead, 'What do you know of Lorienne Royer?'

'Too much, certainly, for her good.'

'That girl of hers – Violaine, was that her name? I'm damn sure she gets knocked about.'

'That's quite an allegation. What makes you say it?'

'I know the signs. There's a kind of posture you – people adopt after they've been clumped a few times. They know where the fist or boot comes from, but not when, so they're always in fear. I'd love to give the poor girl tips on how to fight back. Grabbing hold of somebody's eyelids stops a whole bunch of trouble, in my experience.' She was astonished to hear laughter.

'Take the fight to the enemy? But, Coralie, if Violaine is twenty-nine, she isn't a girl. She can fight her own battles.'

'I'm not so sure. I don't like Lorienne. D'you mind me saying?'

'Do I sound as if I do?'

'La Passerinette's your favourite hat shop, so I supposed you and she must be friends.'

'My love, I go to one tailor in Berlin, to another in Zürich, and always to Henry Poole in London. I don't necessarily like the gentlemen who measure me up.'

'But you wouldn't want me to punch them.'

'No – or to hang on to their eyelids.'

'I'd punch Lorienne if I caught her swiping at that poor girl. I hate bullies.'

Dietrich wound his fingers through hers. 'Let me stop being obtuse. I thoroughly dislike Lorienne Royer, though I hardly know her. She turns out lovely hats, and as it is Ottilia's shop, I take friends there when I can. Happy?'

'I suppose "obtuse" means being a clever-clogs,' she said crossly. *How many 'friends' did he take hat-shopping?* 'How can you dislike somebody without knowing them?'

'Do you like Sir Oswald Mosley?'

The question bewildered her. What had that got to do with Lorienne? 'Mosley the Fascist? I hate Fascists. They're ignorant. Once, we ran out of silk ribbon at Pettrew's because those daft sods burned down the warehouse supplying it because it was owned by Jews. Three weeks we were laid off—' she ended, on an intake of breath. God help her, she'd just accidentally spat out that she was a factory girl.

'So you don't like Oswald Mosley, even though you don't know him, which proves that disliking a stranger is sometimes more than unexamined prejudice.'

She waited for Dietrich to catch up with her error but he went on, 'Lorienne Royer was Ottilia's lady's maid before the present one. Lorienne wanted to go on to better things and Ottilia handed La Passerinette to her to run. They are supposed to share the profits fifty-fifty. Mademoiselle Royer is efficient, but I don't consider her particularly talented.'

'No,' Coralie rushed in. 'Violaine's got all the skill. The way she twisted a simple piece of felt into something beautiful . . . What makes her stay?'

'I have no idea. However, I am certain that Ottilia gets nowhere near fifty per cent of the profits. So, I go in occasionally to remind Lorienne that I am around and have a sharp eye. She knows I'm in constant touch with Ottilia.'

Coralie laid her head on Dietrich's chest. Every conversation led to another woman. She remembered the key in Dietrich's hand. Whose door did it open? 'Who are you meeting tonight?'

'Business connections from Berlin. They're here to see the Exposition—'

'You promised to take me!'

'And I shall, but tonight it's just men. We will be speaking German and you would feel left out as we outbid each other in vulgar arrogance, as men invariably do at a business dinner.'

She drew shapes on his chest, waiting for the shortening of his breath. This new power might come in handy. 'Dietrich, what exactly is it you do for a living?'

'I effect the transfer of items from Person A to Person B, taking a commission.'

That was clear as mud. 'What items?'

'Art. Jewellery, sometimes, or rare books. Oriental antiques. Even old instruments and musical scores. If somebody has something rare or beautiful and is willing to sell it, I will transact the exchange.'

'You're a dealer.'

'I prefer to call myself a middle-man.'

'It's not very romantic.'

'You'd rather I were a handsome prince?'

'Yes.' She laughed, because it sounded as if he'd forgiven her. But still she wasn't at ease. A wife in Germany she could deal with, but not rivals in Paris. And already he was shifting away, immune to her caress.

After putting on his clothes, he leaned over and kissed her. 'I'm going up to my suite to take a bath. Shall I start yours running?'

'I don't want a bath yet.' She belted her arms around his waist, feeling the grain of his jacket, finding the flap of a pocket. 'Why don't you stay?'

He kissed her nose. 'No, and don't you go back to sleep.'

The door closed behind him. She waited a minute then opened her hand. Bit devious, picking a man's pocket as he kissed her, but his secretive ways were driving her mad.

Chapter Five

The key was like the one to the coal-shed at Barnham Street, though less rusty. The tag read, 'Von Silberstrom, Flat no. 1'.

'Von Silberstrom' sounded German. She sniffed the tag, in case some identifiable perfume clung to it. Then, feeling stupid, she flumped back on her pillows. Now she had to get the blasted key back into Dietrich's pocket without him knowing.

She could intercept him on his way out, though if he'd changed his jacket, and his manservant had hung it away, she'd be in trouble. She hadn't a key to his suite and could hardly ask sniffy Mr Brownlow to let her in. She closed her eyes, thinking she might just put the key on the floor of the lift to make Dietrich think he'd dropped it.

She woke, as from drugged sleep. Someone was calling her name.

Cora, get up! On your feet! Behind her eyelids, a face formed. A face framed with yellow-grey hair, a shaggy moustache obscuring the top lip. Opening her eyes, she saw the same face staring down. 'Dad,' she whispered. 'Don't hurt me. Marry Sheila if you want. I won't say anything to anybody.'

'Wake up, *Liebchen*. You did not order dinner.'

Her vision cleared. 'Dietrich?'

'Who else would be leaning over your bed?'

'What did I just say?'

The mattress dipped as he sat beside her. 'You said, "Cora, get up," and mistook me for your father.'

'He calls me Cora. *Called*, I mean. He's—'

'Dead. You told me on the train that you are an orphan, that you have nobody in the world. Do you often recall your father to life in your dreams?'

He *knew* she'd lied to him. It was in his voice, but she tried to duck the inevitable. 'Did your meeting go well?'

'Perfectly well. But I had intended to call somewhere beforehand, only when I looked for the key to get in, it was missing from my pocket. Have you seen it?'

'I expect it dropped out of your jacket.'

It was Dietrich who found it, nestled between her arm and her side. 'To know it was in my jacket suggests that you took it. Am I right?'

She thought of denying it but, in the end, nodded. 'I was curious.'

'To know my private affairs, where I go, whom I see? If I wished to share such things, I would do so. Don't you understand that, Cora?'

'Don't call me that. I'm Coralie.'

'Since we are playing the game of truth, you are Cora Masson from a place called Bermondsey. You came to Paris with me to escape a cruel situation.'

Her breath scraped. 'How do you know?'

'You took my manservant's seat on the train. You recall me having a conversation with Brownlow, just before the train left Victoria? I was instructing him to make enquiries about you.'

'That's beastly!'

'It was good sense. You had no luggage, you looked as though you had spent all night being chased by bloodhounds. I wanted to know who I was travelling with. Before becoming a gentleman's gentleman, Brownlow was a London police officer.'

She groaned. A bloody copper. No wonder the man gave her that bring-out-the-handcuffs look every time they bumped into each other.

'When you ran up to me at Victoria Station, calling at the top of your voice, it was your true accent everybody heard. Brownlow used to walk the beat in Greenwich, which I believe is a little way downriver from Bermondsey. A few telephone calls unearthed the name "de Lirac" because it seems your father always gave – should I say "gives"? – that name when arrested for being drunk and disorderly.'

'Why didn't you say this before?'

'I've been waiting for you to tell me. To warn me that I have abducted the daughter of a violent man.'

'Oh, he won't follow me here, no chance of that.'

'You misunderstand. I am not afraid of your father. Rather, I object to being . . . what's the word? . . . hoodwinked.'

'I've been trying to confess for days but the words sort of get stuck.' Coralie lay waiting for judgement. Liars were not lovable. Liars only got away with it by being sly, using their power. She wouldn't do that. No eyelash-fluttering, no persuasive caresses.

'Do you wish to tell me now?'

Yes. It would be a relief, actually. 'But you have to promise not to interrupt. Even if I can't find the words.'

Dietrich fetched her robe and held it for her as she got out of bed. 'You will talk and I will listen. When morning comes, there will be no more secrets between us.'

So Coralie told him everything about Pettrews, Donal and Mid-day sun, though when she got to the part about confronting her father and Sheila, her voice almost gave out. 'So now you know. I ran away because I'm scared witless of my dad.'

'You still think he might hurt you badly?'

'More than a black eye?' She gave a dry laugh. 'I'll say. The bricks on the floor in the shed where he works, he's dug them up and re-laid them. Something's buried and I'm afraid . . . terrified . . . it's my mum. I've always wondered why she didn't come back.'

She waited for soothing words, for an acknowledgement of her uncanny intuition or, better still, an expression of utter disbelief. But Dietrich said the worst thing possible: 'Then we should return to London and ask questions.'

'No! What if I learned that I'm right?'

'Surely that's better than not knowing.'

She dragged at her hair. 'I can't go back. Whatever's under those bricks, my father will do anything to keep it secret. Kill me, if he needs to. He's killed before, he boasts about it. "The first time is always the hardest," he used to say. "After that, it's easy."'

'It is not easy, Coralie. Forgive me, but you don't know what you are talking about.'

She tried a different argument, wanting to smother any notion of returning to London. 'I'd be homeless and jobless. Pettrew's wouldn't have me, not after I left without giving notice, and they wouldn't give me a reference. And once my dad's known to be walking out with a policewoman, I'd get the cold shoulder from all sides. People don't trust coppers where I come from. In Paris, at least, I have a chance of making new friends.'

Dietrich came and put his hands on her arms. She was shivering, though the open window let in a caressing southern breeze. 'Friends are not so easy to make in a strange city, and the French are quite introverted. Family-oriented,' he explained, seeing that the word was new to her. 'Don't expect to be drawn into a warm circle very quickly.'

'Being lonely among strangers beats being lonely among old friends. I can invent a new life here, a different me. I can imagine my mother living happily in New York, with a new family, still thinking about me from time to time. That way, there's hope.'

He sighed, accepting her arguments though clearly without sharing her logic. 'If you intend to change identity for ever, you must begin right away and be serious about it. You must destroy everything that refers to your past.'

She knew he was right. She couldn't play at being Coralie de Lirac. She had to *be* Coralie de Lirac. 'I threw away the clothes I travelled in. They reminded me too much of what I'd escaped.'

'You must eject every memory of that old life – even the memory of those you still care for.' Dietrich pulled her tight against him, absorbing the unexpected burst of weeping his words had provoked. He helped her to the bed and they lay side by side, Coralie's hiccuping the only sound.

Eventually, she said, 'So you won't make me go back?'

He kissed her. 'Not if you are completely certain about staying here.' Reaching for the bedside telephone, he called down to room service, ordering a light supper and two brandies. Minutes later, she was propped up against the pillows, marvelling at the way the liquor snaked like fire down her throat. 'I want to stay. I can't explain why, but I feel anything is possible in Paris.'

Dietrich took her glass from her so he could kiss her again. 'And I like having you here with me. It's a good feeling to be needed. We need each other.'

Chapter Six

As June gave way to July, Dietrich went often to the Paris Expo but always alone, explaining that his compatriots had flocked there to buy artworks and were congregating at the German pavilion. During his trip to England, he had acquired paintings of a kind that were very popular in Germany, and was set to make a year's income in a matter of weeks. 'The less reassuring the real world becomes, the more my fellow Germans want rustic vistas and cosy family scenes.' He had snapped up crate-loads almost for nothing, he told her, which would be auctioned in Paris. He was busy whipping up interest.

He couldn't take Coralie to these meetings because his contacts knew his wife in some degree or other. 'It would be disrespectful to Hiltrud,' he explained.

'Dietrich, do you and your wife live completely apart?'

'Emotionally – yes. But I imagine our neighbours think us a conventional family, for all I'm absent much of the time. We have to consider the children's feelings.'

His personal apartment was just off Potsdamer Platz in the middle of Berlin, he told her. As for his wife, she rarely stirred from their townhouse in Hohen Neuendorf, a short train journey north of the city. Claudia, who was twelve, was spending summer at home with her mother. Waldo, fifteen, was at a summer camp with a lot of other boys, and Coralie sensed that Dietrich had reservations about this. The boy was not strong, owing to a heart problem that affected his breathing. Coralie remembered her first weeks at Granny Flynn's, also aged fourteen. Nobody had given a damn about her lungs.

Did Dietrich call his wife on the telephone for intimate chats? Or write pages to her in the privacy of his room? He wrote post-cards to his children several times a week, dashing them off as they sat at their favourite outdoor tables. Those to his daughter were posted as they were, but those to Waldo always went into a sturdy envelope and Dietrich would run the heel of his hand over the gum-strip, ensuring there were no weak spots in the seal. 'No privacy at camp,' he'd say.

One night, when he'd left her to her own devices, she found herself missing Pettrew's. Missing the tea-break chatter, the walk home, arms linked, with Donal's sisters, Doreen and Marion. She even missed working with her hands. Had anyone asked her a month ago her opinion of idleness, she'd have said, 'Perfect! When can I start?' Yet it seemed she wasn't fitted for it. So uncom-fortable did this knowledge make her that Coralie went up to the very top of the hotel and invited the manservant, Brownlow, to take a drink with her in the bar. With a glass in her hand, her fingers might forget their yearning to be busy.

Brownlow's answer was short. 'That would be inadvisable, Miss. In any case, I don't drink.'

So that was that. It would have to be the wireless, or reading. Dietrich had taken her to a bookshop on rue de l'Odéon, the street where her French teacher Louise Deveau lived. Steering her away from romance writers, he'd chided, 'You don't need the euphemistic alternative, you have me.' He'd bought her a book by Ernest Hemingway.

'Everyone should read *A Farewell to Arms*, most particularly men who like war. It should be required reading in Germany, but we burn it instead.' The shop's owner had offered the German translation, *In Einem Andern Land*. Dietrich had bought that, too, saying, 'Read the two together, and you'll learn German without trying.'

The first week of July drifted by. Dietrich and language lessons by day, alone by night. Brownlow was now accompanying Dietrich on his nightly excursions which was the worst snub of all.

Her downcast manner must have impinged on him because one evening Dietrich cancelled his plans and took her to Montmartre, to boulevard de Clichy for a taste of nightlife.

The Rose Noire was darkly anonymous. Little danger of Hiltrud von Elbing's acquaintances chancing upon them there. The resident band were playing swing, slow and seductive, perfect for swaying in Dietrich's arms. In their second set, they upped the tempo for the Lindyhop.

Dietrich sat out the fast dances, but when a black man called Dezi Rice, who had previously sung onstage, approached and invited Coralie to partner him, he waved her off, saying he didn't mind so long as she came back afterwards. She assumed it was a distaste for wild American rhythms that kept Dietrich in his chair, but he insisted it was more to do with ligaments.

'What's ligament?' she asked later, as their dinner was brought to them.

'The tissue that joins bones to bones. It stretches.' They'd been served trout mousse in oyster shells, a house delicacy that took the place of Île de Ré oysters during the hot months of summer. He bent an empty shell backwards, showing how it was hinged. 'Damage a ligament badly enough, it snaps. See?' He broke the hinge.

'You damaged yours?'

'Ruptured. And this' – he raked his hair back to reveal a scar to his hairline, raised like the pith of an orange – 'I crashed.'

'Driving too fast?' She remembered the lipstick-red Mercedes Roadster.

'You've heard of Baron von Richthofen?'

'The bloody Red Baron? You're not him, are you?'

He put oyster shells on her plate, offering her the black truffle sauce that came with the mousse. 'No, but I flew with him in 1915.'

'In the war?'

Dietrich nodded. 'Richthofen called me "Kleiner" because, for a while, I was the youngest pilot in the army air service.'

'Were you an air—' She bit her lip. She'd been about to say 'air ace'. She had to keep reminding herself that Dietrich had been on the wrong side. 'Did you get shot down?'

'Winged, otherwise I wouldn't be here. I was hit by a Canadian pilot flying a DH.2. That's a British plane, and it was a dog-fight over the British forward lines near Arras.'

'I suppose the Canadian thought he was doing his job.'

'Of course. My gunner would have got him, given a chance. We went into a spin but I straightened out, landed in a ditch, and fractured my patella. My knee,' he translated. 'And gained this.' He indicated the scar.

'You should pretend it's a duelling scar.'

'My father had one of those across his left eye, like all good Prussian aristocrats – he despised mine because it did not come from the edge of a sword.'

Coralie sipped her wine, a chilled Pissotte from the west of France recommended by the club's friendly sommelier, Félix. How strange life was. Last month, she'd been a factory hand whose favourite tipple was Guinness. Her opinion of Germans had been pretty cut and dried. Now look at her, in steamy cahoots with a man who'd won his spurs shooting down British boys over France. By the time their oysters shells were empty, she'd learned he'd been sixteen when the Great War started – which made him thirty-nine now – and eighteen when he flew his first mission for the Kaiser. She'd been a babe in arms.

A new conversational topic was in order. Looking around, she asked Dietrich what he thought of women dining in hats. Several expensively dressed women were doing just that. 'I'd feel funny, eating with a hat on.'

'In my mother's day it was *de rigueur* except at private dinner parties. Since you cannot Lindyhop in a hat any more than you can march in rubber flippers, why bother?'

Maybe. She'd enjoyed being hurled round the dance floor but, still, these after-dark hats with their diamond pins and cowlicks of net were very desirable. She could imagine herself perched on a window-seat, the wireless on, constructing satin pillboxes for wealthy clients. Trimmings in a basket . . . busy fingers. Only this time, working for herself.

'I'm going to order steak for us next.' Dietrich leaned back to catch the eye of a waiter.

'Make sure they cook mine properly.' She'd seen plates go past with blood-gravy.

'You must to learn to eat meat pink, not grilled to the texture of a pilgrim's sandal.'

When she said, 'Pink for hats, brown for meat', he took her face between his hands and kissed her until a waiter coughed discreetly.

'Or we could go home?' Dietrich said. He consulted his watch, which had luminous hands and a worn leather strap.

'We don't have a home.'

'No. We have freedom, now you've unburdened yourself.' When the waiter had left, he continued, 'You have unburdened yourself? Or do you need to tell me more about this friend, Donal? Was it he who took your virginity?'

So he had noticed. Course he had. 'It wasn't Donal. He and I have never been more than pals. Can I tell you another time? I feel raw with so much telling.'

'I have no business to ask, but do not blame me for minding.'

'When I'm ready.'

'And until then you are free to be yourself. Free to be Coralie de Lirac, who walks down the boulevards of Paris with fifty pairs of eyes following after her.'

He was a little drunk, she decided. Fifty pairs of eyes? Maybe, if she had her skirt tucked into her drawers.

'I want you to imbibe Paris, Coralie, absorb her so that I can see her through your eyes.'

'See her through your own!'

'You understand that to us Germans, Paris, La Lutèce, is the mythical white hart we chase through the dark forests. She is our quarry, our fantasy, for ever out of reach.'

Two bottles of Pissotte was probably why she answered, 'I'm going to get hold of her by the tail, just you see. But would you buy me a hat shop? Like Ottilia did for Lorienne?'

It was probably why he laughed and said, 'Of course, just not yet.'

That night, in each other's arms, he murmured, 'If you intend to remain in Paris, your papers, your language skills, your history must all be impeccable. All traces of Englishness must be erased, including overcooked meat.'

'You're frightening me.'

'Coralie de Lirac must have a history nobody can dispute. You told me your father was Belgian?'

'From Tubize, in Brabant.'

'Then we will start there. You must have photographs taken. Easy enough. Louise Deveau can take you to a booth in one of the big department stores.'

He said nothing more about it until, around mid-July, he handed her a parcel. 'Your new identity.'

They were sitting on a bench in parc Monceau, filling in the time between making love and having dinner. Men in overalls were fixing *tricolor* bunting between the trees in preparation for the 14 July celebrations. Taking documents from an envelope, she discovered that Coralie de Lirac had been born Marie-Caroline, daughter of Guy de Lirac, a lawyer from Nivelles, Belgium. 'What's wrong with Tubize?'

'Why give the hounds an easy trail? Go to Nivelles some day, familiarise yourself with it.'

'All right. But come on, a lawyer? My dad hates the law.'

'*Hated.* He is dead, your poor father from Nivelles.'

'Why Marie-Caroline? Why give me something extra to remember?'

'In Catholic France and Belgium, children are invariably named for saints and I cannot find a Sainte Coralie.'

'I was called Cora for my grandmother, but Mum said Coralie had a nicer ring. She said it would stand out on a billboard if I ever followed her into the profession. Theatre, I mean.'

'You can still be Coralie. The French have nicknames too. But you were baptised Marie-Caroline.'

Her mother had been given the maiden name of Marlène Decorte, also from Nivelles. There was a French passport, artfully aged, giving Coralie's occupation as a *modiste*, which, Dietrich said, was the nearest the French had to 'milliner'. Her birthdate was given as 8 November 1915.

She exclaimed, 'I'm October the twenty-second!'

'Not any more. Learn every word of these papers. Repeat them to your reflection in the mirror night and morning. November the eighth is my birthday, which means we can always celebrate together. Wherever we may be.'

'In Paris, I hope.'

'I hope too, but I can't neglect my other life for ever. Like the little bird on Ottilia's shop window, I am *passerine*.'

'Is that where "La Passerinette" comes from? I've always wondered—'

'She is a little migratory bird. Pretty, grey and rose-pink and she breeds in southern France, in dry thickets, but winters in Africa.'

'So . . .'

'Like la Passerinette, I perch, I fly away. These documents will get you a residence certificate.'

'If you say so.'

'Coralie, what is the matter?'

'I won't remember a new birthday, and if you'd grown up in London, you'd hate November. Fog, beginning to end.'

'From now on, talk only of Paris.' Taking the papers from her because she was crumpling them, Dietrich added, 'On November the eighth, I will take you to the Tour d'Argent and afterwards, love you in ways that transcend your experience and stretch my imagination. Then you will remember it.'

'So you're staying until November?'

Dietrich moved a curl that had dropped over her eye. 'I'll stay until I know you can fly unaided.'

*

They danced in the hot streets on 14 July and she slept till noon the following day, when Dietrich telephoned her room to tell her to put on one of her La Passerinette hats, 'Whichever feels most comfortable, and a simple dress. You must be able to move freely. I need your help.' Coralie sat up. He sounded serious.

'Ready in no time,' she promised, then remembered she had a fitting at Javier at two, for autumn suits. Four summer ensembles had already been delivered: one black, three white. She hadn't worn them. They were gorgeous but, she hated to admit it, the waistlines were too tight. Blame croissants and jam. 'Dietrich, I forgot – I have that appointment . . . but I can easily cancel.'

'No, don't do that. We'll visit Javier, and then on to rue de Vaugirard afterwards.'

'Where's that?'

'Left Bank, by the Palais de Luxembourg.'

'I'm scared, Dietrich.'

'Of what?'

'Of needing to be useful. I've forgotten how.'

He only laughed.

Coralie sang as she put on a spotted linen dress and one of the soft, sisal hats Lorienne had made for her. She even laughed later as the fitter at Maison Javier exclaimed, 'I think that you are finally learning to enjoy, and not endure, Mademoiselle. Though, pardon, you have put three centimetres on your middle since I first met you. Another adjustment to your *toile*, I fear.'

Afterwards Coralie met Dietrich in the salon, and they set off for the Left Bank, taking the Métro two stops further than necessary for the pleasure of walking back through the Jardin du Luxembourg, whose fountains and geometric lawns freshened a blazing day. On rue de Vaugirard, they stopped at a four-storey house overlooking a corner of the gardens. Imposing double doors contained a wicket, a smaller door cut into the right-hand side. Dietrich rang a bell, and the wicket was eventually opened by a man whose empty left sleeve was pinned, Nelson-style, across his front. *Old soldier*, Coralie thought. Though not that old, in fact. Mid-fifties, her father's age. Her *former* father's age. The man demanded to know their business.

Dietrich replied patiently, 'I am Graf von Elbing. Madame Corvet has been letting me in without fuss every day for a month.'

So this was where he'd been coming. Coralie stole a glance at the name plaque to one side of the door, reading 'von Silberstrom'. What was the likelihood that Dietrich would shortly produce the key they'd fallen out over?

The concierge was refusing to summon his wife. 'Before this, you came with another man. Where is he?'

Dietrich sighed. 'Is that really your business, Monsieur Corvet? Kindly let us in.'

Corvet wrapped his good arm around his empty sleeve. 'Only my wife and I are authorised to enter this property without Madame la Baronne being present.'

'That is not correct. I am also authorised to enter, whenever I wish, by the express desire of Madame la Baronne.'

Corvet jutted his chin. 'Think you can take over everything, don't you, you Germans? And now you're bombing the hell out of Spain. Murderer. Go away, before I call a policeman!'

Coralie smothered a giggle. She'd never seen Dietrich so completely flummoxed. But it was too hot to stand about waiting for a declaration of peace. With a soft groan, she reached for the wall and gave at the knees. 'I'm going to faint—'

A moment later she was seated in a cool courtyard, and the concierge was fetching water. Without giving him time to return, Dietrich drew her into the lobby, where he pressed the lift button

for level two, *deuxième étage*. As they went up, he kissed the side
of Coralie's head. 'Well performed. I'd have been standing outside
all evening. Memories are long, very long.'

'I'm not surprised, if he lost his arm fighting you lot. What did
he mean about Spain? They're having a civil war, aren't they?'

Dietrich said nothing while the lift was in motion. But as he
opened the lattice cage-door, he said, 'German air squadrons are
supporting Franco's Nationalists against the Spanish Republicans.
They've bombed Madrid and some smaller towns.'

She didn't know who Franco was, but she'd heard the porter
at the Duet grumbling about 'damn Fascists' trying to overthrow an elected government. For her part, she was on the side
of the people being bombed. But Dietrich? His tone had given
little away and there was nothing to read in his profile. She tried
fishing: 'D'you wish you were there?'

'Flying? Sometimes. You never lose the love. Change the subject, Coralie. You are very good at that.'

'Who are we visiting today?'

'Nobody.' Dietrich steered her towards a door that was a single
sheet of walnut veneer, brass knob and fingerplate polished to a
sheen.

Coralie had already admired the wrought-iron stair balustrade,
with its gleaming brass handrail. Elbow grease was clearly in good
supply here. This building, like virtually all those she'd entered in
Paris, consisted of separate flats linked by service stairs, but this
was the finest so far. The floor below would contain the best flat,
with high ceilings and lacy window balconies. This one, the door
to which Dietrich was unlocking with the predicted silver key,
would house people a social step down. 'Who is the "Madame
la Baronne" Corvet mentioned?'

'Ottilia, of course.'

'She's an aristocrat?'

'No.' Dietrich let her precede him and closed the door behind her. 'Titles have no sway in Germany. All they do is get you tables in restaurants. Sometimes they get you into trouble.'

'I've come across barons in fairy tales and they're always wicked.'

'Ottilia's father was Freiherr von Silberstrom, an industrialist from Berlin, though the family came originally from Austria. Ottilia was born "Freiin", which translates as "Baroness", or "Madame la Baronne", and she has no trace of wickedness.'

'I'm sure you told me she was married. So why does she use her father's name, not her husband's?'

Dietrich flicked on a light, saying, 'Go ahead but take care, the place is hazardous. To answer your question, Ottilia's husband is Franz Lascar, who was a famous singer in Germany but fell out with the Berlin Gestapo – they're our secret police force. His songs insulted our leader. Ottilia reverted to her maiden name, hoping the Gestapo would overlook the fact that she was married to a traitor.'

'Did they?'

'The Gestapo do not overlook anything. Lascar is, and always was, bad for her.'

'Like too much jam? Ouch!' Her knuckle struck a tea-chest edged with metal. She sucked, tasting blood.

'I said be careful.'

In the front room, shutters blotted out the daylight and a smell of resin took her straight back to her father's workshop. When Dietrich switched on the main light, followed by a pair of standard lamps, Coralie counted two dozen tea-chests and as many shallow crates. It was like Rotherhithe docks when a ship was being loaded. The resin smell came from sacks full of shavings – presumably to protect the valuables inside the chests. What looked to be hundreds of unframed pictures and prints were stacked against the walls. 'You bought all this in England?'

'No, no. My English purchases are in a vault near the Hôtel Drouot, the auction house where they will be sold.' Dietrich was removing his jacket and tie. '*This* is Ottilia's art collection.'

'It has its own apartment?'

'Not just its own apartment.' Dietrich threw open the shutters, flooding the room with sunlight. The vista was of the Jardin du Luxembourg, summer leaves behind wrought-iron railings. 'Look – it even has a view of the Orangerie. That's the building through the trees. Nothing but the best for Ottilia's pictures. They are, theoretically, worth a million pounds.'

She gaped. As a kid, she'd played a game with Donal that began, 'If I had a hundred pounds, I'd buy . . .' They'd considered a hundred pounds quite sufficient for the purchase of their wildest dreams. Dietrich dropped his cufflinks into his pocket and rolled up his sleeves. 'With Brownlow's assistance, I have spent every day since June the nineteenth updating the inventory, wrapping and packing.'

Coralie brushed shavings from the top of the nearest chest, which contained paintings wrapped in near-transparent paper, sealed with gum-strip and labelled. Rolls of the same misty-white paper stood at one end of the room. 'What a job! I wouldn't want to be stuck with Brownlow for nearly a month,' she said.

'No. Brownlow is ill-suited to an artistic environment. Show him an apple, he thinks, "Apple dumpling", not "Still life by a north-facing aperture".'

'I wouldn't think that either. I'd think Eve's pudding, or fritters with vanilla sugar.'

'Still, I doubt I would have to explain everything twice to you. But, seriously, you must also see I am nowhere near the end, and already I have found pieces missing – for all Monsieur Corvet's watchfulness.'

She sensed his anger. 'Someone's been stealing?'

'Small items, but those are often the most important. It is why I am so determined to finish, to get these crates away to safety.'

'So what's my job?'

Dietrich took a leather-bound book from a shelf. 'This is the inventory I drew up two years ago, when the collection left Berlin. I will read you a name from the list, and a description, then you will find the picture. I will inspect it, make a comment as to its condition and tick it off. You will wrap and label. Only when we've catalogued every last thing can I judge what is missing. You, with a mind that sees in pictures . . . I should have asked you before.'

'I wish you had.' Coralie surveyed the unframed works against the skirting boards and wondered if Brownlow had been sacked. That'd be a turn-up. 'Where's it going, this collection?'

'To Neuendorf, as soon as Ottilia gives her permission. She never gets round to things, and her husband always has better ideas on how to handle her wealth. He would like the collection but my job is to prevent all swindlers getting their hands on it, whether they be light-fingered outsiders or famous tenors.'

He held up the ledger to the light the better to read it. 'Right. This is where I left off last time. "View of Oxford colleges across the meadows, George Pyne, 1867, mixed medium, pencil and watercolour." Think you can find it for me?'

Coralie's confidence plunged. She so wanted to help – to outdo vinegar-chops Brownlow – but the nearest she'd ever got to art was saucy seaside postcards. And what the heck was a mixed medium? Walking across the room, selecting a stack at random, she pulled out a glum-looking study of buildings and a meadow. 'This it?'

Dietrich took it from her. 'My God, you are an extraordinary woman. Keep this up, we'll be finished in time for dinner.'

It took them four days, and by the end Coralie felt she'd passed through a cultural baptism. At times, tired out by the task, they'd snapped at each other. But mostly they'd worked, joined by an invisible thread. Madame Corvet, as obliging as her husband was sour, brought them coffee and bags of brioche while they worked. At the stroke of six, Dietrich would uncork wine, and by midnight they were crashing into the tea-chests but laughing about it. When each chest was full, they nailed the lid down and toasted it with more wine. Dietrich was intrigued at Coralie's deftness with a hammer.

'When I was little, my dad worked at the Old Vic theatre. He'd take me backstage—'

'Your father was a lawyer from the town of Nivelles, remember?'

By the time the taxi dropped them back at the Duet, they were good only for bed, where they would lie entangled until Brownlow knocked at the door at around seven, informing them, in what Coralie called his coffin-voice, that he had drawn Graf von Elbing's bath and laid out his clothes – '*Upstairs.*' Brownlow was, Dietrich hinted, sulking. Coralie had usurped him again, but she was too absorbed by her new occupation to care.

At six twenty-nine on Tuesday, 20 July, Dietrich closed the ledger with a snap. 'That was the last picture signed off.'

'What about the ones beside the window?'

'Those I am negotiating to sell on Ottilia's behalf. She needs cash, her husband being too much of an artist to work for a living. Still, now I know what is missing.'

Coralie slid down the wall to the floor. Her fingers felt like butcher's sausages. 'You mean "stolen"?'

'It's possible that Ottilia gave some pieces away. She does that – gives things to people to please them.'

'Like giving La Passerinette to Lorienne?'

'I try to make her understand that if you don't respect what you have, people will take it from you. The more they rob you, the less they value what you are.'

His voice goes to velvet when he speaks of her, Coralie thought.

Madame Corvet came in just then, bringing peach tart fresh from the oven, and Dietrich's next words were for her: 'Madame, I want the lock to this flat changed, and a double one to replace it. Tonight.'

The concierge stammered, 'Without Madame la Baronne's instruction?'

Dietrich took a letter from his pocket. 'Here is her instruction. She gives me *carte blanche* to do as I see fit here. Do you doubt that I have Madame la Baronne's best interests at heart?'

Madame Corvet cast an uncertain glance at the few unpacked pictures, but all she said was, 'A double lock, as soon as it can be done.'

They walked back to the hotel. A fine drizzle was falling, the streets filled with a musty sweetness. 'I love Paris in the rain,' Coralie murmured.

'I love Paris at every season.'

As they crossed the river, Coralie asked, 'Dietrich, are you in love with Ottilia?'

He kept his eyes ahead. 'We were to be married, but it couldn't happen.'

'That wasn't what I asked.'

Dietrich stopped, turned Coralie to face him. 'I love her, yes.'

Not much you could say to that. Actually, saying anything was out of the question because Coralie suddenly felt sick. The rest of the way to the Duet, she breathed deeply and when they arrived, she took the stairs rather than wait for the lift, making it to her bathroom just in time.

Next morning, she called at a pharmacy on boulevard Malesherbes for something to deal with sickness and, returning, found Brownlow in the lobby. Usual dapper self, even the silk panel at the back of his waistcoat ironed smooth. He was collecting post from the desk clerk. They both noticed her and she fancied Brownlow said something crude. Had a *lady* pinched his seat on the Pullman, he'd have got over it. But a Bermondsey chiseller like her? The affront was eternal.

She hung back as he left the lobby, not fancying a ride in the lift with him. When it came down again, she found a letter on the floor. A German stamp and 'Herr Graf von Elbing' on the front suggested Brownlow had been careless.

What made her tear into it like that, though? Appalled, she tried to re-seal it, but there was no disguising what she'd done. Pulling the letter from the envelope, she read the first line: '*Mein lieber Vater*'. My dear father.

She'd sunk, really sunk. The lift made its whining, decelerating noise and she heard a man's cough. Brownlow, waiting for her – or, more likely, waiting for the lift because he'd laid out the letters and found one short. Where to hide it? Her dress had no pockets. She had no stocking tops to push it into because she'd gone out in ankle socks. There was a mat on the lift floor. She shoved the letter underneath with half a second to spare before Brownlow opened the door.

115

Chapter Seven

At last, Dietrich was taking her to the Expo. Forty-four countries had designed pavilions for the event, though, as Dietrich pointed out, only Frenchmen had been allowed to do the actual building so many remained unfinished two months after the official opening.

'They'd be finished if Germans had built them?'

'Naturally. The German pavilion was the first completed.'

'I thought the Russian one was,' she teased.

'You always have a comeback, Coralie. Tell me something fascinating instead. Tell me what you see.'

They were walking down the Chaillot hill between an avenue of fountains, the newly constructed Palais de Chaillot behind them. In front of them, the Seine flowed molten amber in the evening light. 'If you rolled a huge ball through the middle of these fountains and across the river, the Eiffel Tower would go down like a skittle. Satisfied, Monsieur le Comte?'

'Oh, delighted.'

'Can we go to the Japanese pavilion first? I like Oriental things.'

'Then you'll be disappointed. The Japanese pavilion is modernist architecture in its purest form.'

'Why does everything have to change?'

'Because life would stagnate otherwise. Coralie, tonight I have things to say to you.'

'You do?' Her thoughts flew to the letter, which must be hidden still, like a murder victim covered with a sheet. She turned away to hide her guilty flush. Anything, *anything* but discovery. 'What things?'

'Be patient. First, we are meeting a business associate on the German pavilion's roof terrace.'

She sensed a change in him. A refocusing, as when the wheel is turned on a cine-projector and the picture sharpens.

The German pavilion was floodlit, an eagle dominating its summit. Flags rippled at the entrance, red and white, imprinted with black swastikas. Coralie and Dietrich were held up at the doorway by a group of people conversing in German. A man was screwing a flash-bulb connector to an important-looking camera, talking as he did so. He wore a swastika armband on his sleeve. Dietrich seemed interested in what he was saying.

'What's going on?' Coralie asked.

'This man wants to photograph the Russian pavilion.' Dietrich pointed to an edifice on the opposite side of the boulevard. Two giants dominated that roof: a man with a hammer, a woman with a sickle. 'He reports for his home newspaper in Bavaria and wants to show how inferior Russian work is to German.'

'But it isn't. It isn't as tall as this building but it's still beautiful. I don't understand why everything German has to be the best.'

'I didn't say it was. I am repeating another's opinion.' Dietrich addressed the group in his own language. The man with the camera answered and then, to Coralie's confusion, made a straight-arm salute and cried, '*Heil Hitler!*'

'*Heil Hitler!*' Dietrich replied.

Inside the pavilion, Coralie let him lead the way. She didn't know where to look or what to say. She'd seen Pathé newsreels of the German leader making speeches to crowds fifty rows deep. She'd heard the people returning his name from one throat with fanatical enthusiasm. She'd seen black-shirted boys outside pubs in South London copying them, but it had never occurred to her that Dietrich might share the mania. She felt as if she'd left one Dietrich outside the pavilion and come in with another.

Swastikas everywhere. On the floor tiles, on photo displays, even in the stained-glass windows exalting German craftsmanship. What had become of saints with faraway expressions? Coralie hung even further back as Dietrich greeted two men, clicking his heels, declaring, '*Heil Hitler!*'

What was wrong with them? English people didn't go round shouting, 'God save the King!' at each other. She pretended to be fascinated by photographic panels displaying brand-new roads, *Autobahns*, which looked as if they stretched for ever, not a tram or a delivery truck to be seen. At the same time, she eavesdropped on Dietrich and his companions who were speaking in gruff, rapid German. Earlier that month, she'd asked Mademoiselle Deveau if she could spend one of their twice-daily sessions learning German instead of French. Giving the dry smile that was the nearest she ever got to outright humour, Louise Deveau had answered, 'You plan to astonish Dietrich some day by conversing in fluent German? I wish you well. Not every man likes a surprise.'

Coralie had made good progress, but not enough to make sense of what the three men were saying, beyond their regular references to '*der Führer*'. They made a breathtakingly good-looking trio, though: tall and well-built. Dietrich and the man nearest to him in age were both very fair while the youngest, probably in his early thirties, had light-brown hair. They might have been three film stars stopping for a chat.

At last they shook hands and parted, then Dietrich looked around for her.

She stepped forward. 'Your business associates?'

'No, friends. Good friends. Let's get a drink.'

Trailing him up a flight of stairs, Coralie saw that the railings were formed from interlocked silver swastikas.

On the roof-garden terrace, Dietrich ordered beer for himself and ice-cold apple juice for Coralie, which arrived in a tall glass with a straw. She drank it fast. She could have asked more about his friends – but she didn't really want to know. It should be no surprise that Dietrich was political but, ignorant as she was, she didn't like the feel of his allegiances. He ordered her another apple juice and, while they waited, took something from his pocket.

'I have important things to say to you, but sometimes objects speak louder than words.' He opened his palm, revealing a gold ring with a blood-red stone at its centre.

'Oh. It's . . .'

'Old and dull.' He smiled. 'I am starting to appreciate your tastes, but this is no trinket.'

'Are you giving it to me?'

He looked deep into her eyes, flooding her with emotions that scared her. 'You have given me so much that I want to give something of myself to you. Put it into your bag and look after it.'

She pretended she hadn't heard and put the ring on her middle finger. It was too large so she gave it back, watching him drop it into his jacket pocket with resignation. 'Give it to me again in November, on our birthday.'

'Yes, we need to talk about your future—'

'Herr Graf von Elbing, good evening!' A thin man with a sunburned complexion stopped at their table and extended his hand to Dietrich.

This, presumably, was the business associate. Coralie waited for '*Heil Hitler*', and when it didn't come, wondered if you only did that with friends. Or maybe you didn't *heil* if you were wearing a white linen suit and crushing a Panama hat under your arm, as the newcomer was. Dietrich made introductions.

'My companion, Mademoiselle de Lirac. Coralie, may I present Thierry-Edgar Clisson, an old acquaintance and a fine art dealer, in every sense.'

Clisson laughed. 'You flatter me, Graf. Enchanted, Mademoiselle.' He kissed her hand.

That kiss was Clisson's last moment of silence for several minutes. Spouting like the Chaillot fountains, he told her that he was going abroad for a holiday in a few days and this was his final meeting before he went. 'A whole month, bursting with friends. Fishing, outdoor cooking, lounging, every dissipation imaginable.' Home in Paris was over the shop in rue de Seine, he told her. 'Do you know it? A mere stone's throw from where Baudelaire lived, and George Sand too. I hope you are impressed.'

'Terribly,' she said. 'Were they both painters?'

Dietrich's headshake warned of pitfalls, so she left it at that.

The floors below his apartment, Clisson told her, housed the most exclusive gallery of medieval art in France, and upstairs he entertained the *crème de la crème*. There, or at his château at Dreux in the Eure-et-Loir. 'Thanks to my childhood, I cannot be easy with just one home. Don't you feel the same? My parents separated and I tramped back and forth between continents until I turned twenty-one, when I realised I was bringing joy to nobody but the cobblers who re-heeled my shoes. I wrote to both parents saying that henceforth, if they wished to see me, *they* must travel.'

'That was brave. Did you see them again?'

The waiter arrived, and Clisson ordered champagne, insisting that it was his treat. Meeting his 'dear, dear friend and so charming a lady' demanded the best Pommery. He waited until it was poured before answering, 'My father ended up in a colonial outpost, married a native girl, and spawned a brood of children as incomprehensible as his paintings. Did I say he ran a painting academy for the terminally untalented? He never could afford the passage back to France. Hurrah. It is propaganda put about by sentimentalists that parents always love their children and vice versa.'

He likes cats, Coralie thought. His silver cufflinks had a feline paw-print etched on them.

'Of my mother,' Clisson continued, 'I saw a great deal. Here and in Berlin. She remarried, a German air-force man. Perfectly nice fellow, the general, so I relented. Trains from Paris to Berlin are very good, the journey no trouble when one travels first class.'

'Your mother was an excellent woman.' Dietrich spoke his first words since making the introductions.

Clisson never took his eyes off Coralie. Neither did he blink. Perhaps he couldn't, as his eyes bulged like a frog's. She had no idea if he admired her or was inspecting her for cracks. Even when he spoke to Dietrich, he stared at her. 'Are we dining together tonight?'

'No. Mademoiselle de Lirac and I will return to our hotel.'

'So be it. I shall dine at Le Roi George in the British pavilion while you retire to your bed.' If he'd said, 'while you bed your mistress', Clisson couldn't have been clearer. Then, at last, he released Coralie's gaze. 'Dear Graf, let us get to business. Your note implied that you have some pieces from the von Silberstrom hoard to wave under my nose. Last time we spoke, you implied that the collection was to be kept intact.' Clisson flashed Coralie a roguish glance. 'Mademoiselle de Lirac? What does your Dietrich know of the future that makes him suddenly anxious to sell paintings for cash?'

Coralie could have answered, 'Ottilia needs to keep her husband happy,' but just shrugged, unsure if she liked this gushing Frenchman.

'I am a Sensitive.' Clisson patted her wrist. 'I absorb impressions and, let me tell you, a stroll around this pavilion is equal to ten hours listening to loud martial music. There will be war and Dietrich knows how it will start, and we all know who will start it.'

'The Germans? They're boasting, that's all,' Coralie put in. 'They finished their pavilion first and they're making everyone else feel self-conscious.'

Clisson looked hard at her. 'I'm intrigued. De Lirac . . . Which part of France do you come from? Something in your accent I can't quite place.'

She said hastily, 'You gentlemen want to talk business and I need to visit the powder room.'

'Ladies are not expected to run away the moment the word "business" is uttered. This is France, not England.' Then Dietrich swore, realising what he'd said. He turned to Clisson, clearly intending to divert his attention. 'When we met last, you expressed an interest in some engravings by Albrecht Dürer.'

Clisson's eyes boggled. 'Sublime articles.'

'Well, they are still not for sale. What I *am* selling is a set of delightful Russian icons. If you view them tomorrow, I guarantee you first refusal.'

'But I'm going away on holiday, I told you.'

'Delay it, because I am going away too, and once I am gone, this opportunity closes.'

Coralie made her escape, and was through the doors of the

roof terrace before she allowed shock to overtake her. So, he was leaving. The ring had been an attempt at a parting gift. What was she going to do without him?

She found a lavatory some distance away. Inside a stall, she was sick again. Apples and champagne, not a great mix. Returning to the pavilion, she lingered in the swastika-decked foyer, unable to summon the will to climb the stairs. If someone threw a mattress down, she reckoned she'd lie on it and sleep for a week.

Clisson's talk had scared her. Surely Germany couldn't be planning a second war after the hell of the last. War would mean choosing sides and she had no illusions now as to where Dietrich's loyalties lay.

People dressed for dinner were filtering around her, like waves around a rock, so she returned to the roof garden, choosing a different door because she wasn't ready for Clisson's perceptive eye. She'd look at the flowers, she decided, and maybe even the display of Mercedes cars parked under an awning. She ached to be alone with Dietrich and have him reassure her that his planned trip to Germany was a short necessity, that Paris was where he wanted to be.

The carnations and freesias were at their scented peak in the evening air, but their beauty left her cold. She went to the car display, pretending she was selecting a Mercedes to drive away. For perhaps ten minutes, she inspected burr-walnut dashboards, chrome dials and reflections of herself in black panels. Clisson was still talking, she noticed, waving his hands in the air. Another bottle of champagne was arriving. Frustrated, Coralie went to the garden's edge, staring over the river that flowed like oil through a magenta twilight. Reflections soared from its depths, shimmering piles of gold sovereigns.

A party boat smashed through them, fireworks exploding from

its stern, reminding her of the fireworks that had lit the London sky in May for the coronation of George VI . . . Slipping away from Donal who'd taken her to see the display from London Bridge, she'd run back to Bermondsey. She'd had a rendezvous to keep with a sailor whose eyes were long-lashed and up-tilted. She'd lain with Rishal on the grass of Southwark Park and listened to him talk of his home, 'l'Île Maurice', where people spoke French. He'd been ecstatic to find a girl in London he could talk to. Ecstatic described the five succeeding nights. Then, on the sixth, he hadn't turned up. His ship had sailed and that was that.

Well, not quite. Coralie spread a hand over her stomach. Time to stop pretending all this sickness was down to coffee and funny foreign food. Using her fingers as a rough abacus, she counted just short of eleven weeks since Coronation night. She'd missed her monthlies twice in a row. Oldest tale in the book, wasn't it? Girl sleeps with boy, boy flits, girl is left with a bun in the oven. What the hell would she tell Dietrich? She had to say something before he left for Germany or he might come back and bump into her pregnant belly. She tried out a line: 'Dietrich, I've been a fool but I need help.'

She turned around. The table was empty. Dietrich and Thierry-Edgar Clisson had gone.

Chapter Eight

'Monsieur le Comte has left, Mademoiselle. He checked out and paid his bill an hour ago.'

Coralie shifted irritably. She'd never thought the Duet's desk clerk was quite the full payload. 'Von Elbing,' she said. 'Graf von Elbing.' The man was obviously mixing Dietrich up with some other guest.

'As I said,' the man stated flatly, 'Graf von Elbing paid his account and left.'

Coralie planted her feet. No fainting, no vapours. Dietrich, being a tidy sort, had paid his bill to keep his account clear. He'd saunter back in a moment and she'd be in his arms. 'Where has he gone?'

'I have no idea, Mademoiselle.' Was that a smirk? 'The taxi took him to Gare de l'Est, so I presume Berlin. He has gone home.'

Home. To his proper, respectable life. That's what the clerk meant. Colour stinging her cheeks, Coralie demanded, 'Did he leave anything for me?'

The clerk made a weak show of searching the shelf under his counter. 'It seems not. And, Mademoiselle, the establishment would be obliged if you would vacate your room tomorrow morning.'

A thought struck her. 'Did Brownlow accompany him? That's his man-servant.'

'I believe not.'

She pressed the button for the lift, relief flowing in. Dietrich had been called away on business and would be back, or he wouldn't have left his man in residence. Damn that clerk. She'd have it out with him later. As the lift rose, a prick of conscience made her search for the letter. She'd buy a fresh envelope while Dietrich was away, somehow forge the handwriting and steam off the stamp. It would be waiting for him when he came back.

Except there was no letter. She rolled the rug over. Nothing. A cleaner, she told herself. A cleaner had found it.

The door to Brownlow's room was wide open. A chambermaid she didn't recognise was stripping the bed.

'The man who was here – is he coming back?'

'*Non.*'

Had a letter been left for her? Anything with her name on it?

'*Non.*'

She went down to her room, still confident of a note under the door. Again, nothing. She went to bed, her fist in her mouth, her knees pulled up.

There was no drifting up through bubbles next morning. When the maid knocked, Coralie thought, I bet there's no breakfast. Her stomach growled.

But there was the usual generous tray. Coffee, though, not tea, as if, with her imminent departure, the kitchen's memory had failed. She got the coffee down by stirring in all the sugar lumps in the bowl, and ate every morsel on the tray. Confusion added itself to misery when a bouquet of fragrant dark-pink roses arrived for her. Dietrich was back?

'They were ordered yesterday afternoon, before Monsieur le Comte left for Berlin,' the bellboy told her. And no, Monsieur was not back.

She had about three thousand francs, money Dietrich had given her for taxis and which she'd squirrelled away by walking everywhere. How far would it stretch in Paris? No more hotels, for sure. It would have to be a hostel of the lino-floor-and-calico-sheet kind. The kind that catered for girls who'd been left up a gum tree.

Her first task was to find something to pack her clothes in. In the end, she dressed in her bulkiest garments and stuffed the rest into two La Passerinette hatboxes, keeping the third for her hats. She'd sell the Javier clothes. Unworn, they were bound to be snapped up. If she bumped into her own nice chambermaid she'd ask the name of a second-hand-clothes shop. She bumped into nobody. The Duet was as quiet as Sunday, though it was the last Thursday of July.

In the lobby, the porter coughed, implying, 'Gratuity?'

Bugger that. Hatboxes bumping her legs, she left without looking back. It would sweep around the hotel that Mademoiselle had left no tip and had taken the soap from the bathroom.

Miss McCullum's words nipped at her heels as she headed in the direction of the river: 'You really want to live somebody else's life?'

She'd replied, 'Every minute of every day,' with the impudent certainty of a one who had never truly been tested. Well, here she was, living the life of a girl abandoned in Paris, and it felt hideous.

It was a long walk to rue de l'Odéon, but she needed to talk to somebody who knew Dietrich. Mademoiselle Deveau might have a rational explanation for his departure. If she wasn't too late . . .

During their last lesson, Mademoiselle Deveau had given notice that she would be leaving Paris at the end of July. 'Come August, country air suddenly becomes an urgency,' she'd explained. They would resume lessons at the end of September. They wouldn't. Such luxuries were now out of the question.

When Mademoiselle Deveau answered her knock, the relief was too much for Coralie's fragile self-control. She burst into sobs.

Mademoiselle Deveau led her to a chair in the hall. Through an open door, Coralie saw a pair of suitcases, strapped ready for travelling, and a box of vegetables that was presumably destined for a neighbour who was staying at home. Mademoiselle Deveau stood while Coralie sobbed out her story. Finally, she sighed. 'You aren't the first, I'm afraid. Herr von Elbing came to me for lessons in Berlin not long after he'd broken off an engagement.'

'To Ottilia von Silberstrom. They couldn't marry.'

'"Couldn't" depends on which rules you live by. It was put about that she'd thrown him over, but really it was his doing. I'll tell you this: sometimes passion burns fast and hot, like dry straw. Men are good at walking away, while we women stay around poking the ash. A lesson to learn while you're still young. What will you do now?'

'Find a job. Soon, with luck.'

'I wish you plenty of it – luck – but I have to go now or I'll miss my train.'

One last question. Did Mademoiselle Deveau know of a dealer who bought couture clothes?

'Summer things? Try rue des Rosiers, but don't sell them now. Women are buying autumn wear, if they're buying at all. Wait till February.'

February? If her counting was right, by February she'd have a child in her arms. Fear weighing on her like a wet overcoat, Coralie tramped back across the river, resting a while in the Jardin des Tuileries. As starlings pecked around her feet, she sketched a plan. During her daily ambles down the streets near the Madeleine, she'd counted any number of independent milliners' shops; five on boulevard Malesherbes alone. One or other of them was bound to want an assistant of some kind. She told the starlings, 'I have to have a job by evening or I'll be fighting you for crumbs.'

Boulevard Malesherbes was pleasantly cool on its shady side, boiling where the sun hit. Coralie marched into the first milliner's she came to. Introduced herself and asked if they had a vacancy.

'I'm sorry, Mademoiselle, we're not hiring.'

At the next place, an assistant fetched the owner, who looked at Coralie's hatboxes and asked if she'd brought samples. Resisting the urge to claim La Passerinette hats as her own work, Coralie admitted, 'No, Madame.'

She was asked where her last employment had been.

'London.'

Instead of the flare of interest she'd expected, the proprietress bunched her lips. 'I'm sorry, but you would not be suitable.'

She tried to argue, named Pettrew & Lofthouse, 'suppliers to the British upper crust', only to find it wielded as much magic as Brasso. London, it seemed, carried no cachet in Paris. Different the other way round, she thought gloomily, as she wrestled her boxes out of the door.

At the next shop she waited ages, only for a junior to inform her, 'Madame says we're not hiring. Try again in September.'

By the time she'd worked both sides of the road as far as place de la Madeleine, 'Come back in September' had become a marching song. What was it about September?

Sunlight bounced off the Madeleine's columns and Coralie

regretted her dress of paisley-pattern *challis*, worn with a cerise wool jacket. The air was so humid that even the flies were still.

Directly in front of the Madeleine lay rue Royale, a short street of luxury shops that proved equally disheartening, every bid for employment answered with a negative – sometimes before she'd finished asking. She hesitated outside the famous salon of Rose Valois at number fourteen, peering at lace brims, summer flowers and perfectly angled feathers. They'd lay her bare in an instant and she couldn't take much more rejection. A few paces on she passed the Ladurée tearoom with its platters of pink, mint-green and chocolate macaroons. She shut her eyes, but her mouth still watered. Next, was Suzanne Talbot's smart establishment. A couple of hours ago, she'd felt she had something to offer Parisian millinery. Now – honestly? Even Jean McCullum would struggle in this milieu.

But she had to keep going. How many times had she fallen off a bicycle before she'd learned to ride one? Spotting another milliner's across the street, she took her chances with the traffic and opened the door to 'Henriette Junot' so forcefully that she fell inside. Chance of success? *Scant*, she told herself, as she got to her feet, but as a reward for trying she'd sit down at the next café, order an iced *citron pressé* and maybe a basket of bread.

A *vendeuse* stood behind glass doors, brushing a felt hat as if she were stroking a kitten. Coralie used the silent moment to examine Henriette Junot's spring–summer offering. There was none of the usual proliferation of 'sunflower stalks' – the metal stands milliners used for display. Just a table draped in white satin with four *marottes* on it, sawdust-stuffed heads with prim lips and wide-awake eyes. But what hats! One *marotte* wore cherry-pink gauze with a brim full of clashing yellow lilies. Two green straw hats invoked a summer meadow, flowers apparently lobbed to land where they liked. The fourth had started life as a simple Breton bonnet but had ended up as a scoop of wild strawberries, complete with leaves, star-like flowers and berries. A peacock butterfly fed from one of the flowers, and Coralie was suddenly sure it was alive. She blew lightly on it and its wings trembled.

'May I help?' The *vendeuse* had come unseen from the rear of the shop.

Coralie straightened up. 'Are you good at catching butterflies? You have to be delicate or their wings break.'

The *vendeuse* stared at her, then at the butterfly, and giggled. 'It's fake, you know.'

Coralie extended a finger and touched a wing. Painted silk, veined with wire no thicker than a hair. After years at Pettrew's, stitching grosgrain to felt, she was at last seeing into the soul of a truly beautiful hat. This confection of strawberries and leaves was no mere head covering. It was a mood. A caprice that captured a moment, stopping a butterfly in mid-air.

'Mademoiselle? Do you desire a fitting?'

'Oh . . . no.' Coralie recited her speech in a breathless gabble, and awaited the polite dismissal.

'Where did you train?'

To Coralie's surprise, the *vendeuse* had heard of Pettrew & Lofthouse, agreeing that it was a respected establishment. 'For men's headwear. Their ladies' lines are considered very ordinary, and female millinery requires different skills.'

'But I could learn.' That note of desperation! Armouring herself for a polite, *I regret, but . . .* Coralie was astonished to be invited upstairs to the workrooms.

'We are very quiet today,' the girl explained. 'This house provides millinery to the couturier Javier, whose autumn–winter collection is being launched –' she consulted her watch '– in a couple of hours.'

'Javier? Oh!' Coralie suddenly remembered she had a fitting there tomorrow morning. The prospect of being measured and prodded was surprisingly attractive, compared to the likely alternative, tramping the streets. But as Dietrich wouldn't be picking up the bill for any new clothes, it would be wrong to waste the fitter's time. Coralie enquired if the 'Madame Junot', for whom the shop was named, was in today. Or perhaps she was at Javier, watching the collection?

The *vendeuse* shook her head. 'Madame Junot never sees her collections launched as she has such highly strung feelings. One cruel word, even a sharp glance, can throw her into despair. Her *première* has gone in her place. She is where she best likes to be, up in her studio.'

On the second level, doors with glass portholes offered glimpses of women and girls at work. Neat buns and white sleeves under cotton pinafores. A silent machine, Coralie thought. I could be a little cog if I play my cards right. 'What are they all working on?'

'Rooms one and two deal with clients' commissions. The rest are producing the autumn–winter collection – our in-house collection, I should say. That launches at the end of September. Orders will also come from Javier's clients, so September is *desperate*. If Madame likes you, she may give you a trial. One more flight.' The *vendeuse* pointed up narrow stairs. 'I'm Amélie Ginsler, by the way.'

This flight led up to an attic room where a lone figure sat at a table under an open skylight, stitching a cone-shaped hat, using a *marotte* as the support. Seeing cropped hair, loose trousers and a white tuck-fronted shirt, Coralie presumed she was about to meet her first male milliner – until Amélie addressed the figure as

'Madame Junot'. 'This young woman is looking for employment and says she has worked extensively in London.'

Madame Junot stitched on. Coralie was wondering if she'd even noticed their presence, when she twisted her head in a sharp movement and pointed at the hatboxes Coralie had brought in with her. 'What's in those?'

'My clothes. I've spent so many years travelling between London and Nivelles, where my family live' – believing in a new identity was easy if you practised it several times a day – 'that my worldly goods always end up in the wrong place. Yesterday, I took the Paris train on a whim. No time to find a suitcase.' She added what she hoped was a musical laugh.

'They're La Passerinette boxes. Not a spy for them, are you?'

'Of course not, Madame. I'm here to work. I live to create hats.' To cover all possibilities, she added, 'I can sell them too.'

Henriette Junot stared so intently that Coralie feared she had sweat stains under her arms. The disturbing eye-contact broke only when a girl, not much older than fourteen, sidled in.

'Loulou!' Madame Junot clicked her fingers. 'Go down again and fetch a slouch hat, one of the practice models.' When the little assistant eventually returned with a floppy-brimmed felt hat, Madame Junot threw it to Coralie, then pointed to a pair of scissors. 'Show me what you're made of. Fit it to me. Trim the brim. Make it suit me.'

Suit a woman with a domed forehead and what might tactfully be called a strong jaw? Coralie stammered, 'Of course,' and pretended to sink into thought while desperately fishing for inspiration. Trim the brim? She'd had so many ruler-smacks from impatient needlework teachers in her life that her knuckles throbbed when she even picked up a pair of scissors. It was one of the many reasons she'd preferred to stay in the make-room at Pettrew's, why she'd dodged promotion.

Taking the kind of breath that propels the brave into freezing water, she turned the hat round several times, opened the scissors and cut. The blades had a mind of their own, slicing deep into the brim. No choice now but to keep cutting. When a halo of black dropped to the floor, and she heard Amélie Ginsler gasp, she knew she'd reached the point of no return. Actually, she'd created a pudding bowl for a village idiot. Ignoring the raised eyebrows, she turned the stump this way and that, as if contemplating a beautiful enigma.

Loulou unwittingly came to her aid – by yawning. It told Coralie that she needed an idea, fast. Her millinery skills were sorely wanting but perhaps she did have an eye for shape and proportion. Dietrich had thought so. 'You think in pictures,' he'd said.

'So, I'm going to create for you . . . something absolutely simple.' Coralie asked Loulou for a length of Petersham ribbon, and a box of pins. 'Oh, and would you thread a needle with black?' As the child searched inside a cupboard, Coralie amputated the last vestiges of brim. She folded the lower edges under and secured them with the pins Loulou brought. She was now holding something between a toque and a fez. 'Needle, please.' She made herself relax. Tense fingers always get stabbed.

Her tacking was rough because she could hear feet shuffling. Nipping the thread with her teeth, giving the hat a final stretch with the insides of her thumbs, she asked Madame Junot to sit in front of the mirror.

Henriette Junot didn't so much sit as sprawl, one trousered leg extended, head to one side. *That's right, make it as difficult for me as you can.* As she approached her, though, Coralie remembered how she'd felt at La Passerinette, sandwiched between mirror and milliner. A woman hands over power to her milliner, like a man offering his throat to the barber who shaves him. 'Madame Junot will please say if I do anything to make her uncomfortable?'

'You bet I will,' came the reply.

Henriette Junot's nose was straight and her brown hair hung like curtains either side of her face. As for that chin – 'doorstep' came to mind. Coralie placed the makeshift hat, tilting it to the side and forwards to obscure most of Henriette's right eye.

'I can't see.'

'But we can see you, Madame.' Coralie felt a flicker of excitement. Almost by accident, she'd minimised Henriette's protuberant forehead. Now she needed to give the impression of wider cheekbones to balance the jaw. She reached for some black gauze, scrunching it into a rough flower-head which she pinned to the side of the hat. Something interesting was taking shape.

The woman's best feature was her eyes, black as midnight, and Coralie thought, *Had I the nerve, I'd cut her hair*. She took the less radical option, tucking Henriette's behind her ears. The finished effect was neat. Elegant, even.

But reminiscent of the English nannies Coralie had seen wheeling their charges along the paths of parc Monceau. The hat needed further softening. Henriette Junot needed softening. Some part of her obviously yearned for it or she wouldn't spend her life whisking up fragile frippery for other women. Coralie looked around for more trimmings but the attic studio was as spare as its owner. Not even a vase of flowers.

Flowers . . .

'Loulou, open those hatboxes carefully until you find roses. I want three or four heads.'

Loulou found them, thornless Zéphirine Drouhins, Dietrich's last bouquet. She'd worked out that he must have ordered them via the hotel desk before they'd gone to the Expo. Which meant he'd still cared for her then, even if his feelings had taken an abrupt turn later in the day. Her fault? Something she'd said?

Being a delicate climber, the rose heads drooped prettily when secured to the front of the hat. Their rich hue lent tone to Henriette's skin and lips.

Nobody said anything as Coralie took a length of black lining silk from the back of a chair and draped it around Henriette's neck. Framed in black, the Zéphirines leaped to prominence and Coralie suddenly thought, *Two would have been enough*. Trust her to bung four on. 'A good picture, Madame?'

Henriette looked to Amélie, who answered, 'Very good. Actually, beautiful. Perhaps I have brought you a true talent, Madame.'

'Been looking hard for one, have you?'

Amélie flushed. 'I meant, considering the raw material we gave the young lady, the result is extraordinary.'

'Raw material? You mean, the head she had to work with?' Henriette Junot yanked off the silk mantle. 'I find that very hurtful.'

'Madame, I meant considering we gave the young lady poor materials and a pair of left-handed scissors.'

Left-handed scissors existed? Now she looked, Coralie could see their cutting blade was on the left side. No wonder she'd nearly sliced the hat in half. She let nothing of this escape. 'I hope you may find a vacancy for me, Madame Junot, now you've seen my skills.'

Henriette pulled the hat off. Without looking at Coralie, she said, 'All our starters take a two-week course to acclimatise to our house style. After that, they shadow a senior for a month, learning our customers' likes and dislikes.'

'I'd enjoy that,' Coralie said.

'We don't pay our starters to attend the course.'

'I see.'

Henriette flared, 'Why should you expect it? You'd be getting the benefit of our teaching and expertise. You should pay us.'

'How much would I get after the first two weeks?'

'For six months, we pay apprentice rate. Four hundred francs per month.'

That wasn't enough to live on. But if she didn't find a job before her belly swelled, she'd have to beg in the street, or throw herself on the mercy of the British Embassy – who would send her back to London. 'I will accept, Madame, for the chance to work at such a —' she was poised to utter the word 'prestigious', not sure if she had it right, when the proprietress interrupted.

'Come back in the first week of October and I'll make up my mind. No promises.'

'I can't start now?'

The expression that crossed Henriette Junot's face was growing familiar to Coralie. She'd seen it on the face of the Duet's desk clerk, on that of the chambermaid and on the *visages* of a dozen salesgirls. It was contempt.

'Surely you know that all the best establishments close in August? Nobody worth knowing stays in Paris during August. Our customers have ordered their autumn millinery and everyone else can go hang. I'm off on a month's holiday tonight.'

'The workrooms stay open, though?'

Henriette breezed over the interruption. 'We throw a little drinks party on the last Friday of September when guests view the new season's stock. After that, it's business as usual. Yes, come back early in October. I may even remember your name.'

*

August began with a bank holiday, and Paris gave herself up
to tourists and those without second homes or the means to
bolt to the seaside. Walking up the Champs-Élysées, her hatboxes bumping against her legs, Coralie fantasised about iced
lemonade. The cafés and restaurants on this exclusive avenue
were making the most of the holiday trade. Open doors with
tongues of red carpet under moustache-shaped awnings made
her think of insatiable mouths and mocked the hunger in her
belly. *Let one door open to her today, before despair set in.* For the
last four days, she'd eked out her money by eating nothing but
bread and drinking from public fountains. Home was currently
a hostel dormitory, whose rusted window gave a view of drain-
pipes. Her mattress smelt fishy and was so thin that she could
still feel the imprint of wooden slats on her back. The other
occupants had watched her progress to the last bed in the row,
staring fixedly at the hatboxes she had brought in with her.
Stared at her clothes, at her dusty shoes. She'd slept with *those*
under her pillow.

Today her aim was to get temporary work as a *plongeuse*, a
pot-washer. Low-grade, but it would guarantee one good meal
a day. She'd so far enquired at two places. At the first, the patron
had taken in her pink, flounced dress and the Zéphirine rose
she'd pinned to her hatband and laughed. The second had asked
her to show him her hands. Inspecting Coralie's long fingers and
buffed nails, he'd shaken his head. 'You wouldn't last two hours,
Mademoiselle.'

Seeing a couple rise from a table outside Fouquet's bras-
serie, Coralie lingered until they'd put down their money, then
snatched up their abandoned water glasses, draining them one
after the other. Paris heat seemed to increase with every day.

'*Pardon*, Mademoiselle.'

A man bumped into her, setting her hatboxes swinging. She hadn't dared leave them at the hostel, though the value of their contents was greatly reduced as she'd already sold her Javier pieces. Mademoiselle Deveau had been right. A few hundred francs was all she'd got for those beautiful, unworn clothes. Emotions on a hair trigger, she burst out at the man who'd banged into her, 'Look where you're going. It's not like I'm hard to see.'

'As I said, *pardon.*' The man touched his greasy hat. Clearly, he committed the cardinal sin of picking it up by the pinch of the crown, rather than the brim. You could see where his fingers clawed repeatedly. No amount of re-blocking and cleaning would ever save it. It was what Pettrew's repair department would call a 'brush and boomerang', meaning, give it a brush and send it back.

Nauseous suddenly, Coralie pushed on as the outlines of tables and chairs merged with ornamental box bushes and white umbrellas. Feeling like an insect stranded on a gigantic billiard table, she sank down at the first empty table she saw. When a waiter brought water, she took the glass straight out of his hand, then ordered the cheapest thing on the menu. Tomato omelette, dressed lettuce and bread. Lots of bread. She'd intended to cross the river to the student quarter, rather than pay eighth *arrondissement* prices, but she wouldn't get that far. When her food came, she tried not to wolf it down, but dining room manners were beyond her. It was only when the waiter came to clear and suggest, 'Mademoiselle might like coffee,' that she checked her handbag to ensure she had loose change for a tip. The bag gaped and her pulse sounded the alarm. Five minutes' desperate digging produced no miracle. Her purse had been stolen.

*

She cried. Not noisily, not theatrically but in hunched despair. What did you do when this happened? Offer to come back and pay later? How? She didn't even have enough for another night in that rotten hostel.

'Dietrich von Elbing,' she muttered out loud, 'if I ever see you again, I'll either kill you or myself in front of you.'

'The former, I hope. Murder has a delicious grandeur. Suicide is always vulgar.'

She looked up, trying to join the dots of the figure looming in front of her. She made out a white suit, and a travel satchel over one shoulder.

Thierry-Edgar Clisson placed his Panama on the table. 'May I join you? I was dawdling on my way to the station. I'm booked on the night train to Nice, then onwards to Morocco. I believe I mentioned my holiday to you when we met the other day – a little sojourn among the souks. I delayed it to oblige Graf von Elbing, but he let me down.'

He pulled out a chair, fluffed his cravat and removed a flying bug from his cuff. 'You too, by the sound of it.'

'You know he went without telling me?'

Clisson regarded Coralie with interest, though a waiter was hovering. 'I was intending to tiptoe around a gallery before going to the station, but your predicament promises far more diversion. Will you join me for coffee?'

'Iced lemonade, please, and you'll have to pay. A bastard in a hat stole my purse. What is it with this city?' She craned her neck forward, ready to grab Clisson if he showed signs of leaving. 'Why did Dietrich go? You were the last to see him. He must have said something.'

'We-ell, I may have a piece of the jigsaw, though which jigsaw puzzle are we building? That of the romantic hero you are in love with or the angry, embittered man I met in Berlin ten years ago? Or the Dietrich neither of us knows?'

'You tell me.'

Clisson sighed. 'At the German pavilion, when you were off powdering your nose, somebody brought a message.'

'Who? What message?'

'A deliciously handsome young German. Claus von Some-thing. The message was delivered in a whisper, but I gathered that it was a summons home.'

Their drinks arrived, Coralie's cloudy lemonade clinking with ice cubes, Clisson's coffee dripping through a metal filter into a cup. She asked, 'Did you get to see those Russian icons?'

'Not a sniff. I waited in vain for a telephone call, or, indeed, an apology.'

Clisson said more but Coralie was back on the roof terrace, staring over a river full of reflections. 'Monsieur Clisson, why didn't he tell me he was going?'

'Call me Teddy. One of my American customers gave me the name, and I rather like it. We waited for you – Graf von Elbing was concerned. You'd been unwell and he feared you might have collapsed or got lost. But then another of those glorious, chis-el-featured gentlemen came up to emphasise the urgency. The Graf left then, asking me to wait for you.'

'I was there all the time, by the balcony. You only had to look round!'

Teddy sighed. 'My dear, if you must play the tempestuous Juliet, forewarn your Romeo. The dear Graf was looking towards the door, not at the balcony.'

'I came back through a different one.'

'Schoolgirl error. I didn't wait for you either because I was rather put out. I had been snubbed in the matter of dinner.

Slighted over the Dürer engravings, left to drink champagne alone and treated as a message service. Who would not storm off?'

She took a gulp of her drink, almost moaning at the feel of ice cubes and lemon pulp on her tongue. 'What is this Dürer thing?'

'*He* was a fifteenth-century German artist. *The* German artist. He is their da Vinci, in the same league as any of the Italian greats. The engravings are of religious scenes.'

'Most of the stuff I saw at Ottilia's I wouldn't want on my wall. There were a few nice bits, flowers mostly, and some paintings of fruit—'

Clisson cut in, 'You've seen the von Silberstrom collection?' He might have asked if she'd been present at the discovery of the True Cross.

'I helped pack and catalogue it.'

Clisson went very still, then spooled his hand, meaning, 'Continue.'

'Dietrich told me that Ottilia had inherited a fabulous collection from her grandfather, and he's trying to keep it out of the hands of swindlers. He's sending it into safe-keeping.'

'Where?'

'Um . . . Neuendorf?'

'Hohen Neuendorf, in Germany?' Clisson was almost biting the rim of his coffee cup.

'Is that bad?'

Clisson fanned himself with his Panama. 'The von Silberstrom collection was removed from Germany to keep it out of Nazi hands. To move it back, one or two train stops from Berlin, suggests at the very least collusion. At worst – well, one hardly likes to say.'

'Dietrich isn't a Nazi, if that's what you mean.'

'Dear girl, how would you know? He certainly salutes like one. I was in the pavilion when you arrived the other day. I watched him greeting his brethren.'

'He *isn't* a Nazi. He hates men who like war, and those who burn books. You'd understand if you'd been as close to him as I have.'

'Exactly how close, though? Pardon me, but the bedchamber is not necessarily the place where people reveal most of themselves. Psychologically, I mean.'

'We didn't spend all our time in bed. You say you're his friend but you know nothing about him. For one thing, he's not keen on champagne, but you kept buying it for him. *You don't know him.*' She flushed, because she, like Clisson, had heard Dietrich cry, '*Heil Hitler!*' when there had been no reason to do so, except that he was with like-minded people. Finally she conceded, 'Well, I don't really know *what* he believes in.'

'My dear, has it not occurred to you that Graf von Elbing might be just another swindler trying to separate the von Silberstrom collection from its owner?'

She shook her head. 'Dietrich cares for Ottilia. Far more than I like. He wouldn't do anything to harm her.'

'No? He pulled out two days before he was supposed to marry her. Prostrate, poor girl, or so I heard.' Clisson watched Coralie drain the last drops from her glass. 'Another one?'

'Better not.' Her bladder was uncomfortably full.

'What are your plans now that he's abandoned you in similar vein?'

'A job. Any job.' An idea pushed itself forward. 'D'you want an assistant?'

'To assist me in what?' Clisson signalled for the bill.

'Selling your art. I could be your shop-lady. I'd write lists. Tidy up. Do your accounts.'

'Are you experienced?'

'Not really, but I don't think I'm going to find millinery work, and the way I feel about milliners right now, I don't want it.'

'No family to run back to?' Getting no answer, he said, 'There are agencies. You might get a chambermaid's job . . . though lack of references will hamper you.'

'I need a place to stay. I slept with bed-bugs last night and tonight I won't have even that luxury.'

Clisson shuddered. 'What you need is a protector. I don't see you mopping stairs and sluicing water-closets, but I can imagine you as the paid pet of some man of generous instincts.'

She'd have slapped him then, except that she needed him in good humour until the bill was paid. 'Offering to take me to Morocco, are you?'

That drew a private smile. 'Morocco is boys only. I'd much rather have taken the dear Graf.'

'Taken Dietrich – oh.'

'Is that provincial distaste on your face?'

No. If her face had frozen, it was because being rejected, even by Teddy Clisson, hurt. 'It's your life and there are two sides to every pancake, so my mother used to say.'

'What an enlightened lady, though, actually, there are many more than two.' Clisson cocked his head. 'I could write a note to a charming man with a penchant for Junoesque blondes who would look after you very nicely . . . or I could send you to a house I know.'

'A lodging house?'

'La Nichée, behind Gare Saint-Lazare. Very swish, champagne in the afternoon and never more than ten clients per shift.'

'A brothel?'

'You would earn a thousand francs a night.'

She didn't explode, didn't even rattle her tail feathers. She'd seen the girls clustering outside her hostel, faces stamped with a look she recognised. Tooley Street or Goutte d'Or, city prostitutes always had over-vivid lipstick bleeding into face powder. They all walked with an ambling roll that could be speeded up or slowed down to suit the circumstances. She'd seen pimps in the hostel lobby, sharing out the night's dividends with the manageress. Who knew, but one of those men would catch her in the end? Only – 'I can't.'

'Dietrich spoiled you for other men? Yes, I can understand.' Clisson nodded. 'There will be others, though, one way or another.'

'I can't because I'm pregnant.'

Clisson dismissed the waiter, who had approached with the bill. 'Is it Dietrich's?'

She hesitated. 'Yes' might elicit the result she needed. 'No.' She sighed. 'And I don't rightly know what I'm going to do.'

'Life is sacred.' Unclipping a pen from his top pocket, Clisson wrote on a card he pulled from a slim diary. To himself, he repeated, 'Life is sacred.'

'Until it's born. Then it's just one more bastard for the world to spit on.'

Clisson handed her the card. 'The address of an institution that may take you in. The nuns will have you sewing and mending while they lecture you on the error of your ways, but when the time comes, they will place your infant with a good family and will only turn you out once you've secured respectable employment. Don't thank me.'

She hadn't been about to. 'Place your infant' felt like a claw reaching inside her. 'I'm not going to any bloody convent.'

Laughter broke from Clisson. 'That's brothels and nunneries out of the window. I'm all ears. Tell me what you're going to do.'

'Well . . . I could stay at yours. Look after your flat while you're away prowling the souks.' His eyes were popping like a salmon's. 'Do your cleaning?'

'I have a charwoman.'

'Make sure nobody steals your valuables?' Guessing him to be the sort of man who hated clutter, she added, 'Organise your pictures for you. You know, dust them and stack them.'

He made a noise of horror.

The waiter set down the bill, and the moment's interruption allowed in a wild idea. Coralie leaned forward. 'I'd look after your cat.'

'How do you know I have a cat?'

Because she'd glimpsed his cufflinks the other day. Today's were plain gold ovals and Clisson looked suitably astonished by her insight. 'I'd groom him while you're away.'

'Him? What makes you think Voltaire is a tom? People invariably say "she" when speaking of cats. They always say "he" of dogs. And, perversely, "it" when they mention babies.'

'I just know things sometimes. I'm sensitive, like you.' If Clisson hadn't tucked his legs under the table, she'd have looked for tell-tale hairs, and stunned him by telling him that Voltaire was a handsome ginger, or a fine tortoiseshell. So she took a chance: 'I've always liked black cats best.'

Pleasure burst like a struck match. 'Voltaire is purest obsidian! How extraordinary!' Enthusiasm died. 'I haven't said yes, and I'm back home in September.'

'And then I'll move out.'

'How will you eat? You haven't a franc.'

'You'll lend me money. After all, Voltaire and I can't dine in state every night if I'm skint.'

Teddy Clisson leaned towards her. She smelt coffee on his breath and her stomach turned.

'I never lend. But I'll give you a month's salary . . .'

'Go on.' So long as it had nothing to do with nuns or brothels.

'A month's salary if you swear on your enlightened mother's soul that when Dietrich comes back to you – and the atoms in my body say he will – you will use every shred of charm to persuade him to sell me those Dürer engravings.'

She laughed, momentarily forgetting her misery. 'I'll make sure he sells them half-price. Deal?' She thrust out her hand and Teddy Clisson shook it.

Chapter Nine

Having spent the Monday of the August bank holiday failing to get kitchen work, Coralie rose the following morning ready to give millinery another stab. Though her interview with Henriette Junot had misfired, the image of a plain woman transformed by pink roses excited her. She *did* have something to offer. 'The only other thing I'm any good at is love-making,' she told the muscular tomcat winding himself around her ankles, mewing for a share of the milk she was boiling for cocoa. 'But that's no profession for a girl who still has dreams.'

Clean sheets and privacy had given her the sweetest night's sleep she'd had in days. But, as she put the cocoa to her lips, a bilious wave broke over her. In the bathroom, heaving from an empty stomach, she flung out a proposition to any of the Fates who might be listening: 'Give me a job and I'll never be idle again. I'll be the most loving mother in the world too. I promise, I promise.'

On boulevard de la Madeleine, the sun beat against the back of her neck. Why had she not thought of trying at La Passerinette before?

Because it hurt to come back as Dietrich's discarded mistress.

But back she was, and glad to see hats on display rather than drawn blinds. Nearly every other milliner's was shut – most of them for the rest of the summer. Really, she couldn't have timed her unemployment worse.

Lorienne Royer's hats had not moved on in style since Coralie's visit in June, but instead of pink, this time it was a crescendo of peach tones. Recalling her morning there with Dietrich, Coralie suspected the display was a ruse to entice customers in. Once inside, you got whatever Lorienne had available. Coralie saw no sign of activity.

'I'd stir things up, if the place were mine,' she muttered. She hesitated at the door, remembering Lorienne's sharp nails and the cringing assistant, Violaine. Could she risk taking a job here, in her condition? Touching her stomach, sore from retching, she reminded herself that her condition was precisely why she was about to do this. Lorienne Royer shouldn't scare her, anyway. When it came to bullies, hadn't she worked with the best? She pushed the door – and found it locked. Her eye fell on a card propped in the window:

> *La Passerinette is closed for August.*
> *Work-in-progress will be honoured.*
> *Please telephone to arrange collection.*

Coralie poured out her exasperation in oaths straight from the mouth of Jac Masson – until the sound of a window being opened made her look up. A light voice called down, 'We are closed. Have you come to pick up a hat?"

Dazzled by the sun-baked walls of a building five storeys high, it was a moment before Coralie recognised Violaine. The girl was also blinking – like an animal coming out of hibernation. She wasn't wearing her spectacles.

I've woken her up, Coralie thought. At half past eleven on a summer morning! 'I was hoping to speak with Lorienne. I want a job.'

Violaine's reply was lost in the rumble of a passing bus. Boulevard de la Madeleine was one of the grand boulevards of Paris and always noisy – but not quite noisy enough to disguise the sound of a window being shut.

'And the same to you,' Coralie tossed upwards. Deflated, she looked towards the Madeleine. The church would be cool, and she could rest and put in a prayer, since Fate clearly wasn't coming up with the goods. All she wanted was a chance. One little chink of luck. She was thirty strides away when she heard her name being called. Turning, she saw Violaine on the pavement, waving. Coralie hurried back. The girl had come out of a street door the same colour as the stone surrounding it. It must be the way into the flats above the salon.

'Mademoiselle Royer isn't here,' Violaine explained, making a belated effort to smooth her rumpled clothes. 'She's gone to Deauville – you know, by the sea?' A heavy sigh implied, *All right for some.*

'Can *you* employ me?'

Violaine stepped close to Coralie, almost too close. 'Not unless you're offering your services for free . . . could you? It would be excellent experience.' She'd put on her glasses on the way out of her flat, but still seemed to be struggling to focus. It was like meeting somebody's gaze under water.

Coralie shook her head. 'I already have experience. I need a salary.'

'Of course.' Violaine's face crumpled as if she'd just seen the last life belt whisked away. 'Only, 'I've worked the last two nights straight. I must have fallen asleep. I take work up to my flat because the telephone never stops ringing in the salon.'

There were red marks on Violaine's knuckles, as if she'd scalded herself. *Blocking with hot kettles while exhausted*, Coralie thought. *Left on her own while everyone else goes on holiday*. She wished she could help. 'I'm truly sorry.'

Violaine shrugged. 'Why don't you try Printemps on boulevard Haussmann? They might be hiring.'

It crossed Coralie's mind to invite Violaine to have lunch somewhere, but thrift intervened. Oranges and cheese were waiting for her at Teddy's flat on rue de Seine. Thanking Violaine, Coralie walked away, cutting across place de la Madeleine. She was halfway down rue Royale when her mental map of Paris reasserted itself. This was the wrong direction for boulevard Haussmann. Wiping perspiration from her forehead, she wondered if she had the energy to turn around. Printemps this afternoon, maybe? After she'd rested and changed.

As she dithered, she noticed two smartly dressed ladies on the opposite side of the road trying to enter Henriette Junot's salon. They'd opened the door but were clearly too well-bred to push through the press of women already inside. Were the staff giving away free hats?

Henriette's disdainful treatment of her still burned, but Coralie nevertheless went to the kerb and waited for a break in the traffic. Henriette would be away on holiday by now, and it would be good to nip in and thank Amélie Ginsler, the *vendeuse*, who had been so helpful to her. As she darted across the road, a splash of colour in Henriette's window drew her eye. A single *marotte* stood in the window in a lake of pink rose petals. It wore an asymmetrical black beret, with four Zéphirine Drouhin roses falling forward over its brow.

Fury surged through Coralie.

Employing the elbow tactics she'd used at Epsom racecourse, Coralie drilled through the crowd until she saw Henriette herself, surrounded by women in summer suits, all talking at once. So, the vacation had been cancelled – or had that just been a ruse to fob Coralie off? The moment the noise died down, she'd take Madame Junot in a hard grip, march her to the window and demand an explanation for the rose beret. The woman had made her lick the floor in front of a fourteen-year-old workhand, turfed her out, then stolen her design.

Somebody pinched her shoulder. She swung round and there was Amélie Ginsler, looking stricken. Coralie mouthed, 'What's going on?'

Drawing her to the edge of the room, Amélie said, 'The couturier Javier, for whom we provide millinery? His new collection was plagiarised the day you came here. His entire autumn–winter line was pre-sold to New York. The poor man scrapped the whole thing and locked himself away. It's a disaster!'

Amélie didn't have to explain. A similar thing had happened at Pettrew's when a London department store had gone to the wall. A season's orders, cancelled overnight. A stockroom full of materials that must be paid for. Girls on the payroll with nothing to do. Coralie looked at the mob encircling Henriette. 'Angry customers?'

'Gossip-mongers. They want the inside story, because nobody at Javier will say a thing.' Henriette was on the brink of a nervous breakdown, Amélie added. She had been minutes from leaving for her holiday, her new lover waiting in the taxi, but now, instead of spending September at a lakeside château in Ariège, she had the prospect of saving her business from total disaster.

Coralie sized up the situation. Sized up Henriette, and saw a woman drowning. She felt no sympathy, only a surge of excitement. *You prayed for a chance*, she told herself, *and here it is*. Holding back until the salon had almost emptied, the flock gone elsewhere to feed, she marched up to Henriette. 'You're in a right mess but I've got what you haven't – energy and an empty diary. Give me the reins for a month and I'll sort your business out for you.'

Henriette curled her lip. 'I need somebody with talent and business brains.'

Wordlessly, Coralie went to the window and scooped up the Zéphirine beret. 'You clearly think I have talent. As for brains, I'm a direct descendant of the cleverest financier in history, the Duc de Lirac.'

'Never heard of him.'

Coralie assumed a look of astonishment. 'Never heard of the man who saved Napoleon the Third from bankruptcy? Not only did my ancestor rescue his finances, he made him plant trees on every boulevard in Paris as a thank-you. Next time you find yourself strolling in the shade, look up and thank the Duc de Lirac. So. Deal?'

Coralie had no illusions as to why Henriette accepted her offer. The woman had been ready to close her doors, throw the keys into the Seine. A half-convincing story was all she'd needed. And, as Coralie quickly discovered, the salon ran very well without Henriette. Amélie Ginsler held the front-of-house together. Madame Zénon, the Greek-born *première*, ran the production side, with the help of talented deputies.

For the first few days, Coralie did little more than wander around, fearful she'd bitten off too much. But ambition rescued her. Why not use what Henriette had turned her back on to secure her own future and that of her unborn child? Fate had handed her a salon: she would make her name.

Some fifty models had been made for Javier's collection and Coralie sold them first. Not in the shop, because there was the question of who exactly owned the designs: at the Expo, still in full flow on the banks of the Seine. On her instruction, Amélie and Madame Zénon selected ten of the most attractive, confident salon assistants and workroom *midinettes* and Coralie sent them out to mingle with the tourists, making eye-contact, selling hats directly off their heads. Those model-hats ran out within hours and the workrooms went into full production to make more. Cash flowed in and the amiable accountant, Monsieur Moulin, rubbed his hands in pleasure.

'I was deeply involved in retail in London,' Coralie explained to him, neglecting to add that she'd picked up her technique in Bermondsey's fruit and vegetable market. You didn't need to be a genius to see that the barrow-boys who cried their wares the loudest always sold out first.

September arrived and a tanned Teddy Clisson came home. Finding Voltaire healthy and Coralie busy and radiant, he invited her to stay a week or two more. 'I have so many traveller's tales, I need an audience.' Studying her waistline, he asked, 'Are you really expecting, or was it a hoax to invoke my pity? I see no signs of a baby.'

'Believe me, there's a baby.' She'd been disguising her swelling shape under loose blouses belted at the hip. Teddy apart, only Madame Zénon and Amélie so far knew of her condition. Give it a few weeks, nothing would hide her bump. 'I shall find a place of my own,' she promised him. 'I can't stay here – people will start gossiping about us.'

'What fun.' He handed her a box containing a watch of filigree silver with a black enamel bracelet. 'For being a friend to Voltaire. No, I don't need to be hugged.' He became businesslike. 'My landlord always has property to rent along rue de Seine, if you aren't fussy about airy views or reliable lifts. He's quite reasonable.'

Within days, they had found her a place a few strides away towards the river end of the street. It was on the top floor of a very old house, and had no lift, but Coralie took it. The building was only three storeys high, and she reckoned that going up and down with a baby in a basket would keep her trim.

Henriette Junot's 1937 autumn–winter line launched on 9 September. Henriette travelled up from her rented château to preside, bringing her lover – the two of them posing in the new models, giggling like schoolgirls. She then spent a week upsetting Coralie's work regime, sacking juniors and getting on everybody's nerves. The day she left, Coralie felt a silent cheer run through the building.

'When she's in love,' Madame Zénon confided, 'she doesn't give a fig for her business. But when the break-up comes, she is like a mother bear robbed of her cub.' The *première* dropped her gaze to Coralie's midriff, hidden under a pleated tunic. 'I hope you're putting a little money aside. Madame may have female lovers, but it does not follow that she likes women. You understand?'

'I'm saving like mad.' Coralie was also racing to build up a portfolio of designs and to amass the experience that would allow her to open a salon of her own. All she needed was for Henriette to stay seven hundred kilometres away for the next few months – oh, and not discover that Coralie was pregnant. The vile sickness had stopped, thank goodness, and the baby must be small, because Coralie could still get into her skirts with elastic loops attached to the buttons. But all secrets come out in the end.

One mid-October afternoon Coralie was watching Madame Zénon sketch the profile of a hat they were designing together when she realised that one of the *petites-mains* – a millinery assistant – was staring at her side-on, a shocked look in her eye. Coralie quickly pulled her stomach in but later she was aware of staff members whispering behind their hands.

Right, she thought. *Time to face the guns*. She called an evening meeting, at which she informed a crowded salon that she was due to give birth in February. Ignoring the gasps and whispers, she injected a bit of humour: 'From now on, I won't be running about the place and I'll be taking the stairs two at a time, not three.'

'Does Madame know?' asked one of the older *secondes*. She was one of the few people Coralie disliked there, as she was known to spy for Henriette.

'Of course,' Coralie lied cheerfully. 'She's going to be god-mother. Meeting dismissed.' *Give me Christmas and one more season*, she prayed that night in her poky bedroom. If her dates were right, she could squeeze out a spring–summer collection in early February before she went into labour.

November answered her prayers, though in the form of dis-turbing news. Henriette was ill. A cold caught while bathing in the lake beside her château had gone to her lungs. Pneumonia, pleurisy, blood on her pillow. It was unlikely, she informed Madame Zénon and Coralie in a shaky letter, that she'd be back for Christmas. She trusted them to shepherd her business through this vital season.

Of course, with Henriette, 'trust' went only so far.

Friday, 5 November, was stormy. In the salon, arranging ivy and Christmas roses on the display plinth, Coralie contemplated an unpleasant journey home. She shivered as hail pelted the window. Her flat had a fireplace, but she had nobody to make a blaze for her. At the counter, Amélie was writing up the day's sales, also in no rush to face the weather. The door crashed open.

Assuming the wind had forced it and anxious for the glass, Coralie ran to lock it, ivy trailing from her hand. Colliding with the man who stepped in from the darkness, she managed to drape it over his shoulder. He plucked it off, laughing. Deep, black eyes, swarthy colouring and a thick moustache lent him the air of a brigand. Coralie reversed back to the display table, and picked up her scissors.

Amélie, however, was all smiles. 'Monsieur Cazaubon, how nice to see you! Have you brought news of Madame Junot?'

'I'm just back from seeing her.' The stranger kissed Amélie on both cheeks, then looked sideways at Coralie. 'I left Henriette slightly improved but, I'm afraid, very unhappy. Her friend has left her.'

'That's a shame,' said Amélie, though her voice held little surprise.

'I wanted to take her to our parents at Céret, which is only ten kilometres from the Château de Jarrat, where she's staying, but she wouldn't agree. So I appointed a pair of nurses to look after her and I hope to God they don't strangle her.' The man laughed at Amélie's pursed lips. 'Come on. My sister is difficult enough when she is in health, we all know it. When she is ill – *I* would strangle her!'

He spoke fast, almost too fast for Coralie to keep up, and with the accent and rolling *rs* of a southerner. *Cazaubon* . . . Was this really Henriette's brother? He looked more Spanish than French, but perhaps there was an explanation for that. Henriette, she knew, had taken the name 'Junot' to distance herself from her roots, which lay in French Catalonia. Whoever he was, he must have come on foot from the Métro because his hair glittered and he'd left wet prints on the carpet. He caught her disapproval. 'You are Mademoiselle de Lirac.'

Coralie folded her arms. 'I think I know who you are.'

He bowed. 'The apple of Henriette's eye.'

Yes, and I'll stake my new watch you've been sent to check me over. Her heart bumped, and it wasn't just anxiety. For the past four months, the only males in her life had been Teddy Clisson, the accountant, Monsieur Moulin, and Voltaire. Cazaubon's stocky masculinity, the teasing gleam in his eye, promised a taste of something richer. *There will be others, one way or another.* She blushed.

'So, is it true, Mademoiselle?'

'Is what true?'

He made an apologetic gesture. 'One of the old cats upstairs wrote to my sister that you are in the family way and –' he whispered theatrically '– unmarried.'

Coralie held his gaze, knowing instinctively that he was searching for weakness. Moving her Christmas greenery to one side, she allowed Cazaubon an eyeful of her shape. 'One baby and no ring.' She presented her left hand. 'Have a proper look.'

He did. When he met her eye again, the gleam had sharpened. 'Tell me, are you eating for two?'

'What are you, a doctor?'

'A civil engineer. Because if you are, I'd like to take both of you out to dinner.'

Laughter jumped from Coralie's throat. Astonishment colliding with relief. Whatever this man wanted of her, it wasn't her immediate downfall.

Ramon Cazaubon *had* been sent by his sister, he told her later. Henriette had asked him to poke about the stockroom, to go through the accounts. 'She is afraid of you, Coralie, and I understand why. Unlike her, you do not wait for life to unfold. You ride after it, like a gaucho roping a steer.' It was crystal clear, he said, that Coralie could out-business Henriette blindfolded, with her hands tied. 'Anyway, I will write and say all is well.' As for looking over the books, for his sins he spent his days staring at lines on paper. Evenings, he said, were for friendship. And nights were for pleasure.

Against her better judgement, Coralie allowed him to take her out that first time, then a second and a third. Soon, she was looking forward to the bump of the door, the energetic wiping of feet that announced his arrival in the salon. She'd told him off for spoiling the carpet.

Ramon shared his sister's brusque impulsivity, but his nature was warmer. Fiery, even. He never flagged. By midnight, when she was begging to go home and sleep, he was suggesting they go on to Pigalle or boulevard de Clichy, to this or that nightclub. He seemed to know every dance band in Paris. Working by day in one of the drawing-offices of the national railway company, he descended by night into vaults and basements, and soused himself in modern music. He lived several lives in parallel, he told her.

'I adore Paris, but I am also at home in the foothills of the Pyrénées. I am an intellectual, a wage-slave, a hunter and also a Bohemian. I am a politician who hates politics, an anarchist who believes in God. I am a warrior who loves peace. Life is short, Coralie. My parents are like oak trees, growing one slow ring at a time. Henriette, with all her talent, is like a field of standing corn waiting to be cut. To me, life is a rampaging bull. I throw myself over the horns, daring it to gouge and trample me.'

'It might, one day,' she warned him.

'Then I hope I have you to bind my wounds. I am not comfortable to live with, but I know my mind.'

A week into December, he asked her to marry him.

She said no. Twice in her life, she'd thrown herself into uncharted love. Twice-deserted and pregnant, she was wiser. And she didn't love him. 'And you, in your middle thirties, a steady wage-earner . . . there's a reason no woman's caught you yet. What's in it for you?'

'I have bedded many, many women, but never until now have I wanted to marry one. I like your spirit and I want your body.'

'With another man's child inside it?' She'd intended to shock him. She failed.

'I love children.'

Still, she held back. 'I'm not a charity case.'

'Far from it. But your child is.' He knew how to aim his attacks. 'Being a bastard is a bad deal. If you don't believe me, wait till you go into hospital. See how the nurses treat you, and the officials at the *mairie* when you register the child's birth and can't put a father's name to the form. Your little one will come home from school every day, crying. And just think, if you marry me—'

'I get you every night!' Could she live with his relentless vigour? She had not yet slept with him. He didn't mind her belly, but *she* was sensitive about it. He would be a red-blooded lover and she needed to be strong.

'I was going to say, if you marry me, it will really annoy Henriette. She cannot bear me liking other women. She is jealous when a fly lands on her food. It's her nature and I smell the rivalry between you. You like to win.' And the final persuasion: 'I like you, Coralie, and respect you. I am willing to try to be a good husband. I think you need a man to care for you.'

The word 'care' broke her and she began to cry. He put his arms round her and it felt good to be held. They married a week before Christmas.

On her wedding day, she presented her false documents at the town hall and saw the presiding official accept them without a blink. Even the page of mad scrawl from Henriette, railing at her for having the temerity to marry *her* brother and palm off a bastard on 'one of the oldest families in France' – even that failed to dent her new-found security.

On the afternoon of Christmas Eve, 1937, Coralie was lighting candles in the shop window, dreaming up ideas for the spring collection, when pain tore through her, followed by a gush of liquid down her legs.

An American client in the fitting room heard her howl of dismay. As the salon girls fluttered about helplessly, the American came and helped Coralie to her feet. Supporting her until the pain passed, she said, 'Honey, you're going to be pulling Christmas crackers in hospital. You, Mademoiselle,' she beckoned a *vendeuse*, 'go holler at my chauffeur, have him drive right up on the pavement. Someone get towels and somebody else fetch the husband. This lady is in labour.'

At seventeen minutes past midnight on Christmas Day, Coralie's daughter was born, weighing a shave over five pounds. They named her Noëlle Una. Noëlle because the midwife suggested it,

Una in honour of Madame Una Kilpin, whose Rolls-Royce had ferried Coralie through the Paris traffic, and who later offered to stand as godmother.

Coralie took December and the whole of January 1938 off work. On the first of February, however, she left baby Noëlle with a nanny and took a taxi through the chilling rain to rue Royale.

It was a wrench, leaving her newborn, but Coralie knew that, professionally, she was riding a wave. At Ramon's strong suggestion, Henriette had reluctantly made Coralie *directrice* and head designer, effectively giving her full creative control of the business. Then, still unwell and feeling ill-used by the world, Henriette had left for Italy. Her doctor had recommended the warmer climate for her lungs and she'd taken one of her nurses with her. Rumours soon reached Paris of a new relationship. Everyone agreed: Henriette would not be back for a while.

As 1938 unfolded, and profits rolled in, Coralie thanked Providence for her job. For all his promises, his passion, Ramon was not a good provider. His desire for her had not waned. He was an ardent, if sometimes thoughtless, lover. But his salary somehow always melted away before rent day. He had stopped going out to nightclubs so often, but was still addicted to dark basements. Only now it was to attend meetings of left-wing political groups. Coralie knew he was personally funding two or three, and supporting political refugees too. His only useful contribution to their household was coal, which he 'liberated' from the freight-marshalling yard alongside his office.

'Be fair, Coralie,' he would say, when she blasted him yet again for failing to pay her any housekeeping. 'I gave you the best gift. My name. You are Madame Cazaubon.'

True. Thanks to her marriage, she was now a fully fledged French citizen. The secret English part of her slept.

PART TWO

PART TWO

Chapter Ten

Germany, 6 November 1938

He'd stood motionless for so long that his feet seemed to belong to some far-off frozen continent. The leather coat protecting him from the icy rain was beginning to let the moisture through. His ears felt raw, but there was no point putting his hat back on because that was dripping wet too.

Hiltrud stood like a fur-clad pillar, seemingly untouched by the cold. He started to say something, then gave up. It was implicit that whoever broke silence at the graveside was the one who cared least. The one guilty of recovering from intolerable bereavement. It was invariably him.

Rain made the letters on the headstone shine darkly. 'A beloved son, Waldo Dietrich von Elbing, 16 September 1921 to 28 July 1937'. Above Waldo's name, the words '*Blut und Ehre*'; 'Blood and Honour'. Above that, a tilted swastika. Hiltrud and her father had instructed the stonemason to make the swastika larger than the Christian cross at the base. It was Hiltrud who insisted they come out to this graveyard on the banks of the river Havel every Sunday, but what did she see here? That trumpeting stone or the pitiful mound under which lay their son?

Like many other youths of his age, Waldo had been sent to do his *Landjahr*, his year of service, learning to farm. Sent in spite of

an inherited heart condition that resulted in defective oxygena-
tion of the blood. Hiltrud and her father had hidden it from his
supervisors because, in perfectionist Germany, inborn weakness
was a cause of shame.

My shame, Dietrich railed at himself, though he hadn't known
just how far Waldo's health had deteriorated, that he was col-
lapsing after long stints of outdoor work. Or that the other boys
were mocking him, calling him 'girl' because he was so pale.
Had Waldo said any of this in his letters, Dietrich would have
stepped in. Instead, he'd persuaded himself that his son would
emerge fitter and stronger from his experiences. He, meanwhile,
had thrown himself into his love affair, into his Paris adventure.

His poor, beautiful boy. Taking advantage of Dietrich's
absence, Hiltrud and her father had arranged for Waldo to
move on from farm work. To military camp, to learn artillery skills. Ultimately to become a member of an anti-aircraft
battery. They'd been determined to make a soldier of the boy.
The moment he'd learned their plans, Dietrich had left Paris
for Hohen Neuendorf. It was unthinkable – a military camp,
where boys were made to run miles every day with weighted
backpacks? Where they loaded and fired guns, dragging them
across rugged terrain while a *Gefreiter* screamed orders and
smoke-bombs were thrown to mimic real warfare? For strong,
war-minded boys, no doubt it was the best kind of life. For
Waldo . . .

Arriving back in Germany, Dietrich had discovered that his
son had already started his military training. During a tense
family summit, Hiltrud had begged him not to rock the boat.
Her father had called in so many favours to gain this cherished
posting, it would be an insult if Waldo were recalled. Hiltrud's
father had thrown his weight behind his daughter, declaring he

would not stand by and watch his grandson denied the opportunity to grow manly.

At artillery camp the bullying had worsened and Waldo's letters to Dietrich that summer had echoed his grandfather's phrase: 'If I show them I am a man, they will stop.'

They hadn't. Waldo had begun to fall behind in his studies and practical training, so his instructors had added their own threats. He'd been in Hell, and he'd finally written to Dietrich, confessing to daily black-outs. '*Mein lieber Vater*, I cannot go on. Please fetch me away."

That letter had not reached Dietrich until it was too late.

On this occasion, it was Hiltrud who broke the silence. 'We'd better go. I promised Father an early lunch. He has so many duties these days.'

'Come, then.' Dietrich offered his arm, but Hiltrud walked ahead of him towards the gates and his car. As they drove from the Lutheran cemetery, the swoosh of tyres on wet roads masked their silence. Only as they swept through the fringes of Hohen Neuendorf did Hiltrud speak again.

'You will stay and dine with us? My father has a birthday gift for you.'

He'd planned to drive back to Berlin and fill his day with paperwork. He and Hiltrud had been living fully apart for more than a year, a brief reconciliation after Waldo's death having proved unsustainable. He visited the family home only a couple of times a month now, to see his daughter. As for his birthday, what was a fortieth birthday when your son hadn't reached beyond his fifteenth? 'No presents, Hiltrud. Anyway, my actual birthday is two days off.'

'I know that. But you'll be with your mother that day.'

He wasn't planning that either. He was going to Munich. To

the beer hall where the Führer was to make his traditional annual speech.

'So, will you take lunch with us?'

'All right.'

His father-in-law's gift was a framed photograph of himself at the wheel of his new Mercedes 540K and a sugarplum of news for which Dietrich had to wait. Lunch was tense, everybody so civilised, their knives and forks squeaking. Glancing at his daughter, Dietrich wondered if these Sunday rituals were setting Claudia up for a lifetime of chronic indigestion.

When, at last, the coffee pot was brought in, Hiltrud excused herself to make an urgent telephone call. Before she left, she added fresh logs to the fire in the grate.

Dietrich told Claudia she might leave the table. 'Give me a hug, then go and devour *Frauen-Warte*.' He'd spied the magazine of the National Socialist Women's League on the hall table, guessing Claudia was saving it for the quiet of the afternoon.

She slid from her seat, but instead of coming to him, she went to peck her grandfather on the cheek. 'You don't mind me leaving you to slurp coffee alone, Opa?'

'"Slurp" isn't a polite word to use to your grandfather, and he won't be alone since I am here.' The sight of Claudia's red-gold plaits against his father-in-law's thatch of white made Dietrich realise that all through lunch he'd been trying to see Waldo in her. Failing, because she possessed all the rude health that had been denied to her brother. He held out his hand. Claudia ignored it.

'Opa says you never talk to any of us.' Almost fourteen now, her self-confidence matched her ripe colouring. 'Grandpapa talks to me about the Party. *He* listens when I tell him I want to advance the glory of Germany and save the honour of our family.'

Dietrich had been schooled never to flinch, from either word or blade. Dropping his hand, he said, 'If it's glory you're after, you will no doubt find me wanting. Honour I believe I can supply, though perhaps not in the form you expect it.' When she'd gone, he turned to his father-in-law. 'Are you teaching her Nazism, Ernst?'

Ernst Osterberg squared his jaw. 'Don't use that filthy term with me. We are the National Socialist Workers' Party, with the emphasis on "workers".' Something malevolent danced in the old man's eye. 'And Claudia's right. The future belongs to such as she, and I'm proud to have shown her that.' As if to prove it, Osterberg went to the dining-room door, and called after his granddaughter, 'Like to come for a ride in my new car after school tomorrow, *Sternchen*?'

'Yes, please!' Claudia called back.

Ernst Osterberg returned to his seat, leaving the door open. As Dietrich stirred a quarter-teaspoon of sugar into his coffee, he heard Hiltrud talking in an uninterrupted stream on the telephone about knitted squares and her certainty that their local women's circle would produce more blankets this winter than any of the other welfare *Bunds* in Berlin. *We survive*, he thought. *I in my ice-cube in Berlin, she with her knitting needles. Claudia expresses her grief in cold contempt for me, egged on by her grandfather.*

Rain pattered against the window. Ernst Osterberg took out a pocket watch and said, 'You won't want to leave it too late to drive back to the city.'

'There was something you had to tell me?'

Osterberg had heavy bulldog jowls, which limited his range of expressions. He gave what might have been a smile. 'My news, yes. Silberstrom's companies are all now Aryanised. The paint division was finally signed over to a new board on Thursday. The whole lot, purged of their Jewish directors. So, a good birthday present for you?'

'You're on the new board? A "trustee"?'

The brisk nod implied, 'Of course.' Osterberg said, 'You know, you can tell a Jew by his ear-lobes?'

'You told me that once.'

'We will inspect every employee, ten at a time, outside my office.' No twinkle in the heavy-lidded eyes to suggest a joke. 'Max von Silberstrom appointed Aryan board members as his surrogates.'

'As he had been required to do since April.'

'But they worked for *him*, not for the state.' Ernst's fist came down. 'A Jew can't help being a Jew, but a Jewish stooge is a knowing traitor. The Chamber of Commerce will push for harsh punishments.'

'Mm. You mishandled Max von Silberstrom badly, you know.'

The jowls quivered. 'You spent too much of your childhood playing in the Silberstroms' damn garden. Max and Ottilia should be as foreign to you as . . .' Osterberg searched for imagery, first inside his head, then, finding nothing, within the room '. . . as that coal scuttle. We were all too soft on foreign parasites. Now, thank God, we're ridding ourselves of them. I'd like to have seen Max von Silberstrom in jail, but he escaped to Switzerland. Somebody helped him.'

'Men like Max have friends everywhere, I'm afraid. I hope you have some, Ernst. Your institute mismanaged the seizure of Silberstrom Industries. Arguing among yourselves as to who should run the place.' Dietrich tutted. 'Your dithering gave Max time to sell his chemical formulas abroad.'

'What do you mean?'

Dietrich sipped his coffee, enjoying the sight of his father-in-law squirming. The fire had erased the freezing vigil at Waldo's grave and, though Dietrich wanted to get home, he was reluctant to leave the warmth. He certainly had no intention of allowing Ernst the last word. Ernst Osterberg: a natural bully, he'd blighted Dietrich's marriage, crowding him and Hiltrud in the early days when they should have been getting to know each other. Finding fault in Dietrich, training Hiltrud to see those faults for herself. But that was nothing, *nothing*, to the evil the man had sown latterly. 'You know Silberstrom Industries pioneered coloured paints for cars.'

Osterberg returned an impatient movement. 'I considered their Bear's Claw Red for my new vehicle. I decided in the end that a man of my age and position—'

'Thanks to their scientists,' Dietrich cut in, 'you can have your green or blue or sunshine yellow, whereas a few years ago it would have been "Any colour, sir, as long as it's black." But do you know that Silberstrom's laboratories also developed a camouflage paint for aircraft?'

'I'm running the place! Of course I know!'

'Paint using polymers to reduce drag and improve aerodynamics. It gives our fighter planes greater agility.'

'Which is why the factory was Aryanised.'

'But not fast enough.' Dietrich gave a smile that was not quite a smile. 'It was this paint formula that Max sent abroad. "Americanised", you might say. You will enjoy explaining the consequences of that to Reichsminister Göring. Ernst, you may have lost us the next war.'

Now a frightened old man sat at the table with him. 'There's no certainty of war.'

'There is. We are armed way beyond the point of merely defending ourselves and you, Opa, have bungled.'

Osterberg stared at the fire, perhaps imagining his position as head of the local Chamber of Commerce and deputy to the Gauleiter of Brandenburg going the same way as the apple logs Hiltrud had piled on the embers before she left. 'You could help me. You're Göring's friend. You could go and see him.'

'I'm his art supplier – one of many. And he's a busy man, air minister as well as guardian of our economy.'

Osterberg wiped sweat from his upper lip. 'You flew in his squadron, you wear the same medals. Brothers in arms.'

'Ah. There you touch my weakest side. I always wanted a brother.' Dietrich twisted the ring on his middle finger and its dim ruby caught a little firelight. The jewel had been in his family since the 1300s. 'I'll see Göring in Munich in a couple of days. I'll put in a word.' Raising his coffee cup to his lips, Dietrich unexpectedly smelt Paris. His stomach flipped and, for a moment, he was lying in a bath at the Duet, a satin thigh in his eye-line, breasts falling forward as Coralie leaned in for a precarious kiss—

'What are you thinking?' Osterberg demanded. 'What are you seeing?'

Dietrich was seeing Coralie de Lirac. He had given her his trust, a new identity and, briefly, a precious family ring. In return, she had carelessly robbed him of the last chance to see his son alive. He prayed he never saw her again because he wasn't sure he could behave as a civilised man ought.

Chapter Eleven

5 October 1939

The salon was crammed – with customers, journalists and girls in hats. Trays of champagne were still coming out and going back empty. In fact, the only thing flagging was Coralie's feet. Slipping off a shoe, she took a moment to reflect on the afternoon. Many people considered this, her fourth solo collection for Henriette Junot, to be the best the house had ever produced. One fashion journalist had even insisted that this 1939 autumn–winter line should be billed 'Coralie de Lirac *pour* Henriette Junot'.

The sixty hats paraded by mannequins wearing Hollywood-style evening dresses unarguably reflected Coralie's personality. She just wasn't sure if she'd strayed too far towards theatricality and away from style.

Style, the tyrant with a permanent position at her elbow. Nothing to do with fashion or chic, style was indefinable when present and screamingly obvious when absent.

Through an edgy spring and summer, as free Europe woke up to the certainty of war, Coralie had groped for inspiration for this collection. As Polish–German negotiations started up and broke down, she had prowled art galleries and museums for the spark to ignite her imagination. As German troops marched into Bohemia and Moravia, she'd held powwows with her technical staff, trying to summon up the elusive brilliant idea that would get fashionable Paris talking. A night out with friends at the Gaumont-Palais cinema on boulevard de Clichy had finally shoved the answer in front of her face.

All hail, 'Alexander's Ragtime Band' and Ethel Merman in a black top hat. This collection was a salute to Hollywood, with a nod to English restraint. She'd launched it despite war having been declared just over a month earlier. *War? What war?* Blackout was in force, thousands of men had been mobilised, but Paris could still have fun. That was the message at Henriette Junot. There were still plenty of Americans to swell the party – British, too, and even Germans. Only the South Americans were lacking. An Allied blockade of the Atlantic had choked them off.

'Honey, you've given us a blast of London!' A confident beauty in her middle thirties approached as if cameras were trained on her. The accent was American, but such a cocktail of east coast and Deep South, Coralie never could pin down where her friend Una actually came from. For her part, Una Kilpin masked her past which cemented the affinity between the two women. Both were self-made. Both had much to hide and, sensing this, they kept their probing to a minimum.

They often spoke English together, and enjoyed confusing those around them by jumping between English and French at will. With every new person she met, Coralie always stuck to the life-story Dietrich had created for her but she'd made an exception for Una, divulging her work for Pettrew & Lofthouse. She'd called it her 'foreign apprenticeship'. She'd had to; Una had jumped on her cockney accent.

'I spent five years in London and every housemaid I had there said "butter" the way you do. Whenever you talk English, Coralie, I hear Bow bells ringing.'

When it came to the truth about Noëlle's parentage, Coralie was equally frank with Una.

'In a London park? I hope there was a nightingale singing,' came the response. Amorous lapses never shocked Una Kilpin.

Una *McBride,* as they were to call her now. Separated from her shipping-magnate husband, who was in the service of the British government, Una had reverted to her maiden name. 'I've scuttled the Kilpin ships,' was how she'd announced her new identity.

'You must be boiling.' Coralie returned her kiss. Una was stunningly turned out in a Javier *tailleur* of zingy tartan cloth, a tam o' shanter perched on her rippling blonde hair.

'A little snug, but I love showing off this suit. D'you know, I was the only client to get one of the maestro's Scottish ensembles? Javier's 'thirty-seven autumn–winter show was scrapped, as you know.' Una made a 'don't ask' gesture. She'd been implicated in that disaster. 'I had lengths of this fabric made privately and a girl I knew copied the design.'

Coralie had never questioned Una about the demise of Maison Javier or the pirating of the collection. As with a good country sausage, it was sometimes best not to know all the ingredients that made up her friend. All she'd asked was that Una never steal or copy any of her designs and, to the best of her knowledge, Una had not. She didn't really need to as she was the salon's unofficial ambassadress, taking as much stock as she liked for free.

An exacting client, who only ever wore shades of biscuit, toffee and cream, Una McBride was rarely out of the fashion magazines and women bought what she wore. Monsieur Moulin always entered her name in the books in red, but freely admitted that she earned her eternal credit.

Now Coralie frowned at Una's tam o' shanter. 'You should

be wearing one of my hats. People will wonder if you've fallen out of love with us.'

'One cannot wear anything else with this suit, but from tomorrow, it will be all Coralie de Lirac. Oh, sublime!'

A mannequin was sauntering past, demonstrating the effortless *glissade* of her trade. Her gown had the sleeves and shoulders of a Southern belle. Her hat was black plush, with an organza bow secured at the front with a diamond butterfly. Drawing on her Pettrew's roots, Coralie had created equestrienne top hats. Tipped low at the front, high at the back, they complemented the new trend for lush hairstyles. Though not a single German boot had stepped over the border with France, war seemed to have awakened a desire in women to be feminine again. Clothes were becoming curvier, bosoms were 'in'. Along with top hats, Coralie had also produced berets. War's first winter demanded something practical for women walking to and from work in the blackout. She'd chosen bright colours, adding flowers and pom-poms in opposing shades. The lights might have gone out, but working women didn't have to disappear from view.

Please, God, there'd be a full order book after today's show because Henriette was back. Recovered from her illness, but minus her latest lover, she'd swept into the salon as if she'd been away just a week or two, not for two years. Her first act had been to sack Monsieur Moulin and appoint a new accountant. This man, Soufflard, was utterly unmoved by millinery. As far as he was concerned, hats existed to keep off the rain and to make a profit. He was standing beside Henriette right now, watching a tray of caviar canapés going past. Probably counting the fish eggs, Coralie thought, totting up the cost. As for Henriette, she was tête-à-tête with a journalist from the *New York Times*, Mrs

Fisk-Castelman, who had wanted to interview Coralie. Henriette had thrust herself forward, saying, 'One voice speaks for this salon – mine.'

They said jealousy was a green-eyed monster. If so, Henriette had more green eyes than a cage full of cats. Having offloaded her business when it suited her, she now deeply resented Coralie's success.

Coralie had not felt so vulnerable since Dietrich had left. These days, she and her child were completely alone. Ramon had gone – a mutual decision. He now lived a few Métro stops away in Montparnasse and had a new woman in his life, though he and Coralie remained married. Apart from sporadic gifts of coal, Coralie got nothing from him so her dream of owning her own salon had gone cold. Noëlle, at twenty-two months, required either a full-time nanny or her mother at home. The frightening truth was that Coralie needed Henriette more than Henriette needed her. Una, half a bottle of champagne under her belt and blissfully unaware of tensions, announced, 'Dear Coralie, you've brought us not just London style but English class. In Paris, that is supremely brave. I declare you Queen of Hats!'

Coralie shook her head to quieten her, but Henriette had heard. Coralie steeled herself for an angry encounter, but when Henriette approached it was to report how excited Mrs Fisk-Castelman had been by the show.

'One of my best, she says. She assures me that America still keeps its finger on the Paris pulse . . .' Henriette paused long enough to nod icily at Una '. . . and says that I will always have a market in the United States.'

'Sure you will,' Una gave back just as coldly, 'if you open up your next hat shop on board a warship. Nobody plies back and forth across the Atlantic for fun any more.'

Henriette's smile slipped, but she pulled it back. 'As you say, Madame Kilpin.'

'McBride, honey. These days, I paddle my own canoe.'

As Henriette stalked away, Coralie whispered, 'If you're going back to the States, Una, how about taking me and Noëlle with you?'

'I'm not going anywhere. Gladys Fisk-Castelman has been begging me to sail with her when she goes next week, but I won't desert the city of my heart. And you are about to become famous and doesn't Henriette know it! When Mrs F-C writes a person up, the world agogs. Is "agogs" a word?'

'Don't ask me, but I reckon the world will soon be too worried about conscription and food shortages to agog at anything. We may be having a quiet time of it here, but I hear it's Hell in Poland.'

'Whenever you talk like that, I know you've seen Ramon.'

'He visited a few nights ago – he loves to see Noëlle. Say what you like about him, Ramon understands politics. He thinks the Nazis will turn west soon, and invade us.'

'Oh, just stick to hats, Coralie. If truth is the first casualty of war, then vanity is the last. Let the bombs fall, ladies will still want what you make. You have a terrific future.'

By nine, the salon was empty, the collection boxed away. Discarded programmes littered the carpet and the room smelt of perfume and flat champagne. Time to go home. Coralie ached to hold her child, who would be tucked up in bed by now.

She looked around for Henriette – not to speak with but to avoid her. Tomorrow was soon enough for putting the collection, its cost and likely success through Soufflard's mincer. As to who was rightful queen here, Coralie didn't give a kipper's eyebrow.

Not after sixteen hours on her feet. Straightening the belt of her coat, she called goodbye to Amélie and Madame Zénon.

Her mistake was choosing to leave by the main door. Henriette was front-of-house, leaning against the display plinth. Head thrown back, eyes closed. Soufflard was speaking, but he broke off when he saw Coralie.

Henriette opened her eyes, then narrowed them at the sight of Coralie's outdoor clothes. 'Off, are you?' She sounded surprised.

'It's quarter past nine. We don't do a night shift.'

'Still living in that flat on rue de Seine? Isn't it too big for a lone woman and child?' Henriette painted the word 'lone' with audible glee.

Coralie could have answered that, actually, the flat was a touch too small for two, but she'd probably still be living there when God sent the next flood. Getting her huge, rustic bed – it had been a gift from Teddy – up the stairs had taken military logistics. She doubted there were any men left in Paris willing to help her get it down again. 'Yes, Henriette. I'm still on rue de Seine.'

'Good,' said Henriette. 'I'll have your things sent there. You, I don't want to see here again.'

Coralie stopped herself swaying by grabbing the nearest solid object, which happened to be Monsieur Soufflard. 'You're telling me . . .'

'To buzz off.'

'You can't!'

'Give me three reasons.' Henriette had gained weight in Italy and her complexion had sallowed. It had not been an entirely happy residence by all accounts – she'd fallen foul of the Fascist authorities there.

'Three? All right. I've delivered you a collection everyone agrees is stunning. Two, I kept your business together so you had something to get well for—' Henriette's mouth twisted. She was waiting for one more reason. Right, she could have it. 'Three, I'm your sister-in-law.'

Something darker than fury filled Henriette's eyes. 'Not any more. He left you.'

'I threw him out, actually, but we're still married and you have no right to dismiss me.'

Soufflard cleared his throat. 'We do. The books don't balance.'

'They never do straight after a collection.' Coralie hardly spared him a glance. 'When the orders come in, the holes fill up.'

'That's not what I'm saying, Mademoiselle de Lirac.'

She considered reminding him that she was legally 'Madame Cazaubon'. She'd kept 'de Lirac' as her professional name, but was entitled to be addressed as 'Madame' – unlike Henriette, who called herself 'Madame' to increase her status in the business world. In the end, she said nothing because Henriette was thrusting a piece of paper at her.

'Sign it,' Henriette commanded. 'It's you agreeing to leave, without claim on us.'

Coralie refused. 'I do have a claim, not least because I'm owed commission. And I won't give up my job while I've a child to support.'

'Why aren't you at home, looking after it?' Monsieur Soufflard seemed genuinely puzzled. 'I do not approve of working mothers.'

'"Her" not "it"!' Coralie hurled at him. 'And I don't give a damn whether you approve or not. I work because I have to.'

Staff were trickling into the shop, Amélie and Madame Zénon among them. Coralie was glad to see them. They'd stick up for her. Ignoring them, Henriette tried again to get Coralie to take the document. 'We are offering you sixty thousand francs to leave, but you have to sign, releasing me from all obligation to you, now and in the future.'

Sixty thousand? Now, that made a difference. Sixty thousand would start her up in her own place, give her some buffer if sales were slow. Still, a warning bell rang. What had Donal told her, years ago, when she'd picked a fight with a big lad at school and got a bloody nose? 'Rule one: if the other man looks relaxed, it's because he's got a brass knuckle in his glove.' She said, 'All right, I'll sign . . .' the triumph Henriette was not quite sly enough to conceal proved her suspicions were valid '. . . when I've shown it to a good lawyer.'

Henriette stamped her foot. 'I've tried to be fair! You all heard her,' at last, she acknowledged her staff, who drew back nervously, 'hurling my generosity back at me.' Henriette tore up the paper and nodded to Soufflard, who took out a pen. Using the display table as a surface, he began to write. Coralie twitched at the pedantic scratch of his nib but, at last, he held the results out to her.

It wasn't a disclaimer, or a promissory note. It was a bill. Coralie read: 'Stock advanced to Madame Kilpin-McBride from February 1938 through September 1939, 72,000 fr 50'. Payment to Mademoiselle de Lirac in lieu of notice, 60,000 fr. Mademoiselle de Lirac to pay Henriette Junot 12,000 fr 50.' The last figure was underlined. 'We will take cash, Mademoiselle.'

Coralie looked at Soufflard, then at Henriette, whose smirk shouted, 'See?' 'You and your American friend have been robbing my business for months,' Henriette crowed. 'It's all in the ledgers. Leave, or we take you to court.'

'This is unjust! Una's brought millions of francs in custom. Half the order book is thanks to her.'

'I find that highly offensive. This is *my* business. *My* success.'

But it was mock-anger and Coralie knew that she was check-mated. She contemplated all the things she could do. Punch Henriette on the nose, or Monsieur Soufflard. Throw *marottes* at the mirrors. Or be dignified. She walked to the door, murmuring, 'An egg. A bloody egg.' She turned and said sweetly, 'Let's see who brings out the better collection next April, Henriette.'

'Not you. Nobody will employ you. You'll understand soon enough the price of stealing my friends, my staff and my little brother.'

'Henriette, your brother is many things but "little" is not one of them.'

She let the door clash behind her. Here she was again, chucked out on the pavement, and this time she had a child to feed. She *would* feed her child, and send her to the best schools, too. Henriette Junot had pulled the rug, so Coralie would just have to weave herself a fine carpet.

She didn't turn for home, but walked cautiously up blacked-out rue Royale to boulevard de la Madeleine, where a half-moon enabled her to find La Passerinette and a white card in the salon's window. It was sandwiched between glass and blinds and Coralie had no reason to believe that it was anything other than the one that had been there since June: "We regret, La Passerinette has closed down. Please ring the bell for uncollected commissions."

Paris millinery was a small world. The gossip was that Lorienne Royer had left Paris to open an independent shop in some other town. She'd abandoned her assistant, Violaine Beaumont, to deal with irate customers and to claim her salary from the Baronne von Silberstrom in London. Coralie could well believe it, but she hadn't yet heard that La Passerinette had been sold.

She flipped open the letterbox and sniffed the air inside. Vaguely mushroomy . . . Chances were, the shop was still empty.

Violaine's flat above the salon was in darkness. The whole building was as dark as a coal-hole, not a crack of light escaping from any of the windows. As it was too late to ring door-bells, she turned for home.

On the pont des Arts, she stopped to catch her breath. Paris sprawled on either side, like badly raked embers, dots of light everywhere. The blackout had been in force since the declaration of war, but people were getting careless. If German bombers ever came at a full moon, they'd follow the Seine as easily as a white-painted road. There had been regular alerts since September, sirens screaming, people tumbling out on to the street, gas masks bumping as they tried to work out where the nearest air-raid shelter was. All false alarms so far.

They called it the '*drôle de guerre*'. A joke of a war.

The country that invests everything in defence will fall to the nation that invests everything in attack. Dietrich had spoken those words to Coralie at the Panthéon, beside the tomb of Napoleon Bonaparte. He'd known what was coming. Perhaps, instead of fantasising about setting up on her own, she ought to be thinking about leaving Paris. Children were already being packed off to the countryside and schools were closing. Just the other day Julie, her young nanny, had asked Coralie if she meant to join the outflow. 'Some people I know are moving to the Haute-Vienne for safety. It's remote there.'

'So remote I've never heard of it,' Coralie had replied. Truth was, she had no safe haven. No friends or contacts outside Paris. Like most people, she was relying on France's vast wall of defence, the Maginot Line, to keep the Germans at bay. She was relying on an army of two million men, and doing what that Gypsy

woman had predicted for her in a field two long summers ago
– 'stitching and shaping'.

In other words, just carrying on.

Rue de Seine was a street of galleries and antiques shops
including – she glanced up – Galérie Clisson. She tutted at the
chinks of light showing in the upper windows as she passed.
Teddy argued that if the Germans were to bomb Paris he'd rather
like his street to go first. Generosity and selfishness were united
in him: he was living proof that you could love a person without
actually finding much in them to admire.

Her own place stood at the junction with rue Jacques Callot.
Running lightly up the stairs and closing doors silently, she
stopped in the hallway and listened. Breathing, from a tiny set
of lungs and the drizzle of the nanny's snores. Julie must be in
the sitting room, asleep in a chair.

Coralie crept into a little bedroom and knelt by a truckle bed,
stroking the smudge of black curls on the pillow. Her daughter
was deeply asleep, fists clenched. Coralie bent to kiss each fist in
turn, and when little arms rose in a reflex movement, she sucked
the child into a cuddle. Settling her back down, she sniffed. Fish.
Dropping a last kiss, Coralie tiptoed out, preparing to do tactful
battle with Julie. Noëlle must never eat fish. Born two months
premature, she was still tiny. The smallest bone could choke her.

Passing the kitchen door, which was ajar, Coralie noticed
crocks piled on the drainer. Even for Julie, an indifferent wash-
er-upper, it was a mess. The smell of fish was very strong.
Bouillabaisse soup, if her nose told her right. Coralie went to
the sitting room and turned on the light.

A figure slumped in an armchair woke with a rough grunt.

'Ramon – what the bloody hell?' Coralie instinctively searched
for a second figure in the room, but he was alone. That was some-

thing. Julie was only nineteen, and came from a respectable family of booksellers on nearby rue Jacob, but that hadn't stopped Ramon flirting shamelessly with her. Coralie cringed at the memory. The passionate, hot-blooded man she'd thought she'd married merited a simpler definition: womaniser. She looked around. How did one man make so much mess? He'd disembowelled a newspaper. He must have read it in four different places. He'd been smoking, too, a full ashtray alongside the messy remains of a meal. She stood over him, and poked his leg. 'Where's Julie?'

'Uh? Oh. She went home. No point us both being here.' His shirt was wide open displaying a crop of body hair.

'I hope she left before you started undressing.'

Ramon looked down, as if trying to see his nakedness through another's eyes. 'I showed her a bit of chest. It's hilarious, the way she squeaks when I look at her. The more prudish, the more they secretly want to be deflowered.'

'She squeaks because you're an oaf. Honestly, this place smells like a homecoming trawler. You know I don't allow fish.' *Damn this blackout*. 'I can't open a window unless we sit in the dark.'

'Let's lie down in the dark, then.' Ramon reached for her, teeth feral and white. She turned away. There'd be none of *that*. The shock, a year ago, of learning that Ramon was being unfaithful had almost felled her. She'd begun to let her guard down, to feel the protective passion that, in a maturing relationship, replaces superficial attraction. Rejection, anger had been razor blades to the heart. Why did men always betray her? Was she so worthless?

'Passion burns . . . like dry straw,' her former tutor, Mademoiselle Deveau, had once told her. 'Men are good at walking away . . . We women stay around poking the ash.' Recalling, in those words, the dangers of victimhood, Coralie had let Ramon go. They got on all right, these days. When he was in good spirits

– and her stocks of energy were sufficiently high – they could share a laugh. Noëlle adored him so he was free to come and go. But not to get spicy with Coralie.

'You didn't leave Noëlle alone when you went out for food?' Coralie carried the remains of Ramon's supper through to the kitchen.

He followed her. 'Course not, she came too. And, yes, I gave her some fish and, no, she won't die.' Ramon nuzzled her neck.

Coralie had her hands in the sink by this time, and had found a soiled nappy among the cups. It occurred to her to slap Ramon round the face with it, but her anger failed to boil over. She was still too angry with Henriette to turn on anyone else. She shook him off. 'If you knew what kind of day I'd had—'

'Ah! Your show . . . Of course! You're still wearing a hat, so it must have been good.'

'I don't get the logic but, yes, I was pleased. Afterwards . . .' She related the rest of the story.

Ramon gave a burst of hilarity. He never half laughed. 'I told you Henriette would come back and claim her own. I suppose she cheated you?'

She told him about the promised sixty thousand francs, which had somehow turned into a bill for a higher sum.

'My sister is like a whale, mouth open. They don't understand, all those little fish, that when they swim into that great mouth, they are dinner. You are one of those little fish, Coralie.'

'I am not!'

In her bedroom, Coralie put her hat into its box and shuffled round the gigantic *bateau-lit*. Teddy's wedding present to her, the bed took up most of the floor, leaving just enough room for a single wardrobe. As she reached up to put the hatbox on the top, Ramon pulled her down again. 'Can I stay, *chérie*?'

'What's wrong with your own mattress? Or should I say "mistress"? I'm going to warm up the last of that soup. I hope you've left me some bread.'

'It's too late to eat.'

'For you – I've been on my feet all day.' Slithering off the bed, she added grudgingly, 'You can stay on the sofa, but don't badger me, ha? Get carried away and I'll do to you what Teddy's always threatening to do with Voltaire.'

'That magnificent cat. It would be a crime.'

'Yet so tempting.'

As she lit tea lights in the sitting room and laid a place at the table for one, Coralie reminded herself that, even if his taste for fidelity had been short-lived, Ramon had made her safe. He was human too, in a way she was not, caring about the underdog and the poor of the world. For all her grumblings at him, a stubborn affection remained, So really, she decided, she could make up a bed for him in the sitting room. Just for one night.

Midnight. She lay listening to Ramon's breathing. His left arm was crooked around her, and she could hear the tick of his watch under her ear. She gave in too easily, that was her problem. Had Dietrich abandoned her because she'd given herself too readily? Men didn't value what came for free.

What about the ring Dietrich had offered her? It hadn't dropped out of a cracker. That man was incomprehensible. 'I sow the seeds of my own downfall,' she murmured. 'Sow them, water them and tend them. I'm very thorough but, of course, I am my father's daughter.'

Snuffling sounds from along the hallway warned Coralie that Noëlle was waking. With a tired groan, she threw back the covers and reached for her slipper-satin dressing-gown, the one Dietrich had bought her. It still had its rose-petal sheen because she washed it in soap flakes.

When she finally returned to bed, Ramon was sitting up. 'I've a favour to ask.' Laughing at her response, he said, 'Not *that*. I need lodgings for some friends. That's really why I came to see you.'

'I'm flattered.'

'They won't stay for long and they'll sleep on the floor. Soon as they get new papers, they'll be gone.'

'What kind of friends?' He always referred to himself as an anarchist, pledged to smash the corrupt framework of society. 'Friends' could mean anything. 'What are you mixed up in?'

'In war, *chérie*. Like it or not, we all are. So, can you find room?'

Chapter Twelve

A few days later, Ramon came back at six a.m. with a bunch of very-yesterday flowers and two down-at-heel men, whom he referred to as 'evaders'.

Wary-eyed above black, ragged beards, they could have been a vagabond double-act that had just been booed offstage. *Those clothes will have to be burned*, she thought. She'd put them on the fire with a pair of tongs. 'Do you speak French?' she asked them.

The men stared mutely at her, fuelling her irritation. They'd not only woken her, but Noëlle too. A distant cry of 'Maman!' was followed by the bump of a small body rolling out of bed.

'They'd better not be call-up dodgers,' she threw over her shoulder. When she returned, Noëlle on her hip, she gave them another inspection. One had a violin case under his arm, and a battered suitcase seemed to be their joint luggage. Their smiles at the sight of a child seemed genuine, though, and she realised they were younger than she'd imagined. 'So, what's an "evader"?'

'A person who needs shelter. How about some breakfast?' Ramon strode past her to the kitchen. She found him throwing open cupboards.

'Where are they going to sleep?' she demanded.

'In the roof. Ah, *voilà*!' His hand closed around a tin of condensed milk. 'Have you got butter?'

'They're going to sleep in the loft?' Her flat occupied the

building's mansard roof. Somebody at some time had added a ceiling. The space above, accessed by a ladder, was too low for a man to stand. 'It's for storing junk and I'm sure there are birds' nests in there.'

'It's more comfortable than they're used to and all they want is to lie down somewhere safe. I'll bring blankets and sleeping rolls.' Ramon dropped his voice. 'They were in Spain, fighting in the International Brigades, but after demob they were pushed over the border to our side, then shoved into Gurs. That's an internment camp for people whom France can't think what to do with. They walked out and now they need to be laundered.'

'I'll say.'

'Given new identities, I mean. They're musicians and want to work here in Paris. That's why I'm helping. Music lovers stick together.'

'Are they Spanish?'

'Hungarian.'

'Why can't they go home to Hungaria, or wherever?'

'They're Gypsies. Romanies.'

'Oh, no. I won't have Gypsies here. Gypsies steal. They steal children.' She drew Noëlle so tightly against her hip that the child wailed.

'Coralie! I am ashamed of you.' Ramon took Noëlle into his own arms. 'If that prejudice is true, then all prejudices are true. This infant could be despised her whole life – some will say she carries your sin on her head. And you, being born in Belgium, must be thick and I, as a Frenchman, must be a glorious lover. Well, that last one is true, *hein*?'

He always rounded off his attacks with a joke – he knew that, despite herself, she found his humour infectious. Well, she wouldn't smile this time.

He took her hand, and she flinched because his was cold. They'd walked through a chilly dawn. How far had those two lads walked in all? A long way, if they'd come from the Spanish border.

'They aren't wanted in their country, Coralie, and they certainly can't travel through Germany. They are stuck here.'

'All right. I'll make coffee and eggs, and I'll think about the rest. Butter's in the larder cupboard. Looking at it won't fetch it down! I'm not the maid-of-all-work, you know.'

Over breakfast, she extracted a price: 'Ramon, I need coal, enough to last all winter.'

He made discouraging noises. 'Supplies are low. The factories are burning it night and day, armaments and all that. '

'So you want your daughter to freeze. You're all heart, Ramon Cazaubon.'

'I'll see what I can do. Now pass the jam.' Seeing her expression, he laughed. '*Please*, Madame.'

'Tell these boys they can't smoke here. Not anywhere in the flat. I don't want my child smelling like an ashtray. And smoke's bad for children.'

'It never did me any harm.'

She made no answer, just glared, until Ramon tutted in exasperation and called, 'Comrades, there are house rules!'

Shaved and bathed, the two men were revealed to be only a little older than herself. Arkady and Florian. Coralie laughed when they shuffled into the sitting room wearing blue suits Ramon had found for them. Having survived on prison rations for a year, they looked like forced labourers abducted from a rice field. 'The boys', as she would always think of them, listened gravely as she laid down her house rules. Lavatory seat down after use. Knock before entering the bathroom. Whispering only after Noëlle's bedtime. And no smoking, ever, whatever Ramon said on the subject.

From then on, whenever one of them reached thoughtlessly into his pocket, the other would hiss, 'Not allowed!'

They smoked in the street and Coralie worried about that. Any half-awake gendarme would question two identically dressed loafers, or follow them back to the house. So, in the end, she allowed them to smoke in the stairwell, with the window open. The shop on the ground floor was run by a couple who lived elsewhere, and who used the flat above as their stockroom. They met only occasionally on the stairs but, even so, she instructed the boys to curb their native Hungarian, not even to whistle their own folk tunes, in the shared part of the building. Going down one morning to hang out washing, she caught Arkady sweeping up ash. Bright, Arkady was. Never had to be told twice.

He took the linen basket from her and carried it downstairs. He had true musician's hands, like a lute-player's in a Renaissance painting. He'd carried his violin intact from Hungary, preserving it through battle and bombardment between 1936 and demob in October '38. It had survived Gurs, a place of pigsty dormitories and mud. 'Because he sleeps with violin,' Florian explained. 'He is his baby.'

Florian's 'baby' was a hammered dulcimer. That was what had been in the suitcase, padded under a few items of clothing. Coralie watched, fascinated, whenever he hung it round his neck like an ice-cream vendor's tray. When played with metal hammers, it sang like a harp and Noëlle would go into a trance. When Arkady added accompaniment, it was like no sound Coralie had ever heard. Noëlle would grab Coralie's hands, squealing to be danced on her feet.

★

Two weeks flashed by, filled for Coralie with washing, cooking and conversation. Laughter, too, all the better for being unexpected. It eased her frustration over La Passerinette. She'd returned to boulevard de la Madeleine a couple of days after her moonlight visit, and pressed the bell marked 'Beaumont'. Getting no answer, she'd pressed the one above. An older woman had come down and told her that Violaine certainly had the keys to the shop. And, no, it had not been sold. Violaine had been put in temporary charge by the Baronne von Silberstrom, but neither woman was available.

'Poor Violaine collapsed. Nervous exhaustion and I'm not surprised, the way that woman, Royer, drove her. She is recovering her health in a clinic outside Paris and, before you ask, I don't recall its name.'

Without Ottilia von Silberstrom's London address, Coralie was defeated. Taking over La Passerinette had become a need, a dream with a pragmatic lining. She knew she could shake the place up, and she also knew she could never again work for another woman. Those closed blinds! They taunted her, as had a glimpse, on her last visit, of a white-clad female leaving the place. Red-gold hair, an enveloping fur collar, it had to be Ottilia.

Grinding her teeth, because the traffic was too dense even for a suicidal dash, Coralie had watched the figure climb into the back of a taxi which disappeared round a corner into rue Cambon. Coralie had later telephoned Una McBride.

'If you hear that the Baronne von Silberstrom is in Paris, will you find out where she's staying? I tried the Ritz on rue Cambon, but she isn't there.'

Una had promised to keep her ear to the ground.

'I met her in London once, but I can't say we're well acquainted.'

To fill her time, Coralie started teaching the boys 'proper'

French. Julie joined in. Nineteen, with long brown hair and full lips, she enjoyed having two young men vying for her attention and Coralie grew uneasy. Duelling musicians would be bad enough. Enraged parents, demanding the identity of their daughter's seducer would be more dangerous than neighbours or policemen. As she couldn't turn the boys out, she tried, gently, to point Julie towards alternative employment. She couldn't afford a nanny at the moment, she said – but the girl burst into wild tears. 'My parents' house is so gloomy, nobody talks, and you need me. I am Noëlle's second mother!'

Was she? Not a wholly welcome idea, but perhaps inevitable, considering the long hours Coralie had always worked. She relented. Julie could stay on reduced hours, but could she please not wear those tight little cardigans? And please not speak in that breathy way so the boys had to lean close to hear her. 'Arkady and Florian have been starved of female company for months. You know the facts of life, Julie.'

Julie continued to act as if she knew them all too well and eventually Coralie asked Ramon to find alternative accommodation for the boys.

'It isn't that easy,' Ramon retorted. 'As for Julie, let her have a lover.'

'When she's under my roof, I'm responsible for her.'

'No – you only think you are.'

Her anxiety made some impression, however, and Ramon arranged for the boys to audition in nightclubs where he knew the management. Once they got work, they'd be able to get lodgings of their own. From Pigalle to Clichy they played short sets every night for free in the hope of winning a permanent job – and came home with ever longer faces, the evening suits Ramon had acquired for them ever baggier on their frames.

Arkady explained, 'When we offer our homeland music, clubs say already they have quota of foreign talent. When we say we can play American swing music, clubs say we are not black enough.'

'Or white enough,' Florian chipped in.

'Or American enough. But in our own country, we are always too much Gypsy.'

A month into their stay, Ramon delivered their new identity papers, with sleet on his shoulders. November had arrived, but the coal had not. Ramon explained that it was easier to steal the wheels off trains than coal out of the freight trucks. Depots had armed guards, these days. So, they huddled around a two-bar electric fire and made the acquaintance of two new human beings, Arkady Erdös and Florian Lantos.

The boys had been reinvented as wild-boar trackers and itinerant musicians, the former to explain their battle scars. Ramon insisted that boar tusks left similar puncture-marks to bullets. They'd elected to keep their given names, taking surnames that would mark them out as ethnic Hungarians, but not Romany. Arkady believed that changing the name your mother gave you brought bad luck — 'Besides, I could drink one day and forget it.'

'What you need is a gimmick.' Coralie was combing Noëlle's curls. Curls black as a beaver's pelt. The little girl's eyes had an exotic up-tilt and in them Coralie saw Rishal, her sailor lover. Everybody else saw Ramon. Even those who had known her for a long time assumed that Noëlle was his. As an impatient Noëlle squirmed away, Coralie offered her comb to Arkady, whose corkscrew hair was tangled like a fisherman's net. 'You need something to make you stand out.'

'We are not a variety act.'

'You are. As immigrants, you have to play folk music and dress up as a novelty act. It's the law. I'll put my mind to it.'

On 8 November, they all crammed around her small dining table, toasting her birthday. Her official birthday, the one Dietrich had chosen for her. Arkady and Florian, Julie and Ramon, they all sat so close that no one could move unless everybody did. Noëlle was on Ramon's knee, her cheek flat against his shoulder. Someone had put a spray of pink flowers into a tin mug. Cutting her cake, chasing off thoughts of Dietrich, which always came on this day, she made a wish: 'Health and happiness to all!' Then a private one: *A bunch of pink roses, from someone who has the guts to stay faithful.* Her thoughts veering, she suddenly said, 'What about the Rose Noire?'

Everyone looked at her.

Ramon caught on: 'The place on boulevard de Clichy? They shooed us out. It's in chaos. The man who owns it was locked up in La Santé.'

Coralie nodded. 'Seven years' jail for ripping the ear off his American singer. Got carried away making love, m'lud. *She* says he attacked her when she gave in her notice. But listen . . .'

Coralie had heard that the Rose Noire needed musicians. Struggling under the management of its elderly sommelier, Félix Peyron, they couldn't get decent bands to play. 'They have an outfit called Les Hot Boys, but the trumpeter's seventy, and it's never the same line-up two nights running. The club's desperate for a resident band.'

'But we are not Hot Boys,' Florian said sadly. 'We are cold boys, often.'

'Teddy goes there,' Coralie said, 'and he told me they're running an open night. You get up, play a short set, and the band that gets most applause wins a six-week contract.' The boys were straining to follow her French. 'You'd have to find a couple of other band members.'

Ramon answered for them. 'You can't take a piss in Paris but you're standing next to a refugee with a guitar on his back . . .' His expression clouded. 'How would you fix the biggest round of applause?'

Coralie stood up and demonstrated enthusiastic clapping.

'Very funny, Coralie. There's only three of us, even assuming we drag Nanny along.' He winked at Julie, whose chair was so close to Florian's, their thighs must have been touching.

Julie said, 'I'll come. I like to dance.'

'Well, I was joking,' Ramon answered. 'You're too immature for the Rose Noire – and who'd look after Noëlle?'

He was trying to sink her idea, Coralie realised. Mentioning Teddy had done it. Her friend's elitist profession and country château were sandpaper to the eyeballs as far as Ramon was concerned. Well, Ramon could have his politics, but she *really* wanted her flat back, her life back. Being unable to settle down to work was akin to being in a boat without paddles, drifting ever further from the shore, a feeling that had intensified when she read a piece in *Marie Claire* praising Henriette Junot's 'astonishing and witty line of equestrian-inspired hats'.

'I'm sure Julie's mother would mind Noëlle. She's offered before,' she said, ignoring Ramon's objection. 'As for an audience, I'll rent a rabble and Teddy knows people . . .' *Don't ever play poker, dear estranged husband, because your face gives you away* '. . . and I'll get Una McBride to join us. Some of Henriette's girls might come, too, if I promise them half-decent men to dance with. You boys,' she put on a face that drew nervous laughs from Arkady and Florian, 'must play up the Romany look or it'll be the same

old moan – "Foreign players putting French ones out of work."
That means costumes, untamed hair and eyes a-flashing.'

Julie giggled.

'We have no costume.' Arkady plucked at his clothes.

'And I don't have time to run round finding them.' Ramon
gnawed his thumbnail, meaning he wanted a cigarette. At any
moment, he'd lead an exodus to the stairs, where they'd disappear
in a fug of Gauloises.

'Costumes are my department.' Coralie held up ten fingers.
'These haven't held a needle for over a month. We'll have white
shirts and red sashes. You and I,' she turned to Julie, drawing
the girl into her excitement, 'will wear matching hats. Hats for
everyone. Why not?' she demanded, as Ramon scraped his chair
back. 'I could launch you and re-launch myself on the same
night.'

Chapter Thirteen

The streets glittered with freezing frost on the last Saturday of November but the Rose Noire's dance floor was as hot as a bread oven. Coralie was dismayed – and not just because her dress was sticking to her. Having confidently predicted an easy victory for 'Arkady and His Vagabonds of Swing', she was discovering there was stiff competition. Ten bands at least were vying for the chance of a long-term booking. War had hit nightclubs hard. Half the men of dancing age had been mobilised into the armed forces. Clubs had closed their doors rather than struggle on. Singers and jazz musicians were falling out of work. Of the American bandsmen who had once flocked to Paris to feed the passion for jazz, the better-off had sailed home. The rest were saving up to buy third-class or steerage tickets. Meanwhile, they needed to eat and were willing to hustle.

Una McBride had already sent her Alabama-born maid, Beulah, home and bought passage for a couple of jobless drummers as well. 'Paris won't be a ball for black men and women if the Germans arrive,' she said, following Coralie's gaze to the stage, where the first competitors were tuning up. 'But don't start feeling sorry for *them*. You have your boys to look out for.' Una was scintillating in a backless sequined sheath, her hair styled in a single wave that broke on her forehead in a hundred kiss-curls.

'The Germans won't come,' Coralie answered. 'I know,

because you're still here. If you were afraid, you'd be on your way to London. There are still boats leaving Brittany for southern England.'

'Dear heart, I'm just too lazy to go. I expect I'll regret it.'

'Don't! No more war talk. I want to enjoy tonight.' To do that, she needed to stop worrying about Noëlle, left in the care of Julie's mother. The child had fallen asleep straight after her tea, so no opportunity to introduce her to Madame Fourcade. Coralie knew she should have insisted on Julie staying home. It was why she paid the girl!

The first band took to the stage to the sound of applause. When Julie started clapping. Coralie shushed her crossly. 'Remember whose side you're on.' But Julie just smiled. She looked lovely, Coralie admitted, a spray of silk flowers in her brown hair, a butterfly perched over the largest bloom. Coralie had made the decoration for her, shamelessly stealing Henriette Junot's wiring technique. Una had lent Julie a peach-pink dress, one of the coloured ones she bought each season and never wore.

When Coralie asked why she did that, Una had given a genuinely bemused shrug. 'You know how some people steal from stores and can't stop themselves? I love every dress I see and I have to have it. Oh, I pay. Or, rather, Mr Kilpin, from whom I wrestle a monthly dress allowance, pays, but the moment colour touches my skin, I feel I've rubbed myself with poison ivy. If you can explain my neurosis, you're worth a hundred dollars an hour.'

Coralie wasn't sure how much she was worth. She'd been cutting silk all week, and stitching till her eyes crossed. The eight other girls in her party, *midinettes* from Henriette Junot, all wore a '*cache-misère*' – a silk turban drizzled with tassels, beads and feathers. Seated across three tables, sipping champagne provided by the elderly gallants Teddy Clisson had brought along, they looked like so many Queens of Sheba. Or perhaps Princesses was nearer the mark. Coralie fully intended to be the queen of the evening.

Her own evening dress of ivory bias-cut silk was one that Dietrich had bought her. A little old-fashioned now, she'd added gold vermicelli to the hips, giving it a touch of Mata Hari. And she'd made herself a hat, a real stunner.

Before Henriette sacked her, she'd taken home a couple of top-hat and brim blocks to practise on. Handcrafted from poplar wood, they went some way to make up for the commission Henriette had cheated from her. She'd made herself a top hat for tonight. Silk plush being beyond her skills and her purse, she'd used buckram, a linen cloth impregnated with starch. Once blocked and dry, it kept its shape and she'd reinforced it with cotton-covered wire. She'd painted the hat with rabbit glue and, finally, gold leaf. Burnished with a squirrel-tail brush, peppered with gold lamé roses and butterflies, it shone like a Byzantine crown. If gold leaf brought a blast of her father back to her, she could ignore that. And with her hair a cascade of fat curls, Coralie reckoned she looked all right.

Una certainly thought so. 'I'm going to buy that hat right now,' she said, opening her purse.

'It won't fit you and, anyway, this is my calling card and I want people to look at my head, not yours.' Leaning close to Una, Coralie shared her long-held hopes of acquiring La Passerinette.

Una made a face. 'Don't. It's not worth anything. Sure, take on the lease and buy the stock, but there's no goodwill left there. That awful girl has seen everybody off.'

'Violaine? It's not her fault.'

'Lorienne. Last time I was there, she snicked me with her nails. And all those peach hats in the window. Would she sell me one?'

'You don't wear peach.'

'That's not the point. And it's not fair that you didn't make me a hat for tonight.'

'It's a punishment because you still buy from Henriette.'

'I'll defect, I promise. Give me yours.'

'Gold isn't your colour.'

'Sure it's my colour. Gold is only beige with ambition. Oh, you're too mean.'

A new band was on the stage, their matching white suits complementing Mediterranean complexions. 'Come on, let's shake a leg,' Coralie said. 'I didn't come here to sit on a chair all night.'

'Won't your husband dance with you?' Una injected a shot of malice.

'Ramon's keeping an eye on Julie. The boys are fearful she'll get corrupted. Haven't you noticed Florian's sweet on her?'

'And he trusts *Ramon*?'

Going up to Teddy, Coralie held out her hand. 'Ladies' excuse me. If you don't dance, your legs will go to sleep.'

Teddy cocked an ear. 'I hear no music.'

'I know. If those boys don't blow one end of their instruments soon, they'll be thrown out and the next lot put up. All the better for our Vagabonds, eh?'

The music did start eventually, like a locomotive grinding out of a station. Performing a sedate two-step with Teddy, Coralie shared with him her conviction that the musicians were a bunch of Corsican bandits.

'Indeed they are.' Teddy indicated a second group of swarthy men lined up in front of the baize curtains that stopped light seeping up the stairs and violating the blackout. Wide-shouldered and wide-trousered, they were staring hard at the stage. 'Black-marketeers from Marseille,' Teddy whispered into her ear. 'A turf war's broken out and they're trying to take over here. No, don't stare. They're shy and have guns in their pockets. The band are their creatures. They will win, by the way.'

Coralie wailed, 'Our boys don't have a chance?'

'About as much chance as me throwing you over my shoulder while performing a knees-bent shimmy.'

'I was up three nights sewing their costumes.'

'The world never was fair, my dear, and now it's less fair.'

Arkady's Vagabonds of Swing were the last on the bill, and by the time they stepped up to play, people were leaving, including performers and their supporters, as if they'd also heard the game was up. Arkady threw a fatalistic glance and Coralie sent an encouraging one back. The club wasn't empty by any means. People had walked a long way in the dark to hear music and dance. They would dance.

Arkady's boys – Florian and two recruits, a Spaniard and a Portuguese – had rehearsed a set designed to get people on their feet. They were worth a second look too, in their red and white costumes. 'Come on, girls.' Coralie beckoned to her crowd. 'Grab a partner and get ready to shout.'

The first song was a slow lament for lost love: 'Vous Qui Passez Sans Me Voir'. Arkady and Florian hadn't wanted to play popular tunes but Coralie had been blunt. 'Gather together everyone in Paris who wants to hear Hungarian mazurkas all evening, and you'll be playing to fresh air. People want the music they hear at the films, on the radio, at the Casino de Paris. Give it a Romany twist and you've got something different.'

The Spanish guitarist provided the melody. The dulcimer added a silvery resonance, the Portuguese double-bass player gave the rhythm, while Arkady's violin swooped and sobbed. At the end, there was strong applause. Then the Corsicans moved forward. 'Keep playing!' Coralie shouted, through cupped hands, and Arkady swung into Fats Waller's 'This Joint Is Jumping'. There was a rush for the dance floor. Dezi Rice, with whom Coralie had Lindyhopped all that time ago, grabbed her hand. 'Does that hat stay on?'

'If it doesn't, don't you stand on it!' She and Dezi danced directly beneath the main light, an art-deco extravaganza of pink glass that had been the proprietor, Serge Martel's, parting touch before a police wagon had taken him away. A rose motif shone down on them and as they danced in and out of its shadow, their shapes flickered like a speeded-up film.

Coralie was back in the canteen at Pettrew's, kicking up her feet. She danced on after Dezi stopped – until she saw what was troubling him. The Corsican musicians were trying to get back onstage. Their gangster friends, family, whatever they were, had formed a line behind them. Arkady was oblivious, as he always was when he was playing. Florian had seen the danger, though, and so had the guitarist. The bass-player had also stopped, but his gaze was on the stairs.

What the devil? The baize curtains were bulging open to admit a platoon of soldiers. Moss-green uniforms, patch pockets, black berets.

'English Tommies!' Dezi whistled through his fingers to attract their attention.

Twenty or so Tommies stared around as if they'd stumbled into Fairyland. 'Have the British invaded?' Coralie asked.

'They're stationed in Normandy, along the Belgian border, but they're let out occasionally. They'll be on a three-day pass. Lock up your daughters.' Dezi laughed.

Félix Peyron was greeting the newcomers cautiously. Working out how much champagne they'd drink, Coralie reckoned, and getting his disappointment over with early. The girls in the club were more enthusiastic. They peeled away from the sides, heading for the boys. As Félix and his staff set up new tables, Coralie noticed a smattering of slate-blue uniforms among the green.

'Royal Air Force,' Dezi told her. 'No. 1 Group, stationed near Reims.'

'Are you a spy or something?'

'I was there a couple of weeks ago, playing a morale-booster concert, and I met some of the lads after hours. Bomber crews, mostly, attached to the Expeditionary Force.'

Coralie didn't know whether to be glad to see them or not. They looked so foreign. After two and a half years in Paris, she'd got used to French colouring. Apart from a few dark heads, the Englishmen all seemed mousy or ginger. The Corsicans had stopped their assault on the stage and were eyeballing them.

Blood and teeth before the night's over, Coralie predicted. She ought to warn the Tommies, though the RAF boys would be easier to approach because they were sitting a little apart. One caught her eye. Tall, with good shoulders and a gleam of dark hair under his cap, he seemed to be singling her out too. The pay-off of wearing a gold hat, she supposed.

Dezi whispered, 'Seen something tasty? Don't let your husband catch you.'

'We go our own way.' Ramon had one of Henriette's *midinettes* in a clinch. He must have decided Julie could look after herself.

Dezi said thoughtfully, 'That German you used to come here with? The fella didn't fix on me like I was a threat. I'd say he didn't see me at all.'

'He saw you . . .' Coralie didn't want to talk about Dietrich. All evening, she'd felt his ghost alongside her. Heard his voice, far off, telling her why he was choosing this or that wine and why she should appreciate meat that was cooked rose-pink. The Corsicans had begun chanting 'The winners, the winners' in heavily accented French.

Coralie asked Dezi, 'Who won? My Vagabonds or their people?'

'Theirs, of course.'

'I don't mind my friends losing to better players but that hairy lot couldn't hold a tune in a bucket— Oh!'

A bottle thrown from the foot of the stage had just hit Arkady in the face. He stopped playing, and Coralie saw blood on his shirt. After a string of untranslatable oaths, he tucked his instrument under his chin and played on. *The joint was still jumping.*

The Tommies were on their feet now, clapping. It was getting tribal. The *midinettes* looked frightened, and it occurred to Coralie that if she sent them back to work bruised, she'd have Henriette on her tail. Ramon looked as if he was about to charge the Corsicans like a bull. His dancing partner and Una were holding him back. Teddy and his chums were nowhere to be seen. Probably hiding under a table. One of the gangsters got up onstage and grabbed the microphone, shouting, 'It's over. We have winners.'

Arkady head-butted him and that was the cue for more bottles to fly. One broke against the double bass. The Vagabonds held a five-second conference before resuming 'This Joint Is Jumping', after which they played a bridging piece, which would take them into 'Alexander's Ragtime Band'. This final number was intended to win ear-shattering applause – had it been a fair contest. A Corsican trumpeter was now on stage, blasting out noises like a suffering elephant.

'Right.' Coralie hitched up her dress. 'Now or never.' She'd started off playing by the rules, but now there were no rules.

'Girls!' she shouted to the *midinettes*. 'Watch me and copy.' Running to the stage, she stuck out her hand for someone to pull her up.

'Too dangerous!' Arkady shouted. 'No woman!'

So she heaved herself up unaided. 'Ignore him,' she bawled at Arkady, meaning the gatecrashing trumpeter. 'Forget ragtime. We'll give them . . .' She shouted a song in his ear.

Arkady looked bemused. 'That? Now?'

'Don't you know it?'

'Everyone knows it. All Europe sings it, even in Spain, and in Gurs we sing it. But we have not practised.'

'You want Tommies on your side?'

'What is Tommies?'

'Never mind. Blaze away and you'll have that lot in the black berets roaring along. Give me a bit of instrumental, and I'll come in with the words.'

'You sing, Coralie?'

'I certainly do, and my girls are going to dance.'

'They know how?'

Well, like he said, everyone knew this song and the dance that went with it. It wasn't exactly complicated. All the time she'd been creating tonight's outfits, she'd thought about getting up onstage. A little finale, to steal the evening. It was a risk, because if anything was going to broadcast her true nationality to the world, it would be this song. But seeing these Englishmen had made her feel just a little bit homesick. Proud, too. They were here to sort out the Germans. They deserved something home-grown to sing along to. The Corsican trumpeter had stopped blowing and was making an obscene hand-show at her. Coralie walked up to him and punched him in the jaw, knocking him clean offstage.

She strutted to the microphone. 'That's called manners where I come from. Ready, boys?'

Arkady turned and mouthed to the others, 'One, two, three, four . . .'

Coralie winked at the Tommies, who were shouting, 'Come on, Goldie!' She tucked her thumbs into imaginary braces and sang, '"Any time you're Lambeth way, any evening, any day . . ."'

People rushed to pair up. 'The Lambeth Walk' had been a huge hit in '37, spreading from London across Europe, like a dose of flu. It had stormed New York. Even Germany had its version. Maurice Chevalier had made it a hit at the Casino de Paris. The Cockney walking dance with 'oi' after the chorus was everywhere from public ballrooms to diplomatic receptions.

Coralie sang on; according to the lyrics, everything in life was free and easy. People could do as they damn well pleased . . . In Lambeth, or anywhere for that matter.

The Tommies certainly thought so. They were mobbing the stage and the Corsicans were piling in behind, pulling off caps, tearing collars. Soon fists were flying, women screaming. A bottle crashed at Coralie's feet. She hurled it back. '"You'll find yourself, doin' the –' one of the gangsters got hold of her leg '– "Lambeth walk, oi!"' On 'oi' she kicked him but he pulled her down anyway. Shrieking, she grabbed her hat to protect it. Arkady got her under the arms and heaved in the opposite direction. Coralie shouted at him to let go. If she didn't split in half, her dress would. She landed with a thud on the dance floor, and before she had time to refill her lungs, she was hauled up. Shutting her eyes, she softened every muscle to withstand the coming blow. *Not a black eye, please.*

The blow didn't come. Instead she was pulled to her feet

and hustled away towards the stairs. She staggered along, her hand in a stranger's, gold hat over her eyes. She hoped Julie, Una, the *midinettes* and Teddy had run for the exits too. Ramon could look after himself. She stumbled through the lobby, past the cloakroom, whose attendant flashed a muted torch, and out on to boulevard de Clichy where the air was as cold as sea spray. A smudge of moon gave just enough light to make out the outline of a man with padded shoulders, wearing a cap. He had a belted middle. She realised she'd been pulled out by the tall RAF man she'd admired earlier. '*Merci beaucoup*,' she panted, continuing in French, 'You ruined my chance of an encore.'

Hands linked behind her head and she was looking up into a face that was lean and serious, faintly familiar. A second later, she was being kissed so hard she could hardly keep her feet on the ground.

When it ended, his lips stayed on hers and he said in English, 'Do you know how long I've waited to do that?'

Without thinking, she shot back in the same language, 'Bloody cheek! I'm a married woman and my husband is down in that club.' That was another of Ramon's roles: to be the eternally jealous husband whenever she wanted to discourage an over-enthusiastic man.

'Married? Cora, what have you gone and done? And what the hell are you doing here?'

Cora . . . She stared up, trying to impose on the hard face the soft features that matched the voice, which had grown deeper, the worried inflection gone. 'Donal Flynn. Donal . . . what the hell have *you* gone and done?' She pulled a serge sleeve.

'Joined up, of course. You didn't think I'd still be pushing laundry carts now we're at war? Cora, why did you go? Why did you run? I looked high and low for you. I thought you were—'

'Shush.' Her gaze scavenged the frosted boulevard. It was empty. 'Donal, don't call me Cora. I'm *Coralie*, Coralie de Lirac. Never call me anything else.'

'I went looking for you after the Derby. I looked for you for days, and then for your body, on all the waste sites and the culverts, and down by the docks—' He broke off, pulling her to him again.

'You thought I was dead?'

'I thought Jac had done for you. I cornered him in his shed, got him by the throat, but he swore he hadn't touched you. I knocked him down. Oh, Cora. Alive and three times as beautiful. Cora—'

'Coralie! And, hey, you owe me an explanation too. Leaving me stranded at Epsom Downs—'

He groaned. 'I know. I went home – I was fuming and it never dawned on me I had your ticket till I woke up in the dead of night. I fetched my jacket and there it was. I swear I went straight round to your house and knocked on the door, but nobody answered. Cora—'

'*Coralie*. I'm Coralie now.'

'But why are you here? Why didn't you go home while you still could?'

'This is home. And I'd rather face the Germans than my father, or your bloody sister.'

'But that's it. Your dad's gone and so has Sheila.'

'Where? To hell in a handcart?'

'They're in Ireland, lying low, so my dad thinks. The knives came out for them when you disappeared. Secrets came out. Their love affair was the talk of the streets and Sheila got a formal reprimand from her inspector. Which was nothing to what she got from our gran. Then the big rumours started.'

'What rumours?'

'First your mother disappeared, then you. Then your mother's actor-fellow resurfaced.'

'Who? That Timothy Cartland she ran off with?' Coralie's ears hurt from the pressure of her pulse, from forgetting to breath.

'She didn't, that's the point. I read in a newspaper that a play had opened in Shaftesbury Avenue, and it mentioned a Timothy Cartland. I went to see him after a matinée. I thought you'd want me to.'

No, she thought. *Why can't you leave well alone?*

'I asked him, "Where's Florence Masson?" He didn't know but when I said her stage name, Florence Fielding, he remembered working with her about twenty-five years ago. "A slip of a woman with a big, loud voice." He swore they'd never had a fling. He *had* been to New York but he'd travelled alone and come back alone, in 1938, and in all that time, he said, he'd never heard a squeak of Florence Fielding. I went away, thinking, If Florence didn't go to America—'

'That's enough, Donal. Leave it buried.' Coralie reached up and kissed him, the better to shut him up, and was completely unprepared for the physical yearning that coursed through her. It was more potent than sexual desire. Donal had grown into a handsome man. He was in uniform, serving his country, and that was excuse enough, but until this moment she hadn't realised how desperately she missed love. Missed the comfort of a shared existence. If anybody was safe to be with, it was Donal. They'd shared the same air, the same dust. Yet as he pulled her hard against him and possessed her mouth, her assumptions altered.

Bring down the shutters, she told herself. *You can't risk him asking questions and seeing too much.* She pulled away, asking, 'What do you fly?'

'I'm not meant to say . . . but I suppose it can't hurt. Fairey Battles, light bombers. I'm the observer-navigator and we fly night missions — but listen, Cora—'

'*Coralie.* You've become rather a good kisser, Navigator Flynn. Had a bit of practice?' She felt the knot of his tie move with his throat, and recognised his old diffidence. Good. Let him get tongue-tied. One day she'd be strong enough to hear the ending to Florence's story. And one day she might sit down with Donal and tell him all about Coralie de Lirac. But not now. She'd invested too much in her life here to risk being unmasked as a fraud. She stepped back.

'Cora, don't go!'

'*Coralie.*' It wrenched her heart to deny the hope and desire in the hands that reached for her. God knew, she might never see him again. That silver wing above his left pocket was the real thing, not like her cheap glitter. Donal risked his life every time he took to the air, while she danced and sang. 'I'm going, Donal, and I don't want you to follow.'

Was he even listening? 'I'm in Paris till tomorrow night. We could—'

'No. I'm sorry I kissed you — but doesn't that tell you I'm as bad as I ever was? I'm not only married, I'm a mother.' She cinched her waist with her hands and took another step back. 'I've filled out, see? A little bit matronly, these days.'

'You've got a shape like a film star. Please don't go.'

She walked away, refusing to turn even when it dawned on her that she'd left her comfortable shoes in the club, along with her coat, and that she had a long trek home. And she was still wearing a gold hat. If she avoided being robbed, the first gendarme she met would book her for soliciting.

'Coralie!' Donal's anguish reached her, but he wasn't chasing her.

'Be safe up there in the skies, my friend,' she whispered. 'Don't let the buggers bring you down.'

Chapter Fourteen

Christmas 1939 froze the pipes and put such thick rime on the windows that Coralie prepared a festive dinner in the kitchen with gloves on. She'd invited Una, Ramon – who had ditched his latest woman, or been ditched – Arkady and Florian to her table.

As she trussed the skinny goose she'd bought at the market at ten times last year's price, she was interrupted by a knock. She was astonished to find Julie at the door, clutching a basket of apples and trying to hide a party dress by holding her winter coat closed at the neck.

'Julie? You were meant to take today off.'

The girl answered with a nervous giggle. Heavens, had Coralie really expected her to stay at home? Never mind, she was here now. Her parents, uncles and aunts were all dozing with their mouths open, except one aunt who kept making comments on Julie's new hairstyle.

Coralie took in the mass of curls and interwoven ribbon. 'It is rather . . . Hollywood.'

'I know!' Julie went straight to the hall mirror. 'The girl at the hairdresser's said I look just like Bette Davis in *Jezebel*.' She took off her coat and turned to Coralie, revealing a cardigan straining over an uplifted bosom. 'I'll help you cook and I'll serve at table.'

'I'll find you a nice big overall to wear.' Coralie couldn't resist adding, 'It's just us girls. The men can't come.' Seeing Julie's face drop in dismay, she laughed. 'Joking. Shall I put you next to Florian?'

Everyone brought something: coal, wine, a nip of cognac, potatoes, smoked sausage. Una contributed a case of champagne, a gift from a wealthy admirer who worked for the government. Yet more unexpectedly, she brought Ottilia von Silberstrom.

Una had met the Baronne in London in 1937, but hadn't given her much thought until Coralie's brief glimpse of her on boulevard de la Madeleine. Una had afterwards made enquiries, but everybody said the same thing: 'Poor darling Tilly? Didn't she take refuge in London? Why would she return to Paris, the way things are?' Una had been inclined to think that Coralie's eyes had deceived her.

Then, a few days ago, Una had found herself standing behind Ottilia in the queue at a tobacconist's off quai d'Orsay. 'Turns out, she's been living like a hermit in rue de Vaugirard since the summer,' she told Coralie, in a low voice. They both looked at Ottilia, who was bending down to make the acquaintance of Noëlle. She was draped in thistledown fur. Noëlle was stroking a sleeve, clearly bewitched.

Ottilia looked towards them and smiled, and Coralie returned a nod. The silent exchange was as good as a conversation: *We've met before. A man we both love stands between us and we will not speak of it.*

Una, seeing none of this, went on in an undertone, 'I hated to think of her all alone through Christmas so I dispensed with European etiquette and invited her. Don't say you're offended! You asked me to find her.'

'To discuss business. Oh, Lord, look at that.'

Ramon was now kissing Ottilia's hand and, like Noëlle,

seemed to be slithering under a spell. Had Ottilia had this effect on Dietrich too?

Suddenly aware of her grease-spotted apron and red cheeks, Coralie escaped to the kitchen, dispelling her emotions by lifting pan lids and slamming them down again.

Una trailed after her, opening the oven door. 'Oh, joy! Roast goose, my favourite. Forget work for a day, and get to know Tilly better. When the moment feels natural, we can mention La Passerinette. Let me tell you something, the girl under all that fur and those pearls is a sweetheart.'

And indeed, over champagne aperitifs and an *hors d'oeuvre* of braised chicory, Ottilia displayed none of the grandeur that had so offended Coralie on Epsom Downs.

Later, as Ramon carved the goose, Coralie recalled Dietrich explaining that Ottilia floated through life, the implication being that she didn't quite 'get' the world. The impression solidified when Ottilia said that she'd returned to Paris to oversee the freighting of her art collection back to England.

'My husband insists we bring the paintings to London.' Franz had been angry with her for leaving them in rue de Vaugirard, she said. 'I thought they were safe, but he does not trust the French or anybody. And certainly not me.' Ottilia laughed shakily. 'He said I must go to Paris to arrange for the boxes to be shipped, only . . . So many!' She'd sat in her flat all the summer, unable to lift a telephone to seek advice. 'Graf von Elbing used to do that sort of thing for me.' She met Coralie's eye briefly. Not in challenge, in a bid for understanding. 'I called his home in Germany, but his wife told me he wasn't living there.'

Coralie was cutting up meat for Noëlle, checking for bones. 'So where is he living?'

'Berlin. She gave me a number but told it me wrongly. Deliberately so, I'm sure, because it was like no Berlin number I've ever seen.'

'Has he no friends who could get hold of him for you?' Una asked.

'I tried some galleries, and an auction house he deals with, but as soon as I said my name, they cut the call. In Berlin "von Silberstrom" is as well known as Rothschild in London, or Rockefeller in New York. Only, these days, our name makes people put down the phone. I rang my brother Max in Geneva, and he thought Dietrich might be in Shanghai.'

'China?' Julie gasped. The word circled the table, gathering incredulity.

'I loved *Shanghai Express*,' Coralie said, 'but I wouldn't want to be on that train. China's at war, isn't it?'

'With Japan,' Una said.

Ottilia sighed. 'Dietrich went to buy Oriental art, which is going cheaply now.'

'One man's war is another man's profit.' Una said it with a half-smile but Ramon growled, 'Damn capitalist.'

Not a capitalist, just *passerine*, Coralie answered silently. Flitting from tree to tree, feeding as he goes. 'None of this explains how you got stuck in Paris,' she said to Ottilia. It was dawning on her that this stranded creature might some day become a liability.

The answer was simple. Once war had been declared and the night-ferry to England suspended, Ottilia couldn't conceive of any other means of returning to London.

'What about travelling through Spain and Portugal?' Una chided.

'Or Marseille?' Coralie put in. 'You could have sailed to Gibraltar. Or crossed from Brittany to Portsmouth.'

Ottilia stared. 'Where are they, though? Any of those places?'

Such helplessness clearly appealed to the males around the table, particularly Ramon. The scourge of the bourgeoisie stared moonstruck, missing his lips with his glass, quietly mouthing, 'Such white skin, such auburn hair.' Meanwhile, Coralie thought that six months' hard labour under Granny Flynn would have done Ottilia von Silberstrom the world of good.

For her part, Ottilia was besotted with Noëlle, wanting nothing but to hold her. And, of course, today wasn't just Christmas Day, it was Noëlle's second birthday and after lunch came presents. Coralie had made a rag-doll. Una had bought Noëlle her first pair of proper shoes, cream kid with round toes and ribbon ties. Ramon produced a wooden dog on a string and made them scream with laughter by barking as the child pulled it across the floor. Ottilia presented a beautifully wrapped box containing a platinum and diamond bracelet.

'We can't accept that,' Coralie said awkwardly, and Ottilia's eyes brimmed.

'But you must. I love to give and so much has been stolen from me. Really, take it because it will spare me pain.'

When, later, Coralie tentatively broached the subject of buying La Passerinette, Ottilia breathed, 'Of course you must have it. Yes, take it.'

Now Coralie understood Dietrich's frustration. Ottilia had been born to boundless wealth, but she'd lost most of her assets when she fled Germany. What she had left needed to be protected. From swindlers and, it would appear, from Ottilia herself.

After dinner, the men elected to walk down towards the river to stretch their legs and smoke, and once they'd muffled themselves against the weather and left, Una found paper and pencils.

'Let's wrap up business while the men are away. Coralie, you want that shop. Tilly, you'd like to sell. You need ready cash, I guess?'

Ottilia nodded. 'I do not properly understand, but when I go to the Chase Bank, they say my money is frozen.'

'Well, it's jolly chilly out.'

'I only have the money in the suitcase I brought from London.'

Una found Radio Paris on the wireless and, to the velvet strains of Maurice Chevalier, helped Coralie and Ottilia carve out a deal. Coralie would take over the shop lease and buy the business for fifty thousand francs, to be paid in monthly instalments. That would include all the stock and whatever goodwill had survived Lorienne's fingernails. Coralie would also employ Violaine Beaumont, who was shortly to be released from medical supervision and would return to the flat above the empty shop.

Ottilia explained, 'La Passerinette is her home and she is frightened of leaving it. My dear Dietrich – I mean, Graf von Elbing – says that she is a little brown bird who builds a nest and sits on the eggs, invisible to all. What bird is that?'

'A chicken?' Coralie hazarded.

'Wren, surely,' Una offered.

'Dietrich speaks in pictures. Did you not notice that when you met him?' Ottilia's eyes sought Coralie's.

'Not really,' Coralie hedged. Did Ottilia know of her affair with Dietrich? The childlike gaze offered no clues. Coralie had given Una a hazy outline of her early days in Paris, mentioning a German who'd 'looked after' her but without mentioning a name. Una, fortunately, was fiddling with the radio dial, trying to get a sharper signal, so the awkward conversation died. 'Let's talk about fashion,' Coralie suggested. 'I need lots of ideas if I'm to pay you on the nail every month.'

Ottilia took the bait, and they drew hats until the men came home.

Just under five months later, in May 1940, German forces attacked the Netherlands. On the tenth of the month their air force bombed the heart out of Rotterdam. On the fourteenth, the Dutch surrendered. The German Army swept on into Belgium.

In Paris, people assured each other, 'The Low Countries don't have our defences or our fine army. Or our Maginot Line. The Germans won't get this far.'

The Germans reached the Ardennes forest, the ancient and supposedly impenetrable boundary between Belgium and France, smashed through it and turned along the Somme, to cut off the Allied troops in Belgium.

The British Expeditionary Force, which had thought to stop the enemy's westward advance, was driven back towards the sea. On 27 May, a massacre was averted by the evacuation of hundreds of thousands of troops from the beaches of the Flanders coast. 'The miracle of Dunkirk' left France with a demoralised army facing *Blitzkrieg,* lightning war: formations of German tanks and armoured vehicles, supported by bombers and fighter planes, moving at breathtaking speed. The Maginot Line, stood un-breached but useless. The enemy had cut around it, outflanked it.

On 3 June, an air raid on Paris was announced by wailing sirens that shocked people from sleep. Guns pounded, impossible to know how far away or quite from which direction. The press kept up an optimistic tone. *We will conquer because we are the strongest*. Even so, people spoke of leaving Paris, of crossing the Loire, which would surely provide a second barrier to an advancing army.

On 13 June, those who remained in the capital felt the ground shake from artillery fire. They saw shells streaking across a sky dark with smoke, and heard a sound like mill wheels grinding. An army approaching. Refugees spilling in from the north spoke of German fighter planes strafing them on the roads, and thousands dying as they tried to outrun the enemy to reach France and its supposedly safe countryside. In the parks and boulevards, people looked into the sky, and thought of Warsaw and Rotterdam. They noticed birds collecting in the trees, flying up, like fountain jets, then migrating in dark flocks.

Humans took warning and began to leave too, in cars, trucks, on bicycles and horseback, grid-locking every road out. Julie and her family went, taking Florian with them. Ramon Cazaubon, though technically outside the age range for military conscription, left to offer himself anyway. Coralie and the friends who stayed with her barricaded themselves into the flat on rue de Seine.

On 14 June, the Germans entered Paris. In tanks, in armoured vehicles, in huge numbers.

Reichsminister Göring was one of the commanders at the forefront of the occupation. He brought with him a special adviser, a man who knew Paris well. A man who cut a fine figure in a Luftwaffe uniform and who cherished long-held vengeance in his heart.

PART THREE

PART THREE

Chapter Fifteen

Coralie stepped out on to the pavement, blinking in the light, Noëlle's small hand in hers. Four days shut indoors, waiting for invasion, bombardment and death, had been as much as she could bear. If they were going to die, let them die breathing fresh air.

Paris had fallen. The news had been barked around the streets, in harshly accented French, from loudspeakers mounted on trucks. Electricity had been cut, telephones, too, but at least the shellfire had stopped.

Everything looked strangely peaceful. Too peaceful. On a Saturday in the middle of June, rue de Seine should have been a hive of commerce, yet every shop and café had its shutters down. Most of the population had gone. Those who had stayed, like Coralie and her friends, were still cowering indoors.

Had things been normal, she would have been at La Passerinette. Making, selling, celebrating nearly six months of ownership. But La Passerinette and place de la Madeleine lay on the other side of the river in what, for all she knew, was a war zone.

'*Maman!* Look!' Noëlle toddled a few steps, pointing eagerly. It took a moment for Coralie to see what was exciting the child.

'Oh! Voltaire! He's come home. No, darling, I'll catch him.'

Teddy Clisson had left ahead of the Germans' entry into Paris, heading for his country house at Dreux. Around that time

Voltaire, terrified by nights of shelling and the crump of bombs on the western suburbs, had vanished. Coralie had joined with Teddy, calling his name frantically through the traffic-clogged streets, fighting through the exodus of terrified citizens, all the way to quai Voltaire where Teddy had first found the cat as a stray.

He'd be overjoyed to know his darling was alive, though how she'd send the news, with the postal service suspended, Coralie couldn't imagine.

'You've been fighting,' she accused the cat. Voltaire was decidedly less glossy than before, and one ear hung oddly. 'That needs bathing. Maybe I should fetch your basket . . .' But as she bent forward, Voltaire shot away. 'Never mind,' she comforted Noëlle. 'He'll be back when he gets really hungry.'

Coralie herself was starving, her belly tucked inwards like a dented tea tray. She and her houseguests – Una, Ottilia and Arkady Erdös – had dined well on the first day of their self-imposed incarceration, less well on the second, and for the past two days, only Noëlle had eaten. Coralie craved bread, but would any bakers have stayed open? They needed fresh produce, too – fish, milk.

Turning back towards the house, she saw her companions looking up and down the street as if they feared she, like Voltaire, had vanished. She called, 'It's like the plague's been and we're the last people left alive.'

'Let's go forage.' Una had a shopping basket over her arm. She'd locked up her avenue Foch apartment on the same day Teddy had left town, feeling uncomfortably close to the undefended edge of the city. She'd collected Ottilia from rue de Vaugirard and arrived at Coralie's, announcing, 'We're going to pool resources and your place is easiest to heat, being small.' Discovering that one of Coralie's two 'evaders' was still in residence, she'd added a cheer. 'I've always hated all-women affairs. Gorgeous Arkady can play us to sleep with his violin. Though, hah, his *glissando*s do put fire in my veins . . . Does one still have to climb a ladder to get into his roof-space?'

Coralie had suspected an attraction between the two at Christmas and told Una that Arkady had jolly well better pull up his ladder whenever he went to bed. 'Una, you can share mine – it's huge. Ottilia can have Noëlle's, and Noëlle can snuggle next to me.'

'You're the boss.' Una had brought linen and blankets, a steamer trunk of clothes and 'a box of gold-dust', which turned out to be a dozen bars of hard soap stacked on top of wads of French francs. She'd emptied her bank account a month before, she'd said, when it seemed clear that the *drôle de guerre* was going to stop being funny all too soon.

Ottilia had arrived with her makeup case, two fur coats, a canister of Indian tea and all the currency she'd brought from London, stuffed into a hatbox.

After consulting with Arkady, they agreed that rue Mouffetard was their best bet for provisions as its market had traded almost without pause since the Middle Ages. There, they found a few stalls open and filled Una's basket with red-stalked chard, potatoes, radishes and bruised apples. From a *traiteur*, they bought chicken baked with tarragon, and pigeon breast with Puy lentils. Best of all, they found a café open.

They ordered coffee, fresh bread and butter. The Germans had shipped in bread flour, the patron said. 'They are well organised, and we won't starve. But our army . . . how could our magnificent army simply collapse? I blame the British, taking to their ships, leaving us undefended. *Perfide!* Another pot of coffee?'

'Might as well,' Coralie said. Ramon had taught her to love coffee. It had been a slow affair, but once she'd finished breast-feeding Noëlle, the smell no longer nauseated her. He'd failed to convert her to his other vice, cigarettes. She could see Arkady rubbing his fingers together, a sure sign he'd run out of tobacco. Hiding a smile, she said, 'The Germans won't be sharing theirs, Arkady. Better try to give up.'

After breakfast, Arkady and Ottilia went home with the shopping. Coralie, Una and Noëlle continued towards the river. Time to brave the unknown and find out how her business had fared. She was anxious for Violaine, whom she'd not seen since the day panic had gripped Paris.

Coralie's first season at La Passerinette had proved more interesting than profitable. Without the capital to finance a full collection, she'd created a range of house models. Customers chose a basic shape, taking away a hat trimmed to suit them. But every time Coralie or Violaine finished a model, somebody would buy it. They could never keep the window full and, after a while, word spread that they'd gone out of business.

Coralie's response had been to shut up shop for two weeks in April while she and Violaine did nothing but make hats. They blocked *baku* and sisal shells into summer shapes. Taking La Passerinette's signature pink and grey as their theme, they'd added swathes of net and silk flowers to give the impression of opulence. With millinery supplies ever harder to come by, Coralie had experimented with layered tarlatan and buckram, which, when covered with silk, organdie or taffeta, transformed low-cost materials. In Violaine, Coralie had a fast-fingered helper who made three hats to her every one, and who was seldom discouraged by *outré* ideas. For her part, Violaine had greeted Coralie's arrival with pleasure, once she was assured that her job was safe. Her poor eyesight made her fearful of the world beyond a few familiar streets and she was happiest in La Passerinette's work-room, behind the salon. She liked to work without interference, to be allowed a lunch hour and to have her salary paid on time, modest requirements that Lorienne Royer had found impossible to meet. From their first day together, Coralie had been deter-mined to show Violaine that she was valued.

She'd watch Violaine sewing millinery wire through two thicknesses of buckram, or painting shellac on to silk, and be reminded of a favourite bedtime story of Noëlle's: 'Once upon a time, a shoemaker took on too many orders. Kindly elves slipped in at night, and stitched for him till dawn . . .'

With Noëlle between them, Coralie and Una's first promenade through occupied Paris was necessarily slow. Expecting burned buildings and bomb craters around every corner, they were pleas-antly astonished by the complete absence of damage. Paris had fallen, it seemed, with the grace of a lady swooning on to her sofa. Only when they reached the river did they encounter their first field-grey uniforms. Sentries stood guard at pont du Carrousel. Two stepped forward, sub-machine guns at the ready. '*Halt!*'

'I leave all my worldly goods to you, honey,' Una muttered – dangerously – in English.

'Likewise,' said Coralie. But they were politely waved through.

'Why have men got pans on their heads?' Noëlle demanded. At two and a half, her speech was already well developed – Coralie put it down to her being the only child among garrulous adults.

'Not pans, darling. Helmets. So their heads don't get hurt.'

'How hurt?'

'By birds dropping from the sky,' Una ad-libbed. They'd told Noëlle that the bombing of the Renault car factory at Boulogne-Billancourt was men practising drums for the 14 July parties.

Mindful of the guns behind them and uncertain what lay behind the hulking Palais du Louvre on the opposite bank, Coralie tried to maintain normality. At least the Seine hadn't changed, glinting platinum where the morning sun smashed its surface. From her first days in Paris, Coralie had loved the river. Crossing it was to be suspended between different lives – troubles always belonged to one side or the other.

'Dear God, will you look at that!' Una had stopped and was staring back towards the Left Bank. Above a skyline of grey roofs poked the Eiffel Tower. A banner fluttered from its summit. 'I'm certain that's a swastika.'

Coralie thought so too.

'Want to go back home?'

'Maybe . . .' Coralie knew if she turned tail, it might be days before she summoned the courage to try again. And the sentries *had* smiled. They made it to the Right Bank without hindrance, but on quai des Tuileries, a line of khaki motorbikes and sidecars screened the embankment wall. 'Looks like a whole platoon has gone swimming.'

They peered over the parapet down to the wharf below. Where lovers used to stroll and artists would sit sketching, soldiers walked with a steady, patrolling beat.

On place de la Concorde, the familiar sight of the Egyptian obelisk swaddled in sandbags was almost comforting. Not so the machine-gun posts at each corner of the square. Important-looking staff cars, swastikas flying from the grilles, shared the road with military trucks crammed with troops under canvas tilts. Not a French vehicle to be seen.

Coralie said, 'Listen.' From the head of the Champs-Élysées came the sound of martial music, underscored by a rhythmic pounding, like neatly sliced thunder. An old man – the only other civilian in the square – told them what it was.

'A victory parade. That is the noise of a thousand goose-stepping boots.'

'Noëlle, no!' Coralie stopped the child from reaching out to pet the man's dog, a wiry terrier. Friends were always telling her that she was over-protective. How stupid to be afraid of a dog when armed soldiers were about to engulf them. La Passerinette was so close. She could see the Madeleine at the top of rue Royale. A trick of perspective put it right between the French naval headquarters and the Hôtel de Crillon. Five minutes' walk at most.

The old man followed her gaze. 'The Crillon's theirs now, headquarters to the German commander of Paris. *German commander of Paris.*' He turned away, calling his dog to heel.

Coralie's nerve broke. 'Let's get home.'

It was five days before she tried again. A little after midday, alone this time, she unlocked La Passerinette's front door and called, 'Violaine? It's me.'

A terrible stench stopped her dead.

She thanked the caution that had made her leave Noëlle at home. Swatting through a wall of flies, she went straight upstairs to Violaine's flat. Getting no answer to her knock, she tried the door. It was unlocked. 'Violaine?' Dust on the dining-table and a pot of mould-pocked coffee suggested the place had been empty for some time. Had Violaine joined the mass exodus after all? It seemed so unlikely – a stampeding crowd would be Violaine's worst scenario – but she might have been swept along in the frenzy . . . But that smell, and the flies . . . A more probable story offered itself. Tying a silk scarf around her lower face, Coralie went downstairs to face the inevitable.

At the door to the ground-floor workroom, Coralie selected a key from the bunch in her hand. She unlocked, pushed, stepped in. An outrush of flies and a stupefying reek made her gag.

Violaine lay curled on the floor. A basket was upended, something vile oozing out of it. Mackerel, rotting. Afraid to touch, even to look, Coralie darted a glance around a room as familiar to her as the back of her hand. It was *empty*. Hats, blocks, machines and tools, gone. Rolls of fabric, gone. Another story began to form in Coralie's mind. Robbers, looters. Violaine knocked down, locked in.

The workroom had no window, just louvred slats that sucked light from a walled courtyard beyond. The slats were open and a chair had been pulled up beneath them. Violaine must have screamed for help but, with a million people leaving town all at once, her cries had gone unheard. Without water—

Muttering unintelligible prayers, Coralie crouched beside her assistant. She brushed the hair off Violaine's face and felt warm flesh. Lifting an eyelid, she saw the pupil flicker. 'Violaine? Thank God! I'll get help. No – water first.' Upstairs, she filled the first suitable vessel she found and a minute later was spooning water between cracked lips. 'I'm going to get help. Stay here.'

Stay here? Shock made you say the most stupid things. 'It may take a little while because—' No. Not the moment to reveal that Paris had become German. She considered knocking on doors higher up the building, but brooding silence hinted at abandonment. Only Violaine still lived there, she realised.

A minute later, she was haring down rue Royale towards place de la Concorde, wishing she'd put on flat sandals and a more sensible hat. At least she'd worn a loose summer dress. She could have gone to the nearest police *préfecture*, but knowing Violaine needed help fast meant she was going to the one place she knew had working telephones. The day after the invasion, German soldiers had been seen laying cables across the courtyard of the American Embassy on avenue Gabriel in order to connect the Hôtel de Crillon to the exchange. Let the Germans call an ambulance.

Sunshine lanced off the rifle barrels of the guards marching up and down in front of the Crillon. Coralie approached, eyes lowered. So far, she'd found the Germans to be polite, respectful, even. She supposed that finding Paris open to them, they felt more like guests than conquerors. And they were men, after all. At just the right moment, she'd look up and smile. The hat she was wearing, which Una had christened 'Daytime Seduction', would declare her to be the opposite of a threat. She'd be waved into the gilded lobby.

'*Halt, nicht weiter!*'

Gun barrels pointed at her. Not sure whether she was meant to raise her hands, she explained the emergency in the German she'd learned in her time with Dietrich. She was told to go to the nearest police prefecture, talk to her own people. She stood her ground, mostly because she was afraid to turn her back on those guns. 'I need an ambulance or a car.'

Go to your own people.

'But it's urgent! My friend is—' She stopped as a new voice demanded to know what the disturbance was. The guards leaped to attention

'Generalmajor!' the soldier rattled out, in a defensive volley. 'This woman—'

'Stand aside. Let me see her.'

A tall man in a blue-grey uniform strung with medals, a high-peaked cap and black leather boots subjected Coralie to a long stare. The silver eagle above his breast pocket, the Iron Cross in the apex of his collar, the blue and gold cross hanging over the breastbone marked out his rank. But it was his eyes, firing with recognition beneath his black visor, that told her the waiting was over. He was back.

She said in German, 'I need help.' She so nearly added, 'Dietrich.'

'Come.' He indicated she should follow him into the hotel.

'It's Violaine,' she said. She was addressing his back. 'At La Passerinette?'

He walked on, boots hard on chequered marble, forcing her to keep up until they reached an inner office, where military men and a few young women in uniform sat in front of banks of telephones. He called one of the men over, rattled out an instruction, then left.

She tried to follow but the telephone operator caught her arm. Her German deserted her, so she explained her dilemma in slow French. The man clearly grasped her meaning because he noted down her request for medical assistance, asking for the precise address on boulevard de la Madeleine. He would deal with the matter, he said, but she must stay here. 'Order of Generalmajor von Elbing.'

'But my friend's lying on the floor. I have to go to her.'

'You do not understand, Fräulein. You are under arrest.'

Chapter Sixteen

She took the seat offered to her, assuming the tidy posture she'd learned in Javier's salon, and wondered what Dietrich would say to the idiot who'd misunderstood his orders. Arrested? For wearing a pillbox hat with a rose silk tassel? For running in a pink dress with a frivolous pattern of navy-blue cherries? Or because her skirt revealed tanned legs from the knee down? Perhaps she'd offended a new puritan code. Judging by those girls in their uniforms, chic had not made its way into Germany. But, actually, the dress was a boon, with sunshine pouring through west-facing windows. She ignored disapproving glances from the buttoned-up female operators, and she felt like saying, 'You're in Paris now. Get used to us.'

Poor girls, though. In grey smocks, ankle socks and black lace-up shoes, they looked as if they'd been dragged out of reform school and forbidden to smile.

She amused herself by wondering what Javier would have designed for them. When that palled, she twisted the coral bracelet that had been Ramon's wedding gift to her. Irritably, then anxiously. Perhaps an hour after she'd sat down – she hadn't worn her watch that day – her name was called. Two men in plain suits stood in the doorway. One beckoned.

She got up eagerly. 'Where is D— I mean, Generalmajor von Elbing?' she asked in German.

They said nothing, but ushered her down a corridor and on to rue Royale. The sight of a black car swallowed her concerns for Violaine, replacing them with inward-pointing fear. 'Where are you taking me?'

'Please get in, Fräulein.'

It was a long time since she'd ridden so comfortably, but all she could do was envisage a series of ever more menacing destinations. Every street now had a German name sign. She took stock of them as they drove towards the river. At pont de la Concorde, a motorcycle sentry signalled them on. Once over the bridge, they swept down boulevard Saint-Germain.

Then they were on boulevard Raspail and in a moment, they'd reach the intersection with rue de Vaugirard. The hairs rose on the back of her neck. Had Dietrich come to Paris to deal with Ottilia's art collection? Had he found signs of Ottilia living in the house? And . . . Oh, God. What if Ottilia had given more pictures away and Dietrich thought she, Coralie, was to blame? That would account for his frigidity.

To her relief, the car stopped in boulevard Raspail, in front of the Hôtel Lutetia. A swish place. She'd been there a couple of times with Teddy and, suddenly, she was glad she'd worn high heels and a snazzy hat. If Dietrich meant to meet her here for a drink, she didn't want to look like a drab who had spent two years pining for him. She intended to rage at him, let him know what she thought of him, while appearing peerlessly groomed.

A haven for foreign refugee artists, the Lutetia had been very much Teddy's kind of place. But as she climbed out of the car, she saw that it had suffered the same fate as other grand hotels. From its windows spewed elongated swastikas, like stair carpet spat out to dry.

In the marble foyer, icons of Nazism were everywhere, superimposed on the lush decor. An immaculately suited man was being walked towards them in the grip of two soldiers, and for a moment, Coralie thought they'd collide. His face was sheened with sweat. She'd seen such a face once on Tooley Street, when a man had been knocked down by a tram. Shock. Shock and a haywire heartbeat. As he was dragged past, the stranger mumbled in a strong Spanish accent, 'This is wrong! So wrong!'

'Come.' One of her escorts urged her forward. From the heart of the building came the clink of crockery, the growl of voices, alerting her to the fact that the dining room was nearby and she was hungry – until the smell of baked fish collided with the recent memory of Violaine's shopping basket. *Those flies*. Her gorge rose and she wasn't sure she'd hold it down if they took her nearer the kitchen.

No – they were ushering her up the central staircase, then up another set of stairs, and another, to where the decor was plainer, the corridors narrower. She felt every passing stranger's scrutiny and wondered how she looked to them. Flushed pink, probably, to match her outfit. She'd walked, then run, on a hot June day and sat in a stuffy room without a mouthful of water. And another thing – 'Gentlemen, if you don't mind, I need the Ladies.'

Instead, she found herself in a room whose single window was blanked out with brown paper. One of the men switched on a light, revealing two chairs and a desk. Not wasting money on furniture, obviously. They hadn't even run to a lampshade.

A moment later, the door closed and she was alone.

Locked in. Hammering, she shouted, 'My friend is dying. Let me out!'

She was still shouting when a key turned and Dietrich came into the room. He was still in uniform, his cap under his arm. 'Sit down,' he said.

What happened to 'please'? She'd comply when he asked nicely.

He took the seat at the far side of the desk and laid a book in front of him. It reminded Coralie of the ledger they'd compiled together in rue de Vaugirard.

He said in French, 'Stand, if you like, but you will be here longer.'

'Did you call an ambulance?'

'Sit down, Fräulein.'

Fräulein? Had he forgotten their hours in bed together? But she sat, making a show of smoothing her skirt so he'd think she was irritated, not scared. Dietrich leaned forward, clasping his hands in front of him. He had on the same watch as before, an aviator's watch, with its well-worn strap. Bare light sucked definition from his face and she couldn't tell if he'd aged in the thirty-five months they'd been apart. Only that his hair seemed a little greyer.

'Who's going to start the conversation?'

'This is not a conversation. Your full name, Fräulein.'

All right. Silly games it is. She opened her bag, to extract her identity card. The bag he'd bought her, from Hermès.

'I said, state your name.'

Shocked, she stammered, 'Coralie de—' *No, stop.* He meant her real name, the one he'd invented for her. 'Marie-Caroline de—' *Stop again.* Her card bore a different identity, these days. 'Cazaubon. I am Madame Cazaubon.'

Hazel eyes that had so often laughed with her, so often dilated with excitement or softened in passion, bored into her. 'You are married but you wear no ring.'

Stupid to look down, as if a gold band might materialise. 'It lives in a drawer. We're separated.'

'Your husband's name?'

Ah . . . was this about Ramon's political affiliations? Some of the groups he'd supported in Paris had been quite extreme. 'I told you, we're not together.'

'If you don't tell me his name, it will be easy enough to find out, but it might take several hours. If you are content to remain—'

'Ramon. Ramon Cazaubon.'

'Has he a middle name?'

'Course he has. He's French, isn't he?' She hadn't meant to sound quite so insolent, but her mouth was so dry she could taste her tongue. A glass of water would be nice, if a cup of tea was out of the question. 'Maurice André.' Or was it the other way round? She'd only heard Ramon's full set of names on their wedding day and when registering Noëlle's birth.

Dietrich unscrewed the top of a fountain pen and wrote down her reply. 'Your date of birth?'

'I shouldn't have to tell you that.'

'Date of birth.'

'Eighth of November, 19 . . .' Her mind went blank. In the end, she had to look at her identity card. '1915. You're making me nervous and I'm worried about Mademoiselle Beaumont. I need a drink, too. I mean, a glass—'

'Your place of birth?'

'Um, Nivelles.' Or was it Tubize? 'Nivelles, in Brabant, Belgium. But you know that already, Dietrich!'

'Address me as Generalmajor von Elbing.'

She stared at him. Were they playing a game of pretending to be strangers?

More rapid questions followed. Her parents' professions, her place of baptism, her schooling, her training. After that, questions about Ramon. Age, date of birth – thank God that was easy to remember, being 31 October, All Saints' Eve. Hallowe'en. She'd often told Ramon he was her nightmare.

'His profession?'

'Um . . . the army, just now.' Ramon's civilian job had carried a long-winded title which she'd never managed to capture. 'Before, he worked for SNCF – for the railways? He was an engineer. To do with bridges and tunnels.'

'A maintenance engineer?'

'He . . . No. He made drawings with calculations . . . I didn't really understand it.'

Something touched Dietrich's lips. A smile? 'Shall we say he is a structural surveyor, Frau Cazaubon?'

'Yes. Sorry. I don't know where he's posted, I swear it. We don't hear from him.'

The shutters fell back down. '*We?*'

'I have a daughter.'

'Name.'

'Noëlle Una.' Watching Dietrich's pen, fear spread to her nerve endings. Her child's existence was now on paper. 'Why are you writing that down? Who are you now?'

'What I always was.' Dietrich wrote on for a minute or so, then laid down his pen. 'Why, if you live south of the river, were you at the Hôtel de Crillon?'

She told him that La Passerinette now belonged to her. 'You know it's on Madeleine, so when I needed a working telephone, I ran to place de la Concorde. I told your people that.'

'You bought La Passerinette from the Baronne von Silberstrom? Where is she?'

A warning bell tolled. Dietrich's features remained smooth, but what of the soul within? As Teddy had once brutally pointed out, she knew nothing about this man.

This interview might not be about Ramon at all. Perhaps Dietrich wanted Ottilia, who had been on a Nazi death-list since the mid-1930s. Stranded in Paris, Jewish and a refugee, her situation was fragile. *We'll get her out*, Coralie decided there and then. Back to England, God knows how. 'I've no idea where she is.'

Dietrich's gaze roamed to Coralie's neck, then her face, then to 'Daytime Seduction', so named because its silky tassels entwined with the wearer's curls. 'So you did not buy the hat shop from her?'

'No, from Lorienne Royer. She's moved away, though.' And could therefore not be roped in to contradict. 'Can I have a drink of water, before I faint?'

Dietrich leaned back in his chair and she waited for the words that would bring the interrogation to a close, and allow her to escape to the lavatory, which was becoming even more urgent than the need for water. The silence went on so long, she broke it.

'What else can I tell you? My shoe size? You already know how many sugars I put in my tea and which side of the bed I like to sleep on.'

A twitch. A reaction. So, he wasn't a completely frozen fish. Without taking her eyes from him, she summoned a picture of their Duet bed, placed herself on it wearing nothing at all, and brought him into the scene. She remembered how he had sighed her name as she caressed his body from breastbone to navel and lower . . . She watched the real Dietrich and knew that he was fighting arousal. The muscles of his face and neck were taut as piano wire. She leaned across the desk, laid her hand over his and said, 'Boo!'

She waited for the smile, the surrender. It was so close. When he picked up his pen, she wondered that it didn't snap in two. But all he said was 'Let us go through these questions again.'

*

'How utterly dreadful. Oh, darling, how fearfully humiliating. Dietrich von Elbing did this to you? Ottilia's hero? Should we tell her?'

Coralie gulped down the tea Una had made for her. 'I don't want to think of him ever again. Though I say it myself, I performed one of the great heroic walks of history. I finally got through to him that I was about to burst, and never did a man shift so fast.'

If she ever recovered from her fright, Coralie believed she might one day smile at the memory of Dietrich flinging open doors along the corridor, only to discover that every room was a stationery cupboard or an office. 'I followed behind like chief mourner at a very slow funeral.'

'You shamed him. Good for you.'

'More likely he was protecting the carpets. When I came out of the lavatory, he sort of shrugged and let me go. I still don't know what it was all about, and you must never tell Ottilia. We have to get her to safety, though, before he finds her.'

Una nodded.

Coralie shuddered. 'You think, when they come for you, that you'll fight back . . . but you don't. You drop like a dog. There was a man at the Lutetia, Spanish, I think . . .' But she didn't want to speculate on his fate.

Violaine's fate, on the other hand, would hopefully be revealed shortly. Coralie had been too scared to go back to La Passerinette, so Arkady had gone for her. The air in the flat vibrated with shock. Noëlle had cried herself to sleep, apparently. Una had described playing interminable games with the little girl, promising every minute, 'Maman's coming home real soon, honey.'

Ottilia had cried, too, when Coralie appeared, shaking and dishevelled. She was still emitting muffled sobs in her room. Una fidgeted, then picked up Coralie's cup, taking it through to the kitchen.

'Arkady's been such a long time,' she fretted when she came back into the sitting room.

'Not if he keeps having his papers checked.'

Una seized on that. 'Yes, he's Hungarian. They'll wave him through.'

'Except he's a Gypsy,' Coralie pointed out.

'His papers don't say that.'

No, but his features do, and I shouldn't have let him run my errand. Though her legs were ready to buckle, Coralie stood up to prepare supper. 'Keep busy, girls, that's the ticket,' she said, in Miss Lucilla Lofthouse's voice.

Una called after her, 'I've said it before, you do the darnedest English accent, honey. How long did you live there in all?'

'Oh . . . a few years. I pick up accents. Coralie, the human parrot. Shall I do my Marlene Dietrich impression of a woman throwing together vegetable stew and salt beef?'

Arkady arrived home minutes before curfew. He'd been stopped eight times, he said, but his papers had held up. A German guard had even given him a cigarette.

'What about Violaine?'

'She is at the American Hospital in Neuilly.'

Neuilly was to the north-west, a well-heeled suburb of Paris.

There had been a note, Arkady told Coralie, stuck through La Passerinette's letterbox. 'With a signature I am not reading.' And everything else from the salon had gone, he said.

Coralie had temporarily forgotten about her ransacked workroom. A little voice nagged, *Now what will you do?* Buy more stuff, she told it.

Arkady couldn't tell her who had organised Violaine's transfer to the American Hospital and Coralie gave up caring because Noëlle suddenly woke, screaming for *Maman*.

Chapter Seventeen

On 21 June 1940, Maréchal Petain, hero of the Great War, and his deputy Paul Laval met Adolf Hitler in a railway carriage in the forest of Compiègne, some fifty kilometres north-east of Paris. It was the very same carriage in which the Germans had signed terms of surrender in 1918. Pétain secured peace for France on heavy terms. The financial and human cost would wring the people dry.

Pétain was now free to form a government to work *with*, not against, the invaders and France was to be split into two zones. The new map showed a jagged line running westward as far as Tours, then straight down to the Spanish border. It gave the Germans control of the Atlantic and northern coastlines. Their army would occupy the northern zone, including Paris. The southern section remained under French control and people quickly named it 'the free zone', which made Coralie wonder if she and her friends were now prisoners.

The following day, they gathered round the wireless to hear the words of an exiled army general, Charles de Gaulle. Curtains drawn, they listened as he urged all free Frenchmen to fight on. Never to submit to slavery.

Arkady muttered, 'I will get to England and join his army.'

'You stay right here,' Coralie told him. 'There's more than one way to fight a war.'

'No, there is just one, with blood.'

'Speaking of which,' Una was clearly unhappy with the turn of the conversation, 'how is your assistant, Coralie?'

'Violaine? The hospital sent her home — poor thing's spent more time in hospital recently than anybody should. Thankfully, her neighbour came back from the country and is looking after her. I'll go later in the week, make sure they've got enough to eat.' And face her ransacked workroom: she had to plan how to get her business back on its feet.

Meanwhile, there was plenty to worry about at home. Confidence in German goodwill was running short, as was food. As Parisians returned, shops reopened and the streets bustled once more, the pressure on supplies was showing. For the occupiers, the city still resembled an open banquet, German soldiers consuming everything while ordinary people queued for whatever was left. 'Haricot beans and spinach!' Una complained that evening, pushing her fork through her meagre supper. 'German command has requisitioned any number of restaurants. They call them *Soldatenheime*, which means "canteen", and you can bet they don't serve the lentils and sawdust we get. Meanwhile, our hospitals ration medicines for our war-wounded.'

Una had walked home that evening from the American Hospital in Neuilly where she was now working as a volunteer. Coralie would never have imagined it of her glossy friend, but Una had trained as a nurse in America. She'd done it, she confessed, to shock her socially ambitious mother and escape her grandmother's matchmaking. 'I grew up being told, "McBride ladies do not work," so I chose the toughest profession I could, just to show 'em. Turned out I was quite good at it, and I might still be nursing had I not fallen in love with a Frenchman and wound up in Europe, only to fall into Mr Kilpin's clutches

– but that's another story.' A twelve-hour shift had left her hol-low-cheeked. 'You've never seen such wounds, such infections, and the place is full to bursting. Why do men do it to each other?'

'Make war?' Coralie thought about it. 'Because, like child-birth, they think it's going to be a breeze until they're in the middle of it.'

'I so wish for a child,' Ottilia said sadly. She rarely concentrated on what was being discussed around her, and would randomly fish out fragments. 'When I was engaged to Dietrich, we would plan the children we would have. Two girls, two boys.'

'We *have* to get her to England,' Una whispered, 'before she bumps into him and offers to have his babies.'

Coralie muttered, 'I had to explain the other day why she had to pay at the counter for eggs. She actually said to the shopkeeper, "Have them delivered to rue de Seine."'

'We'll get her away, though "to England" means across the demarcation line, through Free France to Spain, then on to Portugal.'

Coralie made a face. 'Getting her to Gare Montparnasse without her nerves snapping will be hard enough.'

'I'll talk to people at the hospital,' Una promised. 'There's a network among the staff getting American Jews out of France. I can't ask them to help – they're taking enough risks as it is – but I'll pick their brains. Meantime, take Tilly to La Passerinette with you today. Remember, hats are God's way of reminding women that they have heads with brains in them.'

Good idea. They could make a tea party of it. Coralie went to the kitchen and searched out the last scrapings of butter. She had a bag of flour too, so a cake of some sort was not out of the question.

★

In her workroom, replaying the moment she'd found Violaine, and the shelves stripped bare, Coralie let out a hiss of rage. Sewing machines, hat-stretchers, ribbon boards, *marottes* and sunflower stalks could all be replaced. So too, eventually, could her precious hat blocks.

It was the thought of thieves stepping over Violaine that angered her most. A Gypsy at Epsom Downs had once told her that she'd kill. She had come to understand what a lethal mix hatred and impotence could make.

Locking the workroom behind her, she collected Noëlle and Ottilia, who were bouncing on their bottoms on the salon sofa, and together they went upstairs to Violaine's flat. They were let in by Jeanne Thomas, the neighbour, whom Coralie had met once before and who had taken over Violaine's care. A spare woman of around sixty, she greeted Coralie with recognition, but her curiosity was for Ottilia, who, in a spring outfit bought at Javier in 1938, held the eye like a newly opened magnolia blossom. Her auburn hair made a shining frame to her face.

By contrast Violaine, propped against pillows, her curls lank, her spectacles keeping her place in a large-print book, was a pitiful sight. 'Violaine, it was my fault!' Coralie exclaimed, grasping her hand. 'I'd have found you earlier but I chickened out of coming. Got as far as place de la Concorde, then legged it. All that time you were locked in by that scum-of-the-earth—'

Violaine cut through Coralie's emotion: 'It was Lorienne.'

Coralie studied Violaine, wondering if her marbles had come loose during the ordeal. 'Lorienne left Paris ages ago. Went to Dijon, I heard.'

'She did not leave. Good day, Madame la Baronne.' Violaine gave her hand to Ottilia who, until that moment, had been

concentrating on removing her skin-tight gloves. Coralie felt
something flit between the two women. *Sympathy?*

Violaine repeated that Lorienne had not left Paris. 'The Dijon
story was to save face. You terminated her tenure, Madame, did
you not?'

Ottilia bit her lip. 'Dietrich assured me she was understating
her profits to cheat me. So distasteful, dismissing people, and in
the end, I had my London solicitor write the letter. Lorienne
replied in the vilest terms, calling me a . . . I won't say it.'

Violaine nodded, seemingly unsurprised. 'She took a job in
another milliner's — with Henriette Junot, in fact. One of our
customers saw her there. She has some kind of role as Henriette's
deputy. She calls herself "*directrice*".'

'What can you remember about the day she came back here?'
Coralie asked.

Violaine made a face. 'It was the twelfth or thirteenth of July.
The streets were in turmoil and I feared the shops would close and
I'd be left without food. I couldn't cross the road at my usual place
— so many cars nose-to-bumper, honking their horns. Finding a
fishmonger and a grocer's that had anything left took me hours.
Back home, I unlocked the street door and someone shuffled me
inside.'

'Lorienne?'

'That white-blonde hair is unmistakable, I should think,'
Ottilia murmured.

'She had two others with her.' Violaine closed her eyes. 'Lorienne wanted to know why the hats were gone from the window. I
told her they were locked away, that we'd closed for the duration.
She said, "The hats are mine now. Mademoiselle de Lirac sold
them to me." I didn't believe her, but she pushed me to the workroom and flattened me against the door until I gave her the key.'

'You said three people?'

'Three women. One,' Violaine's lips bent in disapproval, 'wore trousers. She had short hair and a gruff voice.'

Henriette – who else? It stank of revenge. Coralie asked, 'They cleared the shelves?'

'In laundry bags that they brought with them.'

'And shut you in deliberately?'

'I'd bought peaches and apples at the shops, and there was water in the kettle. Otherwise I would have died.'

'Didn't fancy those fish, then?'

Violaine turned unfocused eyes to Coralie, but proved herself equal to a joke. 'Oh, no, not raw.'

Noëlle, who so far had sat quietly beside Ottilia, pointed to the basket containing Coralie's cake and lisped, 'Oh, no, not raw.'

Everyone laughed, chasing away tension. Madame Thomas went to make tea, Coralie accompanying her. As the water boiled, Madame Thomas spoke of her pleasure at having somebody to care for again. She'd given up her work as a bookkeeper during her late husband's illness, she said, nursing him until his death five years ago. 'And after that, a silence descended.'

Coralie heard herself asking if Madame Thomas would care to take on La Passerinette's accounts. 'I was going to put a notice in the window. I'm reopening in October, and I need to run things more professionally. I'm all right with figures, but I'd rather make hats!'

'October?' Violaine cried, when Coralie repeated her plan over tea. 'Why so long? We may be struggling, but it's not the same for everyone. Fine goods are *flying* off the shelves. Madame Thomas, tell her!'

Ottilia got in first. 'You can't buy stockings or lingerie because the shelves are stripped bare by German soldiers, sending gifts home to their wives and sweethearts.'

Madame Thomas pursed her lips. 'Or buying them for a certain kind of girl here. It's the old story. If you're prepared to shame yourself, you'll do all right.'

Very well, September, Coralie conceded. Two and a half months in which to find a workshop's-worth of new tools and make new stock. 'What's gone is gone.' She could barge into Henriette Junot's and demand the return of her property but she'd be met by innocent faces, laughed out on to the street.

Paris was teaching her the lesson she'd first learned in London – a working-class girl who dared to reach for her dreams found plenty of people ready to shove her back down. Down she must go . . . only to bob back up again, like a champagne cork. She watched Ottilia eating cake with a silver fork – Violaine's kitchen drawer had yielded just the one and everyone else was eating with their fingers – and thought, *I reckon I have problems, but Tilly has ten thousand enemies in Paris, and if she's shoved under, she won't resurface.*

Chapter Eighteen

Six days later, on the last Friday of June, Coralie de Lirac and Una McBride sat at a table in a low-lit nightclub, dressed as if war belonged to a different universe. They'd left Ottilia at home, watching over Noëlle, and Coralie was looking forward to a few hours' unfettered fun.

The Vagabonds had been given a spot at the Rose Noire, and tonight was their debut. Nursing their drinks, because wine here was now shockingly expensive, Coralie and Una waited for the music to start. The electricity had just blown again. The lights were back on in Paris but supply was erratic up there in Montmartre.

When the Vagabonds finally trooped on, Una whooped.

'Last time they played here, they only just escaped with their limbs intact,' Coralie reminded her.

'Oh, those Corsicans are long gone,' Una assured her. 'They made hay while Martel was in prison, but now he's out, they've melted into the free zone. It's illegal to move currency from one zone to another, so professional criminals are having to choose. The Vagabonds of Swing are in business and the light of civilisation shines once more.'

Looking round, Coralie couldn't see much proof of it. And when she saw a party of six German officers sit down at a table nearby, she questioned her sanity in being there at all.

Dietrich was among the group. Thank Heaven the lighting was so low, Serge Martel's glass centrepiece having been turned off so as not to overload the circuit. 'This wine's too warm,' Coralie complained, reassigning her anxiety. 'We should ask for an ice bucket.'

'Honey, we'd get an empty one. Who's delivering ice?'

'And we're outnumbered by men. Lucifer's mother would get a dance here tonight. I don't want to talk to any bloody Germans ever, let alone dance with one.'

'Too bad, because one of them is gazing at you most intently. Nice-looking, if you go for the frozen-warrior type.'

So, he'd seen her. Coralie stared fixedly at the stage. The Vagabonds began with Edith Piaf's 'Ma Coeur Est Au Coin d'Une Rue', a melancholy number. Arkady's playing was as assured as ever, but Florian seemed tentative. He had returned alone to Paris and had a lost, neglected look about him His crimson shirt hung loose. At some point, he'd discarded his dulcimer for a rhythm guitar, and looked as if he was regretting that, too.

After 'Ma Coeur', Arkady swung into a blistering 'That's A Plenty'. Coralie murmured, 'Poor Florian can't keep up.'

'His fault for bolting to the country. All the proper musicians stayed put, got drunk and played "La Marseillaise" as the Nazis closed in.'

'Did he and Julie marry?'

'No. Even Florian can do better than that silly girl.' Una sniffed.

'Julie's not silly, just young. Oh, Lord, brace yourself.' Two men in badly pressed suits were stubbing out cigarettes, preparing to advance. They looked French, but that was all that could be said for them.

'Dancing, ladies?'

'Sure, why not?' Una allowed the taller of the two to lead her to the floor.

'So?' The other faced Coralie. She vaguely recognised him. She was sure he'd once been a doorkeeper here. Why wasn't he in the army? He seemed to read her and said aggressively, 'Something you want to say?'

'I'd rather dance than talk,' she said. A few circuits of the floor would keep the peace.

Afterwards Coralie accepted another glass of warm wine, and asked about Martel. 'They say he's out of jail . . . Really? After what he did?'

All true, her companion said. Martel had been pardoned by the new regime. He'd have been here tonight, except he'd been sent to a holding centre.

'Getting used to open spaces again?'

'Being deloused, more probably.' The man gestured over his shoulder. 'He won't like this lot.'

At first she thought he meant the Germans, until he turned to glare at Arkady's Vagabonds.

'Third-rate foreigners. They only got the spot because they're instrumentalists. Singers are too much trouble now that lyrics have to be vetted for anything anti-Nazi.'

'I didn't know that.'

He shrugged. 'You do now.'

'Where did you fight? Normandy was it?' It was a hostile question. This loafer had never felt the inside of a uniform.

'Bad lungs.' He coughed thickly to prove it. 'I've joined the Passive Defence Force. I'll come and check your blackout curtains any time.'

'Thanks but no thanks.'

After that, conversation stretched so thin, Coralie was forced to mention the weather. 'It's stifling.'

'What do you want in June? Snow? What's your friend up to?'

Una had changed partners for one of the Germans from Dietrich's table. Coralie hid her exasperation with a shrug. 'She's dancing. This is a nightclub, it's allowed.'

'Knows where her bread's buttered.'

'Buttered?' Coralie hit back. 'There's no butter.'

'That lot are Luftwaffe officers. I told old Félix to give them free drinks because they downed two hundred and fifty British bombers over France last month.'

Only self-preservation stopped Coralie throwing her wine into the man's face. Donal flew bombers. Light ones, whatever 'light' meant. He was a navigator-something, she'd always regretted not listening better. Two hundred and fifty down. Not Donal's. *Please not his.* 'You're glad they shot down those planes?'

'Sod the British. They left our troops high and dry in Normandy.'

'They took thousands of French boys with them. It was go or die.'

'What does any woman know?'

'Go to Hell!'

He walked away, stopping to call back, 'If you ever want a good seeing-to by a proper man, you know where I am.'

She held her tongue. If he'd rather see France under German rule than continue the fight, well, he'd got his wish. Dammit, she was stuck at the bar now. She couldn't find her table without passing Dietrich. She was damned whatever she did – wallflowers sat alone at tables and prostitutes sat alone at bars.

She was wearing her coral bracelet, its spiny edges bit as she pressed it into her flesh. Una was dancing with Dietrich. *Her* man. Bitter she might be, but he was still hers. In her mind, at least.

When Una finally joined her, Coralie snapped, 'Six partners one after the other.'

'It's called co-existence.'

'It's called "selling your wares".'

Una perched on a bar stool and fitted a cigarette into her holder. Her hands weren't entirely steady. 'Shut up and listen. When I was dancing with the first, I heard his colleagues chatting. One of my grandmothers was German and I have a smattering of it.' She put her elbow on the bar and used her lighter to shield her lips. 'As of three days ago, all refugees who fled Germany for whatever reason are to be surrendered for deportation. A special camp has been opened in Poland to receive them. Pétain's government agreed to hand them over as part of the armistice terms.'

'Isn't that against some convention?'

'I have no idea, but it won't help Ottilia.'

'Is Tilly a refugee? I mean, technically, she came here from London.'

'Which is enemy territory. Did you know that her brother Max sent years of valuable research to competitors in America? Something to do with paint chemicals. The Germans were incandescent, so I'd say that Tilly's on every list going.' Una turned to get a clear look at the stage. Perhaps in deference to Florian's rusty technique, the Vagabonds were playing a dreamy 'Mood Indigo'. 'Anybody could betray her. Friends, neighbours, jealous shop girls – what?'

'Imminent peril at nine o'clock.'

'Nine o'what? Oh, we're being navigators.' Two Luftwaffe officers were coming over, followed by a waiter with wine and a silver ice bucket. Turning to glance at them, Una murmured,

'That's your Dietrich, isn't it, headed this way? If anyone could help Tilly, surely he would.'

'No! If anything, he's got a vested interest in turning her— Talk later.' The men were upon them.

Una pouted around her cigarette holder, exhaling smoke in her very particular way. 'Why, gentlemen, chilled champagne. How blissful.'

'Ice for the lucky few, then,' Coralie muttered.

Dietrich asked her to dance and she accepted, as if he were a vague acquaintance and she bored enough to want the diversion. 'Mood Indigo' had given way to 'In A Sentimental Mood' but there was no melting into arms. She didn't want to touch his uniform. All she could think was, *Two hundred and fifty British bombers down*.

He broke the silence. 'I bought you this dress, I think.'

'Yes, when we first arrived . . .' She stopped.

'Straight into the trap. I had told myself how well you held up to questioning the other day. Your answers fitted with the details on your identity card, at least.'

'Why did you do it, Dietrich?' She battled the urge to claw his face. To tear off his uniform, beginning with that swallow-tail cross. Tear it off, find the man he'd once been, the friend, the lover . . . then spit in the face of the man he'd become.

'Question you?' He sounded more German than she remembered, his fluency diminished. Not surprising in three years. 'To discover if, under duress, you could keep to your story. You need to polish your answers. Had I been a professional interrogator, your stumbling would have aroused suspicion.' He tilted his head to examine the headpiece of flowers and ribbon she wore in her curls. 'I had not expected to find you a fashionable milliner. A wife and mother, too. You have been busy.'

'So have you, rising up the ranks, polishing your medals.' *Returning to Paris . . . with what in mind?*

'Tell me about this Ramon, whose ring you do not wear. It was a short marriage?'

'Elegantly brief.'

'But fruitful.'

'My daughter isn't Ramon's child.' She felt his shudder. His expression changed and understanding dawned. 'Dietrich, she's not yours.'

His hands dropped away. 'Let's go to a table.'

He selected one at the edge of the room where he ordered their favourite wine of old, Pissotte. 'Tell me about your daughter.'

Usually her favourite subject, but telling him about Noëlle felt like a violation. 'Just a normal child. She'll be three come winter and then I'll be thinking about nursery school. If there are any open, of course.'

'Is that a dig?' He twisted the stem of his glass. 'Just tell me the facts.'

All right, she thought, here goes. 'D'you remember, we were here having dinner once and you asked me the name of my first lover? I ducked the question. You want the truth? It was a sailor. Rishal. From the island of Mauritius.' She wove a few strands: Coronation night, fireworks tearing the sky, drink running freely. She'd really liked him. 'Though, to be fair, back then I was ready to run away with anybody who showed me a bit of love. We passed a few intimate nights, then he sailed, leaving me pregnant. End of fairytale.'

Dietrich seemed lost in the reflections in his wine glass, giving her a chance to study him properly. At first he'd seemed no different from before, but she saw that lines, like sparrow's feet, ran deep from the outer corners of his eyes. Leaner, too. It grazed her mind that he, too, might have suffered at their parting.

'Why did you leave me, Dietrich?'

'I had to get back to Germany.'

'Why make a fuss of me for two months, then drop me cold? I was destitute, homeless. I hated you.'

He shook his head, distaste in his manner. 'Why should you be destitute with twenty thousand francs, and your suite paid for two months? I may have left you, Coralie, but not to perish.'

'You paid for another two months? They told me to go! Out by eleven sharp.' Memories of that horrible day brought acid to her throat. 'You left no money. I had just enough to keep me from starving.'

'Are you calling me a liar? I left twenty thousand francs, in cash, for you.'

'Who did you give it to?'

'Brownlow, with a letter explaining why I was going and what I had learned of your conduct.'

She flushed, imagining that conversation, imagining the paint-work Brownlow had applied to her good name. Gold-digger, good-time girl. 'Brownlow hated me. He wasn't going to hand over a nice fat wad of cash. Straight into his own pocket, I should think, your gentleman's gentleman. I bet the desk clerk took the money you paid for my suite, too. And you,' her voice throbbed, 'you hurt me when I did nothing but love you.'

'Nothing? Your conscience is clear?' The hard, upward inflec-tion thrust another picture at her: of herself trespassing where she'd no business to go.

Taking a draught of wine, she continued, 'I *did* do something – I took a letter.'

Cold savagery came to his face, and she felt a familiar panic, legacy of her life with her father. 'You took more than a letter, Coralie. You took a life. I can never forgive you, and in my dark hours, I dream of inflicting the same pain on you. I have great power here . . . and you, a mother, an undreamed-of opportunity.'

'What are you saying? Dietrich? What's my being a mother got to do with anything?'

'Your child for my child.' He rose, scraping his chair, and she reached across the table to stop him but he avoided her grasp.

'You'd hurt my daughter? Why? What happened to your child? Dietrich, tell me!'

He was taut with emotion. 'Go. I will have a car drive you home to rue de Seine. See? I know every detail. Even that your last hat collection at La Passerinette was predominantly pink.' He gave a deformed smile. 'I never cured you of pink.' He came to the back of her chair and she flinched before she realised that, in spite of everything, habits of politeness had not deserted him.

'Have you heard from Ottilia since we spoke last?' he asked.

'Yes. I mean, no. She went south. Cap d'Antibes.' That was Una's favourite holiday spot and she often described its white villas and azure bay. 'Baronne von Silberstrom took a villa.'

'Cap d'Antibes, in summer? Ottilia burns like a lamb cutlet. Remember on Epsom Downs, how she wore a coat and gloves? You always were a poor liar, Coralie. She is in Paris, though not at rue de Vaugirard.'

'Cap d'Antibes,' Coralie repeated. 'Send your fellows there for her.'

'And you should know that whoever hides Ottilia risks arrest. No mercy, even for a beautiful, fast-talking milliner. When you wish to bring me information, find me—'

'At the Crillon? Or the Lutetia? Or do you shuttle between the two?'

He pulled her chair back for her, and then they stood face to face. An almost palpable current flashed between them. 'Neither. I have rooms in a place special to both of us.'

'The Duet?' In spite of everything, she blushed, and for a moment she thought he was going to bend to kiss her. She whispered, 'Dietrich, what happened to you?'

He stepped back, clicked his heels and left her.

Just after dawn the next morning, Coralie went out. She wore flat shoes and a plain, belted coat, a headscarf knotted under her chin. She needed to be incognito.

Chapter Nineteen

She walked briskly, hardly aware of an apricot sun misting every surface. At rue Valdonne, a narrow street off boulevard du Montparnasse, she mentally reassembled the directions Arkady had given her late last night, after she'd waited up for him. Brown shutters, a plain house, middle of the street. Middle-ish. Trouble was, everyone seemed to prefer their shutters brown. She was looking for the safe house into which Ramon had taken Arkady and Florian when they first arrived in Paris. Their host, an elderly painter, had later created their identity papers for them.

'Ramon calls him Bonnet. He paints the big pictures.' Arkady had stretched his arms to imply a vast canvas. 'But when he makes forgeries, he works with the touch of a butterfly. He is genius but . . .' Arkady had mimed somebody downing a glass of liquor '. . . Ramon must always check for mistakes.'

Should she be doing this? Commission a drunk to produce similar illegal papers for Ottilia? Brave people did that sort of thing. She wasn't brave. As kids, she and Donal used to play 'chicken' on the railway lines at the end of Shand Street. They'd wait till the steel sang with the vibration of wheels, then perform their own special dare. Hop over the rails on one foot, touch the parapet on the other side, then hop back on the other foot.

She'd never managed it, always pelting back to safety before she reached the far wall. Donal could, though. Funny, that. Hesitant and disaster-prone, he'd had the cooler nerve. Would he say she was doing the right thing, risking herself to help a friend? Or that she was being selfish, putting her child's future in jeopardy?

To get there, she'd walked down boulevard Raspail, her breath shortening at the sight of the Lutetia. The hotel was the headquarters of the Abwehr – military intelligence, she'd learned. Dietrich really had taken her into the wasps' nest. A sensible person, having escaped once, would not seek to return. Would they?

She walked along rue Valdonne until she smelt the bakery and her stomach rolled. You got used to hunger – or, at least, to suppressing it – but oven-fresh bread got through your defences every time. A queue of local women had already formed outside the shop, and when they saw Coralie, they passed hostile looks along the line. Their message was clear: 'Our street, our bread.'

Coralie stationed herself in a doorway a safe distance away. Even hard-drinking forgers liked fresh bread. Arkady's 'genius painter' would emerge eventually. And, indeed, at a few minutes past six, a door bumped open nearby and a man came out. Stocky, with a grey beard and red-veined cheeks, he presented a convincing portrait of a drinker. Whether he was also an artist was unclear. That could be oil paint on his overalls or house paint.

'Monsieur Bonnet?'

He jumped and Coralie thought he was going to scuttle back inside. But he pushed his hands into his pockets and looked at her sideways. 'Who is asking for him?'

She gave a name, not her real one. 'I understand you can provide fake identity documents.'

'Who says?' The thick beard made it hard to gauge the man's

expression, but Coralie could see he had eaten soup very recently. He must live an upside-down life.

'I'd rather not give names, but you can trust me.'

'I trust only two things, Madame. Cognac and cash.' He walked away towards the bakery.

'I'm Ramon Cazaubon's wife, all right?' she hissed.

'Ramon's lady?' He came back and a grin split his beard. 'Quite a man, our Ramon!'

'So, can you help? I have a friend who has to leave town.'

Bonnet hawked and spat the results towards the gutter. 'Man or woman?'

'Woman. Can you also forge an *Ausweis*, a permit to travel? For five people.'

Bonnet inflated his cheeks, letting the breath go slowly. 'I suppose. But I tell you this. I won't forge a police signature, French or German. Signatures you get for yourself, yes?' He drew her into a dingy hallway, which smelt of gas and cooking oil. And something that took her straight back to Bermondsey, to the glue factory on Magdalen Street: decomposing rabbit. Maybe he *was* a proper artist. Her father used rabbit glue to prime his screens.

Bonnet asked, 'Your friend's name?'

'Dupont. Ottilie Dupont. Yes, I know.' She'd seen the beard twitch. Using 'Dupont' was like booking into a hotel in England and calling yourself 'Smith'. She and Una had gone through dozens of fake names, selecting Dupont because it had been the surname of Ottilia's previous lady's maid, which gave their friend a chance of remembering it. 'Ottilie' had been chosen with similar logic.

Bonnet's eyes creased. 'Documents for Mademoiselle Dupont and an *Ausweis*. I'll need the names of everyone travelling on it. How old is your friend?'

'Thirty, and we'll be using her real birthdate because she doesn't remember new things.'

Bonnet made a tut-tut sound. 'You know what happens if she is caught?'

'We know. How quickly can you do it?'

'Two weeks.' When she objected, Bonnet gave a dry laugh. 'For Madame Cazaubon, nine days, but it will cost. A lot. For I am very good.' They shook hands and Bonnet followed her out on to the pavement. Giving her an odd look, he asked, 'You know where Ramon is now?'

'No. He went to fight, and I haven't heard a word.'

'Why not? He's back in Paris. He lives there,' Bonnet pointed across the street, 'with a . . . Sorry.'

With a woman. What else?

'If it's any comfort, she's nowhere near as nice-looking as you.'

Coralie walked away, contemplating the pleasure she'd derive from booting Ramon's backside down the stairs if ever he called on her again.

One more stop to make, then home.

Being a frump in a headscarf has its advantages, Coralie mused. She made it to the Right Bank without being asked for her papers once. She even passed the gun emplacements on place de la Concorde without the soldiers on duty looking up. Under her breath, she sang a revolutionary song,

'"Ah, ça ira, ça ira, ça ira!' It's all going on . . ."' All the way to Henriette Junot's.

Chapter Twenty

Coralie still had a key to Henriette's shop. In the emotion of her departure, nobody had thought to ask for it. The shop was dark. Not even the early-birds had yet arrived.

Closing the door behind her, Coralie flicked a lighter she'd borrowed from Arkady, illuminating four *marottes* on the white satin plinth, angled as if in conversation. Dietrich might mock her love of pink, but if you avoided sugar-candy, it could be subtle. Intriguing that Henriette Junot should be displaying hats of the same *fanée*, faded, shade that she and Violaine had experimented with this spring.

Bringing the lighter flame as close as she dared, Coralie read the hat's labels. 'HJ, Paris.' So – they'd been unpicking La Passerinette labels and inserting Henriette's, using the same stitching holes. Coralie could already anticipate Henriette's defence if accused: 'Prove they're yours!'

Well, she probably could. Flicking the lighter again, she inspected the sizing band inside the hat. Tiny stitches slanted left to right – put in by a right-handed person. Violaine.

But the stitching inside a second hat sloped in the opposite direction. With Violaine's encouragement, Coralie had reversed a lifetime of indoctrination, and now sewed with her left hand. To prove these hats were hers, Henriette Junot would have to produce a left-handed milliner prepared to commit perjury.

But it wouldn't get to court. She intended to take what was hers, now.

She'd start in the stockroom.

That room lay behind the main salon and Coralie had a key, though in fact, she found the door ajar and a light on. Inside, a girl in a raincoat stood halfway up a stepladder. An elderly man held the ladder, which wobbled as he saw Coralie.

Not wanting confrontation, Coralie opened her mouth to justify her presence, when she realised she knew the girl. 'Amélie!'

'Oh, heavens!' Amélie Ginsler, Henriette's head *vendeuse*, stepped down. 'What are you doing here?'

'Fishing. What are you doing?'

Amélie looked guiltily towards the old man, who asked in a whisper, 'Who is this?'

'A friend,' Amélie told him, 'a good friend.' Then to Coralie, 'This is my grandfather. He's helping me.'

'Do what, though?'

'Steal.' Words poured out. 'Henriette means to sack me. I overheard her. She wanted to turn me out right away because I'd been asking too many questions about the new stock, but Lorienne said I should be kept on another week because Rosaire is not quite ready to take over my job.'

'Rosaire?'

'Henriette's – ' Amélie shot a glance at her grandfather ' – newest friend. She started here a few weeks ago, and she's replaced me.'

So, Henriette had brought in yet more 'favourites' to bolster her authority. Coralie felt sorry for Amélie, but there was no time to chat. 'Where's this new stock?'

'Upstairs. I'll show you. I'm collecting my things and Grandpapa's taking them home.' Amélie was cradling something against her chest. Hats made of satin. Not real ones, doll-sized miniatures.

'May I?' Coralie examined one. It was perfect, its flowers and curled ostrich feather to scale. The second was just as exquisite. 'Did you make these?'

'Grandpapa did.' Pride ran through Amélie's voice. 'He carved the blocks, and blocked the felt, and Grandmama trimmed them. They had a business in Vienna once, making antique dolls, and were quite famous. They tried to carry on here, but it's hard to start afresh with nothing in the bank. We have a shop in the Marais, on rue Charlot. Bring your little girl some time. Grandpapa used to sell to the best stores in Vienna and Berlin . . .' She tailed off and Coralie filled in the rest. Of course. Amélie was Jewish. She'd always presumed 'Ginsler' was of German origin, and so it was. German Jewish.

'Did you show these to Henriette?' she asked.

'That's why they're here,' Amélie answered. 'A few years ago, we had a special children's collection. It was my idea, a way to ensure another generation of customers. Our clients brought their little girls along and other little girls modelled hats. I persuaded Grandpapa to lend some dolls, so he might pick up some customers. At the last minute, Henriette demanded commission on any that he sold, and after the show, she made me give her these little hats because she recognised the trimmings. They were offcuts from the atelier floor. We throw away bags of trim every week! But because they'd been turned into something beautiful . . .'

Amélie left the rest unsaid. She took a tape measure from her pocket and a delicate pair of scissors. 'And I have my contact book too, with my customers' names and telephone numbers. After I'm sacked, I shall call them and offer to re-trim their hats. Even rich women can no longer throw away last season's wear.'

The old man presented a fob watch. 'We must go. Already, it is nearly seven.'

'Will Henriette pay the commission she owes you?' Coralie asked.

Amélie gave a dispirited laugh. 'My sales have been put down to Rosaire's account, so, no.'

Rosaire. Number three in the La Passerinette raiding party? Coralie asked how Lorienne was getting on with the other staff.

'She's been appointed *première*. She took over from Madame Zénon, who returned to her family in Marseille – though only after Henriette pressured her to resign.' Lorienne was hated by the sales staff and *midinettes* alike, Amélie confided. 'She blames them for her own mistakes. A monster, except with Henriette, whom she flatters and coddles. The only time I've heard them arguing was after the disaster of the April collection.'

'Oh?' The night she'd walked out – been sacked, depending on whose point of view you took – Coralie had wagered Henriette that she'd produce the better spring collection. With invasion looming, the bet had fizzled out. 'What disaster?'

Amélie addressed her grandfather first. 'Go home, Opa. Take my things and I'll see you tonight. I must show Coralie something.'

'Prepare to marvel.' In one of the upstairs ateliers, Amélie opened a vast cupboard, revealing shelves filled with hats. 'The April line.'

'Good heavens!'

Amélie chuckled. 'We all told Lorienne she was mad, that the timing was all wrong for such colours, but Henriette loved them. "People will say we are taking up the patriotic baton. *Vive la France*." And within ten minutes, it had been Henriette's idea all along.'

Coralie had never seen such a frenzy of red, white and blue. The hats exploded with *tricolor* cockades, feathers and flowers, enough to bring on a flashing headache. 'They didn't launch? I never saw them.'

'No, because suddenly everyone was saying that the *drôle de guerre* was over. Henriette panicked. Unlike most people, she'd always believed there would be an invasion. People she'd met in Italy had a more realistic view of the German Army than we French ever did. Suddenly she had visions of her customers running from the advancing tanks with her designs on their heads. She cancelled the show and ordered Lorienne to start again.'

Only Lorienne had faltered, inspiration used up. With time running out, she'd persuaded Henriette to join her in a desperate eleventh-hour solution. 'Coralie, I didn't know she'd stolen your stock until I found La Passerinette labels on the floor. Lorienne said you'd sold them to her. She said you were—'

'Leaving town? Perhaps she hoped I would.'

'Henriette took over deconstructing your hats, making them up slightly differently to put her mark on them.'

'You can't do that.' Coralie was outraged. 'The shapes won't balance.'

Amélie laughed. 'Balance is the least of Henriette's worries. She's brought new people into her business – Rosaire, Soufflard, Lorienne – and, in their way, they rule her. Sometimes I see Henriette looking exhausted. Well, after today, it won't be my concern.'

They found the bulk of the stolen La Passerinette hats in Henriette's attic workroom: the straw, the sisal, the chintzes and organdies. Amélie fetched a bundle of laundry bags and helped Coralie fill them. They clumped down the stairs, laden like pack mules.

'All my blocks were taken,' she told Amélie. 'Tools, everything.'

'We could check the cellar.'

A search revealed nothing but cartons of felt waste, waiting to be traded on to a company that stuffed mattresses. Amélie said, 'I'd say your equipment was sold within hours. I doubt Henriette has black-marketeers in her address book, but I'd bet my last franc that Lorienne knows a few.'

But Coralie was looking at the bags of felt, an idea forming. Felt offcuts, miniature blocks to shape them on. 'Amélie, does your grandfather accept commissions?' But Amélie was anxious to leave. 'You go,' Coralie said. 'I've one more thing to do.'

It took several trips up- and downstairs, and she was breathless and hot by the time she'd transformed Henriette Junot's window into a tableau guaranteed to stop passers-by in their tracks.

Out on the street, she flagged down a delivery truck, offering the driver all the money she had on her to take her and her bulging laundry bags the short distance to boulevard de la Madeleine. She and Violaine would have to re-sew all the labels, and she still had to re-acquire the tools of her trade, but she had won a victory. An immoral one, perhaps, but what did she care about that?

Chapter Twenty-one

Friday again, 12 July. Her forger had broken his promise over Ottilia's papers. Coralie had been back twice to rue Valdonne. Bonnet had not answered her agitated knocking, though on her second visit, his face had appeared briefly at the window. Well, she'd go back again. And again, until he produced.

They were taking late-morning tea at home – she, Una and Ottilia – when three solid raps at the street door froze them mid-conversation. Coralie felt the crash in the stomach that was becoming unpleasantly familiar. It might be Henriette, ranting about hats. It might be the French police, interested in her visits to a forger. It might be German officials, a black car drawn up at the kerb. Her hands turned clammy as she went down and drew back the bolts.

Ramon was inside almost before she had time to gasp, 'You!'

She noticed immediately that he'd lost weight. His face was hatched with fading scratches. But his clothes were clean and somebody had ironed his shirt. She even got a hint of a woman's scent. Before she could turn on him, however, he blared, 'What the devil are you up to?'

'Talking to Bonnet? Lucky I did, or I might never have known you were back.'

'Bonnet?' Ramon stared. Then, 'You've been to rue Valdonne? Coralie, how dare you? Only *I* deal with Bonnet.'

'Had you told me you were in Paris, I'd have asked you. Ottilia's in danger. We're shipping her out.'

Was that a flicker of shame? 'I was going to call. I've been busy.'

'So I heard.'

'Don't you dare put me in the wrong.' He jabbed a finger. 'After what you did to my sister!'

'To Henriette? Hang on. Not only did she rob me, she nearly murdered my assistant. Go and poke your finger at her.'

'I know what she did, and there's no excuse, but to get her arrested? Coralie – such revenge is beneath you.'

'Arrested? I don't rat, not even on Henriette.'

'You didn't need to. You made a prime show on rue Royale. Those hats, red, white and blue, covered in revolutionary cockades?'

'My window display? A little lacking in finesse,' she rammed her hands on her hips, 'but I made my point.'

'Oh, you made a point. Henriette and Lorienne Royer were arrested the same morning for subversion. Yes, subversion! It is illegal to display the French colours. Do you see any *tricolores* in Paris now? They were taken to the Santé prison. Lorienne's out, but Henriette is still there.'

'I didn't mean that to happen!'

'But it has. You barge ahead, like a lunatic firing bullets in a crowd. It was the same at the Rose Noire, when you dragged us all into a fight, and Arkady and the other boys were nearly beaten up. All so you could be the centre of attention, prancing about in a gold hat. You're dangerously irresponsible.'

'How about you? I thought you were dead, or a prisoner of war.'

His reply was an ironic snort. 'I hardly fired a bullet. I ended up behind the lines, ferrying wounded men to field hospitals.'

'And now you're skulking in a back-street with somebody else's woman.'

He flushed hard. 'What makes you think she's somebody else's?'

'Because they always are. I was the honourable exception. I don't suppose you're working, either.'

'I can't because the German military police are looking for me. I got caught just before the surrender, made a prisoner of war, only I escaped. Me and some other lads jumped out the back of a lorry and ran for it. I pick up jobs here and there now, so don't ask me for money.'

'When was the last time I did that?'

Noëlle must have heard them, because she suddenly wailed, 'Papa, Papa!' from the top of the stairs.

Coralie turned to go up, but Ramon stopped her. 'Once upon a time, Raphael Bonnet lived in Montmartre, but one day he got so drunk he rolled down the slope all the way to Montparnasse.'

'Save the fairy stories for Noëlle.'

'It's not a fairy story. If the Gestapo ever get on to him, he will talk. You've heard of the Gestapo? Geheime Staatspolizei, secret state police. Nice fellows who wear black uniforms or, more usually, grey. Sometimes they lurk in plain suits, trying to look like the rest of us.'

'What's your point?'

'Bonnet knew my name and address and now he knows yours. If he is taken in for questioning, if they torture him, he will betray you.'

So, she had blundered, but she wasn't going to give Ramon the satisfaction of seeing her dismay. 'Bonnet doesn't have this address. I go to him.' She did feel bad about Henriette, though. 'Shall I pack a basket of food to take to your sister?'

Ramon rolled his eyes. 'She has a girlfriend for that. Look, I'll go to Bonnet's now, chase up your papers. Men like him need men like me to kick their arses. It's not women's work.'

Two hours later, Ottilia was staring indignantly at her new identity. 'That photograph is awful. I look sulky and fat.' It had been prised off Ottilia's London Library card. Coralie had been appalled to discover that Ottilia had brought it to France, along with two further proofs of her identity: her passport and a British alien's identity card. This last, a fawn-coloured booklet, revealed every detail of her birth and her former residence in Berlin. Coralie had lit a fire in the grate and put the documents into the flames, ignoring Ottilia's pleas that she couldn't legally re-enter Britain without them. 'Better detained in England than deported to Germany.'

Now she looked over Ottilia's shoulder to assess Bonnet's work. The identity card looked convincing, to the point of being creased and a little greasy at the corners, as if it had been inspected scores of times already. 'Guard it with your life, Tilly, and learn every line of it. Most of the details are true, but not all. See? It says you live in rue de Madrid.'

'But that's an awful street. Once I had a charwoman who lived near there.'

'The point is, it's easy to remember because you're making for Madrid.'

'I thought I was going to Vichy.'

'You are at first—' Coralie stopped, catching Ramon's eye. He considered their plan for Ottilia's escape to be amateur. Such things were men's work, no doubt. 'Una will explain better than me,' she said. 'She'll be back from her hospital shift in time for supper.'

'Why does it say that I am a florist?'

'Your cover story is that you are a single woman, with no parents, going to live with an aunt in Perpignan. Women in such circumstances usually have to work, so we chose a profession you could talk about, if you're questioned. You must have bought enough flowers in your life!'

'That doesn't mean I know about them. I order them and another woman brings them and arranges them. Why should I do it myself?'

Ramon interrupted, asking if Coralie had beer in the flat? He'd run to rue Valdonne for the papers and back again, and it was hot out there.

'We can manage weak tea,' she said. 'Did Bonnet give you anything else?'

'A bill.' Ramon handed her a square of grimy paper with figures scrawled on it. 'And this.'

'This' was a flimsy pink rectangle, their counterfeit *Ausweis*, authorising four male musicians and Ottilie Dupont to cross the demarcation line into the Free Zone. It was stamped with the German eagle and today's date. As Bonnet had forewarned, it required an authorising signature.

'For which you will have to jump through hoops,' Ramon told her.

'We'll queue at the *Kommandantur*, no hoops required. I'll make your tea.'

He shadowed her to the kitchen, and while they waited for the water to boil, she took him through the escape plan in detail.

'It's simple,' she insisted. 'The Vagabonds will play a double set at the Rose Noire tomorrow night. Soon as curfew's lifted, they'll set off for Vichy, taking Ottilia with them.'

'Picking her up here?'

'We're all going to the club. She'll leave with them.'

'Then what?'

'Remember that champagne we drank at Christmas? That came from a friend of Una's. He's now an adviser to the new government in the south, in Vichy. He's pulled strings to get the Vagabonds a week's residence in a club near the Hôtel du Parc. That's where all the top-rank ministers are staying. It turns out Vichy's a bit thin on fun.'

Una had put it slightly differently. 'The ministers, their wives and mistresses are at each other's throats with boredom. Any table-scraps of Parisian culture are welcome.'

'And how do they travel?' Ramon demanded. 'Train?'

Coralie measured tea leaves into the pot. 'By car, courtesy of Serge Martel.'

'You are kidding.'

'Nope.' Back in charge of his club, eager to curry favour with the new, collaborationist government, Serge Martel had not only agreed to release the Vagabonds from their contract for a week but also to loan his famous wine-red Peugeot for the journey. Una had called on him a few days ago, just to make sure. She'd worn her tightest outfit, undone the top buttons . . . Her attention to detail had worked. So far.

Still, Ramon seemed determined to find fault. 'Ottilia will have to hide for a week in a town full of government spies, German agents and security men.'

'It's still safer than Paris and she'll have Arkady to take care of her.'

'And when the week is up?'

'Three boys will come back, and Arkady takes her by train to Perpignan. That's close to the Spanish border.'

'I know where Perpignan is! You're talking about my back-yard. It ought to be me taking her—'

'Well, it isn't.' Coralie poured boiling water on tea leaves, splashing some in her irritation.

Ramon had the grace to shrug. 'I suppose you have to look after Noëlle.'

'I do.'

'And Una—'

'Has her hospital shifts. Arkady will be fine. He's fought in a war, you know.' She bit her lip as Ramon looked away and down. 'What I mean is—'

'I know what you mean.' Black eyes flashed. 'I wanted to fight the Germans, but I ended up digging latrines and carrying stretchers. The war isn't over and one day I will prove that my blood is as good as the next man's.'

'It won't come to that. Look, there is a way you can help. Look after Noëlle tomorrow night. And if . . . if anything happens and I don't come back . . .'

He put his hand hard on hers and the teapot went down with a crack. 'You will, *chérie*, because at the first sign of danger, you will leave the Rose Noire. But don't come back here tomorrow evening in case you're followed. Go somewhere safe and get a message to me.'

She wanted to tell him not to be so over-dramatic, but instead she apologised again for getting Henriette into trouble.

Ramon said grudgingly, 'My sister! Let's admit it, she had it coming.'

After Ramon left, Coralie and Ottilia made their way to place de l'Opéra and joined a line at the *Kommandantur*, where the Germans administered the permits that now governed French lives.

'I'm sure this queue is growing from the front,' Coralie complained after they'd stood for two hours. Arkady was minding Noëlle, but he had to leave at five for the Rose Noire. At a quarter to five, a uniformed functionary came out and shouted, 'Closed. We are closed. Come back again on Monday.'

Monday? 'Couldn't we see somebody now?' Coralie pleaded, stepping in front of him, showing him the pink *Ausweis*. 'We need a signature.'

The man frowned at the paper, reading the names listed. 'Which of you is Dupont? Why have you come here together?'

'We'll come back on Monday,' Coralie said. Sensing danger in his questions, she hurried Ottilia away.

Over supper Una proposed a solution. She'd brought home slivers of smoked ham from the hospital kitchen, a rare luxury, and for Ottilia and Noëlle, a whole chicken leg. Coralie had managed to buy a few potatoes and a litre of rough red wine. It was amazing, she thought, as she laid the table for the adults' supper, how such basic provisions could manifest a feast. Add hunger, and you had a miracle. Noëlle had fallen asleep faster too, having put away a good meal.

'This is how we'll do it. Serge Martel boasts that his club is a magnet for a certain type of German officer.' Una lifted her glass and said, 'Cheers.'

'What type?'

'The old-school kind, which signed up to Nazism but doesn't really swing along with it. Martel told me that he keeps an eye out for them.'

'Protects them?'

Una laughed at Coralie's naivety. 'Garners information on them for the security services. Every night one table at the Rose

Noire is reserved for Nazi police who are spying on their own side.'

'Gestapo?'

'Martel just said police. He points out those officers who might be getting a little . . . shall we say, too French? A little too relaxed. Anyway, we will brush up our charms, and *they* will give us our signature.'

'You think a German policeman will put his name on an *Ausweis* because we smile at him?'

Una topped up their glasses. 'Sure I do.'

They spent Friday evening packing Ottilia's suitcase with plain skirts, knitwear and basic lingerie. If she was searched, there must be no couture labels and, heaven forbid, no London ones.

Coralie struggled to make Ottilia understand why she must jettison her twenty-two-carat Cartier cigarette case with 'von S' engraved on it. Ditto the gold cigarette holder and lighter. Predictably, Ottilia wept. 'They were my twenty-first-birthday present from darling Papa!'

'Choose *one*, then,' a spinster florist might conceivably have one luxury to her name, 'and nothing monogrammed.'

'When I get to Spain,' Ottilia suddenly asked, 'how will I know where to go?'

That was the elephant-sized question and Coralie couldn't answer it. Arkady would deliver her to a safe house, whose address had been supplied by one of Una's hospital colleagues. After that, Ottilia would be on her own.

I could survive, Coralie thought, and Una would relish the adventure. Actually, Una would probably end up travelling first class to Madrid courtesy of a German Feldmarschall, with his entourage carrying her luggage. But could Ottilia sustain the shock of having to make endless difficult choices by herself? Even now, she seemed to be in a trance. She was sitting at the dining table, murmuring in a soft monotone. Her voice, with its German inflection, sounded like a whispering water-pipe.

'Bedtime. I know it's not dark yet,' Una spoke like Matron, 'but we've a big day ahead—' She stopped dead. A car was drawing up outside. She flattened herself against the wall by the window, nudging aside the blackout curtain that Coralie still kept in place. 'Oh, joy,' she murmured.

'What?' Coralie demanded.

'Black Mercedes 260D. And two gentlemen.'

'Are they . . .?'

'Coming to the door?' Una leaned as far forward as she dared.

Hard raps at street level told them all they needed to know.

'Into Arkady's loft,' Coralie whispered. 'Una, grab coats and hats, purses and handbags, so they think we've gone out. Leave them.' Ottilia had begun to pile the teacups. 'Take your suitcase. I'll get Noëlle.'

By good fortune, Arkady had left the loft ladder down – he'd been late setting off for the Rose Noire. Noëlle in her arms, Coralie watched Una scramble through the hatch, then reach down to take the suitcase, coats and hats that Ottilia held up.

'Get in!' Coralie urged as Ottilia climbed gingerly into the roof space. Coralie was halfway up the ladder, passing Noëlle into Una's arms, when a crash told her that the front door had been forced. Just time to drag up the ladder and close the hatch.

They lay side by side on Arkady's bedding, the air heavy with the beating of their hearts. Coralie cupped her hand over Noëlle's mouth, though the child was still half asleep. A louder crash suggested the door of the flat had been opened with a single kick. Then they heard men's voices shouting for 'Freiin von Silberstrom?'

A man called in German, 'Ottilia? Are you there?'

Both she and Ottilia recognised the voice. Coralie hissed, 'Quiet, Tilly!'

Coralie couldn't have said how long it took the men to conclude their search and go. Fearing a trap, they stayed where they were until cramp got to their legs and the continuing silence told them it was finally safe to open the hatch. They spent the night fully dressed, alternately dozing and waking. When the street door bumped open in the early hours, they all woke with a shriek. It was Arkady coming home.

They couldn't risk spending the following day at rue de Seine. Dietrich had come to fetch Ottilia and had not come alone. He might return at any time.

Entrusting Noëlle to Arkady's care – he would take the child to Ramon's house – Coralie spent Saturday strolling in the Bois de Boulogne with Ottilia and Una. They hid among the trees like outlaws. Around teatime, they walked the short distance to Una's building on avenue Foch. Talking in the over-cheerful voice she used when she was scared, Una fitted a key into a lock and said, 'Cobwebs and rotten fruit I can handle, but let's hope there are no Gestapo hiding behind the sofas.'

Inside, their footsteps echoed like the march of wooden soldiers. Coralie was ready to flee at the first answering creak. But there was nothing amiss, beyond a bowl of pulpy apples, busy with fruit flies, and a coating of dust on everything.

Coralie felt as if she'd wandered into a huge, empty hotel. Everywhere she looked, there was a new texture calling out to be stroked. Onyx, suede, marble, burr walnut . . . And no clutter. Una had joked of moving back there with Arkady if – when – he ever got over his awe of her and made a romantic move. But really? Arkady would be a fish out of water in this palace.

She followed Una into a lavish bedroom, conscious of her outdoor shoes sinking into snowy carpet. One wall was lined with mirrored doors. Sliding one back, Una said, 'My wardrobe. This was my maid Beulah's domain – I still feel I'm trespassing. But, for better or worse, I'm my own maid now. Grab what you like.'

Coralie gaped. 'How many evening dresses do you own?'

'Two hundred maybe. Beulah took a dozen trunks back to the States, but I guess there's enough left. To misquote Henry Ford, "Choose any color you like, so long as it's—"'

'Beige. I dare you to wear red tonight, or give pink a go.' Coralie pulled out a floor-length shrimp-pink dress shot with silver thread. She exclaimed over the plastic zipper in the back.

'Elsa Schiaparelli,' Una told her. 'It's the real thing, because nowhere could I get a zipper dyed just the right shade.'

'You've never worn it?'

'*Virgo intacta*.'

'I just don't understand—'

'Must we always come back to this? *Because I can*. Because it used to give me pleasure to run up bills for clothes I never wore, and thus torment Mr Kilpin, the kind of man who would charge a friend to smell his coffee. And,' Una put the Schiaparelli back on the rail, 'because if I had a dress, no other woman could have it. Come on, choose. We need to be at the Rose Noire when it opens to get a good table.'

'Nothing too tight or heavy.' Coralie was thinking of midnight, when the club's walls trickled with human perspiration. They needed to be able to move freely and to run, if necessary.

Ottilia picked up a dress that was little more than a net covered with reflective discs that blinked as they caught the light. 'This,' she breathed.

'Vetoed.' Una replaced it in the cupboard. 'In your heart, you may want to outshine me, but those *paillettes* have a nasty habit of coming unstitched. You'd end up shedding scales like a wind-dried herring.'

Coralie's watch said it was gone five. 'Why don't you just choose for us?'

For Ottilia, it was ivory silk with a lace evening coat. For Una, cream bias-cut with an overskirt of embroidered chiffon that fanned behind her as she walked. For Coralie, a sheath of coffee-cream rayon silk, whose back dipped below her waist, weighted with strands of beads.

'All Lutzman originals,' Una said proudly, 'and there only ever were originals. Yours suits you, Coralie. It needs a long back and heroic shoulders. Mine are too narrow.'

Coralie contorted herself in front of the mirror. 'Are the beads at the back to give dance partners something to play with?' Not that she was going to dance. Head down: that was her plan. 'Who is Lutzman? He obviously shares your love of washed-out colours.'

'Not he, she. Alix Gower – one of Javier's protégées. Lutzman was the name she adopted when Gower became a little poisonous. A story for another time.' Una struck a pose for the mirror, hips forward. 'She absorbed Javier's liking for clean lines but, being female, also understood the desire to seem innocent while being downright sexy. Men never knew where they stood with Alix. Had them all on the hop, even her husband.'

'I never took to Javier's stuff,' Coralie admitted. 'Too plain for me.'

'You don't say. Your dress is called Lutzman Number Ten.'

'Is Alix still in Paris?'

'No, she ran for her life. She's half English, half Jewish and, as we know, both parts would have been locked up if they'd caught her. Hell, where's Tilly?'

In the en-suite bathroom, it turned out, rootling in the medicine cabinet for tweezers. Encountering herself in a wall of mirrors had alerted her to the 'horrendous tragedy' of her eyebrows. A bottle of sleeping tablets without its cap stood on the vanity unit.

'How many did you take?' Una demanded.

'Only a few.'

'Then let's pray they don't start working too soon.'

While Una searched out evening cloaks for them, Coralie turned her mind to evening shoes. Predictably, Una had a phenomenal collection, though none with heels under four inches. Ottilia opted to keep the walking pumps she had on but Coralie couldn't bring herself to go out in the leather brogues she'd put on that morning. She selected a pair of satin sling-backs, amazed to discover that Una's feet were a half size bigger than hers. She made them fit by stuffing tissue paper into the toes.

Finally, they were ready to go. 'I take it we're not going to be spirited to boulevard de Clichy in your Rolls-Royce?' Coralie asked.

Una laughed sardonically. 'I already handed it over to some monocled owl at German Army Headquarters. They'd have taken it anyway, robbed me blind by giving me devalued francs for it – and I hadn't enough fuel to go further than the city limits anyway. I don't care because, in return, I got free passage to Switzerland for two writer friends, who were hiding in one of those refugee rabbit cages in the Marais. You know, ten poor souls to a room in a crumbling *hôtel particulier?* I know you're going to ask,' Una dropped her voice, 'why didn't I buy Ottilia's escape?"

'No. Tilly's far too much of a prize. They'd have issued an *Ausweis* and arrested her at the first checkpoint. We're doing it the only way we can, by stealth. You're a good woman, Una Kilpin-McBride.'

'Aw, and you're not so bad yourself, Madame de Lirac-Cazaubon. So – pony-cab? The Rose Noire's too far to walk, and I don't rate the Métro in evening dress. Oh, shoot!' Una had been inspecting herself in the mirror. 'Hats.'

'Lead the way. I suppose they've got their own wing?'

'No – I want to wear one of those bijou babies Amélie Ginsler made for you.'

'My doll-hats? They're not ready.'

A week or so after her encounter with Amélie at Henriette Junot's, Coralie had walked to the Marais to offer old Monsieur Ginsler a commission. After getting lost for an hour in the maze of streets, jangled by the bustle and smells of crowding humanity, she'd located rue Charlot. The Ginslers' shop had needed no pointing out. Tiny wax faces stared through gauze-protected windowpanes.

Amélie's greeting had been a mix of surprise and delight, old Monsieur Ginsler's more cautious. 'I was thinking you'd want just one or two,' he'd muttered when Coralie announced that she'd purchased twenty bags of felt offcuts from a waste-fabric merchant.

'For as many miniature hats as you can make, Monsieur.' She'd turned to Amélie. 'Think about it. Women spend all day queuing, or going to and from work. They jam a headscarf on because it's simpler. But a doll-hat could go into a handbag or its own bag. Then, at night, off comes the headscarf, on goes the doll-hat, and they can go out looking chic without even having to find a mirror.'

In the end, Monsieur Ginsler's wife took up Coralie's cause.

'You say "no" because we're so busy, Manny?' She glanced meaningfully up at a cobweb-strewn beam. 'Even the dolls sleep.'

At the end of the visit, the Ginslers had presented Coralie with three teacup-sized hats, perfect in every detail. Later Coralie had shown them to Una, only to put them away as she recognised the gleam in her friend's eye. She said just as firmly now, 'I haven't gone fully into production. I'm waiting for September.'

'What's to stop you launching them tonight?'

'Everything. They'll be a sensation, I'm convinced, and the last thing we want tonight is people staring at us.'

'I disagree,' said Una. 'The more we give people to look at, the less they'll notice the thing we're trying to hide.'

'Too bad. They're at home and I'm not slogging back over the river.'

'You have them made in the Marais? I know the Marais. My writer friends lived just down from the doll shop. So let's go.'

The Vagabonds were well into their first set when Una, Coralie and Ottilia arrived at the club. They'd spent half an hour at the Ginslers', sitting in front of a smoky fire, while Amélie and her grandmother feverishly trimmed three little hats for them.

Coralie was in reflective mood as she descended into the candlelit Rose Noire. Tonight she'd discovered that Amélie had a profoundly disabled daughter. The family was so protective of twelve-year-old Françoise that her existence had been entirely unknown at Henriette Junot. 'I told only Madame Zénon,' Amélie had confided.

They paused on the dance floor. The Vagabonds were playing a hot jazz version of 'La Marseillaise' so loudly that glasses shimmered on the bar.

'They know it's illegal to play it, don't they?' Coralie stared uneasily at them. 'Nobody's dancing.' She drew in a breath, steeled herself and tried to avoid the eye of the proprietor, Serge Martel.

Thirty minutes later she was in the Ladies with Ottilia, the near discovery of Ottilia's British alien's identity card still making her breath come short.

Ottilia went straight to the mirror. 'Have I done something wrong?'

Coralie waved the offending card. 'This is more dangerous than a loaded gun. It's even stamped "Bow Street police station"! Don't you get it?' Obviously not, as Ottilia shook her head. Tears were close. Sighing, Coralie took an eye-pencil from her bag. 'Give yourself a bit of definition, go on. You look as though you haven't slept in a month.' As Ottilia leaned into the mirror and drew shaky lines, Coralie said, 'Remember that day at Epsom? We both had a palm reading. I don't know what your Gypsy told you, but mine said I would kill one day. I've realised recently, I could.'

'Me?'

'No, not you.' *Well, sometimes.* 'Kill to protect the ones I love.'

Ottilia feathered the pencil over an eyebrow. 'I envy you. I look for the future and I don't see anything. I only see what is behind.'

'You will be happy again.'

'No. The day Dietrich broke off our engagement, it was like slamming into a wall. I still remember every word he said. "I find it impossible to go ahead in life with you." *Ahead in life.* His went on, mine stopped. I was nineteen. I don't remember what that Gypsy told me at Epsom, but I remember stumbling out of her caravan in despair.'

Not knowing what to say, Coralie retired to a lavatory. The

flush wasn't strong enough to drown the identity card so, very reluctantly, she fished it out again. Standing on the toilet seat, she lifted the top of the cistern and dropped the card inside. She heard the door to the Ladies open and shut. Blotting her hands on lavatory paper, straightening her dress, she unlocked the door to the cubicle and stepped out. 'Good God! Julie!'

Coralie stared at her former nanny, whom she'd supposed was still in the country. Where had that milkmaid complexion gone? The girl in front of her looked more like twenty-nine than the twenty she must now be. In a tight satin dress, scarlet lipstick and a matching pillbox hat balanced on her exaggeratedly rolled hair, Julie Fourcade was a bad translation of a Hollywood starlet. Hiding her shock, Coralie said, 'Have you come to see Florian? Poor boy got so thin without you. But why haven't you visited? Where are you living? Not on rue Jacob, or we'd have bumped into each other.'

Answering with a vague shrug, Julie added, 'Busy, you know how it is. And I'm not back with Florian. I have a new man.'

Yes, Coralie thought. The signs were there. 'I hope he looks after you.'

Julie's gaze skimmed Coralie's gown, upswept hair and the doll-hat with its hot-pink feathers. Her eye dropped to the coral bracelet. 'Ramon gave you that, didn't he?'

'"Coral for Coralie."'

'My man gave me this.' Julie flashed an opal ring, showing it proudly to Ottilia before going to the cubicle that Coralie had just vacated. 'Nice to run into you both. Pop over to my table, have a drink, if you like. Now, pardon me, I'm bursting.'

As the bolt clicked, it dawned on Coralie that Julie hadn't asked once about Noëlle.

Their German officers stood as they returned to the table. A good sign, as it meant they regarded them as ladies, not tarts. Thank God Dietrich had not thought to look for them here — not yet, anyway. Eleven hours to go, trapped, until Ottilia was safe away. Only then could Coralie and Una leave. Coralie saw Una on the dance floor with the senior black-uniformed officer.

'I have an idea,' she said to those remaining at the table. She spoke German and the men stared, too slow to hide their surprise at her educated accent. Mademoiselle Deveau had been a good teacher, and she'd picked up more from Dietrich than perhaps he'd ever realised. 'Two of you dance with us, and the one left behind can order dinner. The chef here's very good. He has nothing to cook with, of course, but his way with fresh air is . . .' She kissed her fingers. Offering her hand to the oldest of the men, she said, 'While we dance, I'll tell you who taught me German.'

Her partner was in his mid-twenties, muscular, with wide-apart eyes and a broad nose. He smelt a bit sweaty, which induced her to lean back rather than copy other women, and drape herself against his chest. Oh, well, charming signatures out of men was Una's forte, not hers. It wasn't long before she spotted Julie, with a German partner, her plump arms around his squared-off shoulders. He seemed rather entranced. Was he the provider of opal rings?

Phrases had been coined to describe the relationship between invader and civilian, but the word 'collaboration' was the most loaded. To some, it meant 'working relationship'. For those like Serge Martel, it meant profiteering, and to certain women, it meant sexual congress. *To others*, Coralie supposed, *it might even mean love*.

Her partner, she learned, was called Ulrich and he came from Lower Silesia, to which she replied, 'Where the coal comes from.'

He seemed taken aback and she wondered if he'd been taught that the French were ignorant and lived in rabbit holes — just as they'd been told that the Germans were starving and smoked cigarettes made from dung. She asked about his regiment, hiding her relief when he pointed proudly to the lightning-strike runes at his throat and said, 'Waffen-SS.'

Presumably that meant he wasn't Gestapo. When she said, 'I thought you might be a policeman,' Ulrich looked so offended that she asked quickly, 'What does SS stand for again?'

'*Schutzstaffel*. It means "Elite Guard".' He showed her a skull-and-crossbones ring on his knuckle.

'We'll all look like that if food gets any scarcer,' she said. It didn't get a laugh. Neither did it get them any nearer a signature on an *Ausweis*. She searched again for Una and instead saw Ottilia, dancing with another of the younger SS officers, lost in her trance. Ah, there was Una – clearly doing her best to stick close to Ottilia. They needed to have a meeting, re-draw their plan, because Coralie was certain of only one thing: Ottilia would not sustain her composure for eleven hours.

'You were going to tell me how it is you speak German so well, Fräulein.'

'Mm? Oh, a teacher, here in Paris. Half the time we'd speak French, the other half German. And I read a few books. Silly romances,' she said, deciding not to mention *A Farewell to Arms*. 'I don't like too much reality.'

She caught Una's eye then, only to see her friend's expression petrify. Four men stood at the edge of the dance floor. They were looking from couple to couple, as if crossing faces off a list. Tall and well-built, they were not typically French. Neither was the cut of their suits. Coralie saw them confer, then signal to Ottilia's dance partner.

Coralie's partner had seen them too. 'They are officers of the Gestapo. It seems they wish to question your friend.'

'They'll have made a mistake. Otill—' She cleared her throat. 'Ottilie is a bit dim, but she's no danger to anyone.' Ottilia was being led off the dance floor, towards the men. *Take your time,* Coralie urged wordlessly. *You are a florist from rue de Madrid, enjoying a last night out in Paris before going to your aunt at Perpignan.*

One of the Gestapo was less heavy-set than his fellows. He had a facial scar, and round spectacles that gave him the look of a scholar. Or even a cleric. A Homburg hat was wedged under his arm and he was taking off leather gloves, presumably so he could search inside Ottilia's bag. She was proffering it meekly. There was nothing alarming in his demeanour.

He raised a succession of items up to the light. A lipstick, a pen, the gold cigarette holder. Finally, an ID card, which he inspected with agonising thoroughness.

When he gave the handbag back to Ottilia, Coralie let out her breath, but relief was short-lived. More questions, it seemed, and soon Ottilia was making the fluttering gestures that prefigured tears or sometimes hysteria. *You are Ottilie Dupont, who trained at a technical school on the Left Bank. You are unemployed because there are no flowers in Paris.*

Had Dietrich summoned these men? Had he followed them, perhaps from the Bois de Boulogne or avenue Foch? Coralie looked at Arkady, a horrible thought stealing in. *He* might have been trailed to Ramon's. The Gestapo might already have taken Noëlle and Ramon, Dietrich making good his threat . . . *Your child for my child.* Stop it, she ordered herself, or you'll be in hysterics before Ottilia. Maybe somebody here had called in the secret police . . . Coralie's gaze found Serge Martel, and he stared back at her for the count of twenty, then put his hand to his heart and gave a small bow.

The Gestapo had Ottilia surrounded.

'Where will they take her?' Coralie asked her partner.

'The Gestapo have a place on avenue Foch, with prison cells and interrogation rooms.' Ulrich put distance between them. 'You went with that woman to the ladies' room. You were gone a long time.'

'We were fixing our faces.' Her voice split. 'Touching up our lipstick.'

'But she *is* your friend?'

'Not really. I hardly know her.'

There. Betrayal was so easy and she was no better now than Serge Martel or her father. *I have to be,* she told herself.

They were taking Ottilia towards the stairs, two Gestapo holding her arms. Four men, to remove a woman as slender as a wine-glass stem.

Coralie muttered an excuse to Ulrich, and, afraid he would try to stop her, ran as if to the lavatories. Changing direction, she cut behind some tables, keeping to the shadows. In her haste, she stepped out of one borrowed shoe, turning her ankle. Excruciating, but she mentally blanked out the pain and pulled off the other shoe. The club's stairs were lit by tea lights, a candle on each step. Coralie climbed soundlessly, knowing the arrest-party was just ahead of her. Perhaps Ottilia had, belatedly, put up a fight. Coralie could hear her demanding her cloak in near-hysterical German. So much for being mild-mannered Ottilie Dupont.

Coralie had no particular plan and her only weapon was a hatpin. And even though it was a nice sharp one, it wouldn't fell four trained policemen. There was just a chance that, as they left the club, she could slide between them and whatever vehicle they drove. If she could get Ottilia running, they might seize their one advantage: the streets of Paris. Coralie knew the back ways, the cut-throughs. If they made it as far as the Butte de Montmartre, she'd find the ancient, rustic lanes where no car could follow. She stepped forward. It was, literally, now or never.

A hand clamped hard over her mouth. Somebody had come noiselessly behind her. She tried to kick but was bodily lifted up the last few stairs, and shoved hard against the wall. A voice said in her ear, 'Don't fight me.'

Dietrich.

'I can't save you both. Kurt.' Another shape loomed. 'Take over and keep her quiet.'

Time to draw a breath, then a different hand covered her mouth. She heard Dietrich shout, 'Major Reiniger, stop, please. I have new orders regarding the woman von Silberstrom.'

A challenge was given in answer, then Coralie heard Dietrich again: 'I am Generalmajor von Elbing and I am to take this woman to Luftwaffe Headquarters. She is of great interest to the Reich and to my superiors. Hand her over, please.'

Coralie got a corner of her mouth free. Her man – had Dietrich called him Kurt? – had a softer grip and must have decided she didn't need to be put in a wrestling hold.

She asked, '*Was tut er jetzt?*'

'Pulling rank. Let him get on with it.'

Dietrich was challenged again. One of the Gestapo – Reiniger, presumably – demanded, 'On whose orders, Generalmajor?'

'On the orders of the commander in chief of the Luftwaffe. On Reichsminister Göring's orders.'

'He isn't in Paris. I must know who gives you orders here.'

'Reichsminister Göring.' Dietrich remained polite, but with an edge. 'Are you questioning the instructions of the man who answers directly to the Führer?'

Silence. Had Dietrich overshot himself? Coralie couldn't see much, but she could hear Ottilia's frightened breathing.

Dietrich tried a more conciliatory tone: 'I suggest, Reiniger, you return with me to avenue Marigny and put your doubts to General Hanesse, my immediate superior. I should perhaps have explained that it was he who issued this order following a telephone call from Berlin.'

'I know the general. We'll take the woman away with us and call on him in the morning.'

'But the general is leaving Paris early tomorrow.' Dietrich made a thoughtful sound. 'Here's an idea. He will be dining at the Ritz, now, at his usual table. He won't object too strongly to our disturbing him, I'm sure. Let's go and find him.'

That seemed to be the secret code, the 'Open, Sesame.' Coralie heard the scuffle of shoes and at last saw a female shape in the darkness. The shape dissolved, but somebody moved fast towards it. A swing door bumped open and closed.

A car engine fired nearby. Ottilia was gone, but was she safe?

They waited, Coralie and the companion she had not yet seen. A muttered discussion took place among the Gestapo men, seasoned with profanities. At last, the swing doors bumped again, several times, and they were gone. The club's majordomo, the cashier and the cloakroom attendant crept out of a side-room. A low-powered light came on.

Coralie glanced up and screamed. The man beside her possessed a face out of a horror film. Much of one cheekbone and the jaw beneath had been cut away, flesh stretched over bone. Scar-like sutures showed where it had been stitched. The eye above, the right eye, was covered with a black patch.

A sardonic smile suggested that her reaction was not new. 'Oberleutnant Kurt Kleber, friend and colleague of Generalmajor von Elbing. And, no, I don't know where he's taking that lady, but I'm to conduct *you* to a safe house.'

That house turned out to be Ottilia's place on rue de Vaugirard. Coralie recalled Dietrich saying that he'd moved into a place 'special to us'.

Kleber helped Coralie from the staff car that had brought them from the club. Her ankle had swollen alarmingly.

'This house is Luftwaffe property,' Kleber said, misreading her hesitation. 'The Gestapo will not force their way in.' He took her arm. 'You are all right? You are not wearing shoes.'

'I turned my ankle, like an idiot.'

Kleber helped her inside to the lift. They ascended to the second floor, where she'd come so often with Dietrich in the summer of 1937. Preparing to hobble around packing cases, Coralie was astonished to find the flat bare, a pristine blue carpet covering the floorboards.

'What happened to all the crates?'

Kleber helped her to a sofa. 'Do you mean the art collection that was stored here? Generalmajor von Elbing shipped it out as soon as he moved in downstairs. I saw the last few crates being loaded up.'

'Where was it sent?'

'You will have to ask him.' Kleber brought up a footstool and talked of sending for a doctor.

'Cold water and cloths will do.' When he came back with them, she asked, 'Where has Dietrich taken my friend?'

'I really cannot say. Is there anything I can bring you to make your stay here more comfortable?'

She felt like saying, 'My daughter,' but in the end requested an aspirin, toiletries, some garment to sleep in. Oh, and something to eat. She was anxious about Noëlle, Ottilia, Una and herself. Yet, somehow, ravenous. 'Who lives in this flat?'

'Nobody. I share the one downstairs with Dietrich. Two other personnel were here for a while, but they've been put back on active duty. I expect you could do with a drink.' Kleber reached into a sideboard and brought out a bottle of pale spirit. 'Kirsch?'

'If it'll help the pain go away.'

He handed her a glass, saying, 'We have met before.'

'I don't think so.' She'd have remembered.

'Oh, we have. You came with Dietrich to the German pavilion at the Expo, though we weren't introduced. You were wearing pink.'

'I was. You're right.' And the shock of seeing Dietrich and two well-dressed men exchanging Nazi salutes had never left her. Neither stranger had looked remotely like this unfortunate fellow, however.

A smile moved one side of Kurt Kleber's face. 'I have changed, I hardly need say. I was caught in an explosion. Perhaps you will remember if I say that I was the elder of the two who met Dietrich, the less handsome one.'

'Is the other man here too?'

'No, at war.' Kleber topped up her glass and promised he'd telephone Luftwaffe HQ opposite, and ask for a dinner to be brought from the kitchens there.

'What about the Corvets, the concierge and his wife? Don't they still live here?'

Kleber looked blank. 'German staff come in daily from across the road to clean. Apart from that, we look after ourselves. Never fear, there is a bed freshly made up. Shall I show you? No? Very well. I will bid you goodnight.'

He clicked his heels and left.

Coralie stayed on the sofa, emptying her glass sip by sip. Kurt Kleber had called this a 'safe house' but that could mean anything, depending on the motives of the people operating it. If Dietrich was really her enemy, she was in deep trouble, but she felt less afraid of him now. Serge Martel, on the other hand . . . an informant. A collaborator. A smiling enemy. As she knocked back the last of her drink, she tested her ankle. The cold compress had done some good and she made it to the bathroom. She wanted to wash away the smell of the Rose Noire, and all traces of the enemy's touch.

Chapter Twenty-two

There is a particular sound a person makes when slipping back into a steaming bathtub. Coralie made that sound, then felt guilty. Noëlle might be awake, calling for her. Even so, she admitted, as she lathered soap into a flannel, a few moments' bliss would not bring down the sky.

Curls wrapped in a towel turban, she was half asleep when the sound of a key turning in a lock roused her.

She heard, '*Guten Abend!*' A man's voice. Someone bringing her dinner? She'd assumed the domestic staff at Luftwaffe HQ would be female, but thinking about it, they were much more likely to be military stewards. She lay absolutely still, except that she pushed the big toe of her uninjured foot into the cold-water tap to stop its loud, giveaway drip.

There came a light rap at the door. 'Take your time, Coralie. Dinner will arrive in half an hour.'

'Dietrich?'

'I'm leaving clothes for you, from Ottilia's cupboard. She will not mind as you are such good friends now.' He spoke French, rather haltingly. 'Unless, of course, you wish to dine in that very revealing evening dress.'

A note of insecurity? She asked, 'Is Ottilia with you?'

'No, and I am not going to tell you where she is. I shall be in the sitting room, waiting.'

He'd chosen a black Javier dress in knitted silk, with a same-fabric belt. 'He probably thinks nuns overdress,' she muttered, as she put it on. But once she saw herself in a mirror, she admitted she looked like a grown-up Frenchwoman. Autumn–winter, five years old, she judged. A dress from the era of sleek hair and near-masculine restraint.

She took peony-pink lipstick from her evening bag. 'We're all wearing mouths big this year,' she informed her reflection. Stroking mascara into her eyebrows to darken them, she added, 'The day I'm seen all in black is when I'm lying in an ebony coffin.' She'd taken off her doll-hat to bathe, and now she put it back on. Hot-pink feathers clashed with her lipstick.

Shame about the ankle, which looked like a piano leg.

She found Dietrich sprawled on the sofa, as in happier days, staring into a glass of wine. *That* had not been his habit before. He'd only ever drunk wine at table.

'Knock, knock,' she called gently from the doorway. He stood up, saying, without inflection, 'I would know you anywhere, Coralie.'

'You look more yourself too.'

He'd changed from uniform to a suit of pale grey-blue, a white shirt and a dark blue tie. Conservative, but human.

'Come, sit down,' he said.

'You'll have to help.' She displayed her tender ankle. 'I did it running after your friends in the club.'

'They are not my friends.'

'You speak the same language.' She sank gratefully on to the sofa. 'I don't know how I'm going to manage. I hate the Métro and buses are rarer than camels in Paris because you lot have nicked all the fuel.'

He did not rise to the jibe. 'You had better get a bicycle, then.'

She couldn't hold back a gurgle of amusement. 'Very sensible.'

'A bicycle will give you freedom.'

'Freedom. I wonder. Pour me another glass of kirsch.'

They sat side by side, nursing their drinks, like strangers who have arrived at a cocktail party on the wrong night. Living in a crowded house, Coralie's ears had grown used to constant background noise. Truth be told, she'd never been good with silence, awkward or contemplative. 'Please tell me that Ottilia's all right.'

Dietrich put down his glass and held out his hands, palm up. 'Do you see blood?'

'Proves nothing. Even Jack the Ripper washed his hands, I should think.'

He gave a sardonic nod. 'You have still an answer for every occasion, like the drummer boy clashing a cymbal after the music has stopped.' He frowned. 'That was badly constructed, but I spoke not a word of French for three years.'

'Well, you're in the right place to brush it up.'

He ignored that too. 'From boulevard de Clichy, I took Ottilia to the house of somebody I trust. In a day or so, that person will take her to another place of safety. I will learn that location when I need to. It is how these things work.'

Coralie knew that. Arkady and Florian had been moved around Paris in similar style until the police had stopped looking for them. 'How was Tilly?'

'Tilly? Oh, Ottilia. Quiet. You had drugged her.'

'No, but . . .' She mentioned her suspicion that Ottilia had found sleeping tablets in somebody else's bathroom. 'And then we made her drink champagne.'

'So. She will sleep, which is the best thing. But why to God did you take her to a nightclub that is a hive of Abwehr and SS?'

Gulping kirsch was her excuse not to answer. She wasn't about to divulge machinations, which, in a colder light, felt every bit as ill-advised as Ramon had judged them to be. Had Dietrich not arrived when he had, Ottilia would now be in Gestapo custody. She and Una might be in the neighbouring cell. Their only triumph: to flush Serge Martel out of the shadows.

'Where is your daughter?'

'In bed, I hope.' She wasn't going to discuss Noëlle. 'When you came up the stairs behind me at the Rose Noire, you said, "I can't save both of you." May I assume that your intentions towards me are honourable?'

'I would not say that.'

Without intending it, they'd moved closer. Dietrich touched her jaw, a fingertip pressure that sent a ripple into her stomach. She looked into his eyes, distinguishing the brown flecks from the green and the gold. If she was going to get under his skin . . . Did she want to? No. Not under, *against*. Dietrich was no more indifferent to her than she was to him. If she were to lean nearer, trace the hard line of his mouth . . . what were the odds that he'd pull her to him and kiss her?

That was what the old Coralie would have done, but she'd outgrown factory-girl manners. She'd learned how to sit with modest allure. To walk with her hips forward, head high, eyes soft . . . Tempting to put it to the test, to find an excuse to move about the room, but her piano-leg ankle kiboshed that. 'Your friend Kurt reminded me that we'd met before.'

'He has been through Hell. As have I.'

He sounded so remorseless, so bitter, that it was easy to re-dress him in his uniform. To remind herself that, during the last war, he'd fired on British pilots, and would doubtless have been doing so in this war had he been a few years younger. They must not become lovers. Innocence had gone. 'Nice and roomy in here,' she said, thinking, Tease him. Laugh at him. Remember how he hates it? 'Heavy job, was it, getting all those crates down the stairs?'

'Are you asking me where the von Silberstrom collection has gone?'

'You can't blame me for being curious.'

'I don't. Not for that . . .' He left the comment dangling. 'It is safe.'

'Who from?'

'A good question.' He got up and went to the window. Not to look out: it was pitch dark, shutters and curtains drawn. He was putting space between them. 'What would you think if I told you that the collection is awaiting inspection by my old comrade, Göring, for his personal acquisition? That what he does not want will be sent to Germany, as a gift to the Führer?'

'I'd think Teddy Clisson was right. That you're a swindler.'

'Teddy is too kind. What if I were to tell you that all the pieces by Jewish artists and the degenerate works of all races will either be burned or sold to fund the Reich?'

She stood up, and hot pins burst in her shin. 'I would remind you of a bookshop on rue de l'Odéon where you told me that, in Germany, they burned copies of *A Farewell to Arms* because it challenged narrow thinking.' Had she hit home? Impossible to tell. 'What about those Dürer engravings Teddy wanted so badly? I suppose they've been spirited into safe-keeping.'

She'd surprised him with the memory. 'They too are safe,' he said.

Staying upright took real determination, but she wanted to say her next words while looking him in the eye. 'You damn Nazi.'

Dietrich came towards her, anger in every line, but before he reached her, a knock came, followed by 'Hello!'

Another knock, at the door to the room they were in. Coralie suspected Dietrich was grateful for the interruption.

'*Komm herein!*'

A man in uniform entered, carrying a tray covered with a white cloth. Dietrich indicated he should take it through to the dining room. After the man had left, he offered his arm to Coralie and said, with a hint of mockery, 'Shall we go in to dinner? We will be gossiped about, you know. Not because we are together, alone, but because it astonishes German chefs to be asked to cook so late.'

She'd never been inside the dining room before. It had previously been full of boxes. It was a pleasant room, with striped wallpaper, shutters fixed back, the window open to let in a night breeze. Chairs and the table were of lime-washed wood, a provincial Louis Quinze style similar to some that Teddy Clisson owned. The steward had left the candles unlit, and they agreed to stay in darkness so they could enjoy the open window. Coralie lifted the lid of a chafing dish and what she saw flummoxed her. 'What are those?'

'*Spätzle*. They're *Knüdeln*. "Noodles", I think, in English.'

'Dumplings, you mean?'

'Without a dictionary, I couldn't swear it. They are dropped into boiling water, then cooked in melted butter and I grew up on them.'

The main part of the meal was a *Rouladen*, a flank of beef rolled around bacon, dill pickles and a grainy mustard. The vegetable was red cabbage cooked with apple, and the combination of sweet, savoury and sharp was utterly intriguing. Coralie would have cleared her plate twice had she not been wearing a dress with a belt.

Dietrich had opened a bottle of wine, whose label announced it to be from a vineyard in the Rhône region, near Avignon. Rich and beautifully balanced, it tasted a world away from the *vin ordinaire* that was all she could buy. Last September's wine harvest had gone ahead in the regions unaffected by the carnage of battle. France was still a great wine producer, but the Germans were getting the best stuff.

'"Where blind and naked ignorance delivers brawling judgments, unashamed . . ."'

'Hey?' His words confused her, partly because he'd spoken English.

'Tennyson, *The Idylls of the King*,' he elucidated. 'Did I tell you I studied at Oxford University, as a Rhodes scholar?'

'You didn't tell me much about yourself at all. Did I tell you I studied at Magdalen College?'

'Magdalen, Oxford?' Only he pronounced it 'Maudlin'.

'Magdalen Street, Bermondsey. Let's see if I can remember something . . . "Don't Care didn't care, Don't Care was wild. Don't Care stole plum and pear, Like any beggar's child." You always used to grow more poetic as the night wore on, I seem to recall.'

'As the night wore on? How will this one end?'

'How would you like it to end?' Blame the wine, her fingers crept across the table to meet his. It had to be the wine. He was despicable and she didn't want him.

And he did not want her, patently, because he left the room. He came back after a few moments with an attaché case, which he put on the table, shooting the clips. Attaché cases were the world's greatest passion-killers, she thought, after bloomers and dirty nails.

After closing the blackout curtains and lighting the candles, he took out a letter. 'You stole from me. I should have taken more care as I had early warning of your habit.'

She couldn't deny it. She'd taken a key from his pocket then a letter, the one he placed like an accusation on the table. Even upside down, she recognised the ruler-straight address and the German stamp. Returning to his seat, Dietrich waited for her to speak, hands clasped. The ruby on his middle finger glowed in the candlelight.

Dodge the opening punch, get a quick one back. Donal's advice. 'You broke into my house yesterday. Kicked the doors in.'

He admitted it without hesitation. 'You were hiding in the roof.' At her reaction, a string of swearing, something like laughter rippled through him. 'You are no Houdini. Where else would you hide? Besides, indents in the hall carpet suggested that an attic ladder had just been pulled up, but the most compelling evidence? Teacups on the table.'

'Maybe I don't like washing up.'

'But you do like your tea, and in these days of empty shelves, I cannot see you leaving a cup unfinished, unless forced to escape. Had you had let me and Kleber in, we wouldn't have had to break your locks. We could have taken Ottilia and saved you much distress.'

'Why didn't you tap on the ceiling?'

He thought about it. 'Had I been alone, I would. To get a panicking Ottilia through a hatch safely or with dignity . . . no.'

'Not much care for my dignity when you questioned me at the Lutetia.' *Crossing my legs for hours.* 'You were bloody uncivilised.' Dangerous words, because she read a matching volatility in Dietrich. Were they to erupt at the same moment—

Dietrich slid the letter towards her, but kept his hand upon it. 'Before I forget, you really should not leave the dial to your wireless set at the frequency for Radio Londres. BBC broadcasts are prohibited and the penalty for listening—'

'Is having your ears shot off by firing-squad, I should think. You buggers are making forty new laws a week, but thanks for reminding me about that one.'

'Listen to Radio Paris instead.'

'And put up with Pétain telling us how much in charge he is?'

'It plays perfectly good music.'

'It plays propaganda. We're supposed to sing "Oh, How We All Love The Germans" to the tune of "Yes, We Have No Bananas".'

'Shut up, Coralie. This letter, how much did you read?'

'The opening line, *"Mein lieber Vater"*. No more, I swear it. I don't even know which of your children sent it. I never got to tell you, but I'd learned a bit of German so I could have had a stab at reading the lot, but it was private. It was yours.'

'And yet you opened it. You have no idea how wrong that was.' He came to stand beside her, took her face in his hands. She felt the band of his ring at the side of her mouth. Then against her temple. She flinched as he drew out hatpins and removed the dainty hat, turning it in his hands. 'This is a ridiculous pretension.'

'It's my living.'

'And you want to live.'

'I have to survive. I have a child.'

'Ah, yes, a child. You want to live for her and you want your child to live.'

Of course she did!

'And yet you should count your life in hours. Serge Martel knows you are English.'

She experienced a sensation that was becoming familiar. The

constriction of the throat, the feeling of insects crawling through the veins. 'He only suspects—'

'He *knows*. We watched you tonight, Kurt and I, from the darkest corner of the club. You, your sophisticated friend and Ottilia, and those Waffen-SS idiots. Martel slithered up to us.' Dietrich adopted an unctuous tone: '"Monsieur le Comte, Herr Kleber, such an honour. How extraordinary, your *petite amie* is also here. But different tables? No quarrel, I trust?" His breath is a kind of poison. "Is it Mademoiselle's alien status that is perhaps distasteful to you? How well she hides her English birth, *hein*?"'

'You must have told him, then. Nobody else ever knew.'

'I have never told, Coralie. It has to be your lapse, your carelessness.'

'So what will you do?'

'Martel hopes I will reward him for silence. He plans a little blackmail, I think. It would solve the problem if I took you to eighty-four avenue Foch myself and turned you over to the Gestapo.'

'You hate me that much?'

'Ten lifetimes could not dispel what I feel towards you.'

'This letter . . . I shouldn't have opened it . . . No, it was hiding it, wasn't it? That was the very wrong thing.'

He returned the letter to the attaché case, shutting the lid with aggressive clicks. 'Goodnight.'

She couldn't get up quickly enough to follow so she turned in her chair. 'Tell me why.'

But he was gone, and she was left contemplating the remains of dinner. To her astonishment, she slept deeply that night and woke as the midday sun blared through a gap in the curtains. She found a letter outside her bedroom door.

rue de Vaugirard, 1 a.m.
14 July

Dear Coralie

Had I more self-command I would have stayed. Did you
really believe I might turn you in to the Gestapo? No, I
am not so debased. I doubt Serge Martel will denounce
you either, as he perceives you to be under my protection.
Should you ever be questioned, I have few qualms, as you
stood up well to my interrogation. I am obliged to leave
Paris, so have arranged for a car to take you home. Before
then I must – I need – to make you understand the grievous
wound you inflicted. Be brave enough to take breakfast
with me, around eight o'clock.

Dietrich

Eight o'clock . . . She found her watch. Only four hours too late.

Chapter Twenty-three

~~~~~~

La Passerinette reopened on 3 September 1940, a full year after the outbreak of war. The hats Coralie had snatched back from Henriette Junot drew a stampede. She'd added black gauze and feathers to the pink models and her customers were enchanted by this departure from the usual autumn tans and russets. Journalists mingled with clients at the reopening party. Fewer pages and ersatz paper took away the gloss, but magazines thrummed with the latest ideas and were desperate to tell their readers how to be chic with less.

As for the doll-hats, Coralie was selling all that the Ginslers could make. The response had initially been cautious, so Coralie had recruited Una, who had not only survived that night at the Rose Noire, but now had a Waffen-SS *Sturmführer* among her troupe of official admirers. 'All above board, hands above the table. He will never put a toe over my threshold, and take that how you please.'

Una had moved back into avenue Foch, picking up the reins of her social life. She was again a leader of fashion *and* a nursing heroine. Having declared that 'To wear a hat no larger than a teacake is not only modish but patriotic', she had established the doll-hat craze in under a week.

They proved popular with German soldiers, who discovered that they could buy an authentic Paris hat small enough to send home to a wife or lover in the regular mail-transport. Men in uniform queued down boulevard de la Madeleine. At the end of September, Coralie deposited twelve thousand francs at the Crédit Lyonnais bank. One day, she hoped, it would find its way to Ottilia.

Of Dietrich, she'd heard nothing since finding that letter outside her bedroom door. She guessed that he had taken her absence at breakfast as a slight.

She thought of him, however, every time she set off to work on her new bicycle. She'd been wobbly at first, horrified to find herself cheek by jowl with cars and vans. The streets were a battle zone, military troop trucks demanding right of way, French vehicles snarling with frustration. Many drivers had attempted to overcome the fuel shortage by converting their vehicles to run on *gazogène* burners that consumed wood and charcoal and belched out smog. Coralie would carve through the chaos, competing with high-stepping trap-pulling ponies for the bit of space granted to them.

She found her confidence, however, and soon she was flying the four kilometres between home and shop twice daily. She created her own style *à la bicyclette*. A short jacket, comfortable culottes, ankle socks, a silk square to keep her hair in place and a hatbox in her front basket. Free advertising. Arkady had attached a klaxon to her handlebars. Friendly shopkeepers would get a toot, and so would German troopers taking breakfast in their *Soldatenheime*. Coralie was happy – as happy as anyone in hungry Paris could be. She was busy and successful and she felt safe. Even though he was absent, Dietrich had somehow erected a protective screen between her and those who might seek to betray her. Noëlle was thriving in the care of a new nanny, and Coralie had her flat to herself again, Arkady having joined Una at avenue Foch.

'As doorkeeper and friend,' Una insisted, though Coralie suspected more. Perhaps the difference in their ages and the social gulf between them made them wary of revealing too much.

One morning in mid-October, Kurt Kleber called at La Passerinette. Would Coralie make a hat for his wife as a surprise? She would be joining him shortly in Paris. His clear eye softened as he spoke his wife's name, and Coralie thought, My God, lucky girl.

Unfortunately, it hadn't occurred to Kurt to find out his wife's measurements. 'She is a little like you in looks, Mademoiselle de Lirac. Well, blonde, anyway.'

'Have you a photograph at least, so I can see the shape of her face?'

'Naturally I have picture of Fritzi.' In his pocket book, next to his heart.

Coralie pinned it to her work-board and created a hat by empathy. When Kurt called back to check progress, he thought the result magnificent. He paid her in occupation currency, which had twenty times the value of the franc, and gave a delivery address on avenue Marigny. 'This is General Hanesse's headquarters, where I have taken an apartment more suitable for a married couple. Did you know Dietrich is back at rue de Vaugirard? You must have thought him a stupidly long time in Switzerland. I did, I can tell you. Will you not call on him?'

So, he'd been to neutral Switzerland. She'd love to ask why, but pride stopped her. And, no, she wouldn't call.

Kurt decoded her expression. 'I wish you would. I saw how proud Dietrich was when he brought you to our pavilion. I saw him look at you. I have known him several years, but never truly happy until then.'

'It didn't last. He left me.'

'You know why?'

'Not really, but, look, I've customers waiting.' She pulled open the door, eager to get Kurt through it. 'I'll have a delivery lad bring the hat as soon as it's done. Tell Frau Kleber to pop in – I'll show her how to wear it and we'll adjust the sizing.' She watched Kurt go. Nice man, but she couldn't risk overstepping the line into friendship. Where was the line? It amused her to sell doll-hats at a thousand francs apiece to the boys in grey uniforms. As she handed over the little poplar-wood boxes, she'd say, 'Your sweetheart will think she's getting a French cheese. When she opens the box – *ooh, là là.*'

She'd hear herself vamping up the sexy accent and think, 'I'm no better than Serge Martel, taking their money with a synthetic smile.' It *was* collaboration, made worse because some of those boys genuinely believed that, in a matter of weeks, they'd be heading north to launch *Blitzkrieg* on England. Every saucy comment, every wad of occupation currency she accepted from a soldier's pocket, betrayed two countries. Liking Kurt Kleber wasn't collaboration, but visiting Dietrich in his flat was. The line was a wiggly one, but she saw it clearly enough.

A few days before the end of October, the roar of engines broke the early-evening peace. A moment later, two glowering youths thrust open the door, barged in and shouted, 'You have Jewesses working here.'

Coralie stepped between them and the client she was serving. Actually, she had just appointed two new backroom assistants, Paulette and Didi Benoît, French-born Catholics. And it was absolutely no business of these louts. 'Get out,' she said.

One of them waved a brick. 'This is going through your window if you're lying.'

Red mist descended. She was not Jac Masson's daughter for nothing. Grabbing the youth's hand, Coralie made the brick collide with his nose. She shouted over his howls, 'Out of my shop, you nasty little shits!' and reached for her scissors. Left-handed scissors Una had given her last spring to celebrate her first collection. 'Out, or I'll slice a hole in your face big enough to post your sodding brick through.'

They backed out, just as one of Coralie's regular clients arrived, escorted by the German officer she was having an affair with. The officer demanded to know what was going on.

The uninjured youth, whose accent and *argot* linked him to the backstreets of Montmartre, made a form of salute and thrust out a card. 'We can do what we like!'

The German inspected the card, shrugged and handed it back, explaining later to Coralie, 'They're with our police.'

'They've joined the Gestapo?'

He made a 'sort of' noise. 'They're under Gestapo protection.'

'So they *can* do what they like?'

Yes, pretty much, was the answer. From that moment, Coralie truly understood that there were two enemies: uniformed Germans with their obsession for new rules and counting '*Ein, zwei, drei!*' as they entered buildings in tight formation, and the home-grown scum, who were finding undreamed-of power and were answerable to nobody. Her new-found happiness and feelings of safety drained away.

The last day of October, All Saints' Day, was a Thursday and quiet. Coralie was sitting over the books with Madame Thomas, sharing a small desk in a corner of the salon. Jeanne Thomas had asked if she might work downstairs because it was warmer than in her flat upstairs. Coralie had agreed because, though nobody said so, they felt safer if they were all bunched together.

As Madame Thomas ruled lines down a clean page of her

ledger, Coralie discreetly eavesdropped on Violaine – or, more particularly, Violaine's new client. A stunning girl with the figure of a fashion mannequin, she'd strolled into the salon with a German companion, announcing loftily that 'darling Rudi' had been recommended to this place by 'darling Jakob', who turned out to be the officer who had helped see off the brick-carrying youths.

Violaine had invited Rudi to make himself comfortable on the sofa, before pulling out a chair at one of the mirror-tables and inviting the newcomer, 'If Mademoiselle would please sit here?'

Mademoiselle had insisted on having the table turned around so that her back was to the window. Perhaps she wanted to gaze on her German prize, or was she even a little nervous of him? Rudi cut an imposing figure in his Stygian-black SS uniform, ice-blue eyes radiating a combination of blankness and rigid discipline.

'. . . must make provision for tax, of course, Mademoiselle de Lirac.'

'Sorry, Madame Thomas?'

'You have made a profit, so must pay tax.'

'Yes, of course. Better to pay a little extra than too little.' The German Revenue imposed heavy penalties for errors and defaults. Coralie's eyes drifted back to Violaine's lady customer, who said sharply, 'Don't stare at me. And don't you stare either, Rudi. Read a newspaper, why don't you? Will you find him one?' She clicked her fingers in Coralie's direction.

Coralie rose, with what she hoped was quiet dignity. 'Of course, Mademoiselle. French or German?'

'German, obviously.'

Coralie bought two newspapers each day, the *Allgemeiner Zeitung* and *Le Figaro*. After passing the *Zeitung* over, she walked back to her place, passing behind Violaine, who was lifting their customer's lustrous black hair to reveal the shape of her head. Rude and uppity she might be, Coralie thought, but this name-less young woman possessed the kind of neck poets write about. Only – Coralie gasped – her left ear looked as if it had been eaten by rats. The girl tensed and Coralie passed on.

Watching Madame Thomas print '31 October' at the head of her new page, Coralie murmured, 'Ramon's birthday.' She'd been planning to buy him a packet of cigarettes and take Noëlle to see him. And, if she were honest, to look over his new woman. But she'd bumped into Bonnet last Sunday at the quai de Montebello and had not quite recovered from something he'd told her. She and Noëlle had been looking for story books among the stalls. Bonnet had been selling some of his own books, and he'd broken off from haggling to greet her. 'Ramon's lady! And Ramon's child?'

She'd introduced Noëlle.

Bonnet had shaken his head. 'A fool, Ramon leaving you for that piece he's with now. Oh, she's pretty enough but she's out every night and, *mon Dieu*, they argue. The language. She slams out, and I hear her tap-tap-tap down the street. He runs after her . . .' Bonnet had mimed a man desperately in love '. . . "I cannot live without you, Julie!"'

'Julie who?'

Bonnet didn't know. 'There are thousands of Julies in Paris.'

True, and even Ramon would not have stolen a friend's girl. Or his child's former nanny . . . She'd stooped to questioning Noëlle. 'Was Papa's lady-friend nice when you stayed with him that time?'

'No lady, just Papa.'

So, he'd got rid of 'Julie' for the day, had he? Keep away from

rue Valdonne, good sense told Coralie. Some things it's better
not to know.

Madame Thomas closed her ledger. 'Lunchtime – and look
at that rain.' A slanting downpour, the boulevard dark with
umbrellas. But, then, it was November tomorrow, the threshold
of winter. What would this one would bring? Shivering under
blankets, chapped hands and chilblains. Frozen bodies brought
out of unheated apartments?

'Shall I tell Paulette and Didi to take their lunch now?'
Madame Thomas asked.

'Of course. Violaine will be a while and I'll have mine when
you come back.' Coralie stayed at the table, running her eye down
Madame Thomas's figures, but when the door shuddered open,
she looked up in alarm, fearing another brick. A lone man stood
in the doorway. Even worse than youthful bullyboys, it was Serge
Martel.

Martel, standing in her light, his hat and the wide shoulders
of his jacket dark with moisture. Coralie rose, and forced a smile.
This man had power, and she had a little girl to protect. 'All this
way in the rain, Monsieur Martel? Not running your car, these
days?'

'I like to walk sometimes, to stroll in the park.'

'Really?' She doubted it, somehow. That pale hair and the
paint-water eyes belonged in basements, or in a prison cell. She
tried to think of something to say that didn't involve the Rose
Noire or Ottilia, whose wraith shivered between them. In the
end, she said, 'Vichy loved the Vagabonds, Arkady told me. The
management of that club they played in keeps trying to rebook
them. Will you let them go?'

'Maybe they can have them. I can have my pick of the best
jazz quartets now.'

'Being nice' snapped. 'No, you can't. Not since the round-up of black musicians.' Dezi Rice had gone and she'd wept for him. He'd been walking away from a cabaret in Montmartre when a windowless van had stopped beside him. Raised voices, the slam of doors. People called those vans Salad Wagons – maybe because victims were tossed inside them. 'The best jazz quartets are at Drancy now, awaiting deportation to nobody knows where.' Only the luckiest had got on America-bound ships before the round-ups started. 'Stick with Arkady. Loyalty means that when you need friends you have some.'

'Recognise this?' Serge Martel dropped Ottilia's British aliens' card on Madame Thomas's ledger. Its fibre-board was swollen from its drowning in a lavatory cistern, but the information inside was clear, the photograph sharp. 'You hid a wanted woman instead of delivering her to the authorities.'

'Who found this?'

'Julie.'

'You mean my Julie?'

'*My* Julie. She knows how to keep me sweet.' Martel pinched Coralie's ear, which hurt because he had found the part where the nerves were close to the surface. He continued, 'We can help each other. You give me information about a certain man's activities. I, in return, tell those in authority that you are an innocent dupe.'

So, Ramon was his target. She'd better get a message to him, fast. 'I'm not an informant. You've picked the wrong woman.'

'I get a pat on the back from Major Reiniger, you get to live.'

'As I said, I'm not an informant.'

'Your little girl has Maman to kiss her goodnight, not a hard-fisted bitch in a state institution. If you're arrested, your kid will go to an orphanage. Did you know that the matrons in those places sometimes sell little girls to supplement their wages. Sell them to men who pass them around until they end up dead.'

'You are obscene.'

'Mm. So there it is. Give me information, and I'll keep a nice table for you at my club. "The best champagne for Mademoiselle de Lirac, Félix. Hurry up, you arthritic old slob." Deal?'

'I'll hand over my husband when Hell freezes.'

Pale eyes blinked. 'Cazaubon? You think I want your wind-up Bolshevist?' Martel spat.

Violaine turned and said, 'What is happening? Mademoiselle de Lirac?'

'Nothing. We're having a chat.'

Martel leaned so close that Coralie smelt acetic acid on his breath. Félix Peyron had confided once that his boss ate only red meat. 'I don't want your husband. I want Dietrich, Graf von Elbing. And if you don't give him to me . . .' He sang the opening bars of a familiar song. " Tell me its name, *Miss* de Lirac.'

'"The Lambeth Walk . . ."' She pronounced 'Lambeth' as a Frenchwoman would and he gave a bow, acknowledging her bravado.

'An Englishwoman who aids Jews, your life will be finished. Think about it.' On his way to the door, he cut behind Violaine, staring into the mirror at the face reflected there. 'Good God, Solange Antonin, back in town and in good company.' Oblivious of the shocked response his greeting provoked, or perhaps enjoying it, Martel stared into the mirror. He departed, leaving the door for somebody else to close.

I have to find Dietrich, Coralie thought.

Chapter Twenty-four

How to get away when Mademoiselle Antonin had flown into a frenzy and her escort was waving his pistol at anybody passing the door? Violaine fetched smelling salts and calmed down her client. Coralie was about to slip out of the door when it opened to admit a tall, thin man, in a yellow-brown suit, who shook his umbrella over the step.

'Teddy, you're back!' Made stupid by shock, Coralie blurted out, 'That suit is a horrible colour.'

Thierry-Edgar Clisson looked a little taken aback. 'Caramel. Made in Algiers and it brings back memories of sunshine. Good day to you too.'

'Your hair's grown.'

'One does not trust those country barbers. I returned from my place at Dreux only yesterday. As we're being personal, what a singular hat.' Teddy raised imaginary opera glasses to Coralie's head. 'A bonbon dish adorned by a pink water-lily . . . Are crowns and brims out of fashion? And who do we have here?'

Teddy turned an appreciative glance at Rudi, who had holstered his pistol but remained defensive. 'Waffen SS? Such fetching uniforms you boys wear. Of course, one can never go wrong with black in town.' Turning back to Coralie, who was mouthing, *Don't!* he said, 'Are you free, dearest? I have a perfect surprise for you.'

She began, 'I can't—' but a little whirlwind burst in shouting, 'Maman! Oncle Teddy is taking us for lunch!'

Coralie's new nanny, Micheline, followed, her raincoat splashed as high as the pockets. She was a dark young woman with country-fed prettiness but Nature had not formed her for running. As she spoke, she hauled up the brassière straps that had given way under stress. 'Madame, may we?'

Everything fled from Coralie's mind but Serge Martel's vile threats. 'You let Noëlle run alone in the street? Anybody could have taken her!' They could have passed that monster just moments before. 'I entrust her to you, Micheline. *Trust*—'

Teddy squeezed her arm, rather hard. 'Noëlle was never out of our sight and, my dear, you're upsetting your child far more than I or Micheline ever could.'

So she was. She held out her arms and Noëlle rocketed into them. 'I'm sorry, so sorry. You too, Micheline. I overreacted.'

'Not at all, Madame.' The girl looked stricken. 'You are right, we forget from time to time, but things are different now.'

'Can I have ice-cream for pudding, Maman? You always buy me ice-cream when you're cross.'

Solange Antonin emerged from her mute state to say, 'If that were my little girl, I would take lunch with her every day and buy her four ice-creams.'

'Four? Yes, please!' Noëlle shrieked.

Coralie heard herself agreeing that lunch would indeed be perfect. 'If you can find any ice-creams in Paris, precious, I *will* buy you four. Let me just put my coat on.'

'And change your hat,' Teddy called after Coralie. 'Unless, like a real water-lily, it closes up in the wet.'

In the workroom, she put on a trench coat and exchanged her doll-hat for a brown felt fedora, tying a waxed silk head-square over it to protect it from the rain. The telephone she'd inherited from Lorienne Royer sat, shiny black and mahogany, in a corner and she wished she knew Dietrich's number. She ought to send a note to Ramon too. Martel had not implicitly threatened her husband, but even so . . . *my Julie*, her Julie, Ramon's Julie, everybody's blessed Julie. If Ramon and Martel were involved with the same Julie, there would be trouble.

Hearing Paulette and Didi returning from lunch, she ripped a sheet from an old invoice book. One of them could take a note to rue Valdonne. What to put, though? Nothing too overt in case the girl was stopped. Coralie chewed her pencil, then wrote: 'Ramon, some gardening advice . . .'

'Unless you have somewhere particular in mind, can we go south of the river?'

Teddy threw Coralie a quizzical look. 'Of course, but only if we take the Métro. I've always considered walking in the rain an overrated pastime, and a certain young lady,' he meant Noëlle who was jumping in puddles, her rubber boots landing each time with a fat splash, 'has no respect for pale shades of trouser.'

He took them to a favourite restaurant on the south side of the Jardin du Luxembourg, choosing an outside table under a waterproof awning. The menu was short – three dishes and no mention of ice-cream or any dessert.

Coralie settled down for a two-hour recess. Teddy's lunches were always long. She chose blue-cheese omelette, her appetite rising at the prospect of eggs. But it was obvious from the first forkful that the eggs had been watered down. As for cheese, somebody had waved a grater over the top. Where once there'd have been golden sautéed potatoes and crisp lettuce, her plate was bulked out with macaroni and more of the interminable haricot beans. Watching Noëlle tuck into strips of pink-braised liver while keeping up a conversation with Teddy and Micheline, Coralie thought, She chose better than I did. I have a raised a perfect little French girl, mannerly, epicurean and chic. And if Serge Martel harms one atom of her, I will tear him to pieces.

'. . . how delightful. I adore coincidence though what one generally calls "coincidence" is either statistical inevitability or bad luck.' Teddy was rising from his seat, extending a hand, and Coralie fought her way back from murderous thoughts.

Somebody spoke her name. 'You,' she said.

'I had wondered if Paris had swallowed you up,' was Dietrich's inscrutable reply. 'Teddy, my good friend, how are you? And?'

Coralie made the introduction. 'Mademoiselle Hascoët, my nanny.'

Dietrich was in uniform and Micheline threw Coralie a shocked look. 'And this lady?' Dietrich asked. 'Is this perhaps Noëlle?' He took off a leather glove and put out his hand. Noëlle took it in both hers, her fingers curling over his. He said, 'You are a beautiful child. Eyes as dark as a woodland floor and as bright as an otter's. Noëlle Una Cazaubon.'

Coralie tensed: she was back in the Lutetia, watching Dietrich note down her daughter's name.

'Do you speak French like a native, little Noëlle?'

Noëlle gave Dietrich an unswerving stare and replied, '*Hering, hering, fass wie Göring*.'

Dietrich tossed Coralie a silent question.

'We . . . overheard it in a restaurant. Army officers – yours.' They'd heard the phrase on Radio Londres, actually, in a satirical verse with a German chorus, comparing Hitler's newly promoted *Reichsmarschall* to a bloated fish. From now on, the radio would stay off until Noëlle was asleep.

At Teddy's invitation, Dietrich joined them. He had been at Luftwaffe HQ all morning, he told them, dictating letters, but had been tempted out by the view from his window. 'There is something irresistible about a wet garden. Trees shine like polished candlesticks. Who would be shut indoors at such a moment?'

'Me,' said Teddy.

'You always were more cat than dog, Clisson. Will you permit me to order coffee?'

'If you mean that concoction of roast barley and stable-sweepings that passes for coffee, these days, no, thank you.'

'Ice-cream!' Noëlle shouted hopefully.

'I will ask.' Dietrich went inside. They couldn't see who he spoke to, but a few minutes later, a pot of excellent coffee came to the table, along with two *crème caramels* floating in a syrup of burned sugar. 'No ice-cream,' he told Noëlle, 'and they had only two *crèmes*, but they have provided three spoons.'

'Not for me,' Coralie said, though she'd have dived in had Teddy been the provider. Then, belatedly, 'Thank you.' She opened her handbag under the table, felt for a pencil and a scrap of paper and wrote, 'We have to talk.' She found Dietrich's hand and pushed the paper into his palm.

When it was time to leave, Dietrich said to Coralie, 'I will walk you home.'

Conscious of Micheline's glances and Teddy's snuffle of amusement, Coralie's courage failed. 'You don't need to. We'll take the Métro.'

'Go with the dear Graf,' Teddy urged. 'I shall linger over the last drops of nectar.' He meant his coffee. 'If I stay here long enough, a friend is bound to pass by.'

'And I might go to rue des Écoles,' Micheline said, 'to call on Florian. If you don't mind, Madame?'

'Not at all,' Coralie said. 'Give him our love.' Florian was a regular visitor now, having taken rooms near the university, a few streets away from rue de Seine. So many students had been called up, or had failed to come back from the exodus, that the building's owner had feared his property would be seized as a billet for German troops so he'd offered rooms to cash-strapped musicians. Micheline often spent her free afternoons listening to Florian, practising his guitar or dulcimer while she darned his clothes. 'They are falling off him and he doesn't know how to thread a needle,' she'd explained, and Coralie hoped that she wasn't about to lose a second nanny. Love was a gross domestic inconvenience, all told.

So it was Coralie, Dietrich and the child who set off across the park. The rain had stopped and the paths steamed in the golden afternoon sun, drifts of leaves giving off a smell of sweet decay. They took a meandering route toward the exit on rue de Vaugirard, and when Noëlle flagged, Dietrich swung her on to his shoulders.

At her door, Coralie took out a bright gold key, and couldn't resist checking Dietrich's reaction to it. He had yet to apologise for kicking her doors in, though she presumed it was he who had sent the carpenter to repair them. When she'd asked the workman who was paying him, the man had replied warily, 'One of *them.*'

Dietrich didn't notice her key, as Noëlle was pushing his cap over his eyes. He lifted her down and the moment the front door was open, she sped upstairs shouting, 'Tante Nou-Nou! Arkady! Papa!' because she still expected the house to be full of adults, even though Coralie had explained that they now lived alone. Dietrich stopped Coralie following.

'What did you wish to tell me?'

She described Serge Martel's visit. 'He thinks he has something on you and wants me to provide details.'

'And if you don't?'

'He will denounce me as an Englishwoman.'

'What do you imagine he has on me?'

She shook her head. 'He might think you've compromised yourself by helping Ottilia.'

'Perhaps I have.'

Not what she wanted to hear. She needed Dietrich to dismiss Martel's threats as the ramblings of a deluded narcissist. To say that he, Dietrich von Elbing, was one of an invincible elite, and that he cared enough for her to protect her and her child. But though he was looking at her, she felt he wasn't seeing her. He didn't even notice when the rain began again, a few drops at first, then a cloudburst.

'Can we go inside, please?'

Dietrich came back from his distant place. 'When I knew I was being posted to Paris, I hoped you would be here.'

Her heart skipped. He *was* hers still, in spite of the uniform and the overbearing manner. Afraid of his feelings, yes, but that was understandable. The world had changed. They had changed. 'Where else would I be? Come inside, please.'

'I hoped you would be here. I wanted to find you. To make you suffer. I wanted to make you feel the laceration of the soul that I endured and still endure every day.'

She gaped at his blasé brutality. 'You had your revenge at the Lutetia.'

'You believe so?' Like German officers of all branches of the army, he wore the *Schirmmütze*, the cap whose exaggeratedly high peak changed the proportions of the face. Rain slewed off its waterproof visor, darkening the stiff collar of his jacket, the ribbon of the swallow-tailed cross around his neck and the Iron Cross on his breast. He allowed her to pull him into the lobby and they stood facing each other at the foot of the stairs, a puddle forming around their feet.

'I believe it!' Coralie didn't trouble to keep her voice down. She hadn't seen her shopkeeper neighbours for months. They'd never reopened after the defeat of France, so she let her anger ring. 'I was in your power and had no idea if I would see –' her voice shook '– see my child again. I know I did a dreadful thing in taking that letter but you put me through the wringer and humiliated me. What else do you need to prove?' She pushed past him and climbed the stairs, pulling the headscarf off her hat because it was dripping down her neck. She heard the front door slam and thought, Good riddance.

He caught up with her at the turn of the stairs. 'What more to prove? I will tell you, Coralie, and you will hear me out.'

She strode on, unbuttoning her coat as she went, but she left the door to the flat ajar. She sensed it would be futile to shut him out. He might kick his way in again.

Throwing her dripping coat into the bath, putting her hat on the hallstand along with her keys, she went into the lounge. Noëlle was spinning in the middle of the floor, arms wide, squealing, 'Papa, Papa!'

Sprawled in an armchair, beret pulled down to one side, the neck of his sweater pulled up over his mouth, was Ramon. A glance behind revealed Dietrich putting his hat next to hers on the stand, removing his leather gloves. She hissed, 'Perfect timing!'

'Papa got bad tooth,' Noëlle chanted, still spinning.

Ramon got up, cradling his jaw. Dietrich came in. What could a soaking wet German officer and an anarchist with toothache say to each other? Nothing, it transpired.

'Ramon, come to the kitchen,' Coralie said tersely. 'Stay here, sweetheart,' to Noëlle. 'Play with your bricks. Herr von Elbing, please make yourself at home. I won't be a moment.'

The kitchen was just big enough for her and Ramon to get inside and close the door. He smelt of wet wool, of some sweet, female scent. 'Couldn't you have taken off your outdoor things before you sat down?'

'I'm soaked to the skin. I got your note.' Ramon pulled crumpled paper from his trouser pocket. '"Black Roses have the sharpest thorns and get everywhere." I suppose the "gardening advice" is to tell me that Julie has left me for Serge Martel?' He gave a humourless laugh. 'I did notice.'

'So you've been living with my Julie?' Seeing the answer in his eyes, she slapped him hard. And then remembered he had toothache. 'Sorry.'

'Yes, it's true, but it's over. Julie went to Martel last night, bags packed, even though I warned her what he was. I told her, "He's a Gestapo lapdog," but she laughed in my face. Her parting words, "You next, Bolshevist."'

'That's awful.'

'I know. I kept telling her, "I'm an anarchist. I am beyond factional politics."' Ramon pulled his jersey down. He looked drawn, but there was no sign of a swollen gum. 'Stupid girl. Greedy, stupid girl.'

Coralie's resentment boiled up again. '"Oh, Julie, I can't live without you." Did you have her here, in my house, with my baby asleep in bed?'

'What do you think I am?'

'A cheat. A liar, even to yourself. If you didn't have toothache, I'd punch your jaw.' She poked his cheek. 'You don't even *have* toothache, do you?'

'It was all I could think of when Noëlle told me that Maman was coming upstairs with a German who calls her an otter and materialises desserts from café kitchens by magic. "Make yourself at home, Herr von Elbing,"' Ramon mocked. 'You have questions to answer too.'

'Go to hell— Oh, God!'

She'd assumed he was scratching his armpit until he produced a revolver with a short black barrel. Its brass plating was worn, as was its grip. All firearms were to have been handed in to the authorities weeks ago and the penalty for being caught with one was death. She mouthed, 'Take it away!'

He swung open the cylinder to show her six empty chambers. 'My father's infantry sidearm, from the last war.' He returned it to the webbing holster under his jacket. 'Shall I try it out on your German? Show him how we French fight back?'

'Yes, do that, because I really want a corpse in my sitting room. It would be the perfect end to the day.'

He grinned. 'Sarcasm is wasted on anarchists – we have already shifted our moral boundaries. Anyway, I'll say what I came to say. This is goodbye, Coralie. I'm calling on Henriette, then leaving.'

'Without a proper coat?' She didn't believe him. Didn't want to. For all her grievances, having him nearby was a comfort.

'I'll steal one of Tattie's.' His childhood name for Henriette. He pulled her into a hard embrace, his moustache like wire on her cheek. 'Be careful, my wife. Life isn't a game, it's a dirty pool full of circling insects all trying to survive. Now there is a new little predator in the pond.'

'You mean Martel?'

'I mean Julie.'

'What's she got against me? I was good to her.'

'We don't always like those who are kindest to us. And,' he whispered against the lobe of her ear, 'women don't like hearing other women's names called out in the heat of passion. I am too careless sometimes.'

She pushed him away. Hopeless, incorrigible. When he died, they'd probably find he'd smuggled a harlot into his coffin. 'How will you live?'

'I'll get over the demarcation line where security is weak and head into the wilds, link up with men like me. If you need me, go to my sister. And, Coralie? Keep an eye on Henriette. She's not what she was.'

'That's no bad thing.' Coralie opened the drawer where she kept tablemats and, at the bottom, emergency currency. She took out all there was, wondering how much she could spare. For all his talk of joining up with 'men like him', she couldn't believe it was so simple. Wherever he went, he'd need food and lodgings. And luck: the moment he made contact with an underground network, he'd be a marked man. In the end, she gave him all she had. 'Happy birthday.'

He gaped. 'So it is! I'm thirty-seven. Dear God.' With a nod of thanks, he pocketed the notes. 'Promise you'll check up on Henriette? Prison ripped the veneer off her. They put her in with drunkards and prostitutes, and during questioning, they forced her head under freezing water until she blacked out. They only let her out because they knew she would die if they kept her longer. Her lungs. . .'

Coralie put a finger to her lips. The sitting-room door had just opened and closed. A moment later, the door to the flat clicked shut.

'Thank God,' she said, in her normal voice. 'He's Dietrich von Elbing and once, long ago, he half loved me but now he hates me.' She laughed shakily. 'We all seem to hate each other, these days!'

Ramon stroked her cheek. 'I am glad you are not keeping a pet German on a lead. Though,' he frowned, 'people speak of lines of uniforms outside your shop.'

'I'm selling hats, to survive.'

'Come the Apocalypse, people will remember the selling, not the hats. Got any proper food? I'll go when I'm sure that bastard's left the street.'

He consumed the last of her olives and a heel of cheese, and downed red wine from an open bottle. Then he put his hands either side of her face, kissed her and said, 'I mean what I say. If ever you see Julie Fourcade, walk in the other direction.'

'Wait.' Coralie fetched a tin of medicines from the cupboard, dribbled clove oil into her palm and slapped it over Ramon's jaw.

'Now I smell!'

'Exactly, and if you bump into Dietrich, he *might* believe you have a bad tooth.'

Ramon kissed her again. 'Now you are beginning to think like a man! Tell Noëlle goodbye for me.'

Coralie wiped off the kiss, then washed the pungent oil from her fingers. The flat was silent. Noëlle often fell asleep mid-afternoon. If so, she'd catch forty winks herself. Heaven help her, she needed it after the day she'd had. When she entered the lounge and saw Dietrich at the dining-table, skimming a newspaper she'd bought a couple of days ago, she was baffled. He'd left, hadn't he?

He looked up. 'What is it?

'Where's Noëlle?'

He looked towards the sofa, then at her. 'She went to find you. You were shut away rather a long time with your visitor.'

'Husband.' The correction was automatic. Coralie was already out of the room, calling, 'Noëlle?' She checked the bathroom, both bedrooms, then the kitchen in case the child had somehow doubled back. They often played hide-and-seek, and there were not many hiding-places. Returning to the lounge, she checked behind the sofa, even under the table and behind the curtains.

Dietrich, meanwhile, folded the newspaper. 'Not here?'

'No.' A dreadful apprehension grabbed her. 'I heard the door go. I thought it was you – oh, God.'

Dietrich followed her into the hall where he reached for his cap and gloves, and the house keys – the speed of his movements suggesting his own automatic responses. 'Put your coat on. She cannot have gone far in the rain.'

'So why isn't she back?'

But he was already on his way out. She followed, calling after him, 'This is your fault. Kicking my doors in? The locksmith only had materials for downstairs, so the top one doesn't lock properly and Noëlle is just tall enough to open it. If anything's happened it's—'

'My fault. All right, but I slammed the front door when I came in and your husband will surely not have let her out as he left?'

All true, but where was she? Coralie tried to see over Dietrich's head, hating him for being just tall enough to block her view of the downstairs lobby.

No sign of Noëlle. 'Can she have got into the shop?' Dietrich asked. There was a service door off the lobby and he pushed it. Solid, padlocked. Impossible for a child to get through.

'She must be upstairs still,' Dietrich said.

'But I heard the flat door open and close.'

'Leaving her on which side of the door?'

But Coralie didn't know, and was thinking only of wasted time.

She ran out into the rain, calling her daughter's name left and right. She went to Teddy's door, because Noëlle might have tried to find him in his shop. But the shop was locked, the shutters down. She crossed the road to the *pâtisserie* where they used to go every Saturday to choose a tart or a cake. Thrusting open the door, she called wildly, 'Have you seen my little girl? Anybody? Small, dark—'

Dietrich caught up with her. 'If you wish I will order everybody living in the street to search. Everybody out of their houses in the rain, to search, on pain of arrest. Shall I do it?'

He meant it, too. Have him act like the enemy, even for Noëlle? 'No, just help me look.' Back on the pavement, she turned round and round, willing Noëlle to appear through the blur. Her hair was streaming, her clothes too.

'If Ramon had found her on the stairs, would he have taken her away with him?'

'No.' Ramon, for all his flaws, was not a man knowingly to inflict pain. 'He would have put her back inside the flat. It's Martel,' she moaned. 'He's got her.'

'How would Martel have got inside your house?'

'I don't know! But he threatened to sell Noëlle, pass her around filthy men until she died. My girl.' Her guts twisted and she bent forward to control the pain. 'Please,' she murmured through desiccated lips. 'Please.' A flash of memory: in a field in England, she'd demanded of a Romany, 'Read my love-line.'

And the woman had said, 'It is unclear. It is severed. I see children. You will kill.'

Now I understand. She gripped Dietrich, her nails penetrating to the flesh under the sturdy cloth of his jacket. 'Why my child, why not me?' She saw a matching pain in his eyes, but this time it didn't frighten her. It was like reading her own emotions in large script.

'Why *your* child?' He spoke in German, slowly. 'Why *my* child, Coralie?'

She struck him with her fists because otherwise the scream inside her would rip through tissue and bone. 'I can't bear it. I want to die.'

'So, perhaps you do understand. Come.' He led her across the road, back to the flat, using the keys he'd taken from the hallstand. 'She must be indoors. Nothing else makes sense.' In the flat, he said, 'You search this side of the hall,' he indicated the kitchen, 'I will search the other. Open everything. *Everything*.'

In the bathroom there was an airing cupboard fitted into a corner, so poky that Coralie had to roll her towels to fit them on the shelves. She opened the door without hope and saw, in the gap between the floor and the bottom shelf, a small form. Head at an angle, knees drawn up. Coralie sank down and reached in. Noëlle came out in the same shape, as if she'd been set in a mould. Coralie carried her to the lounge where she found Dietrich pulling items from a sideboard.

He came over and pressed his knuckle into the hollow under the child's ear. 'She's all right.'

Voice thick with sleep, Noëlle murmured, 'Found you, Maman.'

He put a glass in her hand. 'Calvados. I found it in your sideboard.'

It was left over from Christmas. Coralie sat up and raised it to her lips.

'Are you all right now?'

'Mostly. I can't believe how I panicked.' Her right ankle was throbbing because running up and down the street had strained already weakened ligaments. She hadn't known fatigue like this since giving birth.

Dietrich had lit a fire — the first in the grate since she'd attempted to burn Ottilia's documents, but no warmth reached her. He fetched a blanket and wrapped it around her, sitting down beside her. 'Are you able to talk?'

'Won't they expect you back at work?'

'No. I don't report to anybody in that building. But we are here, and unlikely to be interrupted unless your child wakes.' They glanced at Noëlle, curled like a dormouse on a quilt in front of the fire. 'Or your husband drops in again.'

'He won't, but I'm in no mood for chat.'

'"Chat" is not what I have in mind. I have been waiting to tell you of my life after Paris. I had not the strength the other night, but now feels right.'

She took a slug of Calvados; Normandy apples with the innocence fermented out of them. 'All right. Speak.'

He told her that the letter she'd concealed had been his son's last cry for help. 'Waldo was begging for release from military training and he must have thought I had turned my back. My poor boy. He was desperate. When I left you at the Expo, it was because I had received a telegram, stating that Waldo had collapsed.'

'That's why you went so abruptly.'

He signalled to her to be quiet. 'Once, you asked me to listen while you recited something deeply painful. I ask the same of you now. The telegram mentioned an accident, though nothing of how serious it was. I raced by taxi to Gare de l'Est, got on a train that was just about to pull out, and by the early hours, I was over the German border. Nobody could have travelled faster. Even so, I was too late. Waldo was dead even before I left Paris.'

'What happened?'

Dietrich got up, walked to the window. 'His heart failed.'

'That only happens to old men.'

'It happened. The afternoon he died, the afternoon you and I went together to the Expo, he ran in the heat. He should not have run at all, the oxygen supply to his blood was insufficient. It was a boiling day and each boy carried ten kilograms on his back – considered top weight. Waldo doubled it, because he wanted to prove himself a man. Twenty kilograms. Do you know how much that is?'

She thought of Donal, staggering under the weight of laundry baskets, wheezing, 'These weigh a ton!' Twenty kilos . . . She bought flour in two-kilo sacks. Ten of those.

'I tried it.' Dietrich turned to face her, firelight flickers stripping the years from him. 'I drove to a lake near my family home, to see how far I could run round its perimeter with twenty kilos on my back. Forty years old, that gave me some excuse, but I was near to collapse before I was a quarter of the way round. I could not have done what Waldo did.'

'You think he put that weight on his back, knowing it would kill him?'

'I admire my son—' He stopped and fixed Coralie with a reproach she could not sustain.

'Dietrich, I didn't kill Waldo.'

'No? That letter needed to reach me.'

Shame had nowhere to hide in her face. She looked away, saying, 'Brownlow dropped it on purpose. He set me up.' When Dietrich made no response, she nodded in bitter acceptance. 'I can't pin it on Brownlow, can I? I opened it because I wanted to know who was writing so often, who might take you away from me.' She wanted to express her sorrow, but knew he must have heard trite condolences too often. She waited. Waited for words of forgiveness. Waited until she wondered if he'd even heard her.

At last Dietrich spoke. 'I admire my son for choosing such a courageous and defiant—' He stopped. Breathed deeply. 'Such a defiant—' A muscular spasm gripped him, pulling the line of his chest and shoulders out of shape.

She ran to him, grasping a hand that shook convulsively. Was it his heart too? Was he having a seizure? 'Dietrich?'

A terrible sound escaped him and she saw his face twist. She drew him to her, taking his weight, while something broke inside him. At last she allowed herself to say, 'I'm sorry. Darling, I'm so sorry.' Then, because he didn't throw her off or unleash any rage on her, she said, 'I love you and I want to make it up to you.'

'It is too late.'

'I want to make you happy.'

'That is beyond possible.'

'Then at least let me take away some of your pain. Let me try.' *I can help you*, she vowed silently. I can help you mend and you – she looked to Noëlle, murmuring in her sleep – you can protect us from Serge Martel.

Becoming lovers again required several weeks of tentative courtship, rebuilding intimacy. When, one diamond-cold night just before Christmas, Coralie invited Dietrich to join her in the rustic bed, it was with a new consciousness of him as a hurt and complex man. They loved with a mute intensity because their bond had deepened, beyond words.

He had allowed her to see into his soul, as he had allowed nobody else. She had been hurt and rejected almost beyond bearing, but chose to trust again. Only when some cruelty of war thrust itself in front of them did their closeness waver.

The months marched on; the German clamp tightened. War

raged throughout the world, changing in shape but never lessening in savagery. A mood of resistance grew in France.

On rue de Seine, Noëlle celebrated her third birthday, and a year later in 1941, her fourth, by which time she had stopped asking about 'Papa Ramon' whom she never saw any more. She had learned to look forward to visits from 'Oncle Dietrich', who was teaching her German and was very gentle with her. Life went on.

PART FOUR

PART FOUR

Chapter Twenty-five

Tuesday, 24 March 1942

Coralie opened her eyes to citrus light. She was in Dietrich's flat,
the one that had once been Ottilia's, in a bedroom facing the
Jardin du Luxembourg. It must have been early because the birdsong was louder than the strict-time step of the sentries marching
alongside the park railings. The sentries always turned off rue de
Vaugirard on to rue Guynemer where, after a hundred steps, they
would stamp, turn and march back. She lay contemplating the
day ahead. Today she launched her latest spring–summer collection, and she ought to be up, choosing what to wear. But instead
of flinging back the bed covers, she reached out and stroked a
man's taut stomach.

Just enough pressure to invite him awake.

Dietrich rolled over and took her in his arms, kissing her slowly
at first, with heightening passion as he came fully conscious. He
stroked the curve of her waist, her hip, fingers exploring and
teasing until she was whispering his name and pulling his lips
to hers.

They tangled, with a sense of mischief that came from the very
private nature of their relationship. Dietrich had finally induced
Coralie to relinquish her apartment and move into this building,
though only after a sustained siege. She had insisted on keeping a

token independence, moving herself and Noëlle into the flat one
floor up, where the art collection had once been stored. Micheline
occupied the ground floor, acting both as Coralie's nanny and
as concierge, with Florian Lantos, whom she'd married. Each
morning, Micheline took Noëlle to a nursery school on boulevard Saint-Germain.

Noëlle remained a slight child, and would probably always
be so as rationing and shortages had stripped everyone's diet of
proteins and essential fats. For all that, she was happy, delightfully
opinionated in three languages. French, of course, German and
American English, the latter taught her by her godmother Una,
her Tante Nou-Nou, until Coralie put a stop to it.

Germany had declared war on America in December 1941, after
its ally Japan had bombed the Hawaiian port of Pearl Harbor. In
a stroke, Una and her compatriots lost their neutral status. Just as
Una had handed over her Rolls-Royce before it could be seized,
she'd resigned her flat on avenue Foch to a German intelligence
chief, taking Coralie's old home on rue de Seine, which she shared
with Arkady. 'Musical chairs for the dispossessed.' Arkady was
at last her acknowledged lover. Her SS *Sturmführer* was history,
and most evenings, Una could be found at home knitting jumpers
from scraps of wool – or making dinners from scraps of food.

Most people kept to their homes now, shopping in the morn-
ings when the shelves were better stocked. At night, Paris went
dark, pinpricks of light showing where the brothels and nightclubs were.

The Rose Noire thrived because Serge Martel was now one of
the most powerful black-marketeers in Montmartre. The Vagabonds still played three nights a week, but Coralie never went.

Martel had not denounced her. His interest in Dietrich had
mutated to a cautious truce. Coralie's business was thriving,

miraculously protected from the officious probings of German tax inspectors. She was safe, Noëlle was safe, and they had Dietrich to thank for it.

'Tuesday is a stupid day to launch a collection,' she murmured into Dietrich's shoulder. 'People have hardly got their week started. But we know what's ahead.'

'Do we?'

'Easter.' Which came in early April, and after that, Hitler's birthday on the twentieth. A rumour was circulating that the Führer intended to celebrate in Paris. Whether he came or not, parties and receptions would be held in his honour, and Coralie had planned her launch to give her workroom time to complete the commissions that were building up.

'I shall come to see you late this afternoon,' Dietrich said, against her lips.

'No, come early.'

'Ah, yes. The rules. Never the twain.'

'It's for everyone's good.'

A regime had established itself at La Passerinette. German customers before lunch, French after. Many high-ranking German officers had brought their wives to Paris and these women expected precedence over the French. Coralie dared not offend them, and running La Passerinette resembled diplomatic hopscotch. It was why these last moments in bed were precious.

So why spoil them by picking at a scab she ought to leave alone? 'Dietrich, this month, I'll be depositing the last tranche of my debt to Ottilia. The bank manager is getting suspicious. He thinks I'm a black-marketeer. Which Swiss bank should I transfer it to?'

'Good try, darling.'

'I wish you'd tell me where she is.'

'It is safer for you and her if you do not know.'

'Because I keep imagining her on a train to Germany.'

Suddenly Dietrich was leaning on an elbow, looking down at her. 'Why?'

'Una and I were discussing it. All the Jews who were rounded up last year – the ones from the Marais and the Sentier – were taken away by train to Germany, but even Una can't find out where exactly. She had a friend at the American Embassy who was going to make enquiries, but he skipped the country. We can't bear the thought of Tilly being among the deportees. Some of Madame Thomas's friends were taken.'

'Madame Thomas?'

'My bookkeeper, who Violaine lives with.'

'She's Jewish?'

'Madame Thomas is, though I hadn't known it. She's frightened and keeps asking me if I think it will stop.'

'What will stop? The persecution of Jews in France? Only when the French government puts its foot down, and when my country reverses its stratagem to rid the world of Jews. I think, all considered, that deportations will begin to increase.'

'How can you be so—'

He kissed her into silence, then made the sound that meant, I *really* have to get up. Before throwing back the covers, he said, 'Poland is where the deportees end up.'

Never did she feel more separate from Dietrich when they spoke of the human cost of occupation. He was not a cruel man, but he was pragmatic, seeing a degree of suffering as inevitable. And let nobody think he was anything but a proud and loyal German! Their perspectives were so different. She often visited Amélie Ginsler, and her friend would describe the arrests of Jewish men in the neighbourhood, which had begun as far back as 1940. Those between certain ages without citizenship had been taken to holding camps, and their families had waited in vain for them to return. 'We keep our heads down,' Amélie confided. 'We're afraid, though I often wonder, what if we stood shoulder to shoulder and said, "No"?'

Watching Amélie tend her daughter, Françoise, Coralie had absolved her friend of such responsibility. If the French government, police chiefs and others down the ranks refused to stand up for humanity, how could one mother? How could she herself? How, if she was being fair, could Dietrich?

Coming back in from the bathroom, seeing her sitting in bed with her arms linked around her knees, Dietrich said, 'You are anxious about this collection?'

Was she ever! 'I've taken a risk with the materials I've used.'

'Tell me more.'

'Not now.' She got out of bed, nipping into the bathroom ahead of him. Later, buttoning the waistband of her cycling culottes, she promised, 'All will be revealed at eleven o'clock. I'll keep a standing space for you, so don't be late.'

She arrived at the shop to find Violaine strewing paper chrysanthemums in the window display. They'd put the collection together in spite of the fact that many of the fabric warehouses of the Sentier had closed. Foreign straws, like sisal, *baku* and Leghorn were unobtainable. Fur-felt too, as the trade with America and Canada had fallen victim to sea blockades. Even wool-felt was a luxury, as its main producer, the Low Countries, was occupied and Germany took its output. There might eventually arise a domestic straw-plaiting industry, Coralie supposed, similar to that found in the English county of Bedfordshire, but until that happened, she and Violaine made do with whatever they could find.

She bade Madame Thomas good morning. 'It's kind of you to help out in the shop today.'

Jeanne Thomas was arranging chairs borrowed from the café across the street, placing them in two lines to create the effect of a catwalk. For an extremely short cat, Coralie admitted, but this show should still be an event.

Two events, a morning and an afternoon one. Printed programmes being out of the question, she chalked the running order on a blackboard. Customers would be given a handwritten programme as they arrived, cut from discarded 1941 desk diaries, on which they might note down the hats they wanted to try later. They'd better have brought their own pencils.

Champagne would be served, canapés too: pastry parcels of minced veal and pine nuts, vol-au-vents filled with chestnut and goat's cheese soufflé, the ingredients bought from a local black-market trader who was making a fortune supplying luxury provisions to the Germans. The promise of canapés and a Château Latour 1929 should guarantee a good audience at both sessions, Coralie told herself. She even had a professional mannequin. Solange Antonin, who had modelled for Javier and had a posture to rival that of Queen Nefertiti, had graciously agreed to lend her professional skills for one day, her fee the pick of the collection.

In spite of their unpromising start, Solange had won a grudging corner of Coralie's heart. The girl had suffered. There had been a miscarriage in her past, an induced one, Coralie gathered, although Solange had never provided any details. Dashed hopes a-plenty, too. But what really brought them together was a shared dread of Serge Martel. His fine white teeth had torn off the top half of Solange's ear.

The first parade was due to start at eleven sharp, and people were arriving. Coralie felt her first stage-fright. She had always modelled her own hats – there'd never been anyone else to do it – but today she would parade alongside Solange. She hoped it wouldn't be a case of gliding swan and waddling duck. Violaine had already set up a table and mirror in the corridor. She'd help them into each hat and fix the numbered tags to their wrists, which was how the audience identified each model. Didi and Paulette would show clients to their chairs, or to the stand-ing-room behind the chairs, and serve canapés while Madame Thomas poured champagne. Half a glass only per visitor, or there wouldn't be enough.

'I think this is our best collection so far,' Violaine said as they waited for the audience to settle.

Madame Thomas popped her head round the door to report that the mainly German female gathering had taken their glasses without thanks. The finest champagne was their due, apparently.

'So long as they order my hats, they can be as sniffy as they like.' Coralie shivered in her summer dress. A cold March day, and she was promoting thoughts of sunshine and holidays. The spring–summer couture shows that had finished a month before had finally rung the death knell of the tubular, bias-cut styles of the 1930s. This year's waistlines were nipped in. Not with belts – belts were '*Sooo* ante-bellum', as Una put it – but with darts that followed the contours of hand-span waists. *We all have hand-span waists, these days*, Coralie thought, catching her reflection in the cheval mirror. Skirts were wide, sometimes with spare fabric bunched at the back, giving the illusion of a well-fleshed bottom. Necklines had been getting lower for a couple of years and both Coralie and Solange displayed cleavage. Short bolero jackets restored some modesty. With skirts shorter and fuller, jackets had shifted upwards, ending at the ribcage or just under the bosom. Hat design always followed couture, and this season's were higher and blowsier to balance the new silhouette.

Madame Thomas called around the door, 'Ready, I think.'

Coralie squeezed her coral bracelet for luck and slowed down her mind. *Do it any way you like*, Solange had said, *just don't rush*. Four paces along the catwalk, pause and pose. Walk to the end, turn, pose, hold, giving each side of the room time to study her from all angles and note the model number on her wrist.

Taking her time gave *her* the chance to assess her audience. German officers' wives always dressed conservatively and wore little makeup. Strong faces, bony brows, hairstyles resolutely old-fashioned. These wives, along with the female clerks, typists and telegraphers bulking up the German administration, had been dubbed 'grey mice' by Parisians, who, if they noticed them at all, did so with studied disdain.

Posing in a hat of stiffened chintz with gossamer-silk roses on a frame of millinery wire, Coralie acknowledged that the 'grey mice' took the business of fashion seriously. They were making notes. But whereas Parisian women craned forward, conferring with their neighbours, sketching outlines with their hands – sometimes breaking into spontaneous applause if something delighted them – these women wrote behind their hands as if in competition with each other. And just as they'd taken her champagne without appreciation, she suspected they wanted her hats, but not her.

The first twenty-four models were wide-brimmed Gainsborough styles, designed for sunshine, for race-days – and there still was racing at Longchamps – for outdoor dining or strolling beside the river. She'd created them from salvaged cottons and silks laid over foundations of buckram and tarlatan. Using short-runs of cloth meant she'd never be able to replicate these models exactly.

The selection that she and Solange were about to show would be easy to reproduce, however, because Coralie had acquired quantities of raw fibre from an unexpected source.

A rather disagreeable source.

In the corridor, she let Violaine replace flowered chintz with a sun-hat in an understated shade of grey. As she listened for Solange's returning footsteps, she stroked its crown. Not just the colour of smoke, every bit as light, too. This was the surprise element of the collection, the one she'd balked at explaining to Dietrich that morning..

The silk water-lilies around the brim had begun life as a parachute hooked on a tree somewhere in the Burgundy region. The more informed among the audience might recognise the hat itself as *crinolin*, which sounded romantic, but was derived from horsehair. A consignment had been destined for a furniture factory in Cologne.

'Like the parachute, it's courtesy of the British RAF,' her black-market supplier had informed her, as he produced a whole horsetail. 'The RAF flattened Cologne to stop the Germans enjoying the war too much and the factory I was supplying no longer exists. I've a truckload going spare, and I thought of you.'

Coralie's first year at Pettrew's had been spent in the plait room, stitching strip-straw into rosettes. Horsetail, similarly treated, proved as fine as sisal, and could be blocked just the same. Mixing the strands gave subtle variations in colour. After perfecting the technique, the Ginslers had gone into production, turning their doll shop into an extension of Coralie's workroom.

She adored the result, but would Paris? From the silence that greeted the *crinolins*, Coralie feared not. Pencils bobbed, but eyes were doubtful. Perhaps the hats were too . . . restrained? Coralie de Lirac, restrained? One colour had been banished entirely from this collection: pink. As moderate applause greeted the end of the show, she felt like shouting, 'If you want pink hats for summer, go to Lorienne Royer at Henriette Junot! She thieves my ideas and pumps them out six months later.'

What she actually gave was a polite little speech. The hush was so disheartening, she thought again of Henriette Junot, who famously never attended her own collections.

And Dietrich hadn't come. Clearing her throat, Coralie finished in German, 'If you would approach me or my assistants, *gnädige Damen*, appointments for fittings can be put in the diary. Thank you.'

The tight smile flew off her face as a pack of soberly clad women advanced on her.

Dietrich arrived as the afternoon show got under way. Coralie saw him slip in and gave a mock pout. He mouthed, 'Sorry,' as fifty or so Frenchwomen glared at him. He clicked his heels – a shade ironically, Coralie thought – and Una McBride called out, 'If you'd come this late in 1940, we could have built another fifty miles of Maginot Line.'

The interruption changed the mood. Solange speeded up, her turns getting faster, her poses shorter. Coralie guessed she was wanting her champagne. The chintz sun-hats were well received but once again, the *crinolin* models drew silence – a different texture of silence. Whereas the 'grey mice' had seemed uncertain how to react, the French ladies treated La Passerinette's newfound simplicity with overt disapproval.

In the corridor, Coralie groaned to Violaine, 'Una's the only person smiling.'

Solange came in, unpinning a flaxen yellow pillbox. 'Could

you walk on your hands, do something to wake them up? I saw frost settling.'

Coralie did the only thing she could: she showed the hats she was proud of and willed the audience to see them as she did. She'd never been so happy as the finale hove into sight. Back in the corridor, she slipped into a matelot jacket and held out a matching one for Solange. They'd go out arm in arm to show the last two models, she said, because this collection was feeling like a song with too many verses.

Their hats were nearly identical. Solange's tipped to the right, covering her damaged ear with a silk streamer, Coralie's tilted to the left.

'People don't like newness,' Violaine said, as she opened the door for them. 'Not until somebody else gives them permission. Give them permission.'

Coralie tried, but failing in public dampened even her vivacity. Worse, it was *silent* failure. Unimaginably worse even than that was seeing Serge Martel in the audience. He must have come in while she'd been out of the room. He stood on the same side as Dietrich, his hands resting on the back of a chair. Occupying that chair, a girl whose hair was lacquered into profiterole curls and whose short red dress matched her lipstick.

If ever you see Julie Fourcade, walk away.

She and Solange had agreed to turn and pose in one, smooth movement, but Solange had also seen Serge and swerved away from him. Coralie was a step behind and, in skipping to catch up, her ankle gave way and she fell. After a moment of white-hot pain, she threw out a hopeful joke. 'Who sank the ship under me?'

She was helped to her feet by Dietrich, who murmured, 'Don't let him see your fear.'

A short while later, she addressed her audience while holding on to the back of a chair. 'Mesdames, please excuse the somewhat ragged ending to this show. I always was a better milliner than a mannequin. Please stay for more hospitality, and to discuss the collection —'

Behind her, Solange snarled, 'I will kill him. I will take his eyes out.'

She shushed Solange, continuing '— to discuss the collection and take another glass of champagne. Did I already say that?'

'I live to see his blood!'

Coralie signalled urgently to Dietrich. 'Fetch Solange a drink and keep her occupied.' She continued her speech, but nobody was really listening.

'We want the white hat you fell over in, and we want to take it now.'

Coralie was writing an appointment in the diary and did not immediately raise her head. Following Coralie's disjointed speech, Una had announced loudly that she *adored* everything she'd seen and could she have an appointment immediately, if not sooner? The frost had lifted a degree or two, and a dozen or so other women were waiting to make their appointments.

'The white hat. We want it.'

Coralie met Serge Martel's eye. 'That's not possible.' She turned to Julie. 'You know how it works. Look, the hat won't fit you and we can do better for you.'

Julie pouted. Coralie wondered how she'd got hold of that hot shade of lipstick, when every other woman was reduced to melting down the stumps of old ones, mixing the ill-coloured goo with glycerin, and enjoying slippery kisses afterwards.

'I want the white one.' Julie touched her hair, as if afraid her curls were disintegrating.

'And you can add some fancy roses,' Martel said. 'Why are your hats so boring, Mademoiselle de Lirac?'

'I prefer "sophisticated".' She sent a silent apology to Javier, whose subtle genius had collided with her ignorance back in the summer of '37. 'If Julie would like to come back—'

'Mademoiselle Fourcade to you. We're getting married.'

She swallowed her contempt. 'If *Mademoiselle Fourcade* would care to book an appointment, we will create something she'll be proud to wear and we will be proud to put our name to.' *Though how the girl would get a hat to stay on her head . . .*

'I want it now.' Julie glanced up at Martel, drawing audacity from him. 'Now,' she said, just as Noëlle had started to do at around the age of two.

Coralie realised where the child had got it from. 'Not possible.'

'Anything's possible.' Martel inspected a fingernail. 'Julie and I are dining tonight in a restaurant with a roof terrace and that sailor hat is just right. As your lover would say, a perfect hat for a *Dachterrasse*. You should try the phrase out on him, when you're alone.' Julie giggled as Martel pulled her close and nibbled her ear. She was carrying a handbag made from three shades of leather, one of the new fashionable carry-alls, and she made sure Coralie noticed it by constantly shifting it up her arm. Something about the bag disturbed Coralie, but she couldn't work out what it was. She just wanted the obnoxious couple out of her salon.

When Violaine came over with a question, Coralie interrupted: 'Violaine, can you box up the final model, the white sailor, the one I wore?'

Behind her lenses, Violaine registered astonishment. 'But we never—'

'We're making an exception for Mademoiselle Fourcade.'

'That hat needs flowers,' Martel chipped in. 'I'm not having my girl looking cheap.'

'Heavens, no,' Coralie agreed. 'Violaine, attach cabbage roses and a spray or two of jasmine. There are dove feathers too, all colours, and why not add ribbon curls? The more, the better.'

'And where should I place this . . . salad?' Mutiny edged Violaine's tone.

'On top, dead centre. That way –' Coralie forced a smile at Julie '– whenever the future Madame Martel wears the hat, she will be reminded of her wedding cake.'

That night, Coralie lay on the bed, waiting for Dietrich to join her. A forgettable day, if she could only persuade her brain to it. She knew this collection would not take off, not as previous ones had. She'd held the match to the blue touch-paper, as if to send a rocket up into the sky, and it hadn't caught.

'It'll be a slow burn, you watch.' Una had tried to lift her spirits but Coralie trusted her own instincts. She'd feel better if she could get Serge Martel and Julie out of her mind. Martel had paid generously for a hat that would make Julie look like a Christmas goose. And then, just as Coralie had thought the dramas were over, Lorienne Royer had turned up. She'd misremembered the start time.

She'd brought an escort, a small Frenchman with serious spectacles and oily hair.

'I know him.' Una had sidled up to Coralie. 'He works for the director of police. He creeps around the hospital, checking patients' residence certificates. I hope all your people are *bona fide*.'

'Well, they're all French citizens.'

'What he really wants to find are illegal refugees. Or, preferably, terrorists.' Last summer, a young Frenchman had shot a German naval officer at a Métro station. Eleven Frenchmen had been sent to the firing squad to appease the Germans. It was then that Coralie had felt the heartbeat of Paris change. More attacks had followed and more reprisals. With General de Gaulle's broadcasts from London settling in angry people's ears, new, clandestine groups had sprung up. If you agreed with their aims, you called them '*résistants*'. Otherwise, they were terrorists. Ramon had joined such a group in the Auvergne, in the heart of France.

Seeing Lorienne beating a path towards Violaine, Coralie had stepped in front of her. 'Madame, you cannot expect to be welcomed here. You steal my hats, you steal my ideas. At least have the grace to copy from the other side of the window.'

In a burst of defiance, Lorienne had dodged round her. What had passed between her and Violaine, Coralie had no idea.

'She was drunk,' Madame Thomas, who had witnessed the exchange, confided later. 'Her tongue got the better of her. Let it rest.'

Dietrich came in from the bathroom, bringing with him the scent of soap and toothpaste. 'Are you staying with me all night?'

'Mm. Noëlle's with Micheline and Florian.'

'Good. Shall I carry you out and put you in the bath?'

'Pull me up. I'll go under my own steam.' She extended a hand but, instead of taking it, Dietrich got on to the bed beside her and unbuttoned her dress. She wriggled out of it and offered herself up in apple-green silk underwear. 'I ought to wash first.'

'Why? You smell quite delightful – of other women's perfumes but also of yourself.' He kissed her, a sensuous kiss that travelled from her throat to the inside of her thighs. So tempting to be seduced away from the business of thinking. She could see the top of his head. His hair was going the colour of wood ash but was still thick. Her chosen lover. Protector, too, but now, in every other respect, her equal. As love had once sneaked up on her uninvited, so had self-confidence.

They made love intensely, the sighing of skin against silk the loudest sound.

In his arms afterwards, she listened to him tell her about his day. He'd been to avenue Marigny that morning to call on Kurt Kleber and Kurt's wife Fritzi, and to pay respects to his Luftwaffe superior, General Hanesse, who had insisted on lunch at the Ritz. After that, a rushed meeting with a man who claimed he could acquire a work of art by the Dutch master Vermeer. A painting that Reichsmarschall Göring wanted badly. A painting Dietrich knew to be fake because the man had sold a near-identical one five years ago to Göring's official art dealer, Walter Hofer.

'I told him that Hofer might be duped a second time, as greedy men rarely grow wise, but please, not to waste my time.'

Coralie had her head on his shoulder, only half listening because she was thinking of Julie's arm around Serge Martel's waist, and a leather bag on a plump elbow. The bag had been three colours of leather: tan, mole brown and olive. *Olive.* She exclaimed, 'No – not possible!'

Dietrich broke off. 'More than possible. Göring idolises Dutch masters and Hofer hasn't yet realised that people paint fakes especially for him.'

'No – I've just realised something. That girl, Julie—'

'Too much rouge. Too much everything.'

'Her bag was a new-for-old. You take some worn-out ones to a leather-merchant's and they stitch a new one from the pieces.'

'And now you're thinking that La Passerinette can branch into handbags. Good idea.'

'Listen. One of the colours was olive green and,' she rolled so she could speak straight into his ear, 'I brought a handbag that colour from London.'

'I remember. It clashed with your dress. Why did you not destroy it?'

'Because it was a cheap market bag. No label, nothing to say it was British-made.'

'You think Julie stole it?'

'From the top of my wardrobe. I'd slung it up there.'

'So, she is a thief and that is distressing in a nanny, even a former nanny. Are you fearful you left something in it?'

'Yes.' She made a face. 'But I can't think what.'

He kissed her. 'Nobody can threaten you while you live under my umbrella.'

Umbrella. Sunshine and flowers. 'Martel told me to repeat a phrase to you. "A perfect hat for a *Dachterrasse*". That means "roof garden", doesn't it? Why would he have learned that particular word?'

'God rot that bastard!' The bedclothes dragged off her as Dietrich rolled off the bed, blasting her in sudden chill. The ceiling light came on, its starfish arms illuminating slowly, like an old-fashioned gas lamp.

'What have I said?' Dietrich never cursed; not in front of her, anyway. And though she knew the insult had been aimed at Martel, the shift in his manner alarmed her.

'Get up, Coralie.' He was naked, his body a harsh sculpture in the saffron light.

She swung her legs off the bed, reaching for the underwear she'd pulled off after their lovemaking. Holding it against herself felt like a parody of modesty so she dropped it and walked into his arms. A test of his love. *If* he loved her, he would comfort her. She felt his erratic breathing and it stole in on her that he, too, was afraid.

That word, '*Dachterrasse*', had affected him.

He said, 'Cast your mind back to that July evening at the Expo. Outside the German pavilion, I exchanged friendly words with a photographer. You recall?'

'Yes. And you saluted.'

'Which shocked you. I saw. Inside, I met two men, one was Kurt Kleber, the other a younger man, a mutual friend. All this you remember?'

'You all shouted *Heil Hitler*! Course I remember. I was upset and I wished I hadn't seen it.'

'Did you hear what we said among each other, we three men?'

'No. I was too far away and you were speaking in German.'

'But you knew a little German by then.'

'Quite a lot, actually. I'm good at languages.' It came out defensively. 'Growing up talking French gave me an ear, and I wanted to learn it for you. On your birthday, I was planning to spend the whole evening talking German to you. It was going to be a surprise.'

He brushed this aside. 'Tell me again, did you hear anything of the conversation between me, Kleber and the other man?'

'Not a word, I promise.'

'But sometimes you lie, Coralie.' His hands circled her throat. No pressure, but she was seeing her father, murder in his face. 'Dietrich, please—'

She tried to put her arms around him but he took her to Ottilia's dressing-table where plain hairbrushes and his *Schirmmütze* cap were reflected in the multiple mirrors. Keeping hold of her hand, Dietrich opened a drawer and took out some small boxes, the sort that contain cufflinks. From the same drawer, he removed a pistol.

Her head swam. 'Please don't.'

He put the gun down beside his cap, then opened one of the boxes, shaking it over a cloisonné plate that still had some of Ottilia's hatpins in it. Two bullets clacked into the dish.

'One each,' he said.

'You're going to shoot me?' *And then himself?* As the room began to spin, she watched him unscrew the top of one bullet, and tip something out which rolled like a coffee bean. Then the same with the other bullet.

'These are potassium-cyanide ampoules, Coralie. We take one each.'

'I won't. I can't! I have a child. I don't want to die!' She tried to pull away but his grip did not relent.

'I don't mean now, and perhaps never. It is a safety measure. A reassurance. We must keep them on our bodies all the time. Even in bed.'

He looked serious. He *was* serious.

'You must sew a little pocket into a neck choker, something you can wear each day without attracting notice. Perhaps you would do the same with the ribbon of my *Pour le Mérite*.'

She looked at him blankly.

'My Blue Max. The cross I wear always around my neck, the Prussian order of merit. Don't say you have not noticed it.'

She nodded.

'So. We will wear them all the time, and if we are taken, we put the ampoule between our teeth,' he mimed it, 'and bite down, crushing the glass shell. Death then is quick.'

'If we're taken? You mean—'

'If the Gestapo come, our lives would be worth nothing and our manner of death atrocious.'

She stared into his eyes. Dietrich, her protector, was describing her nightmare. 'You said we were safe! What's changed? Why would they come now?'

'You must make arrangements for Noëlle. I advise you to send her away, perhaps with that girl, Micheline. They should go to the country, or to Teddy's estate at Dreux.' The grip on her wrist was becoming painful. 'You and I are together to the end. Wedded. Adam and Eve.' The allusion to their nakedness came with a dry laugh. He selected another box from the dressing-table and extracted a ruby ring, slipping it on to her finger. 'This ring, you gave back to me because it was too big so I had it made smaller. We must live for each other now, trust each other, face every danger together. Yes?'

He was asking for faith, but without explaining. *And I'm meant to be the one with secrets*. She closed her eyes and scenes from her life spun through her brain. *Noëlle's birth, her first cry*. Ramon saying, 'I like your spirit and I want your body.' Rishal, her sailor lover, saying, 'I cannot believe I have a girl who speaks French.'

And Donal. Donal calling her name on boulevard de Clichy, finally getting it right. The two of them playing chicken on the railway lines at the end of Shand Street. She'd always cheated, darting back to safety, because she was a coward.

'Dietrich, why are you saying all this now?'

'Because what you have told me tonight tells me that my life is in danger, and yours too – you know more than you think. We must keep faith with each other. That is the only choice.'

'Is it to do with "*Dachterrasse*"? When Martel said it, I thought of us on the roof terrace at the Expo, and Teddy, and the man I now know to be Kurt Kleber. You always told me you were an art dealer, a middle-man. Are you something else too, Dietrich?'

'I am much else, Coralie, and will say more after I have consulted with Kurt. Until then, be patient and brave.'

'I will try, Dietrich. I do trust you, but don't ever try to separate me from my daughter.'

Chapter Twenty-six

Fritzi Kleber, Kurt's wife, was a Nordically fair woman and, on meeting her, Coralie presumed she was a typically glacial German-in-Paris. But Fritzi's manner was friendly. Over aperitifs in the Ritz bar, she kept telling her husband to slow his speech so Coralie could keep up. 'Even I cannot follow him sometimes.'

They dined together at the Ritz, then went on to the Rose Noire. Fritzi desperately wanted to listen to authentic jazz, which was banned in Germany now.

Sipping her champagne, Coralie stroked the choker of pewter-grey satin around her neck. From it hung a silver bottle the size of a wren's egg, bought from an antiques shop on the Left Bank. The bottle was hinged like a clam shell and would once have contained a single measure of snuff. Its present cargo was far more lethal.

Dietrich wore uniform, complete with the *Pour le Mérite* the Kaiser had awarded him in 1917. She'd done as he'd asked and sewn a false back to the ribbon to provide a secure hiding-place for a bead of potassium cyanide. In the car, she'd whispered, 'Why are we going anywhere near Serge Martel?'

'Because we are dealing with a wolf, with a wolf's ruthlessness but also its fear of confrontation. We will show it that it cannot win, and first, we must tempt it from its lair.'

It was just gone eleven p.m., and the club was thinly populated. Unsurprising, for a Wednesday night. Had her last visit here really been two years ago? The place had changed, the dance floor reduced in size, extra tables crammed in. French clientele huddled near the bar, or sat at the outer tables. The best, predictably, were occupied by German military. A lot of girls about the place, too. Single girls in cheap dresses.

The Vagabonds were onstage, playing a tune called 'Swing 42'. Coralie waved, but they didn't respond because it was impossible to see beyond the first row of tables.

Would Dietrich want to dance? How long since she'd *really* danced? She was dressed for it, in an evening gown of lemon silk jersey, which she'd bought from Una, who was also here. Coralie waved and received a blown kiss in return. Una was with a couple Coralie had met a few times, a husband and wife who worked at the American Hospital.

'We can invite them to join us, if you wish,' Dietrich offered.

Coralie shook her head. 'They work such long hours that they never stay anywhere late and, to be honest, we're not friends like we used to be.' That wasn't true. She and Una were as close as ever but they maintained a show of distance because Una had joined the Resistance, turning the flat on rue de Seine into a safe house. She took in refugees and stranded British airmen, whose planes had come down over Belgium or France, and who had to be moved, stage by stage, to the Spanish border. Coralie sometimes made hats, or altered clothes, to fit these evaders, working covertly, communicating with Una only when strictly necessary.

'Mesdames, messieurs, the Rose Noire welcomes you as it always welcomes beauty.' Félix Peyron, bent and hobbling after two of the bitterest winters on record, parroted his time-worn salute, and took their order for coffee and brandy. The Klebers got up to dance.

Félix suddenly remembered something. 'Monsieur Clisson bids me say good evening to "the Queen of Hats".'

'Teddy's here?' Why hadn't he come over in person? 'Mind if I go and say hello?'

'Not at all,' Dietrich answered. 'I won't – he is still angry with me.'

'Why?'

'I persuaded him not to offer for some modern paintings stored at the Jeu de Paume gallery, and now he resents it.'

Skirting the dance floor, Coralie was touched by the way Fritzi looked into her husband's disfigured face with steady love as they danced. Dietrich had told her they'd been childhood sweethearts.

At her approach, Teddy rose with exclamations of pleasure. But even as he planted kisses, she felt his reserve. Was he angry at Dietrich's most recent interference, or with her because she'd failed to secure those Dürer engravings for him? She'd really tried, but it was one of the subjects upon which Dietrich was utterly immovable.

Teddy introduced her first to the two women in his group, types Coralie put down as 'middle-aged sophisticates'. They had deep suntans under their makeup. Before the war, they'd probably lived six months of the year in Nice or Cap d'Antibes. They eyed her cocktail hat, a posy of parachute-silk lilies, acquisitively. Two men in dinner jackets sat with them. Teddy introduced the elder of the two as 'my firmest of friends' and the second as 'a very beautiful boy'.

Known to be utterly safe in female company, Teddy was always in demand to squire divorced or married women around cabarets and clubs, often so they could meet their lovers. It struck her now that these women might be acting as his smokescreen too, protecting him from gossip. As Coralie shook hands, the two women squabbled good-naturedly over who should buy the lilies directly off her head.

'Not for sale, Mesdames. Come and see me on boulevard de la Madeleine.' She held out a hand to Teddy. 'Lunch soon?'

'I'll be devastated if we don't. *A bientôt!* Kiss Noëlle for me.'

Back at their table, she said to Dietrich, 'Couldn't you have let him have one little painting from the Jeu de Paume, to keep him happy?'

'Not mine to give and, anyway, they have been burned.'

Suddenly she felt weary. 'Let's not stay too late.'

'We can't go yet. This is a special visit for Fritzi, her first to Paris. And, likely, her last.'

'Why her last?'

'Hold tight. Here comes the wolf.'

Serge Martel approached with a girl on his arm. Not Julie, Coralie noticed.

'Herr Graf von Elbing, Mademoiselle de Lirac.' Martel's smile glided over them to rest on the occupants of a table a short distance away. Coralie pressed her foot against Dietrich's. The same men had tried to arrest Ottilia. Gestapo. They wore loose civilian suits, and while two had forgettable features, the one with the bullet-shaped head she would remember for the rest of her life. He'd been the first to grab Ottilia's arm. As for the one in charge, she'd never forget the puckered scar running down one cheek or his mean, steel-framed spectacles.

Martel accepted Dietrich's offer to join them in a brandy. He didn't pull out a chair for his companion, Coralie noticed, or offer her a drink. Seeing the Klebers dancing, he asked Dietrich, 'How did your friend blow his face off?'

Dietrich let a beat pass, then said, 'He is — was — an explosives expert with the Luftwaffe and was injured in a laboratory accident. The friends who care for him no longer notice his injuries.'

Brandy arrived. Martel impatiently waved Félix away as the old man began one of his automatic compliments to the mute female companion who had found herself a seat. 'Kleber should be careful,' he said to Dietrich. 'Didn't some fellow in Germany try to blow up your leader? He failed and came to a nasty end.'

'You mean Elser, who planted a bomb at the Munich beer cellar in 1939?'

'Imagine if he'd succeeded.'

'Imagine.'

'Do you think there are other conspirators?' Martel stared at Dietrich over the rim of his brandy glass, as if sharing a dangerous idea. 'Other plots for your leader to worry about?'

'My friend, you are flirting with the firing-squad, voicing such ideas.'

Martel laughed and leaned back, his white tuxedo gaping. He was putting on weight, Coralie saw. About the only person in Paris who was. She turned to the girl beside him, who had still not spoken, and said, 'I like your dress. Lovely colour.'

The girl stared, sullen, fearful.

'Is it green or blue? Hard to tell in this light.'

The girl blinked and Coralie realised she didn't understand. She had butter-blonde hair – natural, not peroxide – and round cheeks. The paint on her nails was chipped, as if she gnawed them.

Martel downed his brandy with showy machismo. 'I don't fear the firing-squad. I work with your boys. Look.'

Dietrich looked. 'Not *with* them, Martel. *For* them. The Gestapo do not team up with such as you.'

Coralie tried to kick Dietrich under the table because this game scared her, but the girl squealed in pain instead, and squealed again as another woman came up behind her and twisted her ear.

'Get upstairs.' Julie Fourcade tipped the chair sideways and the butter-blonde girl said something angry. Flemish, Coralie reckoned.

Martel jerked a thumb. 'She's right. Get upstairs, Marijke.'

Julie took the girl's chair, snuggling up to Martel. She wore a greenish orchid as a corsage. The flower could only have come from Spain – another of the luxury goods defying borders – and Coralie felt a rush of outrage. Children were being taken into hospitals perilously underweight. Everyone had dry skin due to the lack of fats in the diet. Yet fuel was being wasted to ship in fancy flowers.

Even as she let her outrage flow, the honest part of her soul acknowledged that she was doing better than most. *Her* child got meat four times a week, courtesy of the Luftwaffe HQ kitchen.

'Married now, you two?' she asked Julie.

Martel answered, without looking at her, 'Not yet.' He turned back to Dietrich. 'You know, von Elbing, I think you're one of those aristocrats who want Germany to lose the war.'

'Which aristocrats are those?'

'The ones who want to replace Hitler with one of your own kind. *Dachterrasse.*'

Dietrich had picked up his brandy, but now he put the glass down. Looked first at Serge, then at Julie. 'If you believe you have something on me, turn me in.' He held them in an unblinking stare. 'My only regret would be to have wasted a fine evening in a badly run brothel.'

'I run no brothel.' Martel's colour rose.

'That this is a whorehouse would be obvious to a fifteen-year-old farm boy on his first visit to the city.'

'I am not running a brothel.' Martel spoke through clenched teeth.

Dietrich concentrated his gaze on Julie. 'Do you live here with this man?'

Julie squeaked, 'What are you suggesting?'

'That you should do a better job of protecting him. It is illegal for a man to be in charge of a brothel. To be so would render him a pimp. It follows that, if you are Martel's fiancée, his consort, you are the *madame*. That makes you liable for the good order of the place.'

'What's he saying, Serge?' Julie hooked a curl off her brow and twisted it nervously.

Martel muttered something. A threat, a denial.

'You are breaking two laws, Mademoiselle Fourcade.' Dietrich took a long sip of brandy and Coralie thought, He's good at making people squirm. I can vouch for that. 'One, you employ foreign girls. That is *verboten*. Second, you have not subjected them to the required medical checks.'

'How d'you know?' Martel flashed back.

'Because I consulted with the chief medical superintendent of Paris only yesterday. You are violating every law there is.'

Serge Martel searched inside his tuxedo and, a moment later, handed Dietrich a card.

Dietrich glanced at it. 'Gestapo membership. I heard they are taking anybody, these days.' He held the card in the candle flame, even as the flame bent around his fingers.

Martel stood up and shouted.

'He's bringing those buggers over,' Coralie warned.

'Let them come.' Dietrich dropped the flaming card into an ashtray, and clicked his fingers at Félix Peyron, who had stayed close by and seemed to be enjoying the spectacle of his employer trying to put out the flames.

Seeing him, Martel roared, 'Do something, you old fool!'

To Martel's horror, Félix pointed a soda siphon, spraying liquid and ash everywhere.

'Idiot. Get out of my sight!' Martel screamed first at Félix, then at Dietrich. 'You will answer for this, von Elbing. I have friends who will make you answer.'

'Understand one thing, Martel.' Dietrich did not lower his voice, though people at nearby tables were straining to catch his words. 'The Gestapo have great power, but it is not limitless. Even they know that it is the Wehrmacht, the army, who will fight and win this war. They know also that the army has three enemies: Russia, the Western allies . . .' he savoured the moment '. . . and foreign brothels peddling venereal diseases to our troops. To catch the pox is one of the greatest dishonours that can befall a German soldier. For the pimp and the *madame* supplying contaminated girls,' he turned to Julie, who looked bewildered, 'there is even less mercy.'

'Is there some disagreement?' The Gestapo officer with the scar and spectacles had come over. He stated in German, 'Something was burning just now.'

'Major Reiniger, good evening.' Dietrich met the major's practised scrutiny without flinching. The *Pour le Mérite* hung over the collar of his shirt and Coralie saw Reiniger take stock of it and mentally change tack. 'Herr Generalmajor. Apologies, I thought, perhaps, there was a difficulty.'

The shaven-headed subordinate standing behind his major regarded Dietrich with almost fanatical respect.

'There is no difficulty,' Dietrich said. 'Merely that Monsieur Martel has accused me of plotting to murder the Führer.'

Martel gulped, then stammered something. His broken nose, old injury though it was, must be impeding his oxygen flow because he changed colour and spittle joined the soda water and charred paper on his tuxedo. Coralie began to see that Dietrich was not, perhaps, entirely mad.

Dietrich continued, 'By insulting me, he insults our army and the air force upon which the Führer's vision of a greater Germany depend. He insults my war record and my name, which, in honour, I must defend.'

Major Reiniger stared at Serge Martel, his lenses shining like the eyes of a fox in the dark. 'You are drunk, Martel. Why else would you insult a German officer?'

Martel pointed at Julie. 'She gave me the information.'

Julie stared, slack-mouthed, at Martel, evidently waiting for him to announce the joke. Coralie said quietly to her, 'Admit you made a mistake. Say you're sorry and we'll all go away.'

Julie thrust a finger at Coralie. 'She's a spy!'

At that moment, the Klebers joined them, seemingly shocked at finding the table they'd left ten minutes earlier ringed by tense bodies. Reiniger and Kurt Kleber already knew each other, and as Kurt introduced his wife, Coralie allowed herself to hope that the situation would dissolve into friendly handshakes.

The Vagabonds had completed their first set and people were streaming off the dance floor. 'You have an office where we can discuss this privately?' Reiniger asked Martel.

A minute later, eight of them were climbing concrete stairs to an upper storey.

Martel's office was untidy, a surprise – Coralie had always judged him on the evidence of a spotless tuxedo. Papers covered his desk and a greasy telephone suggested he made calls while eating.

Julie was blank with shock, and started crying when Reiniger snapped at her in German: 'Explain what information you have heard of Generalmajor von Elbing.' He repeated the question in French. Slowly.

'My fiancé said that he – Graf von Elbing – wants to sacrifice himself to save Germany.'

They all looked to Dietrich, who raised an eyebrow. 'I may well have said that. You may have said the self-same words, Reiniger.'

'I mean, he wants to kill Hitler,' Julie explained desperately. 'Sacrifice himself by killing Hitler. Somebody told my fiancé, somebody who knows him.'

'Who?' demanded Reiniger, but Julie shook her head. 'I don't know.'

A silence followed, so intense Coralie could hear somebody's watch ticking.

Martel was leaning against a wall, arms folded so tightly his knuckles were bloodless. 'You've got it wrong, Julie. Tell Major Reiniger that you always get things wrong. What Herr Graf von Elbing has been overheard saying is that he wants to *sacrifice himself for Hitler*.'

'That's not what you told me!' Patches were forming under Julie's arms, darkening her satin dress. 'He made one attempt and failed. *You* told me that.' She stepped towards Martel, her fingers knotted in a distorted prayer.

'Gentlemen, my fiancée,' Martel pinched his mouth in distaste, 'my *former* fiancée, has a weakness. She invents things to make herself the centre of attention.'

Coralie knew it was over for Julie when Reiniger said to her, 'You accuse an officer of the German air force of this most disgusting, shameful crime for your own amusement?' He rapped to his colleague, 'Get her out of my sight.'

Julie's screams ripped along the corridor, before stopping abruptly. Coralie saw Kurt and Fritzi Kleber move closer to each other. She sought Dietrich's eye but he was gazing beyond her, his expression empty. She looked at Martel, who had thrown a girl he supposedly cared for off a cliff.

Martel made an appeasing motion of the hands. 'If you gentlemen—'

But Dietrich pushed him back against the wall. 'Your woman made accusations against Mademoiselle de Lirac. *A spy*, she said.' Coralie froze. 'Has she special reason to suspect her of espionage?'

Dietrich stepped back and Martel scuttled over to a filing cabinet. He reached deep inside and brought out a white card. 'Julie found it in one of Mademoiselle de Lirac's handbags, but I'm sure it's nothing important.'

'Why keep it, then?'

'I – I had meant to tear it up.'

So there had been something in the bag. Something of hers or of Sheila Flynn's? Or something she'd picked up on her journey to Paris with Dietrich?

Dietrich took the card, staring at it for a good half-minute, an aeon to Coralie. He said, 'It is a race card, from an English racetrack. The Derby Stakes.' He passed it to Reiniger, who gave it to Coralie. Who dropped it, picked it up but could hardly read it, she was trembling so badly.

Priced sixpence. She and Donal had bought one each.

'You were at that race?' Reiniger asked her.

Coralie sought Dietrich's eye but he was staring past her. Her choker ribbon felt suddenly too tight. 'I can't entirely remember.'

'She was there, Major Reiniger, as my guest.' Dietrich shrugged. 'It was 1937 so no crime for either of us. I was there on business—'

'What business, Generalmajor?'

Dietrich gave a small smile. 'The business of art. Using my position, my title, to get invitations to as many great English houses as I could. I made discreet inventories of their art treasures so that when we invade Britain I can ensure that the best pieces are reserved for the enrichment of the German people and the personal pleasure of the Führer.'

'Why take Mademoiselle de Lirac? Why take a Frenchwoman?'

Dietrich laughed out loud. 'You need ask? Because I adored her, as I still do.'

Reiniger clicked his fingers for the race card. Coralie realised from the way he inspected it, his lips slowly moving, that he must also have some command of English. Handing the card to Kleber, he said in German, 'I want to know which horse she backed. One of them is marked.'

Without giving Kleber time to read the list of runners, Coralie said, 'Mid-day Sun.'

'Ridiculous choice,' Dietrich said. 'The odds were impossible.'

'And yet he won,' she said. 'Graf von Elbing backed a horse called Le Ksar. Russian, isn't it? Why don't you accuse him of spying for the Soviets?'

'Generalmajor, Oberleutnant, gnädige Damen,' Reiniger was stiff with apology, 'you have been subjected to filthy slurs. I beg you, accept my deep regret and return to your table. I wish to speak alone with Monsieur Martel.'

Back in Dietrich's flat, they gravitated to the fireplace because the night had turned cold. Tepid ash told of a fire that had burned itself out hours ago. They stood in a circle, holding hands. Dietrich, Coralie and the Klebers. It was Fritzi Kleber who finally said, 'That felt like showing a policeman a dead body and daring him to accuse you of murder.'

Dietrich agreed. 'It was the only way, Fritzi. Martel had his moment and lost it.'

Kurt said thoughtfully, 'He can never make the same accusation again and be believed.'

'Poor, poor Julie,' Coralie said. 'What will happen to her?'

Fritzi sighed. 'You are sorry for her, yet she would have seen you dragged off without a shrug.'

'But Martel . . . I mean, not a word in her defence.'

They digested it, then Kurt said, 'We need to know how Martel got his information. Who knows about Dachterrasse? Who knows of our plans?'

Plans? Understanding crept slowly towards Coralie and she told herself that she was mad or had misunderstood Kurt. She'd presumed they'd all been victims of a distasteful joke spawned from Martel's warped mind. 'Plans?' she echoed belatedly. 'Dietrich, Kurt, you mean you really want to kill Hitler?'

Chapter Twenty-seven

'Not yet.' Dietrich broke the circle and picked kindling out of the fire basket. He clumped the sticks together, held them out. 'One or two can be snapped, but a bundle is unbreakable. Only when we have an unbreakable circle can we act. We have learned hard lessons from previous failure, from poor planning. We call ourselves the Dachterrasse Circle, after the roof garden at the German pavilion, but now we work with others elsewhere, and to them, we are the Paris cell.'

'Is it wise, involving this woman?' Fritzi looked from Coralie to Dietrich.

Am I? Coralie wondered. Involved? 'If you succeed, the war will be over?'

Dietrich answered, 'Only if the right men seize power in Hitler's place. Then we might make an honourable peace, but there can be no surrender for Germany. There can be no illegal and unjust terms as in 1918. We would fight on, if necessary.'

'Unjust' triggered Coralie's anger. 'You're making France pay millions of francs for the honour of being invaded. You bomb other people's cities and take their lands. Why can't you be satisfied with the country you've got and leave the rest of us alone?'

'Enough. Do not speak of what you cannot understand. You know nothing of our history.'

'You've started two bloody wars, I know that.'

'*Coralie*. Enough.'

'Dietrich, she's in shock.' Fritzi's gentle voice cut through the tension. 'That poor Julie – we all stood by.'

Dietrich made a quick gesture of apology. 'As you say, though Julie Fourcade would have sent all of us to the same fate and, in a few days, would have been wearing Coralie's hats about town.'

Coralie doubted she'd banish Julie's screams from her mind so easily.

'We haven't answered the most important question.' Kurt had his arm around his wife's shoulders, but he was looking at Coralie. 'Who is Martel's informant? Who overheard our conversations or listened in on our meetings? It has to be somebody who knows German and who knows Serge Martel. Who is that person?'

Coralie felt doubt stealing into the room. The Klebers looked at each other. Dietrich, at the floor. Out of nowhere, a memory barrelled into her mind. A café table on the Champs-Élysées. Herself and Teddy Clisson talking about Dietrich, she insisting he wasn't a Nazi.

'He certainly salutes like one,' Teddy had drawled, adding, 'I was waiting in the pavilion when you arrived . . . I watched him greeting his brethren.' Could Teddy be the informant? It would make him a collaborator of the worst kind, prepared to betray a friend. But did Teddy see Dietrich as a friend, or as a source of valuable artworks? Perhaps he resented being denied the pick of Ottilia's collection, and had taken his revenge by tickling Martel's ear with vague suspicions, knowing they would quickly reach the Gestapo.

She blurted out, 'Teddy was at the Expo when you all met. You, Kurt and that other man.'

'Who is Teddy?' Kurt asked.

'Thierry-Edgar Clisson,' Dietrich said. 'An art dealer, a friend. Go on, Coralie.'

'We were talking about you once and Teddy said he'd watched you that day, admiring your looks. He remembered "a deliciously handsome young German, named Claus von Something".' Hearing in-drawn breaths, Coralie suddenly wished she'd kept her mouth shut. Selfish and vain as he was, Teddy could *not* be a Nazi sympathiser. His pattern of living was the very antithesis of the Nazi creed. Neither would he turn over a friend. She of all people should know that. 'Forget it,' she said. 'It was a long time ago.'

'He understands German, this man?' Kurt asked.

Dietrich nodded. 'His mother married a German, and they lived in Berlin. Teddy visited fairly often. His German is more than adequate. Fluent, would you not say, Coralie?'

'I don't know,' she said miserably. She'd give anything to retract. 'What I do know is that Teddy is kind.' Not good, exactly. 'Kind.'

'And he has always spoken so well of me, Coralie. Not so?' A sad smile touched Dietrich's lips. 'I do not want to think of Teddy as false. Yet he is one of the few people in Paris who knows me well enough to make sense of my friendships and my public actions, match them against a thread of overheard conversation and come to the truth. And he was at the club tonight. Coincidence?'

'From what I've just heard, I feel certain that this is the man who has betrayed us. We must deal with him.' Kurt Kleber spoke lightly, but his un-shuttered eye glinted. 'Where is he likely to be?'

Coralie shrugged, trying desperately to think of a way to throw the men off the scent.

'When you spoke to him earlier this evening,' Dietrich asked her, 'had you the impression he'd stay late?'

'Yes, definitely.' Actually, he would almost certainly have left the Rose Noire by now. Teddy never stayed anywhere beyond the midnight curfew. If Dietrich and Kurt were to drive out to boulevard de Clichy, which even through empty streets would take some time, there was a chance she could reach rue de Seine ahead of them. Guilty or not, she must warn Teddy, because a stark alternative was in front of her. Fritzi Kleber had opened her evening bag and withdrawn a small pistol. She handed it to her husband.

Coralie expected Fritzi to leave with her husband and Dietrich, to be dropped at home on the way to boulevard de Clichy. But when Fritzi said, 'Coralie and I will wait here for your return,' her heart plummeted.

The men left, and a minute later Coralie heard a car engine being fired. The hunt for Teddy Clisson had begun.

Fritzi was in talkative mood, jarring Coralie's nerves. She asked about La Passerinette, apparently unoffended by Coralie's mono-syllabic replies. 'Paris styles have such mystique and, my dear, you would have stared at me in Munich.' She chuckled. 'So behind the mode! I hardly dared step outside during my first week here – though, naturally, I had the darling hat you made me.'

Coralie's fingernails curled into her palms as Fritzi exclaimed, '*Mein Gott*, it is past midnight. It is April the twenty-third.'

'Is that important?'

'Three days ago was the Führer's birthday. Belatedly, we must celebrate with a drink.'

'Must we?'

Fritzi's beautiful face became a picture of incredulity. 'Do you not believe in us, Coralie? Do you not realise that it might be the last chance?'

'Of course.' An idea struck Coralie. 'There's a new bottle of schnapps in the kitchen. Shall I fetch it?' She walked out, leaving Fritzi trying to poke some life into the fire. In the kitchen, Coralie took a couple of glasses and poured a measure of peach schnapps into each. Then, slipping into the bathroom, she located veronal, the sleeping powders Dietrich had introduced her to and which she occasionally relied on when the stresses of a collection got to her. A generous spoonful went into Fritzi's drink.

'You'll excuse me if I don't join you in the toast,' she said when she returned to the living room. 'I'll drink to "absent friends".' She passed Fritzi a glass.

'To Germany,' said Fritzi, and downed hers in one.

'Health and happiness.' Coralie took a dainty sip.

It took twenty minutes for Fritzi to fall asleep. After standing over her for a few moments, Coralie went to the telephone in the corridor. When the operator answered, she gave Teddy's number as quietly as she could.

At Teddy's end, the telephone rang and rang. 'Pick up, *pick up*.' Dietrich and Kurt had had almost enough time to get across town, to find Teddy gone from the Rose Noire and to have crossed back over the river. Even now, they might be turning into rue de Seine. *Pick up. Pick up.*

Somebody did. A male voice, a little raspy, said, 'Yes, hello?'

Hers was an urgent whisper. 'Teddy, you have to leave Paris, now! They believe you betrayed them, Dietrich and Kurt Kleber. They're coming for you. You have to get out *now*.'

'Thank you, Coralie. Message understood.' The line went dead. Coralie stood frozen to the spot, understanding dawning.

Teddy hadn't answered. Dietrich had.

Chapter Twenty-eight

To be out after curfew was to risk arrest. To be out after curfew in a lemon evening dress was to risk arrest while catching a dreadful chill. Doing it with a child in your arms was perhaps a stroke of genius. If stopped, Coralie could claim that she needed a doctor for a choking infant. Leaving the telephone dangling in Dietrich's flat, she'd run upstairs and slung a few essentials into a bag.

No time to write a note for Micheline, who was sleeping on a divan in the sitting room. Time only to snatch up her everyday handbag, the one containing keys, bank books and other essential documents, and wrap a sleeping Noëlle in a blanket. As she tiptoed down the stairs with her, Coralie reflected on her daughter's ability to slumber through virtually every crisis.

No fixing this latest blunder. Tonight, she had chosen sides – Teddy over Dietrich. And, yes, she might be wrecking Dietrich and Kurt's plan to rid the world of a tyrant for the sake of a man who preferred cats to people, and who might be a despicable collaborator. But when push came to shove, she'd chosen Teddy because he'd reached out to her when she was desperate. She couldn't explain it to herself, except that loyalty had trumped love.

Dietrich might never forgive her. Knowing what she now knew of his double life, he might not even be inclined to spare her. But there was no going back.

Luck was with her as she stepped on to rue de Vaugirard. The moon was behind cloud and the Luftwaffe sentries at the furthest point of their patrol, in rue Guynemer. With Noëlle heavy in her arms, she took the opposite direction, into rue Tournon. A true moment of fear came when headlights flared at the junction of Tournon and rue de Seine. Coming towards her. She ducked into a doorway and Noëlle whimpered.

'It's all right, darling. We're going to Tante Nou-Nou's and we'll pop you into that big warm bed.'

On rue de Seine, Arkady opened the street door at the second rap and it was clear that he'd only just come home. He wore his outdoor coat, his violin case in his hand. 'All right!' He raised his arms, as if fending off ill luck, then dropped them as he recognised her. 'You! Sorry, I thought I was in trouble for breaking curfew. I walk home always after work, because I must get out of the Rose Noire. Filthy place. But what is wrong? Noëlle is ill?'

'No, but I'm in a terrible fix.'

He ushered her up the stairs, where they found Una dozing on the sofa, a candlewick housecoat over her evening dress, her hair in sponge rollers. She sat up, saying muzzily, 'Darling – oh, my stars, what's up?'

Coralie gave them a filleted version of events. Nothing about the assassination plot or of Martel's foiled attempt to denounce Dietrich. All she said was that Teddy had fallen foul of the German authorities and that Dietrich had gone, with another man, to settle the score.

'Settle how?'

'They took a gun.'

Una pulled in a breath. 'I heard a car shortly after I was dropped home this evening. A door slammed and I had three heart attacks because I thought – well, we always think they're coming for us, don't we? Then I heard hard knocking just down the street. Yellow-belly that I am, I kept the lights off and my back to the wall. It was Teddy they were after? *Dietrich was part of it?* Why?'

'I'm not sure.' She wanted to tell Una and Arkady everything but she was ashamed of her own part in the situation, and of Dietrich's readiness to exact revenge.

'We know why.' Arkady was stirring up the fire, adding chunks of broken-up vegetable crate. 'His life is not natural. He goes to bed with men.'

'We don't judge, honey.' Una made space on the sofa so Coralie could lay Noëlle down.

'We do not judge so hard, but *they* do. Often Teddy is seen dining with young men. You want tea, Coralie, or chicory mud?'

'Neither, thanks. Did you hear –' she hated to say it '– a shot?'

'Gunshot?' Una shook her head. 'I heard doors slamming, and men's voices.'

'Shouting, arguing?'

'Fear. I heard fear.'

Arkady offered Coralie a cigarette, and when she refused, said, 'Sorry, I forget. You can stay here as long as you need. I go back up into the roof to sleep, yes?' He gave a rueful grin. 'Excuse me, I am very tired.'

'One more thing.' Just one little thing. 'The Gestapo took Julie tonight.'

Getting no response, Coralie wondered if they grasped what that meant. 'She will talk and she knows that you escaped from the camp at Gurs, Arkady. She was here when you and Florian arrived, one suitcase between you. She knows you fought in Spain for the anti-Fascists and she knows your origins. Florian's too.'

'You think they will arrest me, this Gestapo, because I am *manouche*? Or because I fight on the losing side in Spain?' Arkady took matches from his pocket, only to find the box empty. 'A mean-face woman came up to me the other day. Demanded to know if I was Gypsy. I said, "Are you witch?"'

Una pulled her knees up, hugging her chest. 'It's true, what Coralie says. We sat at this table, talking about costumes for the Vagabonds.'

Coralie nodded. 'And I kept going on about big Gypsy sleeves and playing up the romantic foreigner. At least Ramon should be safe – the Auvergne's a big place. You know he and Julie lived together?' Seeing a glance pass between the others, she slowly nodded. 'Clearly, you did.'

Una admitted it. 'Arkady's shoulder is the one Florian cries on and, yes, we should have told you, but I said you had enough on your plate.'

Coralie reflected that it hardly mattered any more who was in bed with whom. 'I'm scared for you,' she told Arkady. 'They have camps for Gypsies now, just as they have them for Jews.'

'Your German tells you that?' Arkady found a lighter in another pocket and snapped down on it, getting a short-lived flash each time. 'Damn and hell. Out of fuel. Everything runs out but trouble.'

'Here, emergency supply.' Una took a box of matches from under a sofa cushion and struck a light. Arkady crouched in front of her, cigarette glued to his bottom lip, and Coralie watched a tender ceremony take place between them. A moment later, tobacco smoke hit her, transporting her back to her father's yard in Bermondsey. To an iron chair by a wall where Jac would smoke his Navy Cut. She frowned at Arkady. 'Where'd you get that English cigarette from?'

It was Una who replied. 'Nose like a bloodhound. One of our guests left it.'

'Guests . . . an evader, you mean? English?'

'A tail-gunner. "Tail-end Charlies", they call them. His plane crashed just this side of the Belgian border but don't ask more.'

Arkady went to sit by the window, opening it slightly to let his smoke drift outside. Full as she was of brawling emotions, Coralie appreciated his consideration. He returned her look. 'I am not leaving. Who will protect Una if I go away?'

Una blew him a kiss and added, in her brightest voice, 'I was born under a lucky star, and Arkady's mother told fortunes. She always said her son would die on a carpet of leaves. Isn't that right?'

'A bed of leaves.'

'So, as long as he stays out of the park in the autumn, he'll be fine. But how about you, honey? Can *you* be safe?'

The answer was easy. Dietrich had once told her how difficult it was to make friends in Paris and, in defiance of that, she *had* made friends. But, one by one, they were disappearing. Ottilia, Ramon. Even Julie. Poor, silly Julie. And now Teddy, taken to God only knew what fate. 'No,' she said. 'I can't ever be safe.' She looked at Noëlle in her blanket and wondered if Dietrich would follow her here.

Maybe, but where else could she go?

Next to Una in the great bed, she lay awake, trying to dispel images of the gun in Fritzi Kleber's handbag and the look on Dietrich's face as he had left the flat with Kurt. Teddy was beyond her help, and she must plan for herself. More particularly, for Noëlle. She'd known for a while that Paris was unsafe for her child. No putting it off.

As Una turned and muttered in sleep, Coralie went through the names of everyone she'd ever met in Paris. Who among them might offer asylum to a little child? One name jumped forward, one so unlikely, she accused her mind of mocking her.

The following day was Thursday, Una's day off from the hospital. Leaving Noëlle behind, dressed in a plaid Javier town suit her friend had lent her, Coralie took the Métro to place de la Concorde. On rue Royal, she entered Henriette Junot, braced for a fight. She said to the first person she saw, 'I need to see the proprietress.'

A *vendeuse*, arranging narcissi and willow stems in a wicker trug, hardly glanced up. 'Upstairs. Keep climbing until you reach the ivory tower.'

On the stairs, Coralie stood aside to let a young girl come down.

'*Merci, Madame,*' the girl murmured.

'Loulou?' Behind the polite demeanour, Coralie recognised the skinny child who'd watched her fumble with Henriette's left-handed shears five years ago. 'It *is* you!'

'Oh, Madame Cazaubon. I beg your pardon, I was far away. Madame Junot is in her studio, but isn't very well. Please don't tire her.'

'Don't ruffle her, you mean? I'll do my best.'

The sound of a hacking cough made Coralie pause. Was she wasting her time? Henriette in health was a hyena. Henriette ill was likely to bite her head off before she'd got two words out. All the same, she had to try.

Knocking and entering, she inhaled a blast of pine oil and balsam. A figure in wide-leg trousers and a fisherman's sweater was bent over a metal bowl, a cloth over their head.

'Henriette?'

A hoarse 'What do you want?' confirmed the identity.

'I need somewhere to hide my daughter deep in the countryside and I'm hoping you can help. That place you stayed at, the
château de Jarrat in Ariège . . . is it owned by friends of yours?'

The cloth was flung aside, revealing a face the colour of mashed
strawberry. 'Kiss my arse. You put me in jail. Why should I do
you any favours?'

'I'm asking for Noëlle. She's Ramon's daughter, too, and he
would help if he could.'

Henriette walked up to Coralie and slapped her face, buck-
ling over into a paroxysm of coughing. Coralie, reeling from the
blow, watched without pity until Henriette began making a dry,
screeching sound. 'On your hands and knees,' Coralie ordered,
pressing hard on Henriette's shoulder. 'Drop your head and
breathe shallow. Shallow in, deep out. That's better.' She mas-
saged Henriette's shoulder-blades until the spasm passed. There'd
been some terrible lung disorders at Pettrew's, the air being constantly full of fluff and fur particles. They'd all been taught how
to help a colleague having an asthma attack. Looking down, Coralie saw how thin Henriette's hair was. Once blue-black, it was
woolly in texture, like that of an aged dog.

She helped Henriette to a chair and poured her a glass of water.

'I'm dying.' Weakly, Henriette indicated her worktable. Apart
from the pungent bowl and a water jug, there was nothing on
it. 'I spent three months inside La Santé, being plunged twice a
day into ice-water.' She lifted her head, a snake-like movement.
'Help you? I wish you'd never crossed my path, or Ramon's. The
bitch who left him – what was her name, Julie? – you brought
them together and she made a fool of him, so he ran off to join
some band of free-shooters. If he dies or the Gestapo get him,
it's on your conscience.'

'Men like Ramon are born, not made, Henriette. Look, whatever you think of me, Ramon loves Noëlle. I reckon she's the only person he truly loves – next to you, of course. So I'm asking help for his sake. Not mine.'

Henriette made a snarling noise. She'd lost teeth. 'Everyone cheats me. Lorienne, Rosaire, that bastard accountant I brought in, they're taking my world from me, bit by bit. It's "Lorienne Royer for Henriette Junot" but soon, it will be "Lorienne Royer for herself".'

A racking cough took over. Henriette put her hand to her mouth, and afterwards wiped blood off it. 'Ramon said you had a German sniffing around you. He was ashamed of you and so am I. Get lost.'

Coralie had one last card to play. To be precise, a photograph.

Taken at Noëlle's baptism, it showed Ramon cradling her. It could have been any baby, just a crochet bundle with a button-nosed profile. But the photographer had caught Ramon smiling down like a man witnessing a miracle. Henriette stared at it. Coralie knew it could push her either way.

After a minute or so, Henriette dropped the picture and sighed. She opened a drawer and removed a pair of keys, which she tossed towards Coralie. 'Seventeen, impasse de Cordoba. It's a back-street, linking with rue d'Édimbourg in the quartier de l'Europe, good for fast escapes. The flat's above a boarded-up printer's shop. It's cold as charity and nobody knows about it, not even Ramon.'

'It's yours?'

'All mine. You can move in there with your bastard.'

Coralie gritted her teeth. 'What do you use it for?'

'Trysts.' Henriette coughed again, grabbing the cloth that had been covering her head. When she finally looked up, she seemed surprised that Coralie was still there. 'What more d'you want?'

'To say thank you.'

'All right. I'm sorry, by the way.'

'What – for sacking me? Cheating me?'

'Not that! All's fair in fashion. No, for that girl we hurt, the one who works for you.'

'Violaine?'

'Lorienne swore she would return and release her. I didn't know she had not.' Henriette closed her eyes. 'There's a proverb where I come from – "Feed the crow, it will still peck your eyes out." Lorienne knows I'm finished. But . . . I shall evade her.'

'You're going home?'

Henriette found sufficient strength for a flash of disdain. 'No. I'd go back to Italy if I could, but I shall go to the next best place. Switzerland.'

Back at rue de Seine, Coralie found Noëlle in a lather of excitement. 'Oncle Dietrich came,' she said. 'I pull his necklace and say he is an otter. He said, "No, *you* are an otter."'

'It was an argument hopelessly circular,' said Una. 'If he hadn't been wearing that Blue Max, I wouldn't have known him.'

When Noëlle was at last quietly drawing pictures in the margins of a newspaper, the two women sat down to talk.

Una explained, 'He came in the form of a human telegram, delivered a few formal lines, clicked his heels and went. Though had he found you, not me, I suspect a quiver of emotion would have been detectable.'

'What did he say?'

Una took up the stance of a Prussian officer. '"You are safe and have no more to fear today than yesterday. I wish you had understood that I had to take extreme action last night and wish you had not meddled." At that point, honey, he stopped being a telegram and became just a little human. I *have* to know what you did.'

'Another time, Una. What else did he say?'

Una became Prussian again. '"I accept that the time has come for us to part and wish you well. You may return to rue de Vaugirard any time."'

'I can't go back there! I can't see him.' Coralie twisted her coral bracelet, which snapped in two. She gave a cry and buried her face. 'Course it's over. Course it is!'

Noëlle, looking up from her drawing, immediately burst into copy-cat tears, which forced Coralie to pretend the whole thing was a game. Later, she gave Una a broad description of the previous night's events – though saying nothing about the plot to kill Hitler. 'Dietrich and his friend Kurt believe the war will be lost. Somebody overheard them saying it and informed on them.'

'You mean Teddy informed, and that's why Dietrich went after him?' Una thought about it. 'I don't believe it. Know why? Teddy's in love with Dietrich. You only have to watch him when you two are together. The sight of you, so entranced, is unspeakably painful to him.'

'Are you serious?' Coralie chewed her lip. 'I never saw it.'

'Because when Teddy's with you he dilutes the impression by saying rude things about Dietrich. Oldest trick in the book. Here's what I think. Teddy's missing, but if anybody's killed him, it's the other fellow, Kurt What's-his-name. Your Dietrich is not a natural assassin. Sure, he's hurt that you double-crossed him, but he also knows he's drawn you into something murky. So, he's letting you go by going away himself. He's returning to Germany. Actually . . .' Una looked at the clock – just gone two '. . . he'll be on his way by now.'

It took all Coralie's resolve not to start crying again. Even among all this swirling distrust and confusion, she wanted Dietrich. Love had seeped back into her bones. Nothing would kill it. Her eyes brimmed again when Una gave her an *Ausweis* that Dietrich had left for her. It bore Coralie and Noëlle's names, an official Luftwaffe stamp and signature, and carried an open date. It meant she and her child could leave Paris swiftly, should they need to.

Arkady came home with the news that he'd called at rue de Vaugirard and found Florian and Micheline packing. The couple would be out of Paris by the end of the day. 'They go to Micheline's parents' farm, by the sea. So, we will not see them again. Bloody war. Bloody occupation.'

Coralie couldn't stop herself. She wept, and even Una joined in.

The sad, anxious spring of 1942 included one sharp moment of joy. Coralie cycled home one April evening to the *pied-à-terre* on impasse de Cordoba where she and Noëlle now lived, the fingers on her handlebars fuchsia pink because she and Violaine had been dyeing goose feathers all afternoon.

A familiar fragrance on the stairs – Worth's *Je Reviens* – alerted her to a visitor and she found Una drinking chicory coffee with the retired teacher Coralie now employed to collect Noëlle from nursery school each day. 'I have news,' Una whispered, as they kissed cheeks.

'I will say goodnight, Mesdames.' Mademoiselle Guinard put away her books. She was coaching Noëlle in reading and arithmetic. Coralie had struggled with spellings and her times tables at school, but Noëlle loved the work. Probably because nobody had yet told her it was work.

Once Mademoiselle Guinard was gone, Una said, 'Well, this place is certainly snug.'

'Poky is what you mean.' The flat's main room served as sitting room, dining room and kitchen, with a window providing a view of sullen impasse de Cordoba, a dead end, closed off by a railway line. Coralie and Noëlle shared a box-bedroom. The bathroom was little more than an alcove. Coralie had learned the timetable of nearby Gare Saint-Lazare from the shaking of the walls. In fact, the place reminded her of her father's shed. Its one virtue was that only her closest friends knew of its existence.

'Good news or bad?' she asked, as Noëlle put on the radio and began to dance. Dancing was the child's way of celebrating the end of the school day.

As a sobbing soprano filled the room, Una handed Coralie a postcard. A winter scene, city roofs with snow-capped mountains in the background. 'It's from Geneva,' Coralie said. 'Who do you know in Switzerland?'

It was addressed to Madame McBride, and the unsigned message read, 'O, Joyeux Noël, Noëlle.'

'Can you break the code?' Una grinned.

Coralie laughed suddenly. '"O Happy Christmas, Noëlle" . . . "O"! It's from Ottilia!'

'She took her time, but our friend seems to have developed a cryptic turn of mind.'

Coralie thought that highly unlikely.

Una agreed. 'Which is why I think she's living with her brother Max, who inherited all the family brains. He's taken Swiss citizenship and has rebuilt a sizeable business so I might be able to get his address through one of my government contacts. Then we can write a cryptic message back.'

As spring gave way to summer, Coralie immersed herself in work, always the antidote to doubt and loss. As was scavenging for materials. Of course, every day brought reminders of Teddy, of whom not a word or sighting had reached her, and of Dietrich. She missed them both, but Dietrich was the one she called out to in the early hours.

On 1 June, La Passerinette ran out of buckram. Coralie spent the next day, between clients, varnishing linen with rabbit glue and shellac, creating a fabric stiff enough for blocking. She'd snapped up two dozen fire-damaged hotel sheets at a stall on rue des Rosiers and hoped they'd sustain her through the summer. The sister-assistants, Didi and Paulette, complained that the shellac fumes were giving them headaches, so Coralie sent them to parc Monceau, to find feathers. Pigeons were attractive meat, these days, and the grass was often strewn with their plumage – and with city milliners determined to get to it first. She was hanging up squares of linen to dry when Violaine came into the workroom to chivvy her into going home. 'My head is spinning too, so I don't know what yours is like.'

'My head's been spinning since 1937.' They wished each other goodnight, and a moment later, Coralie heard Violaine's tread on the stairs. Seconds later, a piercing scream.

Coralie was out of the door in a moment and found Violaine rooted to the landing, staring in horror at Madame Thomas, who must have come down from her flat with the intention of doing some early-evening shopping. The older woman wore a hat and carried a basket. A bold star had been sewn to the bodice of her dress.

Two days ago it had become been compulsory for all Jews in France to register with the police and wear the six-pointed yellow star on their outer clothes. 'Why?' Violaine's voice shook with more than shock.

'Because we must,' Madame Thomas stammered.

'You trotted along to the *préfecture* because you were told to? Would you jump off the roof of this building if they told you to?'

Though affronted on Madame Thomas's behalf, Coralie felt Violaine was overreacting. 'My friend Una is American and she goes once a week to a police station at Neuilly to have an attendance card stamped. Lots of people have to.'

Violaine turned on Coralie. 'Just because an ordinance goes out, we don't have to obey it.'

'It is the law,' Madame Thomas insisted. 'We have to obey the law.'

'Why? You're a French citizen! They have no right to number you and make you wear a label.'

'No,' Madame Thomas sought Coralie's eye, 'but isn't it better to go voluntarily than have the police fetch you?'

Violaine was beyond the reach of moderation. 'You came to France fifty years ago. You have no accent, you aren't religious, your husband was not Jewish. Who would have known if you had kept quiet?'

'There must be records. Somewhere it will say that I came originally from Prague.'

'So let the Germans search the records! They want you on a list so they can deport you!'

Madame Thomas shook her head. 'The poor creatures being deported are all foreigners and refugees.'

Coralie agreed, to soothe her own apprehensions as much as Violaine's. 'The authorities won't turn on their own citizens, just because they happen to be Jewish or American. They wouldn't dare.'

'No,' Violaine came back sarcastically, 'because then we might vote them out of office.'

★

With four women working together, emotional flare-ups were inevitable at La Passerinette. But the rift grew wider. Violaine never ceased to regard Madame Thomas's yellow star as if it were an open wound, while Madame Thomas regarded Violaine with steady reproach. Was prejudice Violaine's vice? Coralie had never suspected it, but people were deep. Take Henriette, handing over keys. Una, evolving from socialite to dedicated nurse. Silly man-mad Julie . . . No. She still couldn't think about Julie.

Didi and Paulette were openly anti-Semitic. The elder, Paulette, told Coralie one day, 'Madame Thomas mustn't come into the salon. It isn't just that ugly star. She's barred from public spaces now. If word gets out, we could all be in trouble.'

But Coralie couldn't bring herself to make such a speech and took her feelings out on Paulette, and on Didi, standing a step behind her sister. 'If you object to Madame Thomas, we must part company. I will write your references while you collect your things. I don't expect to see either of you at La Passerinette again.' She then told Madame Thomas that she was free to come and go through whichever door she chose.

It was only when Amélie Ginsler delivered the final consignment of the horsehair rosettes she and her grandparents had made that Coralie woke up to the danger she and her staff were in. Amélie knocked at the side entrance. Coralie poked her head out, calling, 'Come in through the salon.'

'I'll use this door. This says I have to.' Amélie pointed to the *étoile jaune* above her heart. Meeting her in the corridor, Coralie saw beads of sweat on the girl's brow. Though it was a cloudless June day, Amélie had on a thick coat.

'I refuse to sew that wretched thing on to my dresses. So I'm forced to wear my one coat everywhere.'

She'd walked all the way from the Marais, with heavy bags,

because taking the bus or Métro had become a humiliation. People would move away from her, she said, or refuse to let her sit down. 'I can't stop at a café table or peer into the window of a shop for fear of being moved on. We must keep moving, like stray dogs, and though some people feel sorry for us, there are plenty who think we're getting our just deserts.'

'If you want to sit in the salon and drink tea, be my guest.' Coralie was astonished to see Amélie's brows tilt angrily.

Madame Thomas came out of the salon just then. She'd been out on an errand and wore a bolero over a summer blouse. Seeing a yellow star that matched her own, Amélie exclaimed, 'If a customer were to report you, Madame, and La Passerinette closed down, we would all lose our work. It is this,' she gestured at the bags she'd put down in relief, 'that feeds my daughter and my grandparents.'

'I will use the side entrance from now on,' Madame Thomas said meekly, and Coralie nodded agreement. It felt like colluding with injustice, but fighting back would only make things worse. Her friends must keep their heads down, tread quietly through life, survive. Then, when the world returned to normal, they could congratulate themselves on having acted right.

The end of a stifling July day. Coralie stepped off the train at Paris's Montparnasse station, reaching to take Noëlle from Una's arms. Arkady unloaded their suitcases and, carrying the heaviest ones, led the way to the ticket barrier. They'd just enjoyed a week away, Coralie's first proper holiday ever. A friend of Una's had lent them a house near Rambouillet, to the south-west of Paris. Standing deep in the woods, the cottage had been basic, but that hadn't mattered. They'd filled their days with picnics and walks, boating on the river Eure, cooking outdoor suppers on fires Arkady had lit in the garden. He had played his violin while they sang English and American songs, and French ones with outrageous anti-Vichy lyrics because nobody could hear them. Coralie had done things she'd never done as a child, with all the pleasure of doing them now with her own little girl. As the Paris suburbs filled the train window, she'd felt a tug of regret.

At the Métro entrance, they were told that lines twelve and six were closed. 'Walk to Duroc station,' they were advised.

They could have separated then, Arkady and Una to walk to rue de Seine, Coralie and Noëlle to take the Métro to the Right Bank. But a strange noise seemed to be coming from the west, from the river, like distant thunder mixed with the roar of a football stadium.

'Sounds like planes.' Coralie scanned a sky as violet-blue as a chicory flower. The RAF and its Allies had re-bombed the western suburbs back in March, targeting weapons plants. Four hundred people had died.

'Such noise would have to be many planes, and they do not come in daytime,' Arkady said.

'Sounds to me like a big game's in play,' Una said. 'Honey, we'll all stick together.'

They headed west along boulevard du Montparnasse. The Eiffel Tower above the rooftops was their beacon as they walked towards Duroc where, by mutual agreement, they proceeded past the station entrance. Noise drew them on. It was when they reached the Champs de Mars, the open space surrounding the Eiffel Tower, that they finally identified where the noise came from. It rose from the Vélodrome d'Hiver nearby. The 'Vel' d'Hiv' was a covered cycle track. Evening sun streaked the western sky, but over the stadium lay a halo of bluish light.

'They don't usually race this time of the year,' Una commented. 'And it's Sunday.'

'That's not the sound of cheering.' Coralie's shoulders were aching because Noëlle had wanted to be carried since Duroc. A headache was taking hold, made worse by a smell on the breeze. Sulphurous – familiar. What exactly?

It came to her. Once, on a hot day, her father had told her to empty the piss bucket in his workshop. It was a metal canister with a lid, like a milk churn. Pouring the stagnant contents into the yard drain, she'd almost passed out.

'A rally?' Arkady suggested. 'Perhaps Hitler has come to visit again.'

'Could be,' Una agreed. 'It's a feral sound.'

'Let's turn back.' Urgency gripped Coralie, as on the day she'd heard soldiers marching down the Champs-Élysées. For all she hated the Métro, she wanted to get underground. She turned on her heel and the others followed. But at Duroc a milling crowd suggested that another line had been shut.

'What do you say we all go to ours?' Una suggested. 'Have tea and wait for the engineers to sort things out.'

A welcome idea. But as they re-crossed the intersection of rue de Vaugirard and boulevard du Montparnasse, they discovered a rough blockade had been thrown up. Gendarmes stood guard, their numbers swelled by cadets and youths in shirtsleeves. 'What's going on?' They were about to find out. Coralie saw the policemen crane forward, as if watching for something.

Within minutes, there came the snarl of engines and a policeman shouted to the cadets to 'stand by'. A moment later, a motorbus chugged by. Coralie saw children's faces, their features indistinct through the sheets of wire mesh that covered the windows. They wore sun-hats and bonnets, and her instant thought was, They're going on holiday. But so late in the day? And why the mesh windows?

It couldn't be a prison bus because it bore the insignia of CTRP, the Paris-region public-transport company. And what prison bus took little children? There were adults too. The vehicle braked, giving her time to see a woman mouthing something at her through a square of window. Her face was locked in disbelief. It was also familiar.

'Amélie!'

Françoise too. The child lay awkwardly across her mother's body, a patchwork blanket rolled for a pillow under her cheek. Coralie ran alongside the bus as it picked up speed, Noëlle's head bumping against her shoulder. She shouted, 'Amélie!'

A hard hand grabbed her, an equally hard voice ordered, 'Don't run!' It was one of the gendarmes.

'I know that girl – she's my friend. Her child's very sick. Where are they taking them?' She was being pulled back towards the barricade. In a moment she'd drop Noëlle.

'Get back, woman. This is none of your business.'

'But where are they going?'

'To Pithiviers, to the assembly camp. They're going to be counted.'

'Counted . . . So they'll be let go?'

The policeman took stock of her smart travel suit, her eighth-*arrondissement* shoes, her La Passerinette hat. 'Of course, Madame. It is just a formality.'

Next morning, Coralie got herself to La Passerinette as early as Noëlle's routine allowed. It was the school holidays, and while Mademoiselle Guinard was away, she was bringing her daughter into work. They walked hand in hand and, for once, the child's chatter failed to divert Coralie. She couldn't get the sights and smells of yesterday out of her mind. Why send people away to be counted in a different town? Last night as darkness fell, she'd walked through an eerily empty Marais, even though she'd known Amélie wouldn't be there. Such silence . . . as though a monstrous machine had sucked the inhabitants away. In rue Charlot, she'd found the doll shop unlocked, Amélie's grandparents sitting side by side on the stairs. Monsieur Ginsler had stared mutely the whole time she was there, as waxen as one of his dolls. His wife's voice had crackled like a worn-out tape-recording, the sound turned low. 'They came on Wednesday. We wait for Amélie. They do not take us because we are too old.'

Too impatient to walk all the way to boulevard de la Madeleine, Coralie waved down a *vélo* taxi, a bicycle pulling a small cabin on wheels. Noëlle sang with delight. Her favourite form of transport!

Expecting La Passerinette to be open, Violaine there to welcome them, Coralie surveyed the locked door, the drawn blinds, and her stomach turned over. Violaine was *always* at work by now. She wasn't the sort to take advantage of the boss being on holiday. Telling Noëlle sharply to stop hopping, Coralie found her own keys.

No hats in the window. Just a couple of dead bluebottles – Coralie shuddered: she retained a horror of flies. The workroom was locked, too. 'Right, up the stairs,' she said brightly, while her heart thudded. Violaine's flat was empty, and in Madame Thomas's, she found the landlord's handyman turning off the gas.

'It'll go back on when the new tenants come in,' he said, giving Noëlle a friendly wink. 'We've a full set of empty flats, all the way up to the roof. You'd get a good bargain, if you fancied moving into one of them, Madame.'

'Where is Mademoiselle Beaumont? Where's Madame Thomas?' Coralie demanded. 'They can't both have left.'

'Jewish, *hein*? The police had a round-up while you were away. Nice and neat, none of us saw it. All the Jews in Paris to the Vel' d'Hiv and shipped away.'

'They've made a mistake.' Coralie wanted to slap the stupid grin off his face. 'Madame Thomas is a French citizen and Violaine isn't even Jewish!'

The man made a face implying, 'What am I supposed to do?' Downstairs in the salon, Coralie found a letter on the mat. It had been there when they came in because Noëlle's small footprint was on it. It was dated Wednesday, 15 July:

You will be wondering why. Her name is Vadia Bermanski and she is a Polish-born Jewess. She thought nobody knew but that is because she does not realise that files can be opened and records searched. She is also obdurate and physically deficient. She always made my skin crawl. I watched the police take her and the other woman away. Vadia dropped her spectacles and a policeman trod on them. Digest that image, Coralie de Lirac. Imagine her final fumbling views of Paris, and you will now understand the cost of sabotaging my life and my work. How will you fare without your 'right hand'? Who will prove herself the better milliner now?

It was signed 'LR'.

'*Maman?*' Noëlle plucked at her sleeve.

'I'm all right, precious.'

A Romany woman had once told Coralie that she would kill and she'd found the idea laughable. Back then, she'd not understood the complexities of friendship and love. Neither had she known that people like Lorienne Royer existed.

She gazed around her salon. *I'm an Englishwoman who loves France and I will fight this evil, whatever it costs.*

It would cost, and she would start paying when a honey-sweet autumn turned Paris once more into a city of gold.

Another Thursday morning, towards the close of September. Coralie dropped Noëlle off at her new school on boulevard de Courcelles. It was a private one, recommended by Mademoiselle Guinard. Noëlle was ready for proper school, she'd said. The child was gifted.

It was just a hop from the Hôtel Duet, and after she'd left Noëlle, Coralie cycled through parc Monceau, where the ghosts of her youthful love affair still walked. She had not given up the business of hats – not with private education to add to her other bills – but because La Passerinette now consisted of herself, alone, she had established a new regime. Arriving at half past nine, she manufactured until lunchtime. After lunch, she took off her apron, turned the '*Fermé*' sign to '*Ouvert*' and became fitter and *vendeuse*. At six, she went home.

There had been no autumn–winter show, the grief-laden summer sucking creativity from her. She now made hats to suit the individual customer, each one absorbing her until it was complete, when she would jump, like a grasshopper, to the next. She had put up her prices and, rather to her surprise, was ridiculously busy. Wheeling her bicycle into La Passerinette's lobby, she heard the telephone ringing in her workroom.

'Possess your soul in patience,' she muttered, digging for her keys, which, inevitably, were right at the bottom of her bag. The telephone rang stubbornly on. At last, she picked up, giving her usual, 'Bonjour, La Passerinette.'

'Please come over – now.' A woman.

'Who is it?'

'I just got home from a night shift and learned that soldiers called at my door at six this morning. Looks like today's the day.'

'Una? You sound like a guitar string about to break. The day for what?'

'They're taking us Americans in. I called the hospital and some of my colleagues have already been arrested. I've maybe got a few minutes, an hour if I'm lucky.'

'Then grab your things and get over here. I'll hide you.'

'And put Little One's life on the line? No, it's face-the-music time.' A shaky laugh. 'This is German–US politics and we're caught in the middle, but I can't think they'll keep us too long. Can you come over, though, fast as you can?'

For once, the Métro ran without stoppages. Even so, Coralie arrived to find Una on the pavement, flanked by German *Feldgendarmarie*. They were burly men with silver gorgets around their necks like over-sized dog tags. They had fighting-dog faces to match. Even so, Una was arguing.

The men were trying to induce her to step into the open back of a troop truck. Coralie saw faces peering out from under the canvas. All female. All, presumably, American detainees. Some were dressed as if for a diplomatic reception. Others were bundled into mismatched clothes as if they'd been jerked out of bed or from their kitchens.

A policemen ordered Una, 'Get in, girl, quickly.'

'Honey, I can't.'

Coralie saw the difficulty. Una had chosen to wear her plaid

Javier suit, the one called Lomond, and its skirt was too narrow to make the step.

Walking forward, Coralie explained the problem in German, at the same time pulling off her coat, making a screen of it so Una was able to hitch up her skirt and join her compatriots. 'My suitcase,' Una rasped.

Coralie handed it into the truck. 'Only field-police,' she hissed in lightning-fast French. 'No you-know-who.' The absence of Gestapo suggested that Una's Resistance activities were not the cause of her arrest. It looked like politics, pure and simple.

'Tell Arkady I'll be back soon as I can.'

'Where is he?'

'Vichy, playing at the Hôtel du Parc. Take care of him and here,' Una dropped her house keys into Coralie's hand, 'use anything of mine you like, and please—'

Coralie was pulled away from the truck so roughly, she felt the cartilage crack in her armpits. The vehicle was revving. A soldier pulled down the canvas flap, knocking Una backwards, but as the truck drew off, an immaculately manicured hand forced a gap. Una's face appeared. 'Feed the dog!'

'You don't have a dog.'

'Sure I do. My bulldog. Take it to my good friends at the hospital.'

In Una's flat – her old flat – Coralie checked every room in case Una really had acquired a dog. An apricot toy poodle, she could believe. Or maybe a Maltese terrier dyed to match the McBride wardrobe . . . but a snuffling, bandy-legged bunch of muscle? That'd be the day.

Finding no signs of canine occupation, she presumed that shock had temporarily addled Una's brain. She unplugged the lamps, checked the gas was off on the stove and that there were no dripping taps. Finding notepaper on the dining table, she wrote a message for Arkady, telling him to call her. The radio was in its usual place among the pots of mustard and honey, and Coralie moved the dial from Radio Londres, where Una had left it. 'You've been listening to the British Broadcasting Corporation – oh!' Bulldog! British bulldog!

Checking that rue de Seine was clear of uniforms, she fetched a broom and tapped on the ceiling hatch, calling out in English, 'You can come down now. I'm a friend.'

Moments later, RAF Pilot Officer Terrence Bidcroft was stretching his limbs and blinking. As she boiled water for coffee, Coralie explained that Madame McBride had been detained. 'Looks like I'm your helping hand from now on. I'll have to find out what I'm supposed to do with you. Meanwhile, how d'you take your coffee? Ersatz, I'm afraid.'

'Who's Madame McBride?' Bidcroft asked anxiously, as he sipped the milkless brew. He had a ruddy complexion, sandy hair and a handlebar moustache.

'Your hostess. The lady who lives here.'

'You mean Paule? That's what I was told to call her. This is dangerous work and operatives have code names. What's yours, miss?'

'I haven't got one. Can't you tell I'm new to this?' As soon as the words were out, Coralie knew she'd re-voiced a pledge. She'd wanted to fight barbarity and the moment had arrived. And with it, lethal danger.

Two days later, she was standing on a platform at Gare de Lyon, sobs splitting her throat. The Resistance had chosen her, forcing an agonising choice of her own. She was sending Noëlle to Switzerland in the company of Henriette Junot. In any other situation, she wouldn't have entrusted a pot plant to Henriette's care but war forced people to the strangest compromises. God protect her darling, and God help Henriette if she botched it.

During the summer, Coralie and Una had exchanged letters with Max von Silberstrom, who had confirmed, in carefully coded terms, that he and Ottilia lived together in a quiet square in the centre of Geneva. Coralie was confident that Noëlle would find a loving foster home with them. Persuading Henriette to take the child there had not been easy, however.

'I don't like children and my memory isn't what it was. I may leave her on the train. Anyway, the girl doesn't have an *Ausweis*.'

'She does.' Coralie produced the permit that Dietrich had left for her. 'It carries my name too, but you can explain that I was taken ill.'

Reading in Coralie an unshakeable determination, Henriette had sighed. 'Very well.' When Coralie had given her the von Silberstrom address, her expression had lifted. 'Goodness, that's the finest square in Geneva. Is it the housekeeper you're friends with?'

'The owners, Henriette. Be civil to them – you might get on their dinner-party list.'

Putting Noëlle on the train, passing up her little suitcase, checking she still had the address label around her neck should Henriette's memory indeed fail, Coralie felt eviscerating pain. 'You have that letter for Tante Tilly?'

'Yes, Maman. Why aren't you coming?'

'It's a holiday, just for you.' The letter read, *Please take care of her and tell her every day that she is all the world to me.*

She left as the train pulled out, and strode home, bellowing like a cow whose calf has been ripped away, heedless of glances and even the occasional snicker. In her flat, she cast herself on to the sofa and beat the cushions until her fists burned. By linking up with Una's people at the American Hospital, taking Pilot Officer Bidcroft to a railway station and handing him over to a Resistance courier, she had crossed a line. She was part of something big, yet utterly alone. At least now she could give herself up to danger without putting her daughter at risk. Now she must wait and see what more the Resistance wanted of her.

Nothing, it seemed. October arrived, the days merging one into the other. Then, around the middle of the month Coralie was closing for the evening, reaching into the window to pick up the last sunflower stalk, when she became aware of eyes watching her. Her stomach flipped but she opened the salon door with a show of confidence. 'May I help you?'

The visitor was a trim woman in a well-made suit. A good-quality hat, which had probably been bought as war broke out, covered her greying hair. 'Mademoiselle de Lirac? Do you not remember me?'

The voice was the key. 'Mademoiselle Deveau!' Coralie embraced her former tutor, squeezing a little too hard because nineteen days without human contact felt like a lifetime. 'How lovely to see you. Have you come to buy a hat?'

'May we talk privately?'

In the workroom, Coralie learned that the American Hospital had passed her details to a Resistance circuit of which Mademoiselle Deveau was a member. Realising that she already knew the person being recommended, Mademoiselle Deveau had made more enquiries and had walked past La Passerinette a few times. 'To see who comes and goes.'

She was a member of the circuit known as Fortitude, she explained. 'Now that Paule has gone, we need somebody to act as a courier for military intelligence and to operate a safe house. I hardly need add, that person must be loyal, intelligent and brave. If you are not that person, please say so now.'

Coralie considered her answer. 'You know that I had an *affaire* with Dietrich von Elbing, and that I serve more German than French women in my shop. Some would say I'm a *collabo*.'

'They might indeed.' Louise Deveau gave an inscrutable smile. 'But I see that as an advantage. You speak German, and you stand over the heads of German women every day. Scraps of information from enemy lips can be sent to the Free French government in London. Every word is as good as a bullet. And should you ever renew your love affair . . . all the better.'

'Dietrich is back in Germany. I reckon we'll get back together the day Adolf Hitler joins the Red Army.'

Louise Deveau made a gesture very like Una's 'Okay, okay' hand wave. 'Come to me at rue de l'Odéon when you've thought about it. I don't need to tell you that it's lonely work. You can trust nobody and confide in nobody.'

'I don't need to think. I made up my mind in July when friends of mine were deported. I can't help them, but I can act in their name.'

Mademoiselle Deveau nodded. 'Your codename will be "Cosette". You will not see me after today. Another agent, Moineau, will contact you from now on. Should you be arrested, you are on your own, though I will expect you to name me –'

'I wouldn't!'

'– as I will name you under duress. It is why you will never know the identities of more than two operatives. We are spokes in a wheel. A couple of spokes can be smashed, the wheel still turns.' She rose. '*Guten Abend, Fräulein de Lirac*.'

Within a couple of weeks, Coralie-Cosette was picking up handwritten intelligence dockets from a butcher's shop in rue

Mouffetard. As the shop opened each morning, she'd buy a piece of meat, then cycle to a private address on avenue Foch, her secrets concealed in the false bottom of a La Passerinette hatbox in the basket of her bicycle. She'd toot her klaxon at German soldiers having their breakfast, singing under her breath, 'Ça ira.'

It's all going on. It'll be fine.

In November 1942, in response to Allied advances in North Africa and the relentless bombing of Italy, the German Army occupied the whole of France. The Vichy government, unable either to respond or resist, was exposed as a toothless regime. There was no longer a 'Free Zone', no demarcation line to cross. For Coralie, in island-Paris, the impact was minimal. Of course, life grew harder, but it had been doing that for three years. German soldiers seemed edgier, more likely to shout and point guns at civilians. But ladies still wanted hats.

A card came from Geneva: 'Merci pour le cadeau de Noël.' *Thank you for the Christmas present.* A few days later, there was a letter from Una. She was being kept at Vittel in the Vosges mountains, she wrote, and could send and receive letters through the Red Cross. 'Write reams, and send books, magazines, anything.'

Coralie did so, and food parcels, warm underwear and a brand new hat in a La Passerinette box. She suspected that the last gift had never reached her friend, as Una failed to mention it in her following letter. That was when Arkady lost hope of her imminent return. He was now in the Auvergne, perhaps with Ramon. Certainly with the Resistance.

The winter of 1942–3 came like a malignant houseguest, reaching into every corner. Into bones and lungs. Coralie worked doggedly at La Passerinette to blot out that bleak, childless Christmas. She'd often sleep in her workroom because it was easier to heat than the flat on impasse de Cordoba.

'Alone' seeped into her soul. Even the Resistance didn't want her, it seemed. Mademoiselle Deveau's pledge that she'd be contacted by another agent had come to nothing.

In January 1943, she received delayed Christmas letters from Geneva, from Noëlle and Ottilia, and cried until she was in danger of washing away the words with tears.

All through that dark season, she gave what work she could to the Ginsler grandparents, but winter hit them hard and the old man died in the middle of January. His wife struggled on, often forgetting who Coralie was or that her family had gone. Coralie kept her fed, paid for her fuel and visited every other day. The old lady called her Amélie, and would snatch her hands to stop her leaving.

February threw out one bitter night too many. Arriving at rue Charlot, wheeling her bicycle because of the snow, Coralie found neighbours in a solemn huddle outside the shop, a light on upstairs.

Coralie begged an Almighty she no longer believed in for something – anything – to prove that life was more than a succession of heartrending failures.

The Almighty obliged.

Coralie was cycling to the salon when a man brought his bicycle alongside her. His black Dutch-boy cap was pulled down against the wind, a scarf knotted under his chin. All she saw were red-veined cheeks and a bit of unprepossessing earlobe. Thinking he was after a view of her pedalling thighs, she told him to buzz off.

'I'm Moineau, idiot.'

'You are? Sorry!' This was her Resistance contact? Somehow, she'd imagined a looker like Robert Donat in *The 39 Steps*, complete with quizzical moustache. What a let-down. Moineau cycled beside her long enough to warn her to prepare for a 'big parcel' that would be delivered to her home.

He slipped a booklet into her coat pocket. 'Rations for Jean-Pierre Vavin, a retired bank clerk in his sixties.'

She understood. Somebody would be needing her hospitality and to feed him she'd draw rations for this fictitious Jean-Pierre, whom she could probably pass off as her father.

'Where shall I bring the parcel?' Moineau asked.

She gave him the address on impasse de Cordoba. 'When's he arriving?'

'It's a parcel. We don't say "he".'

'Sorry. First time.'

'Just get queuing, then wait till dark, all right?'

She did as he said, spending hours in line for food, only reaching La Passerinette by late afternoon.

As evening fell, her heart rate increased. Her first evader might already be on his way. She'd better close the shop and get home. Wheeling her bicycle on to boulevard de la Madeleine, she was hitching up her coat skirts when a shout made her turn. A man in German uniform was crossing the boulevard three or four shop widths away, holding up his hand to stop the traffic.

Dietrich.

She sped away, cycling on the pavement as far as place de la Madeleine. Pedalling blindly into the stream of traffic earned her a fanfare of honks from impatient drivers. Usually, the cycle ride home from Madeleine took her twelve minutes. This time, she did it in six.

★

Moineau delivered half an hour before curfew. Answering his four-beat knock, she opened her door to find the pavement glittering with hoarfrost. She coughed three times; the all-clear.

Instantly, two dark figures peeled out of a doorway a little distance up the alley. One carried a suitcase and seemed to be wearing white gloves. Once inside, both men made a beeline for the electric fire. She had onion soup ready.

Moineau ate his standing up, anxious to get away before curfew fell. After giving Coralie instructions for the next stage, he took spirit bottles from each of his coat pockets. 'One to help the evening go with a swing, hey, Cosette? Take the other with you when you hand this gentleman on.'

Her 'parcel' was Jan Brommersma, a journalist from Rotterdam found guilty of editing an anti-German newspaper. In English, their shared language, Brommersma told Coralie that he'd been on his way to execution, but one of the soldiers guarding the prison van had been caught short. Desperate to relieve himself against the van's wheel, the soldier had left the rear door open.

'His relief is short-lived, I am thinking.'

Jan carried marks of beatings and cigarette burns to his face and neck and Coralie could not bear at first to look at his hands. He hadn't been wearing white gloves; each finger-end was wrapped in scraps of linen, through which blood had soaked and dried.

When he told her his exposed nail-beds were getting infected, she overcame her squeamishness and bathed his hands in warm salt-water, tearing new bandages from one of her own sheets.

They drank a tot of the aquavit Moineau had provided, but Coralie advised restraint. Tomorrow was the hand-over, the most dangerous stage of an evader's journey. After cooking him the

heartiest meal that ration books could furnish – rabbit pie, macaroni and lima beans – she suggested they turn in.

'You take my bed,' she said, realising quickly that his feet
would hang over the end. After elongating the bed with two
suitcases, she lay down on the sofa. Sleep was impossible. She'd
run away from Dietrich, left him calling her name in the street.
Why was he back and what did he want?

Once Jan had fallen asleep, his snores competed with the
freight trains coming in and out of Gare Saint-Lazare. Coralie
got up and, wrapped in blankets, cut out a pair of gloves from
black felt, large enough to cover a Dutchman's hands. Her needle
paused only when Jan began a harrowing dialogue in his sleep,
taking her into his nightmare.

Jan Brommersma had been courteous from the first, appreciative of the risk she was taking but, even so, she felt uncomfortable
to be sharing such a tiny space with a male stranger. One front
door opening on to a dead-end was also far from ideal. She needed
better accommodation.

Over a breakfast of the previous night's leftovers, Jan tried on his
new gloves with a child's pleasure, and asked her how she came
to speak such excellent English.

She lied, by habit. 'From a boyfriend, before the war. He was
an artist who came to Paris to rent a table at a Montparnasse café
and sit in the shadow of Matisse and Picasso. He liked to paint
me, and he'd talk.'

Jan, in his turn, told her the unadulterated truth of the devastation of Rotterdam by German bombers, and also of the
destruction of British towns and cities. He gave enough detail
for her to guess that there must be a trade in intelligence across the
North Sea, probably between the English east coast and Dutch

ports, like Antwerp. He told her that Londoners had christened the nightly pounding of their city 'the Blitz'.

'I met an RAF flier,' she said nonchalantly. 'I think he flew Fairey Battles.'

'Poor damn boy.' Jan Brommersma held his coffee cup between his palms like a child. 'I, too, met a pilot, after the fall of France. He had crashed and my wife and I got him to the coast, on to a fishing boat. He hated those Battle aircraft, called them "lousy crates". You understand "crate"?'

Only too well.

'He said they were too slow to outfly the enemy.' Seeing her face freeze, he said quickly, 'Hey, some blokes are always lucky, like me. Your pilot has been retrained maybe for Lancasters or Blenheims.'

She chose two in the afternoon for them to leave, the hour when shops reopened after lunch and people were hurrying back to work, or joining queues in the hope that a short break had magically refilled the shelves. Walking ahead, her trench coat buttoned against the cold, a pink feather in her hat, she kept to the middle of the pavement so Jan never lost sight of her. If he was stopped, she would pause to retie her shoelaces, dawdling until he was waved on. If it looked all over for him, she'd walk on. And tit-for-tat, she emphasised. No heroics. They were dead meat if they were caught, but the Resistance must go on, the wheel must keep turning.

Their destination was the Île de la Cité, the smaller of the two Seine islands that were the foundation stones of Paris. Knowing how hard it was for Jan's tortured fingers to grip a suitcase, she'd decided in advance to take a bus the length of rue de Rivoli. She'd given him change and coached him on how to pay the fare.

She could hear him, breathing heavily through the scarf he'd tied around his lower face to hide the burns. Lucky it was February, she thought, everyone similarly huddled. The wait at the bus stop flayed her nerves, and when a *gazogène*-guzzler drew up, she stumbled on board. A man laughed at her pink feather, asking where the rest of the flamingo had gone.

Coralie made a playful reply, and Jan was able to find a seat without anyone looking at his face. Still, Coralie spent the short journey convinced that, any moment, the bus would be flagged down and a quartet of Gestapo would order everybody out.

After alighting at the Saint-Paul Métro, she led the way down steep stone steps to quai d'Anjou. Hands in pockets, she strolled along the wharf, stopping just short of pont Marie. There she stared over the water, as if entranced by its colour of silvered teak when in fact she was reading the nameplates of the barges. *Be at your mooring,* Thalassa.

Yes, there she was, a rusted tub, her engine grinding out diesel exhaust. Coralie bent to smooth the ankle socks she wore over her woollen stockings. Left first, then right, as she'd demonstrated to Jan Brommersma. A hearty cackle came from above.

'Parcel for me, *michou*?'

Coralie glared up at *Thalassa*'s deck and hissed, 'Quiet!' An old woman, bare-armed and bare-legged in defiance of the cold, beamed down through ill-spaced teeth. She wore a straw hat a scarecrow would have handed back.

'That him?' The old woman pointed towards Jan, who was hesitating under the bridge. 'Have him throw his bag up first. Last lot were so nervous they nearly left a wireless set behind on the quay. Brought me my medicine, *michou*?'

Last night, Moineau had said, 'The old bird can't steer the damn boat without a proper drink.'

Coralie tossed a bottle of aquavit over the gunwale and the

boatwoman caught it expertly. Two minutes later, Coralie was on pont Marie, again staring at the river. As the chug of an engine became a thick purr and angled wavelets broke against the bridge's feet, she allowed herself to breathe. 'He's away! I'm a proper *résistante* now.'

And she was free to go back to work. At La Passerinette she found a note on the mat.

I must speak with you. Meet me at the café where we last had coffee with Teddy. I will be there at six. D.

The mention of Teddy felt so heartless that she tore the page up without reading it twice. After all, the job of a *résistante* was to resist.

PART FIVE

PART FIVE

Chapter Twenty-nine

It wasn't so much a fresh mood sweeping Paris as the days length-
ened — people were still hungry, angry and frightened — as a
new game, called Bait the Occupiers. Make fools of them, but
never let them know it. It was a very feminine game, and Coralie joined in. As La Passerinette still enjoyed favour among
German officers' wives, the scope for furtive sabotage was
endless.

It boiled down to shape and proportions. The couture collections at the end of February took the previous year's silhouette to
a new extreme and, as ever, hats reflected the trend. Coralie came
up with voluminous shapes to balance bold shoulders, narrow
waists and puffed skirts. The new style suited chic Frenchwomen,
but not broad German frames.

March 1943 arrived with peevish skies sneezing sleet which
rattled against the salon windows and kept clients at home.
One morning, fitting a hat to the head of Frau Pfendt, whose
husband's staff car waited at the kerb, Coralie thought unenthu-
siastically about her journey home at the day's end. No longer
the twelve-minute sprint to impasse de Cordoba. For good or
ill, she'd moved her belongings back to rue de Seine. Una had
paid the rent up to the end of March this year, so it made sense
to occupy it or it would be lost to them. And Una needed somewhere to come home to. Coralie firmly believed that, one day

soon, her friend would stroll into La Passerinette, saying, 'Well, *that*'s what I call a waste of a winter.'

Coralie was glad to be back on the Rive Gauche. She liked being a Right Bank milliner but the Bermondsey girl inside her was definitely Left Bank. Even so, she shivered in anticipation of the squall that would hit her when she re-crossed the river.

She asked Frau Pfendt to raise her chin a little – and felt like adding, 'All four of them, *gnädige Dame*' – 'I want to see if we need a little more height.'

The face in the mirror was round-cheeked with quivering jowls. In happier times, Coralie would have created something dignified. But Frau Pfendt was a victim of 'the game'. Thousands of French men were being sent as forced labour to Germany. Women too. Had Coralie not been married, she'd have been called up, as she was within the age range. The German occupation was siphoning food, labour, health from France – while making the victims pay twenty times over for every scrap thrown back at them. Anger needed an outlet. Coralie had her Resistance work, and this . . .

She stood back to judge the effect of supple, red leather which, when sewn together at the back, would resemble a soft trilby. She'd adopted Violaine's method of constructing directly on to clients' heads, speeding through different shapes until one stood out as a perfect marriage for the face beneath. Or, as in Frau Pfendt's case, as millinery grounds for divorce.

Now that supplies had dried up almost completely, Coralie had put aside her blocks and devised templates to fit any reasonably-sized remnant. The leather she was using for this client had been acquired, by an indirect route, from the bombed-out Renault factory. In peacetime, it would probably have upholstered part of a car seat.

Frau Pfendt would no doubt want some sort of fantastical trimming on it. One of Coralie's current favourites was wood-shavings, which, when sewn in place resembled . . . wood-shavings. She'd never seen the point of pretending that 'found' materials were other than what they were. Ersatz hats were just that. Good enough. Ersatz coffee was unpleasant and walnut-juice 'stockings' fooled nobody.

Taking a handful of stiff ribbon from a basket, she added bows and loops, which quadrupled the hat's dimensions. Red and white, barber-shop colours. Solange Antonin would have carried it off beautifully, but on Frau Pfendt, the result was a hair's breadth away from absurd. Teamed with the woman's outfit, a red and white striped suit from Jacques Fath's latest collection . . .

Showing Frau Pfendt how to hold the hat together on her head, Coralie perched on the sofa arm and invited her to walk up and down. She called out, '*Brava*,' while reflecting that short A-line skirts gave no quarter to stocky legs. Nor had Monsieur Fath designed the blouson jacket for matronly bosoms. Add grey pigskin ankle boots . . . 'over-dressed teapot'.

Coralie kicked one leg comfortably back and forth, watching her client contort. She'd embraced the new silhouette herself and was growing used to it.

She sat Frau Pfendt down again and made some adjustments. She was jotting notes when the gunshot creak above their heads made them both jump.

'Dear me!' Frau Pfendt patted her chest. 'Who's walking about up there?'

Coralie supposed it was the landlord or his handyman checking the place over. The rooms had remained empty through the winter but spring would surely entice new tenants in. Sometimes, at the end of a long day, she'd stand at the foot of the stairs and imagine she heard Violaine and Madame Thomas gossiping or teasing each other: 'What d'you fancy for supper, dear? Lobster Thermidor or *caneton Tour d'Argent?*' In the worst of her loneliness, Coralie had once called out, 'Goodnight, you two.'

'The new tenant's a harp teacher,' she improvised, to drive away those memories. 'He drags his instrument around to catch the light from the window.'

Frau Pfendt's eyes widened. 'I cannot imagine he has many pupils. Who will want to learn to play the harp with a war on?'

'You're right, so to fill the time, he does physical jerks. He crouches and dances like a Russian Cossack. Says it keeps him warm.'

She expected 'Really?' or 'Surely not!' but to her great discomfort, Frau Pfendt began to cry. Tears ran down the pillow cheeks, losing themselves in the many chins. Coralie fetched a clean handkerchief. 'Are you all right?'

'My son Wilhelm is at the Russian front.' Frau Pfendt blotted her face. 'Did you know, during the Russian winter, men freeze to their guns? What is it all about, Coralie?'

'I don't know, *gnädige Dame*.' Coralie took a deliberate step backwards. Keep it formal. Friendship was dangerous, and human sympathy was rationed.

She conducted Frau Pfendt to the pavement, holding an umbrella over her to her waiting car. Another vehicle was parked twenty strides along the street, and the service door to her building was ajar. So, it must be the landlord upstairs. Brrr! She hurried back inside. It was early still, just gone eleven, but even so, she doubted she'd get any more clients as it was Saturday. People would want to stay home with their families. She cleared the window display, pulled down the blinds and took her electric fire into the workroom.

She was hopelessly behind, always having to explain to customers why their hats were not ready. What she needed, she decided, as she drew her stool up to her bench, was that squad of elves. Ten new hats in a line on the bench every morning. She wasn't ready to appoint a human helper.

'Coralie?'

She screamed as a figure filled the doorway. The canvas head to which she'd been pinning pleated felt fell off the edge of the bench. She saw a black leather trench coat with wide lapels, a Homburg hat – and ice-water ran down her spine. The man removed his hat. 'Dietrich!' Or was she meant to call him 'Generalmajor' again? Actually, something more basic sprang to mind. 'You terrified me. How did you get in?'

He displayed a key. 'I am the new tenant upstairs.'

'No!'

'No, I am not. But I am looking over the place, with the landlord's consent.' He sauntered in, checking her workroom in apparent fascination. Once again, he seemed neither civilian nor soldier. The ribbon of his *Pour le Mérite* was just visible inside his leather collar. Did it still contain that cyanide ampoule? Hers was in her handbag.

He said, 'This place is never the same two visits running. I hope you take photographs. One day, they will be a fashion memoir in pictures.'

'I don't even have a camera. What do you want?'

'You. As you will not come to see me, I have run you to earth.'

There was only one door, and no proper window. 'I'll scream.'

'Go ahead. Shall I wait outside?'

'Oh, damn you.'

He was smiling in a way that suggested he was not entirely sure of his ground. 'Will you trust me, Coralie?'

'Shouldn't it be the other way round? I mean, I know too much about you. I've been wondering for months if you'd track me down, to silence me.'

'I think that would be beyond the scope of mortal hand.'

'You did it to Teddy. Dealt with him, without proof he'd done anything wrong. I hate you and all your kind. I'd like to kill you all.'

From beneath his coat, Dietrich took the pistol she'd seen in Ottilia's dressing-table drawer. He pushed back the safety and held the grip towards her. 'It is loaded, seven bullets. Even though you are not an experienced shot, you can almost certainly get one into my head.'

'Just go away.' She put her hands over her face. 'You don't understand what happened here. They took all of them. All my friends.'

'I know. And I am sorry, more than I can say.'

She sprang at him, making a rake of her nails. She got them caught in his medal ribbon and he raised his gun, pointing it up at the ceiling while with the other hand he prevented her from strangling him. 'Do not punish me, Coralie.'

'"Sorry" is an insult. "Sorry" pretends to care yet does nothing. Have you killed Hitler yet? That's why you went to Germany, isn't it?'

'You know perfectly well that Hitler lives still.'

'You should give me the job. I wouldn't keep putting it off!' Her voice was rising. 'I'd walk up to him, pull out a gun and bang! Done. You men talk but you don't act. And I don't believe you give a damn about my friends—'

He got his hand over her mouth. 'You are part of the Dachterrasse Circle, so stop behaving like Julie Fourcade.'

When he took away his hand, she said, 'I'm only part of Dachterrasse because you involved me.'

'I believed in you, as that proves.' He restored the gun to safety and returned it to its holster. 'Come upstairs.'

'What's up there?'

'You will see.' But instead of leading the way, he held her away from him and slowly shook his head. 'What are you wearing?'

What she was wearing was a nipped-in dress with Gypsy sleeves, a skirt that swirled when she turned, a frilly peasant apron tied at the front. For warmth, she'd added a sleeveless bolero. 'It's the latest fashion.'

'There are such shortages of cloth, of labour, of everything. Yet French couturiers are designing marionette costumes for women to traipse to work in. It makes no sense.'

It did to her. She and her fellow milliners might be out of materials, but factories were weaving clothing textiles again. For *French* consumption, defying the pressure to shift production to Germany. 'You lot don't get it,' she said. 'And I mean that both ways.'

They stared each other out until Dietrich said, 'Come on. The young gentleman upstairs cannot wait much longer.'

Chapter Thirty

Young gentleman? He wouldn't explain. Coralie mounted the stairs ahead of him. The door to Violaine's flat was ajar and there she stalled. Her legs refused. 'I can't.'

'It is only floorboards and bare walls.'

'That's why I can't. Where's Violaine? Where are Madame Thomas and Amélie? Where's Amélie's daughter?'

'Lost in Germany or Poland, and I am ashamed.' He ushered her inside the flat, impelling her until they were in the living room, which seemed vast. Violaine's furnishings had been big because she'd needed landmarks to help her get about the room. She'd liked textures, too, and Coralie had watched her steer by them, her fingers finding a *passimenterie* trim or the taut skin of a lampshade. The furniture had been taken out a few weeks ago by a team of men. 'I don't know who they were,' she said. 'German, obviously.'

'They call themselves M-Aktion Kommando,' Dietrich told her. 'The M stands for *Möbel*.' Furniture. '*Kommando* implies, of course, a military operation.'

'All her things.'

'Really, they're just a looting party but they're thorough. I do not suggest you look in the bathroom. Take it from me, there is not even a toothbrush holder, flannel or a sliver of soap left. We have a reputation to keep up of impeccable efficiency. But look,' he ironed the bitterness from his voice, 'something else is here.'

She had noticed the wicker basket in the middle of the floor, assuming it was something M-Aktion had left behind. Dietrich unfastened clips, reached inside. A moment later, he was cradling a cat, whose jet fur made his own leather coat look discoloured.

A baritone miaou made Coralie gasp: 'Voltaire? Where—'

'In the Jardin du Luxembourg. The kitchen staff at the Palais have been feeding him.'

'No wonder he wouldn't go home. Traitor.' She went up to offer a cautious stroke, noticing that his torn ear had mended in lumpy scar tissue. Perhaps she got too close to it because Voltaire hissed and lunged a paw. 'Has he gone feral?'

'I think so.'

'I suppose I'm the lucky so-and-so who gets to look after him?'

'You could, now you have no child to worry about.'

'How did you know?' Because he made no answer, she flung defensively, 'Yes, I sent Noëlle away. You'd given me an *Ausweis* so I used it.'

'You were wise, I think.' Dietrich studied her. Voltaire purred noisily in his arms. 'The permit had both your names on it so why did you not accompany her?'

'I have other ties. I mean, hat-making – what did you imagine?' She'd caught the flash of misgiving. 'I have to make money. I won't let Ottilia pay for my child to live.'

'She would do so with great joy.'

'And I'd still feel I was imposing. I'll take the cat if that's what you're here for. We'll rub along, won't we, Voltaire?'

'*Au contraire*, dear one. Once a daddy's boy, always a daddy's boy.'

Looking into the doorway, Coralie gave a cry of disbelief.

'Teddy! Is it you?' He was thinner, but seemed otherwise well and was smiling in his particular way. 'You utter bastard.'

'Charmed to see you too.'

'I thought Dietrich had killed you.'

Teddy tapped his breast. 'Quite solid, as you see. And, yes, I know what transpired at the Rose Noire and that I was in the frame as the arch-betrayer. Be assured, it was not me. I may tease the dear Graf — and you — with slanderous hints and libellous asides, but I am his friend eternally.'

'I thought they'd chucked you into the Seine or something.' Coralie ran to Teddy, laying her head against his chest.

He stroked her hair. 'It was Dietrich's bomb-damaged friend who had the murderous intent that night. Kleber, fortunately, was decoyed to the Rose Noire while the Graf doubled back to the rue de Seine. Finding me at home in night attire, he became unspeakably domineering. Slapped my face.'

'So I did, Clisson, because you needed to leave Paris at once, only you wouldn't listen.'

Coralie remembered Una's report of raised voices. 'So, when you went to find Teddy, it wasn't to hurt him?'

'I knew he was not our informant.'

'I wish you'd told me!'

She shrugged as Dietrich said, 'How? When?' reminding her that she'd done everything in her power to avoid him. 'Where did you hide him?'

Teddy answered. 'The dear Graf put me on a train to Dreux. I have been living in the gardener's cottage in the grounds of my château, incognito. Tomorrow,' theatricality fell away, 'I go to Switzerland because Graf von Elbing fears I may still be in danger.' He turned to Dietrich. 'Does the Freiin von Silberstrom like cats?'

'Not particularly.'

'You're going to Ottilia? Noëlle's there,' Coralie said eagerly.

Teddy smiled. 'I know, and I'm sure it will be at least eighteen pages.'

'What will be?'

'The letter you will ask me to take to our little sprite. Get to it, as I cannot linger. Goodness, my dear—'

She'd burst into sobs, emotion finally catching up with her. 'I've lost everyone, Teddy.'

Teddy gently detached her. 'You have not. Though our friend here has more layers than an onion – and the onion's talent for stimulating tears – you still have him and must never be afraid of him. Peel him, my dear. Make him reveal everything, and once you have done that, stand by him.'

Chapter Thirty-one

In her villa in Hohen Neuendorf in north-east Germany, Hiltrud von Elbing woke with a painful neck because she'd fallen asleep in her chair. Her knitting lay in her lap.

Voices in the hallway alerted her to a visitor.

'Who is it, Vati?' she called, pushing the half-made sleeve into her knitting bag, then pulling down the cuffs of her jersey to hide the puckered scars that disfigured her wrists.

Her father opened the door. 'A visitor, Hiltrud.'

'Yes, I know, but who – ah—' The *tupp-tupp* of a walking-stick, the uncertain shuffle, announced the visitor's identity. Finding a gracious smile from somewhere, Hiltrud rose and walked forward to greet her mother-in-law. 'Hannelore, you are welcome. How did you get here, though?'

'By train. They are still running, despite the destruction.'

'But so far, in this cold? And you so soon out of hospital.'

'Everybody helps me. Soldiers, passengers, even some French labourers handed me down from the carriage, like a parcel. It was fun. Certainly, it beats sitting alone in my flat, waiting for British and American bombers.'

This was a long speech for the dowager Gräfin von Elbing, and much of it was slurred. Her face drooped and her right foot turned inwards.

'How did you get from the station?'

'Mm?' The dowager leaned on her stick as she made her way to the sofa. 'I paid a man to bring me in his wheelbarrow. Your face, my dear. I paid a man to bring me in his car, better? Is this one going to loom over me?' Ernst Osterberg had shadowed her in case she fell. 'I don't want him next to me. He snuffles.'

Hiltrud made a face to her father, begging him not to react. 'Vati, could you make us coffee?' She said to her mother-in-law, 'It's awful stuff, I'm afraid.'

'Then why offer it? I'll have schnapps, Osterberg.'

Ernst Osterberg left, muttering, 'Since when did I become the butler?'

Hiltrud sat down again, twitching at her cuffs. 'Hasn't the weather turned bitter? Will we ever see spring?'

'No small-talk, I have not the reserves. I want to know why you are still in Germany, Hiltrud.'

'Where else would I be? My father is here. Claudia can still come home when she has time off. And Waldo—'

'Waldo's dead, and weeping over his grave every Sunday won't change that.'

'Don't. Please don't.' Hiltrud pressed herself back in her chair, wanting distance between herself and this drooping, wrinkled reminder of Dietrich. Her father came in with the schnapps, his expression saying clearly, *Alcohol before lunch. I am humouring dissolute customs for your sake, Hiltrud.*

Oh, good God, what if her mother-in-law meant to stay? Hiltrud made a mental sweep of her kitchen cupboard. Dried mushrooms, preserved apples, a jar of pickled eggs. Hardly lunchtime fare for a woman who used to dine in the best houses in Berlin, who'd travelled through Europe in private railway carriages, guest of princes and industrialists. She remembered, then, the reason she'd become upset a few moments ago. 'I am happy to see you, Hannelore, but please do not speak lightly of my son.'

'My grandson. My son's son. Of course I may speak of him. Put that tray down, Osterberg, and leave us be.'

Ernst Osterberg told her he'd stay where he damned well liked in his own house.

'My son's house. Graf von Elbing bought this house with his inheritance from his father and don't you forget it.'

'I heard that the money came from the von Silberstrom coffers. Stick your nose up in the air, but there was a time you weren't above taking handouts from a Jew.' Osterberg turned to his daughter. 'You know this old fiend hid Max von Silberstrom in her house when the Gestapo wanted him? In her bed, knowing her.'

'Vati, please! Forgive him, Hannelore.'

'I *excuse* him. One cannot ask a turnip to be a China orange. But your memory is awry, Osterberg. It was Max's father Bernard who was my good friend. As for my bed, for at least twenty years it has been as empty as your head.'

When her father had stamped out, Hiltrud poured schnapps and the smell of peach-stones filled the air. Her mother-in-law's unflinching gaze was unsettling and she almost dropped the decanter.

'Poor Hiltrud, are you not getting any better?'

'I think so. My doctors say so.'

'Then why are you here and not with my son?'

Hiltrud repeated doggedly, 'Because my daughter comes home when she can. Claudia expects me to be here, and my father needs me.' She'd overfilled one of the glasses. She'd better take it; her mother-in-law had suffered two strokes and now found it difficult to grip small things. 'I am still Claudia's Mutti, and a housewife.'

'You are also Gräfin von Elbing. Listen to me.' The old Gräfin took her glass in trembling fingers. 'Claudia is eighteen, with her own life now. Your father can fend for himself, but Dietrich is in danger.'

'We're the ones in danger! Does Paris get bombed? No! They eat four meals a day in France, Claudia has been told, and all the coal that is supposed to come to Germany feeds their fires. Fires in their grates even in the summer. They burn coal with their windows open so that we go without!'

'The French are for the French. Why should that surprise you? Answer a question. Do you want to lose Dietrich?'

Did she? Hiltrud wasn't sure. She hated him so powerfully, the mere sound of his name made her pulse jerk. But lose him? 'No, I think not.'

'Good, because he is involved in a conspiracy to assassinate the Führer.'

Schnapps spattered the carpet. 'Have you lost your wits, Hannelore?' They had not expected the old woman to recover from the second stroke, and if this was how her mind was going, it would have been better had she not. 'Who spoke this treachery?'

'Dietrich. He thought I was dying last November and made a confession at my bedside. A very full confession, though I am not certain he expected me to understand it. There is a group in Paris called –' the old lady summoned a word '– Dachterrasse. His purpose in returning to Berlin was to confirm the allegiance of this group with a more powerful one here in Germany. I had heard he often visited army headquarters on Bendlerstrasse. Now I understand why.'

Hiltrud drew herself up, wishing she had not put on an old dress this morning and such thick stockings. Shrivelled as her mother-in-law was, she put Hiltrud to shame in her black two-piece and pearls. 'You were at the gates of death. I suggest that you misunderstood Dietrich, who, after all, has taken an oath of allegiance to the Führer. What you are suggesting is foul and dishonourable and I will put it down to your infirmity. I will not hear another word.'

'There is something in my pocket. Take it out, see if it changes your mind.'

A moment later Hiltrud was thinking, *The old woman has certainly gone mad.* It was a piece of card cut from an outdated desk calendar. A French one at that.

'Other side,' her mother-in-law said.

Hiltrud turned it over and spoke the unfamiliar words. 'La Passerinette.'

'A hat shop in Paris.'

Below were numbers, one to thirty-six. After each number, more words in French. 'I never pretended I could speak foreign languages,' Hiltrud snapped. Belle. Séduction. Caprice. Plume. Rose. 'What does it mean?'

'It is the running order of a collection – a parade of hats. The shop is owned by your husband's mistress.' The old Gräfin acknowledged Hiltrud's recoil. 'When in Paris, Dietrich sleeps with a milliner. I said he made a full confession, didn't I? It wouldn't matter, except that this female seems to have charmed him to the point that he spoke of marrying her one day. She is blonde, tall and lovely, so it is perhaps not so remarkable that he should want to make her his wife.'

'His wife – how?'

'After your conduct last year, he might reasonably expect to be a widower soon enough.'

'That is cruel.' Now Hiltrud wished she'd put on a blouse with button cuffs. 'I was not myself last year.'

'Well – are you awake now? Dietrich is being drawn into a conspiracy for which the penalty is death. I cannot travel, so you must go to Paris and bring him back to his senses or, God knows, it may be the firing squad.'

Firing squad? *Her husband?* She wanted to sink down, and beat blood from the floor. Everything around her became slow and unreal. In the next room, her father put a record on the gramophone, a *Volkslied*. The siren-wail tenor mixed with her rising voice. 'He can't betray us! He can't marry a Frenchwoman. He's married to me!'

'Then why do you not wear your ring? The ruby one I passed to Dietrich for you, the one my mother-in-law passed to me.'

'I gave that back to him.'

'Ah, yes. When he refused to join the Nazi Party. I should have said, where is it *now*?'

Hiltrud had no idea. But she understood her mother-in-law's motive. The old woman was goading her into going to Paris to save Dietrich from dishonour and adultery. She doubted she could save Dietrich from the first, given his tepid allegiance to the Reich. But the second . . . loathing him as she did, she had never expected to be replaced. She minded. Minded very much.

Chapter Thirty-two

Coralie had expected Teddy to go by train to Switzerland, and so he would, but Dietrich was driving him to Lyon, the last major French city before the Swiss border.

'He must not be seen by anyone who may recognise him. He must melt away, and the world think him dead.'

'Why?' Coralie demanded. She'd been given an hour to write her letters and wrap presents and was trying to decide which hat to box up for Ottilia.

'I have my reasons,' Dietrich said, 'but I won't divulge them. Not yet.'

'Something else it's safer for me not to know?' Her exasperation bubbled over.

'Exactly. Send the green hat to Ottilia. It's a colour that suits her. Have you chosen gifts for everyone, now?'

'One last thing.'

The men left shortly after, taking Voltaire in his basket, the longest letter Coralie had ever written in her life, a hatbox for Ottilia and a beret for Noëlle. Cherry-red with a pheasant feather, it had been intended for somebody else's child. Coralie had sewn a La Passerinette label into it, spearing her finger in her haste.

She then closed up for the weekend and went home.

*

'*Manna, come on! Come on, my lad, come on . . . Yeees!*'

Now where had that come from? Coralie saw, clear as yesterday, a white, rain-washed rail and jockeys flying past in their spattered silks. She saw her mother's hat dripping dye on to an angry face. Derby Day 1925, and more rain had fallen then than it had on Noah's Ark. The fact that her daughter had just picked the winning horse seemed only to provoke Florence Masson further.

Seated by the front window, eyes closed, Coralie remembered her father lofting her on to his shoulders. *Hup, petite!* 'Manna from heaven! Manna from heaven! Ten pounds I put on that horse to win! Our girl's a natural!'

'That's right, Jac, encourage the kid to be a gambler. When she's a penniless drunk in the alley, picking up the whores' drawers for twopence a time, we'll know who to thank. I'm off.'

Florence had stormed away – slipping in the mud. 'Some bloody day out this is!'

'More fool you,' Jac returned, drunk on the joy of winning. 'Boots next time.'

Florence had got to her feet, her yellow and green outfit plastered. 'I hate you. I hate you to the marrow of my bones, Jac Masson. Lay me in my grave, and I'll still be hating you. And d'you know what?' She'd strained forward like a dog at a fight. 'I've got somebody better. He's a gentleman, an actor, and he knows how to treat a woman. I've had enough of your drink, your stinking workshop, your sulks and your bloody fists.'

And that was the last Cora had seen of her mother.

Coralie opened her eyes. Perfectly evident what had triggered the memory. Dietrich had had twenty-four daffodils delivered to her that morning, even though it was a Sunday and the previous evening he'd set off for Lyon. She'd put them in front of the window as pursed buds. Four hours on, they were singing like canaries. Their scent shouted, 'Springtime!' even though winter had still two weeks to run.

Turning her eye inwards to a rainy Epsom Downs, Coralie saw her mother's yellow shoes picking across emerald grass. She frowned. That wasn't right. For a start, the Derby crowd had trampled the grass to muddy porridge and Florence's shoes had sunk deep. They'd turned brown as high as the instep. And then, any dignity her mother might have salvaged as she stalked away had been spoiled when her heel came off.

The cine-film sequence in Coralie's head went blurry at that point. The only clear and solid fact was her mother's shoe heel in a tin, in a kitchen cupboard in Barnham Street. How had that heel got from Epsom Downs to Barnham Street?

A knock at the street door brought back the bright reality of Paris. There was a car at the kerb, the car Dietrich had regularly borrowed when they lived together at rue de Vaugirard. Running downstairs, she opened the door and pulled him inside. They said nothing until they were upstairs, the door locked behind them. She fell into his arms. 'I wasn't expecting you till tomorrow.'

'In the end I left Teddy at the station in Dijon. He knew how badly I wanted to be back here.'

Back here . . . back together? 'Trust him,' Teddy had instructed her and she so wanted to. 'Peel him.' She wanted to do that, too. Was she ready to be his lover again? Would it be forgivable, honourable, even?

Why not begin safely with small-talk? 'Will Teddy stay with the von Silberstroms?'

'Until he finds a flat somewhere in Geneva. He is excited at the prospect of finally viewing Ottilia's art collection. That was all he could talk about during the journey.'

'I thought those paintings were in Germany.'

'I never said so, Coralie.'

'Don't play games. You sent them back to your home town, to Hohen Neuendorf.'

'When?'

She smacked his arm. 'You told me so, and Teddy said you were sending the collection to Germany as a gift for the Nazis.'

'Teddy says a great many things. The truth? I sent Ottilia's collection to Neuendorf in Switzerland. Her brother Max has a hunting lodge near a village of that name, and the paintings live under his roof.' Dietrich drew her face up to his. 'They are safe. I always said that, no?'

'No. I mean, yes. I didn't know there was more than one Neuendorf.'

'I should think there are plenty. There is even one in Canada.'

'You could have told me so before! I think you should let Teddy buy those Dürers to make up.'

'Absolutely not, because they are not genuine works. All this time, I have been protecting Teddy from gross humiliation and a bad bargain.'

'The Dürers are fakes?'

'Good ones, but not good enough.'

She kissed him lightly on the mouth. 'For not being a swindler after all.'

'If I am to be kissed for everything I am not, should we retire to bed?'

She felt the tug of nature, the counter-force of conscience. There were so many objections to their relationship. Yet she loved this man. Her body had no doubts so she opened negotiations with her conscience by saying, 'I'm not going to apologise for ringing Teddy to warn him that night. I really did think you were going to kill him. As for Kurt, he had murder in his eyes.'

Dietrich let her go and threw himself down on the sofa. Then he got up again, stripping off coat, hat, driving gloves. When he sat back down, he stretched the cramp out of his limbs. 'I left the flat that night every bit as angry, but not as single-minded. I gave the car keys to Kurt and sent him up to boulevard de Clichy before walking the short distance to rue de Seine.'

'Knowing Teddy would be there?'

'In spite of your attempt to send me to the other side of Paris? My darling, I am as familiar with Clisson's habits as you are. I walked, and the night air calmed me.'

'I had to do it.'

'I know. You were torn between loyalties, but you chose Teddy because you have an affinity with the underdog. I am only surprised it took you so long to make the call.'

Coralie recalled digging her nails into her palms, willing Fritzi Kleber to fall asleep. *I won't tell him I laced her drink.* 'I've often pictured you hammering on Teddy's door, him letting you in, white-faced above the collar of his Oriental dressing-gown.'

'We will call it a "firm knock".'

'After that, an altercation – conducted in civilised tones, of course. Teddy calling you "dear Graf" and you insulting him the way you do.'

'The way I do?'

'As if reminding him of something he already knows. I always imagined a gunshot, Teddy slumping, blood on the wall.'

'You are reading too many crime novels. Teddy panicked and his instinct was to hide under his bed. To get him packed and out, I let him think his personal life had caught up with him – as, to be honest, it has. He is on a Gestapo list of degenerates. As for you, I did not blame you for running away – your instincts were correct. The situation that night was deeply unsafe for you, but it did teach me something.'

'What?' She was perching at the far edge of the sofa and he moved to allow her to sit more comfortably. His gaze bathed her.

'That, in fundamentals, you and I are on opposing sides. It does not make me love you the less. But it is so, and being apart is the safest, the correct, thing to do.'

'Oh.' Her heart fell, telling her more about her feelings than any philosophical arguments. 'If that's what you want, complete separation, then I suppose I agree.'

'But do we wish it, Coralie? Our love is full of risk and will offend many, but separation is so cold.'

And she was so weary of being cold. She moved closer and he put his arm around her. They sat silent, Dietrich's eyes on her, hers on the daffodils which were melting into a dazzling paint-splash.

'How did you get flowers on a Sunday?'

'The Duet. I called on my way out of Paris with Teddy, and said, "Flowers, at any cost." How they did it is their secret. Will you tell me now how you passed your time all those months I was away in Germany? With your husband?'

'I haven't seen Ramon since the day we thought Noëlle had escaped. What about you? Were you back with your wife all that time?'

'My wife does not go to Berlin.' It wasn't a chuckle, the sound that caught in his throat. 'Do you know what is happening to my city? Do not imagine a place where people meet in cafés or discuss life and literature strolling along Unter den Linden. Your lot are bombing us to Hell.'

She knew it. Terrence Bidcroft – Una's RAF pilot – had flown in a squadron that was part of a relentless aerial assault. He'd been vague as to whether the strategy was working, but Radio Londres put it more concisely. 'Germany is being pounded towards inevitable surrender.'

Dietrich would tell her yet another version, no doubt. 'Did you return to your wife at all while you were back there?'

'I spent time with my mother, whom I thought was dying. Who *is* dying, though she is enjoying a long finale. Yes, with my wife sometimes. Hiltrud tried to take her own life on the fifth anniversary of our son's death, and for a while I was the only person she would allow close to her. I travelled between Berlin and Hohen Neuendorf as much as air raids and the trains allowed. But now I am back, wanting only to kiss you.'

They moved together, and their kiss became a long rediscovery. Dietrich stroked her face, as if he needed to learn its shape again, then slipped his hand beneath the untidy layers of cardigan and blouse she'd put on because it was cold, and because she'd expected a day alone. He found the swell of breasts and nudged her brassière down to find a nipple, toying with it as she opened her mouth to invite in his tongue.

She let him lead her to the bedroom where they undressed quickly. He wore his *Pour le Mérite*, and she had taken again to wearing her satin choker. They stared at each other's throats.

'Let's hope we never have to,' he said.

'Still, it's nice to know we can,' she quipped.

They laughed at the shock of marble-cold sheets. Gradually, body heat won out. How long since they'd been alone, with a day before them? Coralie sighed as he stroked her belly, hips, thighs. She opened her legs and let him stroke her to the point of climax, then pushed him away, saying, 'My turn. I shall touch every inch of you.'

Peel him, learn everything. She would begin under the blankets, without that most deceiving of senses – sight – to get in her way.

If only they could stop time. Coralie would gladly have signed up to an endless afternoon in that rustic bed. Warm, sated and happy. But Dietrich had other ideas.

'I want you to come back to rue de Vaugirard. Every day, the central heating is turned on and warms nobody. Why stay here?'

'I'm not ready to move again.'

He didn't argue, though she felt it was a tactical retreat.

'At least come for the evening. Bring evening clothes and we will bathe and change in the warm. We are going out tonight. Where is the ring I gave you? You should wear it?'

Five orders in five seconds. He wasn't a *Generalmajor* for nothing.

He explained more as they walked to his flat. 'I have booked a table at the Rose Noire.'

'Are you mad? Last time we only just got away with our lives.'

'We can crouch in the shadows or stride down the middle of a sunlit road. Which do you prefer?'

Later, dressed for the town, they stood in front of a crackling fire. He wore his uniform, the *Pour le Mérite* dead centre between his lapels. She wore an artificial-silk evening dress, one of Una's, in cream and gold print. It had bell sleeves, a flounced neck and a tight waist. The pewter-grey choker didn't look right with it, so she hung her silver snuff-bottle from a fine chain. The ruby ring weighed down her middle finger. Dietrich seemed as wound up as the watch he kept consulting.

'Dietrich, what's tonight about? You seem excited . . . upset . . . I can't tell which.'

'I am impatient. Not with you, not even with myself, but with others.'

'Explain.'

'Berlin has been bombed afresh. Thousands have died. Hundreds of thousands are homeless. My own flat near the Tiergarten . . . uninhabitable. You accused me yesterday of failing in courage, as if I had Hitler in my sights and had failed to pull the trigger. But it isn't that simple. Putting a stop to the blind murder of my country is no less my desire and duty than it was a year ago, and the reckoning is in sight, but others will say when.'

'So – when?'

He made a warning gesture. German orderlies were billeted at the top of the house. Forbidden to use the lift, they entered the main flats only to lay fires and clean, but his gesture implied, 'Ears and eyes.'

He went on, 'In Berlin, I met military friends and we renewed our intention but the pace is slow. Like you, I want to speed up the music and run.' He spanned her waist with his hands. 'I often dream that it is all over. Last night, I even dreamed we had a son. I could not see where we were living. Somewhere very high, with a view over the world, and I knew that you were my wife. If I survive what is to come, I want to live with you and only with you.'

She kissed his forehead, her lips finding the raised scar left by his crash-landing twenty-five years before. She would like Dietrich's child . . . but not yet. She needed her body to be free because, like him, she was tied to a duty. She would never divulge her Resistance activities to him. He had his allegiances, she had hers. It would be tough, being together, with so much to hide.

'Tell me again why you want to go to the Rose Noire.'

'To hear music and see faces. To hold you in my arms.'

'We could do that anywhere. You want to walk into the wasps' nest because it's more fun than waiting for the wasps to find you.'

He gave a slow smile. 'You paint my thoughts. So, shall we go?'

'No.' She put a hand to her hair. 'I can't go out without a hat.'

Chapter Thirty-three

Walking down the familiar shadowy stairs, through the baize curtain that an attendant pulled aside, Coralie was struck by the brilliance. She hadn't blinked like this for months. The deserts of Africa had their oases and Paris had its Rose Noire.

Lustrous lights and candles, quartz-pink tablecloths, wreaths of flowers and polished silver – it had returned to being a refuge for pampered *exils de luxe*. People and hope might die, but money never did. It just crept into ever fewer hands.

How often could the world be remade and still make sense? Her world had changed in the last hour. Dismantled like a wooden puzzle, and rebuilt in a new shape. Not a worse shape, but a profoundly troubling one.

Félix Peyron saw them and managed to bow while still walking. Or, rather, hobbling. *Arthritis up to his knees*, Coralie thought. He struggles on, because he has to. And then Martel was before them, a flat palm accentuating his heart.

'Monsieur le Comte, Mademoiselle de Lirac, when I heard who had booked a table, I reserved the very best one. A pleasure to see you back here. You will discover a few changes. For the better, I trust.'

With Arkady and Florian gone from Paris, the Vagabonds had ceased to exist. A new band filled the stage, nine men, playing old-fashioned swing.

Dietrich asked, 'Have my guests arrived?'

'Just this minute, Monsieur.'

Dietrich hadn't mentioned guests. Coralie frowned. Like an onion, just as Teddy said. Layer after layer. If she peeled too far, what would she find?

As they followed Martel, she felt they were being watched. Dietrich always commanded attention and her dress shimmered like a firebird's wings. With no time to wash and set her hair, she'd brushed it out and let it hang in its natural curl. She must be the only woman there who hadn't used a gallon of sugar-water. As for a hat . . .

When she'd refused to leave the flat without one, Dietrich had insisted, 'You look beautiful as you are.'

'I'm a milliner! I wouldn't ask you to go on parade in a linen suit.'

He'd flicked his wrist, for the tenth time.

'That watch must be getting sea-sick,' she'd said tartly.

'Couldn't you adapt something of Ottilia's? The wardrobe is still full of her things.'

In Ottilia's former bedroom, he'd unlocked an armoire, revealing a treasury of couture. Only one hatbox, and whatever it contained would be years old. Opening it, she'd exclaimed, 'Good God! Tilly's trifle-topping.' It was the hat Ottilia had worn at Epsom, which Coralie had cheekily suggested needed a brim.

Actually, it looked good, though as old-fashioned as she'd feared. It was the wrong weight for evening too. 'I don't think so,' she said. 'We'll have to drop in at my salon.'

'Wait.' Dietrich had been staring at her reflection. She knew he'd recognised the hat and his expression gave way briefly to sadness. He fetched the gauze stole that Coralie had intended to drape over her shoulders and spread it over the hat's asymmetrical peaks. It fell like golden mist. Instantly, a new shape was born.

'A vision from a medieval tapestry. You are Fiametta, Dante's beloved. Ah-ah, do not adjust it, it is perfect. We need something just to secure the veil.' A pearl shirt-stud had sufficed. 'May we go now?'

'One last thing.' She'd applied lipstick, red and bold. Fiametta, little flame. 'I want an answer to something that has plagued me for years.'

'Why now?'

'This hat has let the genie out of the bottle. You remember Ottilia staggering, punch drunk, out of that fortune-teller's caravan? What had she heard?'

A shrug. *Can't remember.*

'Doesn't wash. You remember things and so do I. You told me she'd wanted an answer to a burning question. What was the question?'

He'd sighed. *Must I?*

Yes, he must. She could smell Ottilia's perfume on this hat, and while she'd often been exasperated with the woman, she'd never been indifferent to her sorrow. 'I want to know why, when she had so much, she was so lost.'

Dietrich had capitulated. 'The question she asked the Romany woman was "Did he reject me because of what I was?" The woman answered, "Yes." She left in shock because it was the answer she feared.'

'Because of what she was . . . Jewish, you mean?'

'I believe that is what she meant—'

'Did you dump Ottilia for that reason?'

'I did not.'

'Then tell me why. You cut your engagement just days before the wedding. Tilly's kind and beautiful. She's not the brightest, but you were supposed to be a man of honour. It was as though you opened the car door and pushed her out.'

Behind her at the mirror, he'd spoken to her reflection. 'I broke off our engagement because my mother called me to her private room and confessed that Ottilia was my half-sister.'

'Oh.' *Oh.* 'Your father and Ottilia's was the same man?'

'My mother and Bernard von Silberstrom were lovers, and at the time of my conception, she and her husband – whom the world calls my father – were in different parts of the country.'

'Why not tell Ottilia? Why let her believe it was her you rejected?'

'I told her brother – my half-brother, Max – who urged me to say nothing. Ottilia cannot keep a confidence, as I am sure you have found out.'

'It would have made her feel better. Loved, at least.'

He nodded. 'It would have been the brave thing. I, of course, would have been disinherited by my father and subject to the restrictions – the anti-Semitism – practised against Jews in Germany. As you say, it would have been the honourable thing to stand up and say it. But I did not. What I did instead was look after Ottilia, and Max, to the best of my ability. When they needed to escape Germany, I got them out. I was able to help several of Max's employees to Switzerland, too, with their families. Does that even the score? Had I not been Dietrich von Elbing, I would have been too busy escaping to help anybody.' He gave a bent smile. 'You look upon me differently?'

'Actually, yes. You do look a bit like Tilly, now I think about it.'

'I do not see much of her in me, but I resemble Max in some lights. My daughter Claudia has the same, bright hair as Ottilia.'

They'd said no more about it, but on the drive to boulevard

de Clichy, the enormity of what Dietrich had revealed bore in on Coralie. *He was half Jewish.*

As Martel ushered them to their table, Coralie had a moment to prepare herself to meet Dietrich's guests. Kurt and Fritzi Kleber. On the way over, Dietrich had given her firm instructions not to mention seeing Teddy.

He said now in an undervoice, 'If either of them mentions his name, you cannot bear to think of him, yes? Lower your eyes, look away.'

'And what about Hitler?' she asked. 'Mention him? Don't mention him?'

'This is not a joke, my love.'

'I know,' she hung back, 'but I'm terrified. Fritzi Kleber must know that I ran away the night you went after Teddy. She might have guessed I telephoned him.'

'Impossible. When I got back to the flat, she was dead asleep. Actually, she slept until lunch time.'

Hurray for veronal. 'But, Dietrich, the Klebers surely see me as a threat. I mean, I was enrolled into your plot, then I scarpered. What if Fritzi still has that gun in her bag?'

'Perhaps she does but all this was a year ago. Time has passed and we meet again as friends.'

A moment later, Kurt was kissing her hand in his usual friendly way. Fritzi kissed her cheek. Wine was already on the table and Kurt's immediate intention was for them all to drink a toast. He filled their glasses.

'To a long overdue meeting.' Dietrich raised his glass

There followed a gabble of catch-up, in German. Coralie held back. Fritzi and Kurt were jumping over each other to explain that they'd spent the intervening months travelling across France, visiting cathedrals and Roman ruins. They'd even been over the border to Spain. As for Dietrich, he gave news of Berlin, though that meant describing the devastation wreaked by Allied bombers.

Reminded of Donal, who might still be flying in those slow, rattling 'crates', or even perhaps shot down, Coralie moved her gaze away. It came to rest on Lorienne Royer.

She jumped as Fritzi put a hand on hers.

'I am sorry I have not been to La Passerinette recently.' Fritzi made a face. 'Days hurtle by, but I have seen your creations worn by my friends. What do you think of mine?' She indicated her evening hat, a padded velvet base with clusters of spring flowers.

'Very pretty. But not my design. Put a date in your diary, Fritzi.'

'I will, all the more if this is one of your spring models.' Fritzi stroked Coralie's gauze veil. 'Is it difficult to wear?'

'Well, I wouldn't want to try to eat a lobster while wearing it.' Coralie opened her palms either side of the golden headdress. 'This is the birth of an idea because, like children, all ideas are conceived in hope. What they turn into is anybody's guess.'

Fritzi said no more, as their men had started speaking in low, serious tones.

Realising the women had fallen silent, Kurt broke off. He propped his elbows on the table, and spoke against his knuckles. 'I was asking Dietrich if our oath holds. If we still march towards the same destiny.'

'Dachterrasse.' Fritzi said it softly.

'A year has passed, precious time lost,' Dietrich said, raising his glass. 'But let us drink to Dachterrasse. To friendship. To unbreakable loyalty.'

Coralie clinked glasses then looked away, locking eyes with Lorienne Royer.

The other woman's social smile fell away. Flaxen hair soaked up pink light and her eyes set hard.

'I'm popping to the Ladies,' Coralie murmured. She was an inch away from red mist. Lorienne's letter, describing the arrest of Madame Thomas and Violaine, had been an act of barbarism that, even after a slow passage of time, demanded redress. Except that Coralie did not know how to go about getting it, unless with fists and teeth. 'I'll come with you,' said Fritzi.

In the Ladies, Coralie ran cold water over her wrists and watched Fritzi adjusting her evening hat, lowering it so it obscured one eyebrow. Too low. 'Let me.' Coralie unpinned it and resettled it higher. 'Confession time, Fritzi. Who have you left me for?'

Colour tinted Fritzi's cheeks. 'I love your hats, but after that awful confrontation here with Serge Martel and Reiniger, Kurt felt we had to be careful. We should not meet too often.'

'We haven't met at all.'

Fritzi appeared to steel herself. 'The truth? Kurt fears that Dietrich is not as influential as he was. That business with the Gestapo damaged him.'

'It was Martel who looked most guilty, as I recall. And Dietrich has powerful friends in Germany.'

'You refer to Reichsmarschall Göring?'

The door swung open and two women entered, followed by an attendant bringing in a pile of fresh hand towels. Fritzi said no more. They left the room.

In the lobby, Fritzi hung back. 'Coralie, allow me to know more about the inner workings of German high command than you. Believe me, Göring is not as powerful as he used to be either. Things are not going well for Germany in the war and Göring's command of the Russian campaign is much criticised in some quarters. Oh, I am not speaking treason. We will turn events around. In the end, we will win.'

Coralie looked at her friend in astonishment. 'I thought you wanted peace with honour.'

In reply, Fritzi lifted Coralie's hand, gazing expressionlessly at the ruby ring. 'So I do. Let me warn you as a friend, do not step aboard a ship that may sink. Besides, Dietrich is married and you have already a husband. Where is he, incidentally?'

'Ramon? Down south, working on the railways.'

'I do not like to lie, so I will tell you a truth. I stopped coming to you for hats partly because of this husband who comes and goes. And because I discovered you employed Jewish women.'

Coralie gasped. Fritzi seemed not to hear.

'Since then, I have heard also a rumour that you design hats to make German women look ugly and that you laugh at us in private. For that, you know, you could be arrested. It is sabotage. It is foolish and dangerous.'

'I'd never do that to you.'

Fritzi put a finger to her lips. Lorienne Royer had come into the lobby.

'Frau Kleber, what a pleasure, what an honour.' Coralie might not have been there. 'But one moment,' Lorienne chided. 'Your hat is designed to be worn *over* the eye.'

'So she can bump into things? And *I'm* accused of making people look daft!'

Lorienne ignored Coralie. Fritzi, looking from one woman to the other, said decidedly, 'Perhaps you would be kind enough to correct it for me, Mademoiselle Royer.'

Coralie watched them return to the Ladies. Little electric shocks jumped from her breast to her throat. She touched the snuff bottle at her neck. Fritzi Kleber had turned coat. *Dietrich is not as influential as he was. Kurt felt we should not meet* . . .

Walking back into the club, she paused to watch Dietrich and Kurt Kleber in conversation. A pair of Martel's tarts approached and she saw the men dismiss them. The girls lingered. They were dismissed again and walked slowly away, hips rolling.

Kurt filled two glasses, and lifted his. Another toast in the making, Coralie presumed. To friendship, to a future without Hitler? She thought, *I could walk alongside Dietrich towards any destiny*. For him, and for the hope of humanity. But not for the honour of Germany. I cannot embrace a horrible death for a country that strafed cowering refugees on French roads. That has taken away Violaine, Una, Amélie and her child.

And if this plot failed, if she and Dietrich were arrested, would she have the courage to bite on her pill, invite potassium cyanide into her system? *You will kill*, a Gypsy palmist had promised her. It had not occurred to her that it might be herself *by herself*. She didn't want to die. Noëlle needed her. She had to live.

Dietrich was beckoning a waiter. He is human, she thought. Dangerously human. Aryan and Jewish. It didn't matter to her, but it would matter to Fritzi Kleber. It would matter to *Göring, Göring, fat as a herring*. It would matter to the Gestapo.

If Dietrich's star was falling, and the Gestapo ever questioned her, could she keep his secret? If they arrested her for her Resistance activities – beat her or pulled out her nails, like they'd done to poor Jan Brommersma – would she keep silent?

Not a chance. She'd crack like cheap china. She'd point them to Dietrich and they'd arrest him, throw him in a salad wagon, abuse him, send him to Drancy or another holding camp, then eastwards to God knew what. *Her Dietrich*.

Pulling off the hat that made her as visible as the Eiffel Tower, she made her way to the stairs. Up in the foyer, she asked the cloakroom attendant for paper and a pen and wrote:

It's over. I do care, but Fritzi reminded me that we're both married. Don't come calling –

What phrase would wound that Prussian pride so deeply that he would never come looking for her?

because my husband is a bigger man than you.

She signed it 'C' and wrapped the note around the ruby ring, twisting each end, like a sweet-paper.

She gave the girl a hundred francs to give it to Generalmajor von Elbing when he came upstairs for his cap and his coat. 'If that ring's not in it, you'll spend the next five years in La Santé prison. Got it?'

Astonishingly, snow was swirling as she stepped outside. She walked along boulevard de Clichy, making for the Métro. Unable to hold her hat in place while keeping her hands in her pockets, she took it off and spiked it, like a cocktail sausage, on a railing. Snow would cover it, white on white. A fitting end and, one day, she might make Ottilia a replacement. One day, she might explain her desertion to Dietrich. And he might understand.

Chapter Thirty-four

At dawn on Monday, 8 March, Hiltrud von Elbing arrived in Paris.

Her father had arranged for her to be chaperoned on the journey, not trusting her to travel alone. She hadn't dared to admit that Dietrich knew nothing of her plans to join him. Ernst Osterberg had discovered that a member of the gauleiter of Brandenberg's staff was to visit Paris on official business, and had entrusted Hiltrud to the official's female secretary. She'd had the indignity of overhearing her father telling the secretary that his daughter had been unwell. An infirmity of the mind, for which she took pills twice a day.

'If she weeps, pay no heed, but if she goes white and cannot breathe, use smelling salts on her. You will answer for her well-being. Her husband, Graf von Elbing, is a close friend of Reichsmarschall Göring.'

No wonder her chaperones had regarded her with wary resentment throughout the entire exhausting trip. They had been delayed in Germany by bomb-damaged rails, in France by an unexplained hold-up involving armed soldiers and lots of shouting, and then by snow. The train had finally limped into the station at four in the morning. Seeing all the people sitting where they were, making no attempt to leave the carriage, she assumed there was another delay. But then somebody mentioned that it was to do with a curfew. French passengers could not venture on to the streets until five a.m.

Being German, her party was not subject to such restrictions. A liaison officer from Army Headquarters was waiting on the platform. Such obedience. Such love of duty. Hiltrud's spirits rose, and as they drove through dark streets, wet snow smacking against the windscreen, she looked about with curiosity. For some reason, she'd expected sunny weather. A good thing she'd worn her thickest coat and a woollen hat. Not at all stylish, but if it was good enough for Hohen Neuendorf, it was good enough for Paris.

The gauleiter's representative and his secretary were dropped off at a sprawling palace of a building. It seemed to occupy one side of a square, though Hiltrud couldn't see much. Snow whirled out of a pewter sky, as thickly as at home. Though where was home? Berlin, where she'd been born, had whole districts of burned rubble. Women like her and even women with babies lived outdoors in the cold. The northern suburbs had been pounded and she dreamed often of Hohen Neuendorf being swallowed by a firestorm. No signs of bombing in Paris. Claudia and her father must be correct. Paris had been spared because even those in top authority were seduced by her wicked luxury.

After waiting an hour, the car took Hiltrud on towards her destination. Rue de Vaugirard.

As they crossed a river, the driver said, 'The Seine, *gnädige Dame*. A fine river.'

'It is not as beautiful as the Spree or the Havel.'

On the far side of the river, the streets felt darker, even though the sky was quite light now. She began to cough. 'Why is the air so thick?'

Because Parisians had responded to the lack of heating fuel

458 The Milliner's Secret

by installing stoves in their apartments, the driver said. They burned anything they could get their hands on, and because many of them had no fireplaces or chimneys, they shoved stove pipes through holes they made in the wall. Of course, being near the ground, the fumes did not disperse.

'How unsanitary. They should be stopped.'

The car drew up at a house with an imposing door. To the sound of sentries tramping alongside the railings opposite, her driver rang the doorbell. After a short delay, they were let in. Her driver departed and she said to the man who had opened the door, 'I am Generalmajor von Elbing's wife, Gräfin von Elbing. Will you show me up to his apartment?'

The man took her to the lift, pressed a floor button for her and said, 'Generalmajor von Elbing came in very late last night.'

As the lift rose, she heard him mutter under his breath, 'Good luck.'

She would have Dietrich deal with him. Once upon a time she would have dealt with the man herself. But so often, these days, she felt like a small creature shut inside an over-large body. Her voice was in there but it didn't always come out. Other times, she would erupt in a rage that frightened even her. She must find the right voice if she was to get Dietrich to listen, to come home.

Stepping out of the lift, she knocked on the only door in the hallway. It was opened by a man in a canvas apron, whose sooty hands told her that he was making a fire.

'What time d'you call this, woman? Cleaning duty started an hour ago. And where are your polishing rags?'

She gave him her name, adding, 'And you may inform who-ever employs you that you are dismissed.'

The man stammered an apology. *Sorry, gracious lady, no idea that the Gräfin was expected. The Generalmajor had said nothing. Was expecting extra cleaning help this morning and thought that you—*

'Go back to your task.' She went to find Dietrich.

She discovered him in the bedroom, lying on his front on the bed, clothing thrown about. When she shook his shoulder, he didn't stir. She sniffed . . . Foreign perfume and alcohol. She shook him again and he mumbled something.

He was dead drunk.

She sorted through his clothes, and found among his things a woman's knitted winter stocking, and a pair of ankle socks. She found underwear too, lace-trimmed slipper satin. In the wardrobe, she found more coats and dresses than she'd ever possessed in her life. On the dressing-table – a frippery thing of mother-of-pearl and slender drawers – she found hatpins. And a hairbrush with blonde hairs caught in it.

Also on the dressing-table was Dietrich's *Pour le Mérite*. She picked it up and kissed it. How proud she had been of it, of him, when they were both young. Running her thumb along its ribbon, she felt something and, turning the medal over, saw that somebody had sewn a patch. Cleverly done, so that whatever it concealed could be squeezed out like a pea from a pod.

A moment later, she was holding a brown glass bead. She knew exactly what it was. Her daughter Claudia, who worked with prisoners of the Reich, had shown her one that she'd taken from a female spy. The woman had tried to hide it in her underarm hair but a search had found it. It was a death-pill. So, her mother-in-law had not been exaggerating. Dietrich was indeed planning something that might lead to his capture: even with his hands tied he would be able to get the cyanide capsule between his teeth.

Though not if she had anything to do with it.

Slipping the capsule into her coat, Hiltrud broke the pearl head off one of the hatpins lying on the dressing table, and inserted *that* into the ribbon pocket. She would do all she could to bring Dietrich back to faith with her, and with the Führer. If she failed, he would not have the luxury of taking the coward's way out.

She found the kitchen. It was tidy, too tidy. Nobody cooked there. She could hear somebody clanking in another room and found the orderly who had insulted her at the door. He sprang to his feet.

'Get on with your work,' she told him, 'and then get out.' She discovered she was in a handsome room. Silk wallpaper. A damask sofa, wide enough to seat four. Ornate mirrors, a chandelier dripping crystal. She admired the carved legs of a drum table, and saw a letter on it. And a ring; the von Elbing ruby, hers by right. Where was Dietrich's Frenchwoman?

Where was the female who had turned her husband into a drunkard and a criminal? She knew the handwriting to be his, though she couldn't read the letter because it was in French.

Some words she made out: *amour*. That was "love". *Honneur*. Turning the page over, she found some lines in German, as if Dietrich had written first in his own language.

I cannot believe what you have done. My love for you transcends reason, politics, law and religion. It transcends everything but honour. If it did not yield to honour, it would be worthless. I still believe that I will one day marry you. I do not know how, but that does not undermine the belief that we will have a son together, even if I cannot live to see him grow. I so long for a son with you.

Hiltrud's roar ripped through the walls. Outside, the sentries stopped and tilted their guns in the direction of the sound.

Dietrich woke, catching the tail-end. He put his feet to the floor, tried to stand but everything was spinning. Last night, he had reached for a bottle, needing oblivion.

'Coralie?' A woman had come into his room. He blinked, not believing what he saw. Not believing who was in front of him, holding a kitchen knife.

He believed it when she slashed his face, tearing a line from cheekbone to chin. He believed it when she made another thrust into his leg above the knee, then deep into his arm. Knowing he was fighting for his life, he managed to wrench her arm into the air, twisting until the knife fell. He got her out of the flat, slipping in his own blood, then half pushed her, half fell with her, down one flight of stairs.

Out on the street, he shouted for help and sentries came rushing towards him, guns levelled.

He came round in hospital and learned that it was now 11 March, and he had received two blood transfusions. 'Where is she?' he asked.

His doctor assumed he meant his wife. 'Transferred to a clinic outside Paris, Generalmajor. Le Cloître. The doctors specialise in brain injuries and –' the man gave an awkward cough '– other mental disorders. She will receive the most compassionate care. Poor lady, it seems her mind was overturned by the death of your son. Sons are irreplaceable to mothers, are they not? I believe the lad was killed in the bombing of your home town?'

Dietrich grunted. Let them think that. The agony in his face and shoulder, radiating into his back, was good evidence that he was still alive. He wished he wasn't. The shock of Hiltrud's blade was nothing compared to the shock of Coralie's betrayal.

PART SIX

PART SIX

Chapter Thirty-five

A note from Fritzi Kleber informed Coralie that Dietrich had been murdered by his wife. Gräfin von Elbing had arrived unexpectedly in Paris, Fritzi wrote, and for reasons unknown had attacked Dietrich.

It was lucky, Coralie thought later, that she'd forgotten about the cyanide pill hanging from her neck because she'd have bitten it then. Instead, she threw herself on her bed, beyond tears, until roused by persistent knocking. It was Kurt Kleber, bringing her the news that Dietrich was alive, and had been transferred to a hospital in Germany. 'Perhaps it is a good thing that *all* our plans are so much in the air, no?'

She was too busy picturing Dietrich in hospital, thinking hateful thoughts of his wife, to listen properly. She nearly said, 'Yes,' but caution stepped in. 'What plans?'

Kurt smiled. 'Good girl.'

As summer and autumn of 1943 dragged past, she longed to get the truth to Dietrich. *I only left you because I feared I might betray what you are and for ever bear the guilt.* But Kurt refused to send letters on her behalf.

'Let him be, Coralie, for his sake and your own. And no,' he added, in response to her persistent questioning, 'I don't know what flared between Dietrich and his wife, or even why Hiltrud was in Paris.'

'Might he have asked her for a divorce?'

Kurt sighed. 'Men of honour do not pitch their infirm wives into the gutter to please another woman. Will you excuse me?' Coralie had once again interrupted him at work at the Hôtel Marigny. She should thank him and leave, she knew, but she needed more. Grudgingly, Kurt obliged.

'To dismiss a man like Dietrich von Elbing with a crude note is wantonly to open a Pandora's box. Do not be surprised at what flies out. Why in heaven's name did you do it?'

She couldn't tell him and went home. Looking back over her life, she saw how her impulses had caused disaster after disaster. Stealing Sheila Flynn's clothes. Taking on her dad one time too many. Singing 'The Lambeth Walk' in a French nightclub in her true cockney voice. Filling Henriette's salon window with red, white and blue. Turfing Lorienne Royer out of La Passerinette. Even backing Manna at the 1925 Derby – that had lost her the mother she'd loved. 'People desert me. No wonder,' she told herself.

December 1943 brought freezing pipes and snow, which, because of the stove smuts in the air, turned instantly to dirty slush. Just as cold and long as previous winters. And then, shortly after New Year, a letter:

9 January 1944
To Madame C.
Ma chère femme,

It is perishing in these hills, but I live well enough with a group of fine men (and women!) and our friend with the violin. We are forming a fighting unit and cannot wait to be tested against the enemy and the bastard Milice, whom we hate even more than the Germans. Meanwhile, we amuse ourselves picking off the odd convoy and shooting informants. My old skills are coming in useful. All those years spent calculating tunnel depths and the span of arches have not been not wasted. Do you travel often by rail? I hope you and the child are well, I think of you often.

My love, as always,

R.

Written on onion-skin paper, it had been inserted behind the label of a wine bottle.

The forger Bonnet brought it to her. '*Pardon*, Madame, I drank the wine – I believe I was meant to – and it was a good Côtes-d'Auvergne. Read it, burn it. What a man, our Ramon, eh?'

What a man, but a suspicion of what he might be engaged in made Coralie even more fearful of reaching out to anybody. Her fellow agent, Moineau, had not been near her for months. One morning in mid-January, when she called at rue Mouffetard to collect intelligence dockets for avenue Foch, the butcher shook his head.

'Your usual's not available today, Madame.'

'Tomorrow?'

'The cuts of meat you like are unobtainable now. Try elsewhere.'

It seemed she wasn't even part of the Resistance any more. Fritzi had not honoured her promise to visit, and Coralie now avoided walking down avenue Marigny. It wasn't until early February that a visit to parc Monceau shifted her spirits. If golden aconites and the first snowdrops could push their heads up and smile, so could she, she told herself. She would start the new year afresh, if a little late, by appointing an assistant milliner.

There had been truth in Lorienne Royer's malevolent note: *How will you fare without your right hand?* Coralie had always relied on good technicians, such as Madame Zénon, the Ginslers and Violaine. She missed having people to advise her and help develop ideas. Often, these days, she hit the limits of her skill. It wouldn't be long before people whispered, 'Coralie de Lirac is only as good as her staff.'

On 14 February, she placed a card in La Passerinette's window and in various shops in the Sentier. Within hours, hopeful young women were knocking at her door, eager to relate their experience, as she had once done. They confided how little they were being paid, and how they needed better commission.

'My brother is a prisoner of war.'

'My mother is sick.'

'I have a child to care for, and my husband is doing *service du travail obligatoire* in Germany.'

Poor things. Yet she said, 'No,' to them all. None of them had looked very much like Violaine or Amélie, but she knew that seeing white hands stitching and moulding cloth, curls falling over furrowed brows, would be too much to bear. She took the notices down and struggled on. Then, towards the end of the month, she received a visitor.

'I am told, Madame, that you are seeking an experienced milliner.'

'I was . . . Are you here for your daughter?'

A chuckle. 'No, Madame, for myself. My name is Georges Blanchard and I have been a milliner all my life. I am retired, but . . . ' His savings had been depleted by years of exchange-rate banditry. And he was bored and . . . 'The days are long.' She invited him in, and met a bear with a limp. He was six feet four, a Great War veteran and had suffered shrapnel injury. Her workbenches would be far too low for him and he'd crack his head on the salon chandelier. But he made her smile. She hired him on the spot.

And then Moineau tinged his bicycle bell at her as she cycled home one evening, her wheels crunching over the last of the snow. 'Got a light, Cosette?'

'Hello, stranger.' She pulled over and they pretended to share a cigarette.

He'd been hiding, he told her. Fortitude had been infiltrated by Gestapo informants in January, twelve members arrested. He'd been tipped off by a friendly French policeman before they nabbed him.

'Who was caught?' Not Mademoiselle Deveau, she hoped.

'I can't tell you.'

'Can't or won't?'

'Will it make you sleep better to know, Cosette? Anyway, I only get code names.' He dragged on his cigarette, then held it out to her and, as she took a half-hearted puff, said, 'The fat old bird on the canal? She never used a code name, always Francine. They got her. So, are you ready for a new parcel?'

'Oh dear – I mean, yes, of course.'

'Still at the place on rue de Seine? You haven't gone back to that alley by Saint-Lazare . . . What was it?'

'Impasse de Cordoba. I have the key to it, for emergencies.'

'*Bien*. Get supplies in. Still got that ration book?'

'Of course.'

She tried not to think of Fortitude's twelve doomed operatives. Instead she worried about Una, who hadn't answered any letters since September '43. She took to wearing her choker again. She wasn't sure she would actually prefer cyanide to the Gestapo, but she liked having the choice.

On the last day of February, Moineau delivered a twenty-three-year-old forward gunner who had bailed out over occupied Luxembourg after bombing targets in Germany's industrial Ruhr. Crawford Lesoeur, an officer of the Royal Canadian Air Force flying for the RAF, had broken his leg when his parachute came down in trees. After eight months in hiding, he was only now fit enough to make his way to England.

He was scheduled to stay at rue de Seine for three days, and because he couldn't climb up into the roof space, Coralie donated her bed, taking the box-room that had been Noëlle's. Not that she slept much. Every creak, every night sound was a black Citroën pulling up in the street below. It was the slam of a car door, the approach of booted feet. On what was supposed to be Lesoeur's last day with her, Moineau called to report a problem with the next safe house. She'd have to keep her airman hidden a bit longer, and take him to the next location herself – the usual courier was dead.

Coralie went out and queued for food, eyes skinned for possible danger. She bought small amounts at a time so that nobody would see her enter her flat with provisions for two.

When her guest asked if she was married, she spoke of Ramon, and risked saying, 'He's with the Maquis, in central France.' It made her proud and shone a light on her feelings because, though she missed Dietrich brutally, she was choosing sides again. When Crawford Lesoeur gave his opinion that Germany had to be pummelled to defeat, she nodded agreement. When he said that a well-prepared French Resistance would play its part when the Allies invaded, she took it as the compliment it was meant to be.

'When will the invasion come?'

'It already has, from the air, anyhow. Our bombers are preparing the way for ground troops. I'll think of you, Madame, and when I'm home, I'll tell the boys where to come if they have to bail out.'

Ten days after he'd arrived, she escorted Lesoeur by train to Narbonne where she bought him a ticket for Perpignan. As a Canadian, he spoke French but his accent would give him away. Coralie gave him cotton wadding dipped in clove oil.

'Stick it under your gums, pretend you have toothache.' She gave him a supply of grimy hundred-franc notes to supplement the overly crisp emergency currency the RAF supplied to all its crew. 'Come back to Paris with your fiancée when all this is over.'

'I don't have a fiancée.'

'What do those English girls think they're up to? Tell them to buck up from me.'

There came another evader, and another. They kept coming. British and American bombers were attacking Germany round the clock, and attacking French targets too. The toll among airmen was high. For every pilot, navigator or gunner she helped, there must be ten who crashed to their deaths or were taken prisoner. She'd lie in bed thinking of Dietrich in Germany, at risk from bombs being dropped by Donal. She'd think of Donal, in deadly danger from anti-aircraft guns and Luftwaffe fighters. Trust her to care for men on both sides. Every day, she read German and French newspapers, longing for the headline 'Adolf Hitler Dead!'

One lunchtime in early April, her assistant said, 'Why aren't we doing a spring collection?'

'We've missed the boat, Georges.'

'There isn't a boat. We are free spirits in a land of headless chickens.'

'I'd sell my soul for a roast headless chicken.' Coralie swallowed a spoonful of turnip soup. It was lunchtime, and they were at a Champs-Élysées café that had once guaranteed a decent meal because of its German clientele. Now, to paraphrase Arkady, everything was running out, except turnips.

'I mean it,' Georges persisted. 'We could create a collection in a month, if we really put our minds to it.' His voice dropped coaxingly; 'What about that bet you told me about, the one with Lorienne Royer? Which of you would bring out the best spring collection?'

'That bet was with Henriette Junot, five years ago. I don't recall mentioning it.'

'Bets never die, and now that Lorienne has taken over the Junot salon, she's the one to beat.'

'She stole my medieval idea last summer. Her autumn–winter show was all horns and veils. Some of her models looked like reindeer caught in net curtains. I haven't bothered to check on her this time round.'

'You see? She's beating you. Why don't you want to play the game?'

'Let's just say there are things between Lorienne and me that are more profound than whose collection gets the best write-up in the fashion columns.'

Georges let the matter drop, but on 1 May he came into work and said, 'Sad news yesterday. Paul Poiret has died.'

'The couturier?'

'I worked for him, long, long ago. A fiery character, but if I were a woman, I'd strew flowers in front of his funeral cortège, for he was a pioneer of the natural shape.'

'Then he probably died of shock.' Coralie demonstrated her waistline, cinched to a breathless twenty-three inches. 'I'm afraid we've gone back to being artificially cut in two.'

'If we did a collection, we could pay tribute to him. That way, its late delivery would seem appropriate.'

'Paul Poiret . . .' Coralie envisaged the Oriental-style robes that had shocked and entranced society in 1911. Not that she'd been around, of course, but she'd read the great man's autobiography. Thanks to Poiret, ankles had been uncovered for the first time in three generations. 'That silhouette was long and slim. The style is so different now.'

'Turbans,' Georges prompted.

'Oh, no, I did turbans in 'thirty-nine—forty.'

'Lorienne is giving us big round heads. Again.' Georges mimed a yawn. 'And you know, turbans are so "now". They can be made of almost anything and they lend themselves to every mood. Sharp, simple . . .' Georges leaned closer to her, 'even subversive. Ah, a reaction!'

'Subversive? How, exactly?'

'We could decorate them with secret motifs, seen only from above. A message to the brave boys of the Allied air forces.'

Did he mean something RAF crew could see as they flew over France? 'Arrows saying, "This way to the Normandy coast," embroidered in English? You're a man after my own heart, Georges, but I don't see it working.'

'You're the boss.' Georges made her a cup of coffee, just as she liked it, with powdered milk and a spoonful of honey. The only man in her life ever to make her a hot drink — until she remembered Donal making tea for her once and a witch-hazel compress for her black eye.

'No. No, you're right, Georges. Let's do it,' she said. 'We'll have to be subtle, but it'll be fun.'

Georges rubbed his hands. 'And not all our German ladies have gone home. We could have them promoting a coded message, all unsuspecting. The game, you know?'

She didn't think she'd told him about the game – Bait the Occupier – but then again, she did mutter to herself as she worked, often forgetting he was there.

'How about this?' He took out a notebook and scribbled something. 'A turban, sporting a radio mast with antennae and '*Vive la France*" embroidered under the band, so nobody ever sees it.'

She couldn't explain her sudden rash of irritation. A sense that Georges was encroaching on her territory? 'A design like that could get us a one-way ticket to Drancy!' She flipped his notebook closed.

Georges was quiet for the rest of the morning, and when, later, she invited him to discuss ideas, he said curtly, 'Me? I'm the man who holds the scissors. It is Coralie de Lirac who spins the fantasies.'

She'd hurt him. Her big mouth *again*. 'Georges, I'm sorry. We'll produce a line of turbans. They can be made from silk and cotton waste and I will always say that you originated the idea.'

'Whatever you wish. You're the boss.'

Coralie de Lirac à La Passerinette invites you to
the first showing of her spring–summer collection
on Saturday, 27 May 1944, at 11.30 a.m.,
boulevard de la Madeleine

It felt like a good crowd though many of her German ladies had gone home. They seemed all to leave at once, as if summoned by a call from the Fatherland. Those who remained were either *Hilferin* – servicewomen – tethered by their work – or those made homeless by Allied bombing. Coralie was amazed that stranded women still wanted Paris hats but she wasn't going to argue. She'd been indiscreet in the past, not just in playing 'the game' but in laughing about it with French customers, assuming it would go no further. She, who had worked in a laundry and a factory, should have known that juicy gossip is as uncontainable as a tray of eels. This collection had to repair the damage she'd done to her own reputation: not only did she still have to feed herself and her 'parcels', she was sending money for Noëlle's keep *and* saving for her daughter's ongoing education. Ottilia, however loving and well-meaning, should not assume all of Coralie's maternal responsibilities. The war could not go on for ever and Coralie was beginning to see beyond the daily grind to a time of reunion. Digging between the lines of censored news reports, she detected a tilting of the balance in favour of the Allies. When the time came to collect her child, she wanted to go to Geneva as a successful woman.

As before at La Passerinette, there would be two parades but Coralie had reversed the running order. French first today. Instead of the usual mid-week event, she had chosen the last Saturday in May. Nobody left Paris for country weekends any more.

A few minutes, then they'd start. She'd hired Félix Peyron to act as wine waiter. As hostess, she would deliver the commentary once the parade started. Once again, she had asked Solange Antonin to be her mannequin, and Solange had agreed readily, admitting that her pampered life as the trophy of high-ranking SS officers was, in its way, as limiting as life at home with her parents. Within that gilded incarceration, old insecurities – and her old rages – had returned. With a vengeance . . .

No sign of rage today, thank goodness. Solange was in that semi-trance she always adopted before a show. Georges was in the corridor with her, arms crossed, lips clamped. 'I'm supposed to dress her, but she won't let me touch her head.'

Coralie said, 'Just hand her the hats and let her put them on.'

'What – any old how?'

'You can give directions but don't touch her.' Coralie penetrated Solange's trance by telling her that she looked breathtaking.

Solange smiled slowly. She was wearing a turban of cream silk jersey swathed around a narrow fez, its folds obscuring her 'forbidden ear'. Two plain goose feathers reared up at the front, forming a V.

Coralie had dressed her in a Grecian-style black tunic that was at odds with current fashion but would allow the hats to shine. She said again, 'Thank you for coming. Your being here assures me an audience. You're so famous these days.'

Actually, the word was 'notorious'. On 13 April last year, Solange had shot Serge Martel.

Unfortunately, in Coralie's view at least, not fatally. But she had done it publicly, using a side-arm borrowed from an SS lover. As a result, Solange had gained that special fame reserved for beautiful women driven to a *crime passionel*.

'Bend your knees as you exit or you'll leave those feathers in the door frame,' Coralie warned, before returning to the salon to start the show. She wished Georges would cheer up. He'd worked hard on this collection, his craftsmanship impeccable, but no amount of cajoling had persuaded him to add ideas of his own. To all her suggestions, he'd replied, 'If that is what Madame wants . . .'

He'd not forgiven her, evidently. Still, he looked smart today in his tailed suit and starched collar. And they'd been working together for just a bare three months. Get this collection out of the way, then she'd take him out to dinner and let him lead the conversation. It couldn't be easy for a man of his vintage to deal with a young female employer.

She checked her own appearance. She'd chosen a turban of cherry-red jersey, intricate as a nautilus shell, with twin feathers pointing to the left. Red-dyed goose. Every hat in the collection featured a V-shape, made of feathers, wired fabric or starched linen. The shape was the message.

For many months, the Allies had been landing troops in southern Italy, and an armistice had been signed with the Italians back in September 1943. The country that had been Germany's main ally was now a battleground, casualties on both sides atrocious but the Germans in retreat. Every café-chair general agreed that Hitler could not win a war in the east *and* in the west. On one side or other, he would be overrun. Victory!

The collection showed in just over an hour and applause greeted its end. As Solange posed one final time, Georges joined them and Coralie held her hand out. 'Thank you,' she said. 'Well done.'

'Some credit at last? A bit late, but I'm honoured.'

'I admit, I am the proud owner of a big, stupid gob—'

He walked on, saying, 'I shall take my break now. I'll be back in time for the second show.'

He cut it fine. At two fifteen, she saw him hurrying in, limping hard. He must have gone further afield than usual. Why, on such an important day? The afternoon audience was ready, the German language filling the salon. Old Félix was serving champagne, complimenting every woman present on her beauty – even the cross old dragons. There should be a medal struck for Félix, Coralie thought.

She tried to catch Georges's eye, but he ignored her. All his attention was on the street door. *Who was he looking for?* A moment later, the answer walked in.

No. Georges Blanchard and Lorienne Royer could not know each other.

Dashing into the corridor, Coralie tried to master her panic. Any suggestion that the Allies were winning the war was treasonable. Even being caught painting Victory signs on buildings was punishable by imprisonment. Coralie had once caused Lorienne to be put in jail, and here she was, sharing a Judas glance with Georges, making a V sign with her fingers. Had the woman recruited Georges to settle the score?

'Are you sick?' Solange came up to her.

'I'm thinking of cutting all these hats to pieces.'

Solange nodded dreamily. 'Monsieur Javier used to be the same. Each collection, he would lose confidence and threaten to rip everything to shreds.'

Coralie bit her thumbnail, almost to the quick. Solange didn't understand: this was no creative crisis. She had to decide what to do, now.

'*Fight.*' The word rang out in the empty stairwell above. Last time she'd heard a discarnate voice, in her father's tin shack, she'd run for her life. Nowhere to run this time – but she could stand her ground. 'Solange, can you speed up this next show? Don't stand and pose, keep moving.'

'Surely you wish for people to take notes.'

'Flick your hem, look angry. It's about you this time, not the hats.'

'All right.' An incurious nature was one of Solange's virtues. Coralie thought, *If we're both arrested, she'll wake up fast enough. Oh, God, what am I doing?*

★

Reticent applause lapped over the end of the second show but Coralie was attuned to the nuances of clapping. They liked what they saw, this audience, but their confidence had deserted them. No more finger clicking. No more 'Fräulein, here, quick.' These women had come to Paris in triumph and Paris had curled its lip. In their homeland, unthinkable carnage was taking place. In desiring glamour still, they were hanging on to an illusion.

Félix Peyron tapped her. 'Over there.'

Across the salon, beside Lorienne Royer, Major Reiniger.

Félix heard her murmur of horror. 'What have you done, Mademoiselle?'

'Didn't you see my hats?'

Félix nodded. '*Vive la Victoire!* But V can stand for other things. *Du vin*, for instance.' He put a glass in her hand. She downed it in one, scooped a breath and tinkled a bell. Chatter died down. '*Gnädige Damen und Herren*, I will be delighted to discuss this collection with you and make appointments in the diary. Meanwhile, allow us to serve you another glass of wine.'

Lorienne launched her attack at once. 'Perhaps Mademoiselle de Lirac will explain the significance of the letter V, which is a feature of every hat shown.' Lorienne's German came with a strong French accent, but it brought the room to absolute silence. People stared at Coralie, wanting the answer.

Coralie put down her bell because it was tinkling her fear. 'I'm glad you asked that, Lorienne.' Not 'Madame Royer' or even 'Madame'. Lorienne's air of patrician superiority was as fake as her hair colour. 'What if I wove a V into all my designs as a tribute to a friend?' *Fight.*

'Violaine Beaumont, you mean? Or should I say Bermanski? A Polish Jewess.' Lorienne used the German *Jüdin*. 'Illegally sheltered and employed by you.' Her tone implied, *Got you!*

Coralie felt the mood in the room shift. 'Violaine was – is – my friend. She was also the best milliner I ever met.' She remembered the games of 'chicken' she and Donal had played. Every time she'd turned back, coward that she was. But she wasn't the only coward in the world. Singling out one figure, she admitted, in French, 'Without my technicians I am a second-rate milliner.'

'That's your secret out, then, isn't it?' Georges's voice peaked disdainfully, but he was sweating under her gaze. Or perhaps he was feeling Major Reiniger's clerical spectacles on him more than was comfortable. Perhaps Georges was realising that bringing in the Gestapo was like unchaining an attack dog in a walled yard. The dog's teeth were suddenly in reach of everyone.

'I could never have created this collection without you, Georges. Agreed?' She repeated the question in German.

'Agreed.'

'Georges agrees. So Georges can explain what the V stands for.'

Giving Georges fair time to think of an answer, Coralie climbed on to a chair so that everyone could see her.

'What does V stand for?' she said in a clear voice. 'Let me tell you something that I hope, in future years, you will remember when somebody says the name "Coralie de Lirac". *Gnädige Damen*, Major Reiniger,' she steeled herself to look straight into those glinting discs, 'I am not beautiful, but I have learned how to make others believe that I am. I do it with a hat. I wear one of my own creations every day, even in the bath.' She allowed the titters of amused surprise to die down. 'What is a hat? Is it just moulded felt, steamed straw, or gauze thrown over wire? Yes, it is all of these. But add to that a *je ne sais quoi*. A sprinkle of magic. For every woman there is a hat waiting to transform her. A hat to make a plain face interesting, a sweet face lovely. A hat to hold a straying husband . . .' She paused for effect. Even Reiniger was hanging on her words, though that was not necessarily a good thing. 'A hat to catch a fresh husband if the old one's not worth hanging on to. Pink silk water-lilies to send the blues away. White gardenias to blow away the shadows of time. There is a hat for joy, a hat for sorrow. We are what Nature made us and we cannot send the hands of the clock backwards, but the right hat, a clever hat, a *wicked* hat, can change a face – like that!' She clicked her fingers and the ladies nearby jumped. 'So, what does V stand for?'

Well? Vichy? Veronal? Vick's VapoRub? Always a good idea to know the punch line before you start the monologue. 'V stands for everything a hand-made, personally designed hat should be. *Vivace. Vibrant. Valeureux. Vivant. Originale, mais toujours en vogue.*'

'I was hoping it stood for "Vaugirard".'

She would have fallen off her chair, had she not grabbed the speaker's shoulder. 'How did you get in here?' What she meant to say was, 'You're back at last!'

'I knocked at the side door. Solange, is that her name? She let me in.'

Sunlight between the blinds delineated a scar that ran the length of a lean cheek. She couldn't stop herself looking at it, in shock, in pity.

'Have I changed so much?'

'No. Just . . . why Vaugirard?' Everyone else wanted to know, it seemed. Fifty faces were turned to them. Including Reiniger's.

Dietrich helped her down, but when he spoke, it was for her ears only. 'Vaugirard is where we became lovers the second time, where we forgave each other. Where we recognised that we are navigating the same river. Do you realise we have been apart for more than a year? Another fifteen months, wasted. Hiltrud attacked me on March the eighth last year.'

Touching the scar, she noticed he wasn't wearing his *Pour le Mérite*.

'You find me underdressed? I arrived back in Paris yesterday, late.'

'You're back at Vaugirard? And only just better? Those wounds must have gone very deep.'

He nodded. 'It was a shock, finding traces of my own blood still on the stairs. They took Dietrich von Elbing in an ambulance car to Germany but I am not sure who has come back.' He turned to face the audience. 'None of these hats is for sale, ladies. I intend to buy them all.'

Immediately, there was a scraping of chairs and, within seconds, Coralie was surrounded by women demanding to try on the models and reserve one for themselves.

Later, clutching a pencil worn to a stub, Coralie asked Dietrich, 'Did you know I was in a fix?' Reiniger and Lorienne were still in the salon. So was Georges Blanchard. She had a feeling they were waiting for some kind of climax.

Dietrich nodded. 'On my way home last night, I made a detour by the Rose Noire. I wanted to hear some music that wasn't military anthems or Wagner. Félix told me he was helping you today, but that is not why I am here. I have to warn you of something.'

People were leaving. Good. She was exhausted, wanting only to close up and go home. When Reiniger clashed eyes with her, she said nothing. A moment later, he left. When Solange came to say goodbye, Coralie said, 'Got your hat?'

'The white silk jersey, yes?'

'A good choice.'

When Lorienne arched her eyebrows at her, she raised hers back. When Georges Blanchard shuffled forward and said, 'I will collect my things,' she said, 'No – I'll drop them outside Lorienne's place. Get out and stay out.'

When Félix had been paid, and it was just herself and Dietrich left, she locked the door and pulled down the blinds.

There was pain in the way Dietrich stood with his weight planted evenly on each foot. His hair had yielded a little more to grey and, in the fading light, his scar looked like a badly stitched seam.

In the corridor, she surveyed her hats.

Dietrich came and stood behind her. 'V for victory? A little premature, I think.'

'Help me put them away.'

They boxed them up. Surveying them, piled high on the workroom shelves, Coralie brushed away a tear. Sometimes you saw betrayals coming. Other times, they pinged up, like a rogue bedspring. Georges and Lorienne . . .

She found a card and a pen. Telling Dietrich not to look over her shoulder, she wrote a few lines, which he then read aloud. '"With regret, La Passerinette is closing. Mademoiselle de Lirac thanks her many clients and friends for their support over the years." Coralie, you cannot give up.'

'I keep being pulled down. I lose people, or they cheat me.'

He pinned the card into the soft board behind her workbench. 'Do not let Lorienne Royer grind you down. You are too good at what you do.'

She promised to sleep on it. 'So what bad news have you brought me?'

'The worst.'

Back in the salon, he drew her down beside him on the sofa. 'A few days ago, your husband was part of a gang that blew up a railway tunnel near Auxerre – you know where that is?'

'A morning's journey south of here.'

'On the main Paris to Lyon line.'

She waited for the 'and'.

'A train was caught inside. Over a hundred troops died, and many civilians. Some of the troops were injured soldiers being evacuated to Germany.'

'I'm sorry.' She took a breath. 'For the civilians. Your soldiers had it coming.'

He flashed anger. 'You believe that? Seventeen-year-old boys, dying under a fall of rock, their flesh burned black in the inferno? Had it coming?'

'Blame your bloody Führer.'

He expelled a breath. 'Coralie, no child in any corner of this earth is born to such a death.'

Tell that to the men who took Amélie and her child. 'Is Ramon in trouble?'

'He was seen with other saboteurs and he caught a bullet.' Injured? Dying? Dietrich didn't know or care. 'The Gestapo will sell their souls to catch him. If you're found with him, or near him, I can't help you.' He forced her to look at him. 'If I see him, even with you, I will turn him in.'

'Revenge, because of what I wrote in that letter? I didn't mean it.'

'Because he set explosives regardless of consequence. That is not war.'

'Warning heard and understood.'

'Why do I doubt that?' He laid his forehead against hers. 'Will you come to my flat?'

'Not if your barmy wife is there.'

'Hiltrud is in a secure hospital.'

As Coralie locked up, it came to her mind that Georges still had a key. Maybe she should call in a locksmith. But Dietrich was leaning against the outside wall looking haggard. Chances were, if Georges was planning to come back and strip the place, he'd choose tomorrow, Sunday, when the streets were empty. And she would be waiting for him.

They took the lift up to Dietrich's flat. In the bathroom, she helped him undress, flinching at the scars on his leg. He'd been lucky. A hair's breadth deeper . . . 'I thought you and she had patched things up.'

He shook his head. 'When I was in Germany last, Hiltrud wanted me with her but it was not to whisper words of love. Rather, to void her soul of the cancerous hatred she feels for me. Hiltrud blames me for the loss of our children.'

'Both children?'

'Our daughter lives, but her choice of work has taken her from us. Hiltrud told her doctors that I had made our son a girl, and our girl a man.'

'Will they let her out?'

'Not until I allow it.' He reached over and turned off the bath taps. 'I wish this were big enough for two.'

'I tried joining you in the bath once, and remember what happened? Get yourself washed so I can have some of that hot water.' She perched on the cast-iron rim.

He asked her, 'Why did you leave me? That parting shot . . . To teach me a lesson?'

'No, because I was scared. Before I met you, the worst thing in my life was my dad's temper. Now the worst thing is the Gestapo. Every word is dangerous, every friendship. Even putting feathers on hats brings the buggers through the door! I was frightened for myself and for you.' She frowned down at him, submerged in soapy water. 'Did your mother have you circumcised?'

He gave a shout of laughter. 'What made you think suddenly of that?' More gravely, he said, 'It certainly wasn't my father, the Graf's, choice. But Coralie, didn't we agree, here in this flat, to face every danger together?'

In bed, she caressed him to hardness, to show him that his damaged body still excited her. His wounds were tender still, the nerve-endings still knitting even after so many months, and he joked that it was like two people dancing either side of a barbed-wire fence. But their climax was deep and in step and she told him not to withdraw. She wanted to prove that she trusted him and wanted to shape the rest of her life around him. She could think of only one way to do that.

Chapter Thirty-six

The Lancaster crew had no idea of it, but their bombs had just scored the last deadly hit of the war on industrial Schweinfurt. Ron Phipps, the pilot and a veteran of many tours, asked the navigator for a home course and was given a track south of Frankfurt. It would take them over Luxembourg and onward over France. The navigator advised crossing the sea off Brittany where coastal defences were lighter.

Phipps agreed. 'We're flying too low to risk the Normandy guns.'

They'd been on three engines since being hit by flak on the approach to Schweinfurt and, at just twelve thousand feet, were in danger from a direct strike from the ground. Or from attack by enemy night fighters, as a brilliant moon would be making a silhouette of them against the darkness. The maimed Lancaster bucked and tilted as if maddened by the loss of an engine.

For the crew, it was like being on a fishing boat in heavy seas. The navigator saw the wireless operator clamp his hand to his mouth.

Thirty churning minutes later, the pilot's intercom clicked on again.

'Location, Irish?'

Always 'Irish' to his fellows, for all he kept telling them he was a Londoner, the navigator answered, 'We've just clipped the corner off Luxembourg. We should be over the Moselle river – French side. Keep a course south-south-west and presently, we'll see the Yonne, then the Seine.'

'Roger, understood. Sorry to roll you about, boys. Everyone in one piece?'

One by one, the other six members of the crew switched on their microphones and answered positive.

Irish put his hand into his flying jacket and touched his good luck charm – a scrap of gold braid that had come from a girl's evening gown in Paris, four-and-a-half years ago. Alone in the skies, separated from their squadron and escort, they might just slip home unnoticed. He hoped so. He so wanted to live, to experience civilian life as the mature man that five years of bombing ops had made him.

As they progressed over France, the wireless operator reported a lessening of jamming signals, and was at last able to give Irish some bearings. Wing Commander Phipps was expressing his satisfaction at this when, from the ground far below, came a burst of coloured flares. Anti-aircraft fire from defences on the river Yonne. A second later, the plane shuddered. Flame swept over the Perspex turret and a horrible guttering sound suggested a shell had struck one of the remaining engines.

The Lancaster dropped sickeningly, levelling out after a minute or so. Irish checked his maps and called feverishly for new bearings. If his reckoning was right, they'd shortly be over the Fontainebleau forest. Squeezing crabwise up the fuselage, he stared out through the cockpit cupola at the landscape. He saw the confluence of two rivers, strands of shining ribbon under the moon, and beyond, the dark mass of trees.

He was just back in his seat when the intercom clicked on.

It was Phipps. 'We're losing height fast and I predict an unscheduled encounter with Mother Earth. Prepare to bail, chaps. Any ideas, Irish?'

'Avoid the forest, a correction starboard.'

Phipps wished them all good luck. 'First to the mess bar buys the drinks, the last pays for them.'

What seemed like three breaths later, Irish was falling through the smoke into pitch black. An ice-cold rush knocked the senses out of him and he experienced intense terror, curtailed by a ripping sound, a violent jerk and the glorious flowering of his parachute. For a while, he felt utterly still, but, as the scattered lights below grew larger, he gained a sense of descent. He offered thanks to Our Lady, adding a plea for the other boys to have got out safely. 'And the Wingco, of course,' as Phipps was not a boy and would wrestle with his plane to the last moment.

The Lancaster's death spiral lit up the landscape, showing the two rivers and the thin snake of a brook. Seconds later, a massive explosion announced the loss of another British bomber.

From a second-floor room in Le Cloître sanatorium, a woman watched the distant hillside turn into a raging inferno. The roar of distressed engines had brought her from her bed, and she'd witnessed the impact. She tried to open her window, but it was locked. Pressing her cheek to the glass, she saw figures running across the lawn towards the flames. What did they plan to do? Beat them out with their hands?

This was her moment, her chance. She found her stockings, shoes and underclothes. They had taken her dress, but a cardigan was folded over the end of her bed. She buttoned that over her nightdress. From the bedside cabinet, she removed one small item. The nurses had wanted to throw it away until she told them that it was a bead from a rosary. Clearly, none of them had ever set eyes on a cyanide death-pill before. She dropped it into a wash bag. Looping the bag's drawstrings around her wrist, she left her room. If anybody challenged her, she would say she was going to the lavatory.

A night nurse always sat at a station to mark the comings and goings from the rooms along the corridor. Luck! The station was empty. A cup of tepid coffee and a dish of cherries on stalks suggested the explosion had come as the nurse enjoyed a midnight snack.

Hiltrud pushed cherries into the pockets of her cardigan. On the ground floor the doors stood open, admitting an eerie orange glow and the odour of burning fuel. One of the nurses had left her cape over a chair, and a shoulder bag, which jingled with coins and keys. Hiltrud hung the bag over her own shoulder and threw the cape over the top. She left Le Cloître like a shadow.

On still nights, she'd heard trains passing in the distance. If she kept walking, she would sooner or later come to a railway station.

As dawn broke over the Île de France, Irish woke and attuned himself to the noises around him. He'd had a lucky drop. The chute had caught in the outer branches of a tree, breaking his fall. He'd cut himself loose, dropped five or six feet, then been able to free the parachute and bury it. He dug into his escape pack and found Horlicks tablets, shoved three into his mouth, got up and stretched. A peachy sunrise gave him his bearings and within minutes he found the brook he'd seen from above.

His compass told him it was flowing north-east. Chances were, it would meet the Seine, or one of its tributaries. The silk maps in his escape kit said the next town of size was indeed Fontaine-bleau, on the river Aube.

Using the sheath knife he always carried with him, he cut the warrant officer's stripes and the wing from his battledress and the sheepskin tops off his flying boots. When the boots had been issued, he'd complained they were half a size too small, but that had probably stopped them falling off during his drop. He wouldn't have fancied his chances barefoot.

With profound sorrow, he threw his jacket and flying helmet into a thicket, but couldn't bring himself to hurl his Enfield service pistol after them. After all, he might run into a troop of Jerries, looking for crash survivors.

Hitching his knapsack over his shoulder, he walked out of the fringes of the wood on to a road full of morning sun. He had become an evader.

He reached the railway station of Fontainebleau-Avon shortly after nine, unchallenged. It was Sunday, little traffic about. But he was proud of himself because he'd walked right past a couple on their way to church, and called out, '*Bonjour*.'

'*Bonjour*' was the limit of his French, and he wouldn't get to the next stage without help. After standing for some minutes on the station concourse, eyeing up potential assistance, he approached a man leaning against a wall. Dirty, with jet-black hair poking beneath a beret, the dog-end of a cigarette glued to his bottom lip, he cut an unsavoury figure. Getting closer, Irish saw that one of his hands was bound up in a dirty rag. A vagrant? No use. He needed someone capable of buying him a ticket and getting him on to a train. He was about to slink away when he noticed the man's shoes. They were tan leather with hand-stitched welts, such as professional men wore. Unless they'd been stolen, of course. But by the time he'd thought of that the man had seen him and growled something. Probably, 'What are you looking at?'

Warrant Officer Donal Flynn held out his hand and said, 'I'm a British aviator and I need help.'

Hiltrud von Elbing spent the journey to Paris removing cherry stones with a fingernail. A fiddly job, made no easier by the lurching of the train. The messy results she ate, but after a few attempts she had successfully replaced one stone with the cyanide capsule.

A guard shouted something at her. She thrust out her ticket, but he shouted, '*Identité!*' She produced the card belonging to the nurse whose bag she had taken. The man looked it over, then looked her over. She held her breath.

He was asking her something when a rumpus broke out in the carriage one along. Rudely throwing the card into her lap, he strode away.

A moment later, Hiltrud saw a young man jump from the slowing train. Shots were fired, and everyone in her carriage dropped their heads to their knees. She didn't. It was far more interesting to watch the police leap on to the tracks. Not so much fun being at a standstill for half an hour afterwards. When you have difficult tasks ahead of you, you do not want delays.

At the barrier, a German policeman looked over her papers and called her '*Schwester*'. She puzzled over it until it struck her that her black, hooded cloak and the hem of the cotton nightdress beneath suggested a nursing nun. Where were the taxis? All she could see were bicycles with funny little cubicles attached behind. Yet people were getting into them.

She approached a driver and said, 'La Passerinette.'

The driver returned a mystified look. She pointed to her head, and shouted in German, '*Modistin!*'

'*Modiste?*' he queried, and shouted something down the line of drivers. Somebody seemed to understand and a moment later he was asking her, 'Boulevard de la Madeleine?'

She had absolutely no idea, but nodded nevertheless.

After the bumpiest ride of her life, she found herself in a broad street, as fine as any in Berlin. She dropped coins into the driver's hand, and watched him count them with his eyes before he pedalled quickly away. Within seconds, she had forgotten about him because there was 'La Passerinette' etched on to glass. The shop's blinds were up but there were no hats on show. Nothing to prove that these were the premises of her husband's mistress. Considering what she was planning to do, she must be sure.

The door was ajar, and she stepped inside. A man wearing her father's stiff kind of collar was talking animatedly to a tall, blonde and very lovely girl in a pink dress. They were surrounded by pink and grey hatboxes and Hiltrud had the impression they were arguing over them.

'Fräulein de Lirac?'

They broke off and gave Hiltrud a curious stare.

The girl said something in French through sensual, painted lips. Assuming she was being asked who she was, Hiltrud pulled herself up to a dignified height and said, 'I am your lover's wife.'

The blonde girl took in a shocked breath and colour swept through her cheeks. So. Condemned by her own shame. Hiltrud held out two red cherries hanging from a single stalk. One had a stone, the other . . . Well, she had no actual proof it was a cyanide capsule.

'*Non, merci.*' The girl indicated the door and Hiltrud understood that the shop wasn't open. But, of course, it was Sunday. She'd heard bells as she came through the barrier at the station.

She continued offering the cherries and finally, with an impatient noise, the girl took them.

Hiltrud left, but went no further than the opposite side of the road. After a short wait, she saw the girl leaving the shop, carrying one of the pink and grey hatboxes. Hiltrud followed her to the end of the street, and saw a great building flanked by columns. The girl did not cross the junction, but turned left into another street. At the kerb, she paused and that was when Hiltrud saw her raise her lips to the cherries and bite off first one fruit, then the other.

The girl was halfway across the road when she gave an unearthly cry and doubled over. The hatbox rolled like a drum. Baying like a hound, the girl gripped her throat and fell to her knees. A second later, a black car bearing the flag of the German Reich on its radiator grille ploughed into her.

Hiltrud walked on, ignoring the cries of horror, the running feet. One task complete. She crossed a great square that she recognised. She'd sat here on her first day in Paris, watching eddies of snow falling from a gunmetal sky. She kept walking, remembering the car journey to Dietrich's flat. They had crossed a river and the driver had said, 'The Seine, *gnädige Dame*. A fine river.'

A good enough river, anyway. Shortly after midday, Hiltrud von Elbing stepped off the wharf into cold brown water, completing her second task of the day.

Chapter Thirty-seven

Coralie knew she'd overslept even before she opened the curtains. Georges and Lorienne could have stripped La Passerinette to the floorboards by now, but if they had, they had. She wasn't going to scramble over to boulevard de la Madeleine in yesterday's clothes.

It was after midday and Dietrich was still asleep. She'd nip home to rue de Seine, she decided, change, then return and massage his back until he woke. *The way to a man's heart*.

In her own flat she washed, put her hair up in a bun and changed her pewter-grey choker for one of pale pink. While the kettle boiled, she opened her wardrobe and surveyed her dresses. Was it mischief that made her reach for the pink dress printed with twin cherries in navy-blue?

The last time she'd worn this . . . Well, she'd see if Dietrich remembered. She put on the tasselled pillbox hat that went so well with it, and reluctantly tied a dark headscarf over it because she intended to cycle to La Passerinette. It was such a gorgeous day.

She cycled as far as the river, then wheeled her bicycle across the pont des Arts and again across place de la Concorde. At the top of rue Royale, she was held up by a police block. People were gathered in the road, watching an ambulance slowly drawing up. She heard somebody say that a young woman had been knocked down and killed by a German driver.

Coralie averted her eyes.

Turning right in front of the imposing Madeleine, she wheeled her bicycle into boulevard de la Madeleine, straining her eyes for the first sight of La Passerinette. The salon door was open! 'No!' she raged. 'No!'

When she stormed in, Georges Blanchard, surrounded by hatboxes, looked momentarily relieved. Then, as he recognised Coralie, his fists went up.

Little did he know how many times she'd seen a big man in that stance. 'Put them down, Georges. You don't frighten me. Just know this. If I catch you anywhere near this place again, I will go to the head of the Paris police, the head of the Abwehr, the head of the army and the head of the Gestapo, one after the other, until one of them kicks your backside into jail, and kicks Lorienne's in after it. Look at my face.' She tapped a cheek. 'This is the anger of a betrayed woman. Why did you do it?'

'She promised to make me her *premier* if I brought you down. She was meant to come straight back, with a *vélo* taxi.'

'Better go and find her then, hadn't you? How many of my hats are missing?'

'None.' Georges hesitated, then admitted, 'Lorienne took one with her.'

'I suggest you ask her to drop it back. Now get out.'

Coralie watched him till he'd gone round the corner. Sighing, she closed the door, then opened it again because the shop suddenly felt constrictive. After returning the hatboxes to the workroom, she unpinned her closing-down notice and tore it up.

Seeing her shop threatened again, she'd remembered how passionately she loved her work. Dietrich had advised her well.

Lunch. Why not telephone Dietrich and invite him to meet

her here? She was just reaching for the handset when a man's cough from the salon told her that Dietrich had anticipated her.

Walking through, she began a laughing comment that ended in a gasp. It wasn't Dietrich. Two rough-looking men filled the doorway.

Had she fainted? Because she was on the floor, looking up at the octopus-arms of her ceiling light. Fingers were tapping her cheek. A man muttered, 'Wake up.'

She thought, They're looters. They think there's money here. One of them was breathing harshly.

Fingers tapped her again. 'Come on, sweetheart, wake up.'

Sweetheart? English? Not possible. The faces staring down at her simply could not exist together, not on the mortal plane.

'Ramon?'

'*Oui, chérie.*'

'Donal?'

'Hello, Cora.'

'I'm Coralie. What the hell?'

'We met at a station.' Hard breaths made spaces between Ramon's words. It wasn't her hazy vision that made his face seem grey. It *was* grey. He'd painted his cheeks with some kind of dirt, and dragged it through his hair. Disguise, she supposed. After all, the Gestapo were after him.

Donal finished the story in English, 'He got me on the train at Fontainebleau and stayed with me till I had to jump. We met up at the Madeleine. Lovely church. Whoever built it must have seen the Brompton Oratory because—'

Coralie interrupted. 'Ramon, are you all right?' To Donal, she said, 'He's not well.'

'Caught a bullet in the finger. It smashed bone and it's infected.

He needs a doctor and we both need a safe house. I think Ramon said there were flats above this shop.'

'Too dangerous, but I know somewhere else.' It would have to be impasse de Cordoba.

She let Donal haul her up, then led them into the workroom. Donal looked around, at the boxes, at the designs pinned on the walls, the *marotte* heads sporting unfinished models. 'Who makes all this?'

'I do.'

'They'd fall off their chairs at Pettrew's. I'm proud of you, Cora.'

'Call me Cora one more time, I'll punch you. I'm Mademoiselle de Lirac.'

He grinned. 'And I'm Air Vice Marshal Flynn.'

'You both need a change of clothes. I have to get you out of here.' Dietrich might come looking for her at any time. He would see Donal as an enemy captive, to be treated according to the rules of the Geneva Convention. Ramon might as well have a firing-squad target pinned over his heart. She sniffed him. 'Been sleeping rough?'

'Running, *chérie*, not sleeping. Help me get back to my comrades. I have no money. My new English friend paid for my ticket.'

She took Ramon's filthy beret, replacing it with a trilby that Georges had left behind. It changed his appearance immediately. Ramon's jacket was stiff with dried blood. That was why he stank. She made him take it off and helped him into a trench coat she'd left there when the weather turned warm. Tight on him, but masculine enough not to draw attention. Coralie wished she'd had the foresight to keep a man's suit here as well because Donal's blue-grey trousers, blouson jacket and white sweater screamed 'British airman'.

In the end, she had Donal and Ramon exchange jumpers, and discovered that both men carried pistols in side holsters. She made no comment. For Ramon, she fashioned a cravat from an offcut of cloth while Donal dulled his light brown flying boots with black ink and blue tailor's chalk. After she'd added a slick of glycerin to his hair, he looked more like a local, particularly as he now had a morning's growth of beard. Her finest touch was a black eye, conjured out of the makeup in her bag. Solange had left a bottle of red nail varnish behind and Coralie stippled tiny dots under Donal's eye to resemble burst blood vessels. His face was already hatched with scratches and bumps from his rough landing. 'We might as well make a virtue of it,' she said.

Ramon considered her handiwork. 'You've overdone the yellow.'

'Listen, I've seen a few black eyes in my time.' She said it again in English to Donal, adding, 'I've seen them in the mirror.'

Donal shook his head, and she supposed there were things he didn't like to be reminded of. 'Right,' she told him, 'the story is, I'm taking you home because you were beaten by thugs outside a drinking den. If anybody stops us, say nothing and look dazed.'

It was agreed that Ramon would go ahead and they would meet at the corner of rue de Leningrad and rue du Berne, close to impasse de Cordoba. When it was their turn to leave, Coralie knotted her scarf over her hat and assembled a few useful items, including her left-handed scissors, wads of absorbent cloth, salt and ersatz coffee. Putting them in her bicycle basket, she thought of Dietrich. He would never track her to impasse de Cordoba – it would seem as though she'd abandoned him again.

Outside, she gruffly reminded Donal, 'Traffic comes from the left over here. If we're stopped, I do the talking. Anything goes wrong, run for it and we'll meet at Gare de Lyon, where you arrived.'

'You do the talking, I get to look dumb. Nothing changes, Coralie.'

'At least you're getting my name right.'

In the flat on impasse de Cordoba, she opened the window to air the place. Nobody had been inside since she'd last left it, and the smell of damp was unwelcoming. She made black coffee for them all. 'I'll go foraging in a moment, and contact a member of my circuit. You'll both need money, and Donal needs false papers and a safe sanctuary beyond Paris.'

'You trust your contact?' Ramon demanded.

'Sure I do – he wears Nazi uniform and shouts, "*Sieg Heil!*" every time we meet.'

'Sarcasm is not only wasted, it is uncharitable to a man in my state.'

'Then don't ask daft questions.' She make a strong salt solution with water from the kettle and held Ramon's hand in it until the blood-caked bandage fell away from his finger. When he complained of shooting pains up his arm, she laid a hand to his brow. The bullet had got the middle joint of his wedding finger which was grotesquely inflamed, naked bone under a collar of ragged flesh. More ominously, black streaks radiated from the site. Damn right they needed a doctor.

Donal, meanwhile, was looking around the flat, a two-minute job. He flicked back the window curtain. 'Reminds me of Barnham Street. Grey roofs and mean-eyed windows. I thought Paris was different.'

'Most of it is.'

He turned, unsmiling. 'Still, no worse than I'm used to in

barracks. Cheers.' He drank his coffee without making a face, so she guessed what they got at home was no better. Seeing Ramon slumped on the sofa, Donal said quietly, 'What were the chances of running into him? I nearly fell down when I discovered he was your husband.'

'He has the same effect on me.' She took their cups away to wash. Something about Donal was making her nervous. It wasn't just the physical changes in him she found hard to adjust to, it was his tone, his demeanour. The shy boy had always been easy to brush off and tease. This man was essentially a stranger and he looked at her the same way – as if she were a stranger he intended to know more about.

'Did you mean to come to Paris?' she asked, as she belted on the cheap cotton coat she kept in the flat. 'Wouldn't you have been better heading straight west, making for Spain?'

'I wanted to find you.' Still no smile. 'Ramon was nervous about coming to you – worried the Gestapo might have you under surveillance, but we didn't dare hang about south of the river. Not after I jumped from the train and got chased half a mile.'

'Ramon's a wanted man, you know that?'

He answered instead, 'That time we met at the club, the Rose Noire? You were belting out "The Lambeth Walk". When you told me you were married – ' his voice caught '– I hadn't known until then how much I'd always thought of you as my girl.'

She shook her head.

'No. And you're not his, either.' He meant Ramon. 'There's a German, right?' Donal had inadvertently smeared his painted black eye across his face and he looked like a chimney sweep. A sweep with hard blue eyes, searching her face for clues. It wasn't just Donal questioning either, it was everything he represented. Homeland, King, comrades.

'There are no Germans in my life,' she told him. *Why complicate matters?* 'I'd better go. Don't go outside, stay away from the window and wash your face.' She was out of the door before he could ask her anything else.

The shops were closed, of course, but the patron of her regular café sold her a tin of ham, green beans and a knobbly swede. He also filled the bottle she carried permanently in her bicycle basket with red wine.

Moineau had told her that in an emergency she could go to the Café de Finisterre opposite the entrance to Gare Saint-Lazare. He went there most days for lunch, he said, and always on a Sunday. If she missed him, the proprietor would summon him by telephone if she gave the code phrase 'Cousin Charles'.

Lunch service was tailing off when she arrived at the café at a few minutes after two. No sign of Moineau – she'd probably missed him. Parking her bicycle where she could see it, she squeezed into a chair at a one-person table outside, allowing herself a moment to soak up the May sunshine. She'd have to order something, but it felt mean to eat a proper meal with Donal and Ramon waiting unfed. So she asked for an apple and a piece of cheese and tried to ignore the smell of baked fish and garlic. She paid with some of Donal's emergency currency, and when the girl stared at the brand new note, explained she'd been to the bank the day before. 'Fresh in from the treasury.'

'Long time since I've seen anything so clean,' the girl said – not the greatest advertisement for her café. She took a long time bringing a small plate with a wizened apple and a chunk of Camembert. Coralie was picking the last crumbs when she saw a familiar figure in a Dutch-boy cap parking his bicycle. Moineau called out a familiar greeting to the waitress. 'Bring me whatever you've got, Annette.'

Coralie waited till the girl had gone before hissing, 'Cousin Charles!'

Moineau gave a double-take, then looked around nervously. His corduroy trousers were tied at the ankle with string, the inside leg worn to a shine. *He must cycle a great deal*, she thought.

'What's up?' He came and sat at her table.

She explained the situation, adding, 'And we need a doctor, urgently.'

'An English evader and a Resistance fighter? They didn't come through us.'

'They made their own way. You might as well know, the injured man is my husband, Ramon Cazaubon.'

Moineau gave her a long look. 'Right. Where are they? At rue de Seine?'

'Impasse de Cordoba. Yes, I know, it's a dead-end passage and might be compromised, but I'm out of bolt-holes.'

'So you need to move them on sharpish. Who do you normally link with?'

'Francine, at quai d'Anjou, but you said she'd been arrested.'

'Of course. I'll make some calls.'

'Is there a doctor you trust?'

'Yes, and I'll telephone him from here. Go back to Cordoba and wait. We'll come when it's dark. And, Cosette, take your airman's gun away.'

'How d'you know he's got one?'

'Some carry them. If he's caught and he pulls a weapon, they won't treat him as a prisoner of war, you know that.'

She nodded. 'I'll warn him.'

'No, take the gun from him.'

The waitress brought her wine to drink, even though she hadn't ordered it, and while Moineau went inside to make his telephone call, she allowed herself half a glass. Seeing the waitress serving a nearby table with plates of fish and green lentils, she decided to beg a clove of garlic and a knob of butter from the kitchen. She'd throw it in with the mashed swede, make it more palatable.

She walked through the café and into the lobby where the telephone was housed. Raising her hand to knock at the kitchen door, she heard the click of tokens going into the machine, followed by, '*Hier ist Spatz.*'

She lowered her fist. '*Spatz*' was 'sparrow' in German. 'Moineau' meant sparrow too. Slowly, slowly, she turned.

He was hunched in the alcove, the telephone receiver shoving his cap to one side, corduroy trousers still tied at the ankle. She heard him say, 'Reiniger,' and in German, 'Get me Major Reiniger, quickly.'

Coralie backed away, only to collide with the returning waitress, who dropped the tray she was carrying. Moineau looked out from his alcove, saw Coralie and rushed towards her, grabbing her satin choker which went taut, then broke.

It was that, rather than the incomprehensible betrayal, that made her rage spew over. 'You were calling the Gestapo! You pig!'

'Annette!' Moineau shouted at the gawping waitress. 'Get the *patron*. We need to put this girl in the cellar. Get him!' Then, to Coralie as if wanting to appease her, 'Look, we're on the same side, aren't w— Bitch!'

She'd kneed him in the groin, a half-baked jab because her coat skirts were hampering her. Moineau caught her right wrist in a powerful grip, bending her arm behind her back. 'You sleep with

Germans and I take their—' The word 'money' disappeared in a shout of pain as Coralie's left-handed punch knocked his head sideways. Thanking Donal, who'd taught her that move, she followed up with a second blow that knocked Moineau's cap off. Then she ran.

Both men were asleep, Donal sprawled in an armchair, Ramon face down on the sofa. 'Wake up!' Gasping for breath because she had cycled away like a schoolboy caught stealing apples, she shook Donal. She got a mumble back, so she put her hands inside his shirt, feeling for the cold outline of his gun. Plucking it free, she put it into her coat pocket. Then she pinched him.

Donal woke.

He reached up, drew her face down and kissed her. His chin and upper lip were rough but his lips were soft. 'Cora,' he said, between kisses, 'I have to tell you what they found buried in your father's workshop.'

Not that, not now. 'Shut up and get up. We have seconds to get out.'

Chapter Thirty-eight

They supported Ramon between them like a drunk. His face gleamed with sweat. They were lumbering across rue de Leningrad when they heard the grind of car engines, getting louder. The blasting of horns suggested drivers ploughing across place de l'Europe.

'Moscow,' she panted. 'Run!' They dragged Ramon round the corner into rue de Moscou seconds before tyres screeched to a halt at impasse de Cordoba. They heard the slam of doors, then the crash of a metal bar against wood.

'It won't take them long to see the place is empty,' Donal said. 'Where now?'

Yes – where? Coralie couldn't think of a single safe haven. 'Let's just go. We need to lose ourselves.'

They took the Métro at rue de Liège and spent maybe two hours just riding the lines. She could not take them home, or to La Passerinette. Or to Teddy's, because Dietrich might look for her there, and Dietrich would turn Ramon in. What about Bonnet, at rue Valdonne? Ramon vetoed it, groggy with fever. 'He drinks – never trust a drunk.'

'What about one of your many women?' she asked, quite seriously.

'Never trust a woman.'

She gritted her teeth. Félix Peyron? Only she didn't know

where he lodged. Solange Antonin, who lived in luxury on rue Cambon? Maybe, but what if Solange was entertaining one of her beaux? Una's friends at the American Hospital had all been interned. The butcher on Mouffetard . . . her contact at avenue Foch . . . too dangerous. They might be under surveillance. *Why didn't I make more friends?*

And then she thought, *I know exactly who to go to.*

They alighted at Odéon, south of the river and a stone's throw north of rue de Vaugirard. Leaving Donal supporting Ramon, she went into a bar, paying double-price for the owner's leftover bread. Donal had shared his emergency provisions with Ramon on the train, and that was all they'd eaten today.

Fortunately, she'd had the presence of mind to shove the tin of ham she'd bought earlier into her pocket. Everything else was with her bicycle, thrown down in impasse de Cordoba. Probably by now being shared among the Gestapo.

Unbuttoning her coat because she was hot, and because the tin of ham made her look as though she had some kind of growth on her hip, she led the way down rue de l'Odéon, passing the bookshop where Dietrich had bought her *A Farewell to Arms*. A brief glance showed her a window full of Nazi propaganda.

'Whose flat are we're going to?' Donal asked.

'The owner taught me French and German some years ago.'

'You do speak German, then?'

'Yes, and so does the King of England.'

Clutching bread to her chest, Coralie rang Louise Deveau's bell, willing her to come down quickly. They made an odd trio. Donal, taller than an average Frenchman, wearing peculiar boots and mismatched clothes. Ramon, weak as a stick of boiled rhubarb. She heard footsteps and bolts being drawn back.

Marshalling her apologies for calling on Mademoiselle Deveau in contravention of rules, she stepped inside. Donal followed with Ramon.

The door slammed shut. It was not Mademoiselle Deveau, irritated and reserved. It was a man who put a pistol to the side of her head, saying, 'One terrorist, one evader, one *résistante*. Up the stairs, please, the men first.'

He had turned off the stairwell light, wanting the advantage of darkness. 'Walk slowly, raise your hands. I have seven shots.' He didn't want to fire his Walther PP until he was looking Ramon Cazaubon in the eye.

Inevitably, it was Coralie who objected. 'I don't know how you found me, Dietrich, but I'm not raising my hands because I'm not dropping this bread. I paid a fortune for it. Donal doesn't speak French, by the way, and he can't raise his hands, else Ramon will fall down.'

'Donal,' Dietrich continued in English, 'take Cazaubon through the open door at the top of the stairs. If you try anything, I will shoot Mademoiselle de Lirac.'

'No, he won't.' Coralie sounded perfectly confident. But she gave a start when he moved the muzzle of the pistol to the hollow where her skull met her spine.

'Believe me, I will. Now walk ahead of me.'

The concierge had let Dietrich into the apartment earlier, explaining in the loud voice of the very deaf, 'Mademoiselle Deveau went away suddenly, after New Year. I keep the place clean, but . . . ' Unlived-in places always had a particular smell, and five months' unopened post added a twist of ambiguity. Was Louise Deveau dead or alive?

No sign of Coralie either, but she would come. After all, who else did she know in Paris?

Dismissing the concierge, Dietrich had settled down to wait.

Now he propelled Coralie into the middle of the living room. 'Stay right here.' Pistol levelled, he watched a tall, dark-haired man help a scruffy, black-haired one to the sofa. He recognised Cazaubon, though the man was rougher and thinner than on their last meeting. From the way he fell back against the cushions, he must be suffering the effects of his injury. Was that the bulge of a gun under his jacket?

Coralie looked shocked, as well she might. The Englishman was anxious – bewildered, even. Dietrich returned his gaze. *Yes,* he answered silently. You are seeing a German uniform, a silver breast eagle, a *Pour le Mérite.* You are not hallucinating. 'Both of you, put your hands up.'

Lifting his hands to shoulder height, the young man asked, 'Luftwaffe, sir?'

'Not actively. This time round, I occupy a different role. You?'

'Warrant Officer Flynn, Royal Air Force.'

'Thank you for being honest.' Dietrich nodded at Flynn's boots, which looked as though they'd been pasted with bird muck. 'A pretence of being a deaf-mute farm labourer would have been insulting to both of us.' Coralie was still clutching her hunks of bread. 'I said, hands up.'

She made no move to obey. 'What d'you think I'm going to do, Dietrich? Cartwheel over and strangle you?'

It was the Englishman who answered. 'You know him? This is your German? Dear God, Cora, which side are you on?'

Cora. Dietrich hadn't imagined that his emotions could darken deeper, but the idea of burying a bullet in that muscular young chest was suddenly tempting. 'Get back against the wall, both of you,' he barked. After a shared glance, Coralie and the Englishman backed away until they stood in front of one of Louise Deveau's china cabinets. Like twins. Flynn . . . Hadn't she mentioned the name before? A memory slid into place. *Sheila Flynn.* 'You grew up in the same street.'

'Spot on,' Coralie answered. 'We used to trespass on the railway and sneak into the cinema together. Dietrich——'

He hushed her. Two children growing up together, he could tolerate. But the bastard Cazaubon . . . Going to the sofa, he put his pistol barrel against the man's temple, saying in French, 'I am going to execute you for murder, Cazaubon.'

'Go to Hell.'

Coralie dropped her bread and came towards them. Her headscarf had slipped backwards, holding her curls in a lop-sided snood. Her coat hung open and Dietrich recognised the dress beneath. Pink, cherry print, low-necked. She'd worn it the day he had interrogated her at the Lutetia. Had she guessed, in that spartan room, how he'd been fighting the desire to take her in his arms, to take off her hat and bury his fingers in her hair?

He heard her say, 'Ramon fights for his country. You did it. Donal does it. Even I have a go sometimes. It's war.'

He saw blood on her throat where her choker should have been. Tears in her eyes. He forced himself to look through them. 'Bombing the tunnel at Auxerre was indiscriminate killing.' From the corner of his eye, he saw the Englishman lowering his arms, slipping a hand under his clothing. The RAF issued air crew with side-arms, just as the Luftwaffe did. Not so much for hand-to-hand fighting, but so an airman could put a bullet in his own head if he was trapped in a burning fuselage. That this Englishman had hung on to his suggested an intention to challenge the odds.

Dietrich fired a warning bullet into the arm of the sofa, making Cazaubon duck and Coralie shriek.

'Hands on shoulders, Warrant Officer! You, too, Coralie.'

She folded hers across her chest. 'It's beneath you to kill out of malice.'

'Why? I am as human and flawed as the next man.' Had she any concept of the hours he had just lived through? He had woken to find her gone and had presumed she was at La Passerinette. He'd decided to take the Métro to the Louvre and walk the rest of the way because it was such a lovely day. On rue Royale, he'd passed a huddle of pressmen holding up the traffic. Some were talking to a policeman, and one was photographing what seemed to be blood on the road. A familiar-coloured hatbox. A tag-end of conversation had made his blood run cold.

'. . . hit by a bus, blonde, well-dressed and tall. No name yet.'

He had run to La Passerinette, which was locked. Nobody had answered his flat-handed beating at the door, and the despair that had attended the death of his son had flooded back.

Somehow, he'd got himself back to rue de Vaugirard where an orderly informed him that the matron at Le Cloître had telephoned. Could he call back urgently? He'd learned his wife was missing. A plane had crashed nearby, a bomber, and everybody had run out to see if there were survivors. Unfortunately, somebody had neglected to lock the doors. Would he motor down to Fontainebleau at once?

'No, Madame, I will not. If you had adhered to your duty, my wife could not have walked out. Send out a search party, alert the local police. It is unlikely she has gone far.'

He was going to search Paris until he found Coralie, alive or dead. He was preparing to leave again when the telephone rang. This time, it was the commissariat of police for the Madeleine quarter, requesting he go to the mortuary on quai de la Rapée to identify a body.

That trip, the longest of his life. The surge of joy when he found himself looking down not at Coralie, but at a blue-white Hiltrud had expressed itself in '*Gott sei dank*' followed by deep shame.

Returning home, he'd been in time to pick up a call from Le Cloître, informing him of the shocking news that his wife's body had been found. 'Paris police have just called us. They identified her by a bag belonging to one of the clinic nurses—'

'Hanging around her neck. They dragged her from the Seine. I have just identified her body and you are two hours late calling me with this news.'

'Believe me, Generalmajor, the police only just informed us.'

'Then how did they get my number, if you didn't give it to them? Do not lie, Madame. Do not attempt to shift blame. Were you a member of an army unit, you would be court-martialled.'

He had hung up and mixed himself a fizzing analgesic to dull the pain in his leg and a throbbing headache. He was dehydrated. He drank several glasses of water, and then the telephone rang again. This time, it was Friedrich Olbricht, chief of the General Army Office, calling from Berlin.

'The day of action comes closer, von Elbing. Are you with us still?'

Why this, now? 'Count on my loyalty, General.' In Berlin, he had sworn allegiance to Valkyrie, a conspiracy of army officers, including an old friend, Claus von Stauffenberg, to carry out the decisive stroke against Hitler and his closest henchmen. Valkyrie would trigger cataclysmic events, and the stopwatch had just started ticking. He'd hung up, thinking, Death or freedom. But without Coralie, neither seemed to matter. Where was she?

The physical present had intruded just then, with violent hammering at street level. The orderly must have opened up pretty swiftly because, within seconds, Major Reiniger had his boot over Dietrich's threshold, demanding to search.

Reiniger had four armed thugs with him, and Dietrich's fears swung to Valkyrie. Was his telephone line under surveillance?

'Your mistress has been seen in the company of two wanted men, Generalmajor, the terrorist Ramon Cazaubon and a suspected British evader.' They had escaped from their Right Bank hideout, Reiniger informed him, and Cazaubon was known to be in bad shape. 'Hand her over.'

So she was alive – but with Cazaubon? After everything he had said? 'I assure you, Major Reiniger, she is not here.'

'Then you will not object to a search.'

'I object violently, but you will do it anyway.'

They'd found a hat of Coralie's in the bedroom, which in their eyes was proof of his collusion with French criminals. They could not arrest him on such limited evidence, but Dietrich had no doubt that he now topped Reiniger's list of men to bring down. Would Valkyrie be triggered in time to save him?

Now, in Louise Deveau's genteel sitting room, he knew that taking Ramon Cazaubon at gunpoint to Gestapo HQ would restore his good standing, but such action was beneath him. Cazaubon would get a clean bullet. Dietrich positioned the Walther behind Cazaubon's ear and, with his free hand, searched the Frenchman for weapons, finding a veteran Lebel revolver that he pushed into his own belt.

'*Vive la France*,' Cazaubon said hoarsely.

Dietrich steadied his hand, bent his finger—

'Do it, and I'll kill you.' Coralie was pointing a revolver at him, a heavier piece than his short-coupled Walther. Though her grip shook discernibly, her expression promised no waver.

'An interesting triangle, *Liebchen*.'

'I mean it, Dietrich. I can do it.'

'Bloody hell, Cora.' The English pilot was visibly outraged. 'You've taken my gun. That's military issue.'

'You were always dead easy to rob, Donal. And don't come any nearer because I might just shoot you instead.'

Unperturbed, Donal moved and Dietrich fired into the floor at his feet, sending him back. An armed Coralie he could deal with. Probably. Two armed men in one room would be deadly – which of them would back down? And though there was only a deaf old concierge on the top floor, gunshots would bring the police eventually.

'Back to the wall,' he ordered Donal, who reluctantly obeyed. 'Coralie, you will probably miss me even at this range. Those Enfields are poor aimers.'

He saw Donal Flynn open his mouth to object, think better of it and say, 'He's right, Cora. Sometimes they even fire backwards.'

Ramon Cazaubon was chuckling as if the farce surrounding his own death tickled him, though as far as Dietrich knew, he would have understood nothing that had been said. Perhaps it was like watching a film without subtitles. Nestling his gun right inside Cazaubon's ear, he said in French, 'It will be quick. Better than being carried, crippled, to a firing-squad after the Gestapo are done with you.' To Coralie: 'They will get him, you know that.'

Coralie lowered the Enfield.

He said, 'Put it down on the floor.'

But she didn't. 'Shoot Ramon, you'll have murdered both of us.'

'How so?'

'Like this.' She pressed the Enfield's barrel against her own temple.

'Coralie, no!'

'Cora, put it down!' Donal Flynn stepped forward.

A vision flooded Dietrich's mind, Coralie in his arms, asking him not to withdraw. She had *wanted* his child. 'Cazaubon is not worth the sacrifice and you might be pregnant. It is possible.'

'Well, I don't want to have the child of a murderer. I grew up with one. My dad used to boast how he'd pulped a Frenchman when he was over here, and his eyes would brighten like mine do when I'm describing a new hat. Why kill Ramon? His debt will have been paid by now, you can be sure of it, in blood against a wall in a town square. Murder him, and you'll have my death in your dreams every night, I promise you. I will do it.'

Dietrich stepped away from Ramon. 'Coralie, I thought I had you cornered but you always slip past me.' His desire to laugh was, he suspected, the result of multiple shocks. Only Coralie could get all three of her men together in one room, through a trail of fire and blood, and seize the moral high ground. Determined not to yield, he made his features iron. But she'd won, and she knew it.

'Swear you won't hurt Ramon?'

He sighed. 'I will not shoot him. Lower your gun.'

'Or turn him in?'

'I will not turn him in. He is free to go, your London friend too.' He switched to English, saying, 'Go, Warrant Officer, and take this *Mistkerl* with you. Say goodbye to Coralie and take your chances.'

Coralie stamped a foot. 'Don't be daft. Ramon needs a hospital.'

Ramon, understanding 'hospital' cried, 'No! They will give me ether and I will be trapped.'

'You've got spreading gangrene. It'll go into your bloodstream.'

Ramon showed her his mangled finger. 'Cut it off. He's got a knife.' He meant Donal.

'I can't— Oh, damn you!'

She swore because Dietrich had wrestled the Enfield off her. She swore at him again, then gave up, seeming not to care that he now had all three guns. 'All right, Ramon, I'll cut your finger off, but give me permission in front of witnesses.'

'Permission granted. Get on with it, *ma chérie*.'

Dietrich watched Coralie and Donal prepare an operating table of cushions laid on the floor, and pull a reading lamp close. He heard Coralie ask for a knife.

Donal Flynn bared the blade, but wouldn't hand it over. 'It's not woman's work, Cora. You hold him down.'

Dietrich saw how Flynn looked at her. Such love in his eyes, but it sparked no new jealousy. Just the acid of despair.

'I shan't be able to, Donal. You hold him, I'll cut.'

'You won't have the strength to go through bone.'

This could go on all night, Dietrich thought. Holstering his Walther and locking the two foreign guns in the china cabinet, he took the knife from Flynn's hand. He said to Coralie, 'Find cloths. See if there is a bottle of wine in the kitchen. Louise always kept a stock.' When she came back with both, he said, 'Soak a cloth in wine, to put between his teeth. You, Warrant Officer, pinion him across his shoulders. Kneel on his back if you have to. However hard he screams, don't let him move.'

Coralie sought Dietrich's gaze. 'Thank you.'

He said – or did he think it? – 'I want you only for whatever time we have left, but for that time, I want the whole of you.'

Chapter Thirty-nine

Frauen-Konz-Lager Ravensbrück, northern Germany

Cleaning the windows of the secretaries' building was one of the softer tasks at the camp. Bright afternoon sun sharpened the strokes of her vinegar-soaked cloth, and for the first time in months, Una felt warm. She kept her movements slow but consistent. Since being released from the Hell of the sewing factory, where a broken thread was punished with the whip, she had existed in a state of bated breath. Eyes were everywhere. To be seen to slack, even for a moment, might get her sent back there. Or, worse, to the infirmary, where inmates were assessed for fitness. Fitness to live. To be weak was to be condemned.

From this window, she could see the chimneys of the crematorium breathing white smoke into a perfect sky. June had arrived, in azure. June was the month her spoiled, rich self had always thought of as the end of little-Paris-summer, July and August being spent at Cap d'Antibes. She liked to keep track of the months, though she let the days run one into the next, just as she blurred her eyes to the barracks where she and uncountable other women lived, slept and starved. Likewise, she tried not to see the punishment block or the interrogation block, or the white tent in which the Hungarian Jewesses had frozen last winter. She always tried to talk her nose out of noticing the stench, just as she tried to empty her ears of the wailing screams that marked the days when the trucks transported condemned women away.

How thin she'd grown. She looked almost in wonder at the wrist protruding from her striped sleeve. Every bone showed, and her blotchy skin was covered with a fine blonde fur. She'd caught scabies as soon as she arrived here last fall, from Vittel, and she still carried the crusts on her wrists and hands. Throughout the nightmare journey here, she'd feared her Resistance work had caught up with her. The first few days, she'd moved like a drunkard, shallow-breathing, trying not to catch anybody's eye. Every shout, every door kicked open, had sounded like her name. Except, of course, they took your name from you. Later, because she was fit, they'd put her to work in the sewing factory.

At some point, she'd learned that she had the Abwehr to thank for this imprisonment. German military intelligence had discovered she was married to the Scottish shipping magnate Gregory Kilpin, who had generously loaned his vessels to the British fleet. It made her a *bona fide* enemy.

She'd cursed Gregory. Then, a few weeks back, she'd been summoned before the Kommandant and interrogated about her husband's friendship with Winston Churchill. She'd almost blurted out, 'You're kidding, aren't you? Gregory doesn't have friends.' Thankfully, she'd held back, and by the time she'd finished, the Kommandant believed that Gregory and Winston were old school buddies who did the *Times* crossword together over the telephone every night.

They'd moved her to a less-crowded block, given her this soft job and slightly better rations. They were scared. Scared they were losing the war and that, one day, Winston Churchill would come here and look at their handiwork.

It made her feel almost tender towards Gregory. It had kept her alive because this was a selection camp, the selection being 'work or die'. She shared her extra food and used her nursing skills discreetly. She was teaching English to French, Polish and Russian prisoners. And deportment, how to curtsy and walk into a room in such a way that everybody would turn to look. Maybe not such an advisable skill right here. She liked to think she was scattering rose petals upon the dunghill. To laugh was a miracle. To smile, a godsend, but was it right to try to cheer up girls you knew would soon be selected to die?

The snarling of dogs outside the window warned Una that SS-Aufseherin von Elbing was nearby. Sweet, lovely Claudia kept her Alsatians hungry, tormented them with promises of food, so that when she walked among the prisoners she had demented creatures to terrify them with. Una moved on to the next window and averted her eyes.

One of the secretaries got up from her typewriter and went to the door calling, 'Fräulein? A letter has arrived for you.'

Una watched Claudia come in. How she swaggered, young as she was, clearly loving her connection to the SS – though, in reality, she was as much a civilian as the typists. Dietrich von Elbing's daughter could have been something, Una reckoned. That auburn hair . . . a few months in Paris, well-cut clothes and a decent coiffure. What was it with German women and plaits? And those boots, with a dirndl skirt on the knee? Dear Lord, no.

It was whispered that Claudia blamed her lack of promotion on her father's lukewarm relationship with the Nazi Party. Well, the kid was making up for that.

Una saw her frown at the envelope, then tear into it. That the letter contained a shock was evident from the cry of *'Mutti!'* and the way Claudia let go of her dogs' leads. Any normal dogs would have run off to search for food. Claudia's dropped to their bellies and waited.

At six thirty a.m. on 6 June 1944, Allied forces landed on five beaches in Normandy while bombers destroyed roads, bridges and railways to slow the enemy's response. All over France, Resistance units sprang into action to sabotage and hamper.

Paris basked in heat. Iron chairs under the trees in the Jardin du Luxembourg seemed to have been forged for just such a day as this, the fountains too. Coralie was trying to read a letter but couldn't concentrate. Dietrich had taken a worrying telephone call from Berlin that morning.

He'd come to find Coralie. 'The Berlin Gestapo are on Valkyrie's scent. They have made arrests throughout Germany.'

He'd told her about Valkyrie. More than a plan to assassinate Hitler, it would trigger a military coup that would usher in a new government, and change the leadership of the army. Naturally, the Gestapo wanted to smash it.

'Does that mean it's going to be abandoned?'

Dietrich had managed a wan smile. 'Valkyrie is more than ever necessary. We must show the world that there is resistance to Hitler's Reich.'

They had come into the park in the guise of carefree lovers, held motionless in a long afternoon, waiting for the clap of thunder announcing the storm. Dietrich held out his hand to her. 'I have been selfish, wrapped up in my anxieties. Something oppresses you. You are missing your English boy?'

She folded up her letter, which was from Teddy, who always wrote his news in the style of a cascading brook, weeks' worth of thoughts without punctuation. 'I'm worried about Donal, course I am.' And about Ramon, who had taken his amputation stoically, and would be back in the Auvergne, assuming he'd survived all the identity checks on the way. 'But, like you said, Donal has to take his chances. With luck, the Gestapo and the police will be too overwhelmed by military mobilisation to bother with one lone traveller. Or with us, for that matter.'

Dietrich gave her hand a reassuring squeeze. 'Reiniger is at Dreux, at the military airfield, snuffing out a conspiracy to dynamite aircraft on the ground. While he chases terrorists over there, we are safe. Soon, if fortune is with us, wolves such as him will be stripped of their power. Now talk to me, *Liebchen*, in a stream of consciousness like Teddy, or that wretched American woman.'

'Who, Una?'

'I mean Gertrude Stein, who writes as she talks as she thinks. Tell me everything.'

Pushing her chair right up to his, she tilted her head so the brim of her straw hat meshed with the brim of his and their faces were hidden. She told him how she'd overseen the changing of locks at La Passerinette, picked up her mail and closed the place. The same at rue de Seine. 'Can you tell that I mean to concentrate on you, and you alone?'

She told him how, on the way back from La Passerinette, she'd bumped into Loulou, the milliner's assistant at Henriette Junot, who'd told her about Lorienne's funeral requiem. 'Everyone was shocked at her death, and nobody understands why she was out on the street with one of my hatboxes. We know, and so does Georges Blanchard. Robbing me. I haven't said anything, and I don't intend to. Lorienne betrayed Violaine from pure malice and it makes me hope there's a God and a seat of judgement. But I wonder what made her walk into the path of a car.'

Dietrich grunted. 'The driver claimed she threw herself down in front of him. So it said in the newspaper.'

'Well, the driver would say that. Some of your lot drive at us as though we're pigeons. And guess who has stepped into Lori-enne's shoes? It's now Georges Blanchard *pour* Henriette Junot. What d'you think of that?'

'That treachery pays in the short term. But life is a long arc and every betrayal sows the seeds of our separation from all that we love, all that makes us human. Not a happy subject. It reminds me how deeply I failed Hiltrud.'

'She nearly killed you!'

'She was not in her right mind, and I never wanted her dead. Yet she is, and I am free. Free to marry you, some day. Keep talking, Coralie.'

A movement caught her eye, and Coralie pushed up the brim of her hat, whispering, 'Look, Voltaire!'

'Impossible. Voltaire has Swiss nationality now, remember?' Dietrich lifted his head, but the cat dashed into a patch of shrub. 'Ah, but could it have been Voltaire's offspring?'

'Definitely,' Coralie agreed. 'And black cats are lucky.'

'I thought they were always misfortune.'

'No,' she said firmly. 'Lucky.' She told him about the latest letters from Noëlle and Ottilia. Happy letters, from a different world. 'I can't believe my baby's six and a half. I've missed two of her birthdays. Over twenty months since I saw her.'

'Soon you will see her. But you haven't told me all. Perhaps you don't realise it but you keep falling silent and staring inwards. Donal told you something before he went. I saw you rock on your feet.'

'My father's dead.'

'How and when?'

'A year into the war – September 1940. His yard took a hit from an incendiary bomb that was probably meant for the railway. The blast swept away all the buildings, Donal said, and the fire burned so hot, nobody got near for a couple of days. When the firemen checked for bodies, they found the charred bones of a very tall man and he was identified by a half-melted cigarette lighter that must have been in his pocket. Let's walk.'

Coralie got up, needing to breathe the moist air of the Medici Fountain. The sun, just beyond its zenith, was bleaching her eyes. She continued as they walked, 'The blast ripped away the brick floor of his shed and the men found something buried. Something he was desperate should never be found – so desperate, he was willing to kill me to keep me quiet.'

'It was not, I hope, human remains.'

'No.' A sound broke from her, half laugh, half rage. 'It was a gold chalice, badly damaged, but somebody recognised it. Stolen from the cathedral where Dad used to go and pray. It used to stand in the light of a stained-glass window, St George's window. Used to stand . . . Your Luftwaffe bombed the place in 1942. Nothing but rubble now.' Out came the sobs she'd tried to keep in since Donal told her. 'I always used to say my dad was a bastard but at least he had some faith. Now I know he was just casing the joint. No good qualities, not a single one. But at least it seems he didn't kill my mother. Something, I suppose.'

'Oh, my darling.'

'She's out there somewhere, I'm sure of it. You talk now. Your turn.'

They sat down in the maple-leaf shade of the fountain and Dietrich told her about afternoons spent fishing on the banks of the Havel with Max von Silberstrom, the childhood friend who was also his half-brother. She placed her hand in his so that their

ruby rings ground together. If Valkyrie succeeded, Dietrich and
Max would be able to talk openly about their friendship.

Later in bed she refused again to let Dietrich withdraw before
climax, saying, 'I *will* get pregnant. I'm ready to make another
little life.'

Her father was dead. Hitler was as good as dead, because
Valkyrie consisted of powerful men who were sick to the gullet of
Nazi excesses. The Allies were landing in France. Hitler's armies
were hard pressed, his airforce ground down. Light crouched
behind the horizon.

A few days later, Dietrich told her that Reiniger was back in
Paris. 'Stay indoors as much as you can. Don't let him catch sight
of you.'

Saturday, 15 July

The Walther PP lay ready on the drinks table and Coralie felt like
a tightrope walker, dancing barefoot over a fire-pit.

Today army officer Claus von Stauffenberg was going to kill
Adolf Hitler at the Wolf's Lair headquarters in East Prussia. Once
the call came announcing success, Dietrich would join with the
military governor of Paris, Karl-Heinrich von Stülpnagel, and
other army officers sympathetic to Valkyrie, and enforce a *coup
d'état* here in Paris. Their first target, the Gestapo.

The call came. She heard Dietrich give his name. The stretching
silence made her twist her hands. Then she heard the telephone
receiver dropped back into the cradle.

He came back into the room. 'They called it off.' Driving his
fist into the back of an armchair, Dietrich snarled, 'Reichsführer-
SS Himmler was not present. Who cares? He could be dealt

with later. Poor Stauffenberg. It is a terrible path, martyrdom with a bomb. To be turned back at the last stride, knowing you must walk it again another day . . . ' He swore. Then apologised because, unlike her, he guarded his language.

The final telephone call came on 19 July. The assassination would happen on the morrow. Coralie coped with Dietrich's spiralling nerves, massaging his shoulders, agreeing with him each time he said, 'We cannot let it slip another time. No conspiracy can hold together for ever. The swine has to die tomorrow.'

'He will, I feel it.' If Valkyrie succeeded, the German Army in France would be ordered to pull back to open the way for the Allies – a form of surrender. France would be liberated. The Gestapo, including their French underlings and the loathed Milice, put under arrest. The worst of them executed. The end of the slaughter would be in sight.

It had happened. Hitler was dead. Killed by a bomb in his Wolf's Lair. The news reached General von Stülpnagel's headquarters at two p.m. on 20 July. Kurt Kleber came in person to rue de Vaugirard, bringing Fritzi. As an aide to the new head of the Luftwaffe, General Sperrle, Kurt had heard the news of Hitler's death earlier than most in Paris. The uprising had already swung into operation in Berlin, in Prague, in Vienna.

'I feel guilty,' he told them. 'I was always sympathetic to Valkyrie, but I never swore the oath of allegiance. Perhaps our new leaders will overlook that. After all, I tried all those years ago to do what Stauffenberg has now succeeded in doing.'

'You are as much a hero as Stauffenberg, Kurt,' his wife assured him, kissing the puckered side of his face. 'Everyone knows it.'

They all four stood together as they had before, and Coralie wondered why Dietrich held himself so stiffly until he asked

Kurt, 'You are sure that Stauffenberg is alive? I must know that our friend survived the blast.'

The question was answered at six that evening by a call from one of General Stülpnagel's aides. Stauffenberg had telephoned from Berlin in person to confirm that Hitler was dead.

Kurt and Fritzi left to return to avenue Marigny. After they'd gone, Dietrich holstered his gun and kissed Coralie, telling her to wait up. The mass arrest of Gestapo leaders was under way and he wanted to play his part.

Once he was gone, she was unable to read or even think in a straight line. What was this eerie silence? She went to the window. Of course! For the first time in four years, the sentries in rue de Vaugirard had stopped pacing. She was glad when dusk drew roosting birds into the trees and their chirruping filled the void. She fell asleep on the sofa, waking in deep dark, a key turning in the door.

'Dietrich?'

He came in, turning on the light. Lifting her feet, sitting down on the sofa, laying her legs across his, he said, 'A sight I shall never forget. Sandbags in the yard of the École Militaire.'

'Sandbags?'

'For those rats from avenue Foch to be laid down on and shot. By tomorrow morning, France will be purged of Gestapo command.'

'Reiniger?'

'Locked up on the fifth floor of his building, in the room where he has tortured and beaten his fellow humans with relish.' He patted her ankle. 'Get dressed, my love. We're going to arrest Serge Martel in his own nightclub.'

'For working as a Gestapo informant?'

'Exactly. He has done so from the day he left prison. They even trained him. You can stay at home, if you wish, but I have asked Kurt to join us again. This is a night on which destinies turn.'

She chose the pale coffee evening gown she'd worn on the night they'd tried to smuggle Ottilia away. It deserved a night of triumph. Her hair had dropped out of curl, so she covered it with a silk-jersey turban – the wired ties forming an unmistakable Victory sign. Dramatic eyebrows, dramatic lips though her neck felt naked without her choker. She'd heard the cyanide pill fall when Moineau grabbed her, then crunch as she stood on it. Slowly, she smiled at herself. She didn't need it any more.

She didn't want to go out completely unarmed, though. When she'd moved back to rue de Vaugirard, she'd brought two big trunks with her. Reaching into one of them, she extracted a heavy object.

Entering the bedroom, Dietrich saw what was in her hand. 'Fritzi Kleber once concealed a weapon in a satin purse, but hers was an old duelling pistol, designed to be hidden in a fur muff. That one is too big for you. Here, swap.'

She took his Walther PP, secreting it in an evening bag of quilted velvet. Dietrich stuck Donal's Enfield Mark II into the holster under his jacket. 'Now you are armed and glorious,' he told her.

'I've been thinking. As soon as peace is declared, I'll find Ramon and ask for a divorce. I don't think he'll make a fuss. He's bound to have another woman by now and, though he might talk about pride and honour, losing me won't break his heart.'

Dietrich gave an uncharitable grunt. 'Are you ready? We have a car waiting.'

The Left Bank streets were quiet, but the Right Bank teemed with cars bearing General von Stülpnagel's emissaries and army trucks full of dissident Wehrmacht units. News of Hitler's death had been reverberating between headquarters buildings, Dietrich told her. Stülpnagel was ushering in the new order, fast, to open the way to peace talks with the Allies.

The Rose Noire was packed with German clientele standing in groups on the dance-floor, ignoring a clarinet, trumpet and drum trio sobbing out 'Bei Mir Bistu Shein'. Perhaps only Dietrich and Coralie felt the irony of a Yiddish tune played with a swing beat for German ears. Serge Martel peeled through the crowd in his white tuxedo, squeezing out smiles.

'A less greedy man would have left town by now,' Coralie said.

'Perhaps he has faith in Hitler still being alive, one devil to another.' On the journey over, Dietrich had confided that even Berlin seemed confused about how well the coup was succeeding, with conflicting messages coming out of Army Headquarters on Bendlerstrasse. 'There is a rumour the Führer is not dead, but that's the sort of counter-message we would expect from Hitler's stalwarts. Stauffenberg heard the explosion. He saw Hitler being carried out of the building on a stretcher. He *must* be dead.'

As Martel bowed them to a central table, Dietrich acknowledged the nods and salutes of fellow officers, showing Coralie how much the power-balance had shifted. Dietrich had always been admired and liked by army men, but as a peripheral figure. Now he was at the hub of a new regime. *Should be fun*, Coralie thought, *when eventually we marry* . . . She began to understand the seductive tug of power.

Martel offered Dietrich his best champagne.

'I will choose for myself from your cellar, Martel.' Félix Peyron was already shuffling over. 'Show me to the vaults you're so proud of.'

Martel looked uneasy. 'Félix can go. Tell him exactly what

you want, Monsieur le Comte, and he'll select the best variety. Why would I employ a sommelier and do his job for him?'

But Félix groaned. 'I can't go down those stairs again, Monsieur Martel. My knees are agony. You'll understand what arthritis is one day.'

With a twitch of disdain, Martel yielded, though he turned to Coralie and said, 'Mademoiselle de Lirac, I don't advise you to come with us. The cellar has an uneven floor, and I cannot vouch for the size of the spiders down there.'

'I'm not frightened of spiders.' Linking her arm with Dietrich's, Coralie followed Martel to a side exit. '"Armed and glorious",' she whispered. 'If I see a man-eating spider, I'll shoot it.'

Martel opened the cellar door using keys he'd taken from Félix. He switched on a cobweb-strewn ceiling light and led the way down. Dietrich came last, shutting the door behind him. The cellar was a long room, dug out of rock, its walls lined with racks laden with bottles that mopped up the sound of their footsteps.

'Monsieur is fond of Pissotte, but may I suggest something equally fine?' Martel began describing the grape varieties of a particular region.

Dietrich produced his gun and said calmly, 'Serge Martel, I am placing you under arrest for collaboration with the Gestapo. You have, in return for payment and favours, committed atrocities in contravention of all legal and moral principle. Raise your hands.'

Martel had been reaching for a bottle. He turned to Dietrich, gin-pale eyes flat with shock and fury. 'By what right?'

Dietrich held the Enfield absolutely still. 'I act under the authority of General von Stülpnagel.'

Martel pulled his lips back in a vicious smile, measuring Dietrich's resolve and his own likely fate, Coralie judged. She wanted a gun in her own hand, and was trying to loosen the strings of her evening purse when Martel leaped, fists first. Dietrich fired and, after a moment of strange suspension, Martel crumpled, face down. Blood oozed through the exit hole in his white tuxedo.

'And so the world is remade afresh.' It was Félix Peyron, who had stumped down the cellar steps to join them. 'I guessed your mission, Monsieur le Comte. Nobody saw you leave the club, and no noise escapes this vault. Please, return upstairs and I will lock up. Later, I will throw Martel's father's old war pistol down beside him. I know where it's kept. If the world believes Martel took his own life, it will save you much embarrassment, Monsieur, Madame.' He bowed to Coralie, then addressed Dietrich. 'A Pommery grand cru, Monsieur?'

Dietrich shook his head. 'I hardly think—'

'He is in Hell, Monsieur, atoning for what he did to little Julie and all the other girls he hurt and violated. Go and dance.'

'Dance?' Coralie echoed.

'Did you not see? Our swing band left to join the Resistance and we have a new trio, all as old as me. They have to lie down between sets. Please dance, it will encourage them.'

A mournful tune greeted Coralie and Dietrich on the dance-floor. But they did as Félix wanted, and wound their arms around each other. It was too crowded for them to move much. 'I'd have put a bullet in Martel if I'd got my gun out,' Coralie whispered. 'That Gypsy said I would kill.'

'She said that only to give you your shilling's worth.'

'You may mock, but she also said I'd spend my life making hats.'

'After you told her you worked in a hat factory, no?'

'Have it your own way, but I killed Serge Martel in my mind, so I'm off the hook.'

The band struck up 'Lili Marleen', the song that had become the favourite of the Afrika Korps, translated into French and English and played everywhere. Dietrich sang the refrain in her ear.

They returned to their table to find champagne. Pouring it, Félix said to Coralie, 'Would you do us the honour of singing a number with the band?'

'I haven't practised,' she objected. Sing, with gunshot ringing in her ears? 'I don't have a repertoire.'

'Neither have they.' Félix gloomily indicated the band. 'Keeping them alive the whole night is a triumph.'

Dietrich said, 'I have never had the pleasure of hearing you sing.'

So she sang 'Lili Marlène', the French translation, and calls of 'Encore!' persuaded her to sing it again, in German. Félix came to the edge of the stage, clapping as he walked. 'Will you sing "The Lambeth Walk"? It made me laugh so much when you did it all those years ago. You trounced the Corsicans!'

That was putting a gloss on it, even given Félix's penchant for flattery. She'd actually sparked a fist-fight, having pretty much announced to everybody listening that she was a Londoner. Not her finest exhibition. From her place behind the microphone, she saw that Dietrich was talking with a man, a civilian with a coat slung over his arm, wearing the sort of cap sports-car drivers had worn in the 1920s. Talking . . . He should be watching her! 'D'you know "The Lambeth Walk"?' she asked the band. They did, just. 'Play it slow as you like.'

She sang it in German: '"Do you know Lambert's night-club . . ."' At the end of each phrase, instead of 'oi', she did her best imitation of Marlene Dietrich, purring, '*Nicht wahr*?'

People laughed. But her mind was off her singing because she'd realised that it was Kurt Kleber with Dietrich. Something in his posture drew fingernails down the back of her spine. She held on to the last note for twelve beats, curtsied to the audience, blew a kiss at the band. Hitching up her dress, she hopped off the stage. At the table, Dietrich took both her hands. The scar Hiltrud had carved on his cheek burned red. 'It is over, Coralie. Hitler survived. My friends in Berlin, Stauffenberg and Olbricht, are dead. Executed. It is over. We have failed.'

Kurt said, 'I am taking Fritzi away, I can't risk remaining here. There will be reprisals against anybody seen to be a traitor. Make Dietrich leave, Coralie. Do not wait for arrest.'

Dietrich said fiercely, 'Stand your ground, man. What have you to fear? You were never part of Valkyrie. You were not even part of Dachterrasse.'

Kleber shook his head. 'Of course I was. We swore fidelity in the flat on Vaugirard. We were the unbreakable circle.'

'Unbreakable?' Dietrich had kept Coralie's hands and she felt his bitter, bitter anguish. 'Not you, Kurt. You have been false for a long time. It was you who betrayed me to Reiniger.'

'This is insane!' Kleber's facial scars stretched white, is if they might tear open. 'Betray you to Reiniger? You are my brother officer!'

'True. You stooped even lower. You dared not approach Reiniger directly, in case the information kicked back on you. You used Serge Martel as a conduit.'

'What are you talking about? It was that art-dealer friend of yours who betrayed you. Coralie,' Kurt appealed to her, 'you know it was so.'

'Not any more,' she came back staunchly. 'Not for months.'

Kurt looked at her, then Dietrich in puzzlement. 'You went after him. You believed in his guilt.'

'In the heat of the moment,' Dietrich conceded. 'You, on the other hand, not only accepted a stranger's guilt, based upon a casual word, you were instantly fired up to kill him. Such speed is always suspicious. You had a gun ready, no?'

Coralie, always keen to have facts lined up correctly, interrupted, 'No, Fritzi had the gun.'

'And when I saw it, I knew that another man's downfall had been prepared that evening.' Dietrich looked straight at Kleber. 'Mine.'

'You are raving, Dietrich. You are my friend,' Kurt insisted.

'Fritzi's not a woman to go out with a gun in her bag. That sort of thing is for hard-bitten Annie Oakleys.' Dietrich gave Coralie a smile. 'She was carrying it on your behalf, and she had it with her at the Rose Noire.'

'To shoot you?' Coralie had believed Dietrich to this point, but now her certainty wavered. Hadn't Kurt Kleber nearly killed himself in his determination to assassinate Hitler?

'Not to shoot me,' Dietrich said. 'For me to shoot myself. The scenario was that Reiniger would take us to Martel's office, where Martel would make his accusations. We would be damned as conspirators, you and I. You would be dragged away while I would be offered the honourable way out by Kurt. A bullet to my own head, befitting my rank. That way, neither Kurt nor Reiniger could be held responsible for my death. The plan went awry because Martel did not hold to the line, and Julie fell apart at the first question. Reiniger was never sure enough of his ground to arrest a former brother-in-arms of Reichsmarschall Göring, but he has stalked me ever since. You, Kurt, how do you plead?'

Kurt gave a shrug. 'I plead loyalty to the Führer, except in one thing. I am here in good faith to warn you to leave Paris, or perish. *Heil Hitler!*'

They watched him go. 'Why did he do it?' Coralie asked.

'In the beginning, before the war, he was violently against Hitler. It was his idea to plant a bomb in a Munich beer cellar where Hitler and his commanders held a rally once a year on November the eighth.'

'Our birthday.'

'For so many reasons, an unforgettable date. When we met at the Expo in 1937, Kurt was already laying plans. He thought of the name "Dachterrasse". He was the leader, the one learning to build explosives, the one who would make the bomb. The third man you saw was Stauffenberg, who was to recruit others, and I was to visit the beer cellar in Munich that November 1937 and make sketches of the interior, the position of pillars and so on. We planned to strike the following year. But when I went that first time, the place was so crowded I couldn't record anything useful. We agreed instead that I would carry a bomb personally into another event where the Führer was to speak, and detonate it myself.'

'Kill yourself?'

'Exactly. Easier, really, than trying to plant a bomb and hope it goes off at the right moment. Then that event was cancelled, and the next. Shortly after those failures, Kurt crossed some wires while working in his cellar and he nearly died, but he recovered. The following year, 1938, I went again to Munich, and this time got a better position and was able to memorise the layout of the room. But Kurt, instead of relishing another attempt, began putting it off. The time wasn't right, the political mood of the country wasn't right. I disagreed but did not press. Kurt had been through so much. And, you know, in the first year of war, everything fell to our army. Hitler was invincible and somehow I think that Kurt fell under his spell. Fritzi, who had been solidly behind her husband, lost her nerve too.

She did not want to lose her man, and added her voice to the doubts in his head.'

'So he turned traitor?'

'Not at first. He kept the pretence of Dachterrasse going well enough to convince me, but I think now he was playing a two-sided game. I see it in hindsight, but it was not until we were in Serge Martel's office that I realised there was a traitor and that it had to be a man close to us. One who understood the nature of "sacrifice". That word was spoken several times that night, yet it is not a word ordinary people use.'

'Admit it, you suspected Teddy. And me, just for a little moment.'

'Teddy for a moment, but never you. Not even for a second. I am so sorry, Coralie.'

'Why sorry?'

'For bringing you into something so treacherous. So final.'

She didn't like 'final'. 'Where now?'

'To rue de Vaugirard. You will go to Switzerland, my darling, and I will wait in Paris to see what happens next.'

She tried every argument. 'You are *passerine*. You perch, you fly off. So let's fly off.'

'I lied. I am not that way at all. My home-hopping and country-hopping was due to an unhappy marriage, to my need to find saleable art, and it was the price I paid for rejecting the Nazi religion. It is hard to live in one place when you cannot speak and think the same as everybody else. As for leaving Paris now, I cannot. I knew from the start what I was risking, and had we succeeded, I would have shared in power. I cannot now desert General von Stülpnagel, or the Abwehr and Luftwaffe officers who have jumped side. Kurt was right in one thing. There will be reprisals.'

'I won't let you sacrifice yourself. I love you too much.'

It was just gone three a.m. when they left the Rose Noire.

He would have preferred silence on the journey home, but Coralie had the fidgets. She was planning.

'We'll go to Dreux, to Teddy's château.'

'Dreux is being bombed. The Allies want to wipe out the airbase there.'

'South, then, to Spain.'

'The Wehrmacht is surging north. You have never seen armed columns on the move, Coralie. They are being attacked by the Free French Army, and strafed from above by Allied fighters. It would be suicidal. You will take a train to Annemasse, the French side of the Swiss border, then cross into Geneva. God willing, we will meet there when it is all over.'

She demanded he show her the cyanide capsule in the ribbon of his *Pour le Mérite*. 'I need to know you have it.'

'You no longer have yours. How can I use mine, knowing you cannot?'

'It's different for me. I couldn't take it anyway, not now. I could be pregnant.'

He let her unfasten the ribbon so she could peer at the stitches she'd put in four years ago. He made no objection when she knocked on the soundproof glass behind the driver's head and asked to borrow a cigarette lighter. He had booked a car tonight because he'd been so certain that, by dawn, he would be travelling in dignity to Army Headquarters.

The driver handed over a lighter, before turning the car on to the pont au Change. The river gleamed mirror-black because tonight was the dark of the moon. Had Stauffenberg's bomb been closer, or more powerful, a new moon might have risen on a world remade.

'This isn't my work.'

'Mm?' Dietrich drew his gaze from the river, and saw what Coralie was showing him. 'I watched you make that pocket, and we discussed how many stitches would make the pill secure, while allowing me to bite through.'

'These are not my stitches. They're half as big again as mine.' She kept a chatelaine in her bag, a sewing kit on a chain with a dainty pair of scissors. A minute later, she was holding something. The pearl head off a hatpin. 'Explain.'

'I did not put it there. If you did not . . . Hiltrud.' A last poke from his wife, from the grave, telling him he was a coward? He flicked the pearl out of the window. 'That takes care of that. At home, we will pack a case for you and this car will take you on to Gare de Lyon. You will be safer there than with me.'

'No, Dietrich.'

'By tomorrow night you will be with Ottilia and Max, Teddy and Noëlle.'

'Please come too.'

He kissed her face, tasting salt tears. 'In Berlin, I gave General Olbricht my oath of allegiance, and I am Prussian. To me, such an oath is unbreakable. Valkyrie struck at the heart of power, and there has been no leniency for Stauffenberg, for Olbricht.' He did not want to say, 'And there will be none for me,' but why lie to himself? He had staked everything for Germany's honour, and the account remained to be paid.

Coralie watched Dietrich put her suitcase by the door. He'd had to pack for her and now he put a coat around her shoulders, one of Ottilia's, quilt-lined with deep pockets that engulfed the wad of francs he gave her now. 'Keep some in your shoe in case your coat is taken from you. You have your papers?'

She nodded. 'Please come too, before it's too late.'

He ignored her. 'I need to tell you something important, something you must pass on to Max von Silberstrom. Are you listening?'

'Yes.'

'He must not let Ottilia sell any of the Dutch masters from her art collection because, like the Dürers, they are all fakes. Their grandfather was cheated into buying some of the best forgeries on the market, and I have kept the fact secret for years.'

Astonishment momentarily lifted her misery. 'I always thought you were trying to nab them for yourself!'

'I know you did, my darling, fuelled by Teddy, who could never understand why I sold only select items, and none that he wanted. You see, the perceived value of the collection underpins Max's credit with the Swiss banks. If fakes slip into the market, he will be ruined. Tell him, but not Ottilia. Promise me.'

It was she who heard the sound. The soft click of a closing door. She said, 'There's someone in the building.'

He went still and listened. 'Get your evening bag, quick.'

A panicked search, until she found it on the sofa in the sitting room. Dietrich extracted the Walther and replaced the Enfield in his holster. The Enfield, he shoved under the sofa whose decorative fringe flopped back over it.

Feet on the service stairs. A moment later, the apartment door yielded to a splintering crash. Reiniger was in the room. Three men were with him, pointing handguns. They all wore creased suits and Reiniger's collar was torn. No longer that air of clerical reserve. His face twisted with triumph.

'Generalmajor von Elbing, you joined a criminal conspiracy

to overthrow our beloved Führer and subvert the army. You are under arrest for treason.' He came right up to Dietrich and slapped him hard around the face. 'I thank you for the very uncomfortable night I have spent under sentence of death. Believe me, it will give me the greatest pleasure to repay the compliment.'

Coralie cried out as Reiniger tore off Dietrich's *Pour le Mérite*, striking his throat so that one of its swallow-tail points drew blood. 'I will smash one bone in your body for every year you had the insolence to wear this medal. When I have finished, I will drag your broken, naked body down the Champs-Élysées as a warning to every stinking traitor and terrorist in this city.' He spat in Dietrich's face.

Dietrich kept his back straight, but his voice betrayed his shock. 'I will come with you, Reiniger, but I expect to be treated as a military officer and, dare I suggest, as innocent until trial.'

Reiniger laughed in mock-disbelief. 'We will conduct our trial at avenue Foch. We'll have fun there, and finally find out if your whore really *is* English, after all.'

Dietrich stepped in front of Coralie. 'Leave her. She has had no part in your humiliation. She is a civilian, a non-combatant.'

How many years had she dreaded this moment? Her legs had turned to cold jelly. Her lungs wouldn't fill properly. But her mind raced ahead. Dietrich wanted to protect her, but his power was gone, soaking away, like the blood into his shirt collar. Of course she'd confess to being English. She might hold out a brave hour or two, but sooner or later, she would talk. She would betray Dietrich, and Ramon, and Bonnet, Louise Deveau, Arkady and Una, and anybody else whose name came in on the tide of her terror. When the pain grew intolerable, she would betray Dietrich's last secret. She could hear herself, voice stretched to an animal rasp: 'Ask him why he's circumcised.'

How Reiniger would relish that. The aristocrat who had made a fool of him was the ultimate torturer's plaything – a traitor and a Jew.

Dawn light was stealing through the window. Dietrich stood in its aura, once again her St George. Bloodied and doomed, but so beloved. So human.

He caught her looking and hazel eyes sent her everything she needed to know. He touched his throat, where his medal had hung, a gesture of hopelessness. He caught her eye again and, for a moment, she saw a plea in his own. *You always did have the last word, Coralie. Lawless and unsinkable, pulling keys out of pockets and rabbits out of hats. Can you do something for us now?*

She couldn't see any way out. Those cyanide pills had been their insurance against this moment, and they'd lost them, discarded them, because they had never truly believed it would come. All they had now was whatever they could pull from their human armoury. Defiance, courage . . . Dietrich must have read her mind because he found a smile and mouthed, 'You are brave.'

Brave enough to pull off one last trick? To slam the lid on Reiniger's triumph? Fire a shot into the heart of the Nazi regime? To kill?

Could she . . . Dare she? A Gypsy had told her she would.

'I'm going to be sick,' she said, and plumped down on the sofa, dropping her head between her knees. She reached down through the silken fringe and pulled out the Enfield.

She pointed it and pulled the trigger.

Dietrich von Elbing died instantly.

Chapter Forty

28 April 1945

They would have invoked pity from all but the most war-hardened hearts. Hundreds of women with haunted eyes, the marks of abuse on their flesh. Shapeless coats disguised malnourished shoulders. Knotted scarves kept the wind from emaciated faces.

Two women walked so slowly, they got separated from the main group. One was grey-haired, with anxious grooves running from her nose to the sides of her mouth. Wearing mismatched ankle socks and heavy shoes, she hobbled across the concrete dock, each step a painful kiss. A younger blonde woman waddled after her, breathing in short gasps. She was so pregnant, her coat gaped open. The ragged dress beneath, filling with sea wind, ballooned over her belly. She was supported by two Swedish Red Cross nurses. They'd wanted to carry her off the ferry on a stretcher. She'd refused. 'My feet want to feel free ground.'

As they came in sight of the white buses that would take them to reception centres, to baths, clean beds and nourishing food, the older woman began to sob. 'Why me? What did I ever do in my lousy life to deserve this luck?'

'Can't think, Una.' Coralie dug a knuckle into her swollen waist to dispel a deep, driving pain. The journey from Ravensbrück concentration camp into Denmark had ended months of nightmare. A short sea crossing had brought them to neutral ground, while behind them, Germany was being pounded to destruction. She knew what Una meant. They'd been plucked from likely death because they were French and American. 'Whatever kept you going kept me going. You saved me, Una—' The word dissolved into a wail as Coralie's pelvic muscles went into a violent contraction. She panted, 'It's coming.'

'The baby? Right now? Hey, it'll be a Swedish citizen.'

Coralie didn't care. All she knew was that this baby was skipping an entire stage of labour. Having hung on for friendly soil, he or she could wait no longer. She was going to give birth to Dietrich's child on a bare dock.

Epilogue

Excerpt from *In My Fashion*, the autobiography of Una, Viscountess Kilpin, first published in London, 1960.

It now behoves me to say something about hats, and to introduce you to a dear friend and fellow beater-of-odds, Coralie de Lirac. Who, when not rustling up delicious frivolities in her salon on London's Bond Street, goes by the name of Mrs Donal Flynn. These two ladies are not one and the same and beware anybody who calls her Mrs Flynn at work or Mademoiselle de Lirac at home.

I put her success down to her complete understanding that a superb hat makes a plain woman lovely, a lovely woman beautiful, but is always subordinate to the woman herself. She will not sell a hat off the shelf. Should you go in demanding 'one the same as so-and-so' you will not get it. Bribery and tears won't work.

Let me reveal an insider's titbit: Mademoiselle de Lirac employs only the best technicians and rewards them well, never stealing the credit for their efforts. A working partnership with Miss Jean McCullum of the long-extinct Pettrew & Lofthouse resulted in many scintillating collections. Recently, following Miss McCullum's retirement, Salon de Lirac employed its first male *premier* in the youthful shape of Alexandre Zénon, who is the grandson of a well-respected *première* with whom Mad-emoiselle de Lirac worked for some years in Paris.

I am well known for only ever wearing hats by de Lirac, even in Paris, and have done all a woman can do to persuade Coralie de Lirac to reopen in the City of Light. She is adamant that home is now London.

Derby Day, Epsom Downs, 1961

They had a horse running in the big race. An Irish thoroughbred called Whiter-Than, bought as a two-year-old and in training at Epsom.

'I don't know what made you buy a grey,' Coralie said to Donal. 'Grey horses are never properly white, so even if he wins, it's a bad advertisement for the launderette king of South London.'

Their son, Patrick, eleven years old and now grown up enough to join his parents on a works outing, said, 'I wish you'd called him Scrub-a-dub, Dad. I'd like to have heard that over the loud-speaker. "Scrub-a-dub goes into the straight like a bar of soap off a lino floor."'

Their eldest son Derek, sixteen, wearing a suit with narrow lapels and even narrower trousers, gave his brother a friendly clip round the head. 'The Jockey Club wouldn't let an idiot like you think up a name.'

Their father agreed. 'Even horses need their dignity, Pat. Imagine running as Scrub-a-dub with Her Majesty and the Queen Mother looking on. Did you put my bet on, Cora?'

'Fifty quid each way on the lad.'

'I said "on the nose".'

'I heard. Whiter-Than might come in the first three, but he's not going to win. When we visited the yard yesterday, I didn't feel a thing.'

'Who did you back?'

'Psidium.'

'The one I can't pronounce? You're mad, you know.'

Maybe. Psidium was running at sixty-six to one. 'He's got a French jockey and he's owned by Madame Plesch, who not only has the virtue of being a woman, she's a friend of Ottilia's. *And* I felt a little *whoosh* when I saw his name.'

'Your mother's a witch.'

Coralie kissed Donal's cheek, and asked him to go around the red double-decker party bus, making sure their guests all had a drink. Derek was supposed to have done the honours, but he found the giggling millinery girls too much, interpreting their coy looks as teasing. *Give him a year or two*, Coralie thought, *and he'll work it out.*

They'd hired the double-decker for the mostly female staff at Coralie de Lirac. Donal's washeteria staff were also on board, as were the various accountants and secretaries who kept their two businesses on the rails. Everyone was mingling happily.

A windless day. Sun shimmered off white rails and the air was a cocktail of crushed grass, frying meat and car exhaust. *How could such a brimming place be so full of ghosts?* Yet it was.

There was her father shouting, 'Manna from heaven. Our girl has picked the winner!'

And her mother, saying, 'I've had enough,' and leaving.

There was the ghost of Dietrich, hopping with pain because a cocky girl in a stolen hat had stamped on his foot. There was Ottilia, ashen-faced and remote. Donal, cradling hot sausage buns and ginger beer, telling her she was mad to back a horse called Mid-day Sun.

Taking off her gloves, sending silver and coral bracelets clashing down her wrist, she extracted a powder compact. She checked her makeup, moving the mirror an inch at a time to reflect eyes, lips, cheekbones. 'Forty-six. Where does it go, the time?'

She still had good bone structure and a tight jaw line, but close up, lines and liver spots recorded the starvation of Ravensbrück. She patted on powder to disguise them. A careful diet, expensive creams, a decent hairdresser and dentist made the best of what she'd brought home with her.

At least she could afford good clothes. Today it was an ivory silk suit with a pencil skirt and box jacket, round-necked with big, same-fabric buttons. The hat, from her spring—summer offering, was a straw bowler, high-crowned and shallow-brimmed. She'd gone Una-esque, wearing only white, cream and black nowadays. It wasn't a neurosis, it was a form of discreet and perpetual mourning.

She'd tracked her mother down a decade ago, just in time to say goodbye. Florence had not gone to New York with a fellow actor. That had been a ruse to put Jac off her trail. She'd gone up north, to 'old York', taking her savings. She'd called herself Mrs Mason, given birth to a daughter conceived from a short-lived affair and lived by running a boarding-house for theatrical folk. When Coralie found her, she was in the last stages of pneumonia and pleurisy, being cared for by Coralie's half-sister Gwendolen. A strained meeting, full of emotion and robbed of a resolution because Florence had forgotten so much, and could not speak easily.

She'd cleared up one mystery, however. 'You ran after me at the racecourse, and I didn't wait. You poor little kid.'

The memory that had, for years, spooled through Coralie's

head, like a broken cine film, gained its missing segment. When Florence's control had snapped, little Cora had slithered off her father's back and slogged through the mud, begging her mother to come back. Cora had turned her ankle, and the heel had broken off her shoe. *Her* heel, not her mum's. Florence had bought them matching shoes, two pairs for the price of one, because Cora had been a gangly child with the same size feet as her pint-sized mother. Just ten years old, she'd stuffed the heel into her pocket and struggled on, shouting, 'Mum, come back!' until she realised she was shouting at strangers.

Gwendolen was nice, if sometimes a little 'actress-y'; she'd followed Florence on to the boards. They wrote to each other once a month, and Coralie sent Gwendolen a hat from every collection.

Talking of which, over on the other side of the course, in the members' enclosure, Noëlle would be soaking up the sunshine and, hopefully, buckets of admiration. Coralie had made her daughter a coolie hat of white sisal with hot-pink daisies for this gala race. Worn with a sleeveless white dress, it perfectly suited Noëlle's exotic, elfin style. Donal had put Whiter-Than in Noëlle's name, as a surprise Christmas and twenty-second-birthday present. So it was Noëlle, accompanied by Ottilia and her second husband, who was rubbing shoulders with the racing elite today. If in the extraordinarily unlikely event the horse won, Noëlle would lead him out in front of the Queen.

Coralie didn't grudge her daughter the honour, and Donal preferred being on a bus, ladling out the champagne. He was never wholly at ease among public-school types – too much the self-made barrow boy – whereas Noëlle had grown up among intellectual refugees and expatriate aristocrats. She spoke four languages, attended university in Zürich and weekended in Paris. It hadn't hurt her prospects in life that she'd also inherited much of Teddy Clisson's wealth on his death. Ottilia's husband, an American called Tom Finkelman, who had replaced the vain wastrel Frantz Lascar, had encouraged Noëlle's intellect. He'd foreseen a career for her in industry or international diplomacy. *Good thing she has a sweet nature*, Coralie often thought, or she might have floated away from them, like a helium balloon. Though family life in Coralie and Donal's London home assaulted her refined senses, Noëlle visited several times a year. Maman, Papa-Donal, Derek, Patrick and the twins, Amelia and Donny, were her 'other family'. *We share her*, Coralie acknowledged. The price of sending her away.

It was Patrick who announced that the big race had begun. 'Mum? Can't you hear everyone shouting?'

'I was miles away. Here, borrow my binoculars.' She clasped the front rails of the bus, aware of her girls crowding behind her. Tipsy. They must be, or they wouldn't be getting so close. Her staff lived in awe of her. Not because she shouted or found fault. The loudest noise she ever made was to rattle her bracelets, her way of making sure they always knew she was coming so she didn't catch them talking about boyfriends, or making cheeky remarks about her. They kept their distance because she worked in a quiet bubble, impenetrable except by loved ones. They knew nothing of what she had survived because she never talked of it. They didn't know that she'd been taken away in a car by the Gestapo, or what those beasts had done to her. They didn't know about Ravensbrück. This clean, modern world screened out such things.

She carried the memory in limbs that could not dance, in a fear of elevators and a terror of Alsatian dogs. A Gypsy not half a mile from there had told her she would kill, back when her idea of evil was her dad's drunken fists. Back when the notion of a loving execution lay beyond her mind's boundaries.

'Whiter-Than didn't make a good start, I'm sorry to say.' Donal pushed through the press of shrieking girls to put his arm round her. 'You're not using your binoculars.'

'I gave them to Pat. They make my mascara claggy. You do the commentary.'

'All right. They're round the first big bend, careering down towards Tattenham Corner. A whole lot of brown horses are in the lead, and there's a white one at the back, taking his time. I think the jockey's getting forty winks before the next race.' Donal let the loudspeakers take over. Later, when the winners were written up, his jaw dropped. 'Psidium first? Sixty-six to one? How do you do it, Cora?'

'If you have to ask, you'll never know. Don't look glum.'

'This is the face of a man who just lost a hundred pounds.'

'Fifty, you said.'

'I put another fifty each way on that bloody white horse.'

'Then it's a good thing you've got me, Donal Flynn.' She put her hands to his face. Her left hand carried her wedding band and pearl engagement ring. On her right, she wore a heavy gold ring with a ruby, and one of coral in memory of Ramon Cazaubon, who had been killed at Mont Mouchet, in the Auvergne, in June 1944. Of those dear, Paris friends, only Una and Ottilia remained part of her life. Louise Deveau had survived the war, but now lived almost as a recluse in her flat on rue de l'Odéon. Arkady Erdös had died upon a bed of leaves, as his mother had fore-told, falling in the Tronçais forest while fighting with the Maquis d'Auvergne. His fellow Vagabond, Florian Lantos, thrived. He lived in Brittany with Micheline and their children, having taken over his father-in-law's farm. Coralie had visited a few years before, and had found Florian looking and sounding almost like a native Breton. Only the dulcimer gathering dust on top of a cupboard linked him to the hungry, nervous lad who had come to her for shelter.

'Where are you, my love?' Donal asked anxiously. 'I sometimes think your mind is in Paris, along with your heart.'

She held his gaze until she found the words that expressed what she felt for the man who had mended her, married her, taken her firstborn son as his own. He was still handsome, though his black hair was flecked with grey and his frame had filled out with good living. 'My heart is here, with you. You are the best of fathers, the best of friends, the best of lovers.'

'There's a "but". There's always that with you, Cora.'

'But . . . you're a lousy picker of horses. Leave that to me, Donal Flynn.'

Acknowledgements

Second novels have a reputation for being hard to bring into the world, and while I dislike clichés, or indeed, being a cliché, I have to say that there were some tears wept over the keyboard. You have all your life to write book one. Book two comes with deadlines attached and not a few expectations, so thanks to everyone who helped me through it. *The Milliner's Secret* would never have been revealed had I not had support on the way.

Firstly, my agent Laura Longrigg and editor Kathryn Taussig for being stalwart champions of my writing. Thanks to Nikki Dupin for the beautiful cover design and to Hazel Orme for her exemplary copyediting.

Heartfelt thanks to the Suffolk friends and neighbours who have hauled me through some pretty tough stuff this last year. Rusty and Amber have honourable mention, for being unconditionally loving Labradors and getting me off my chair at regular intervals. To Sam L.E., thanks for being yourself. To Chrissie, my sister Anna and Mel Hayman-Brown for always being at the end of a telephone. And to Mattie, Benita and Travis, three beautiful souls who will always remind me that life is best when it's lived simply, in the present and with friends.

Natalie Meg Evans
Suffolk 2015

Some Hat-Making Terms and Techniques

A hat is usually made up of three parts:

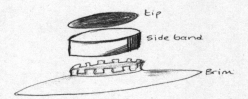

It can be made of anything – velvet, silk, felt, woven straw, leather or even rhubarb leaves if you so fancy. However, the classic hat-maker's and milliner's art is to fashion stiff fabric into shapes that hold their form, in sympathy with the contours of the human head. One traditional method is to build a foundation, using fabrics such as:

Millinery buckram, a woven cloth of cotton or linen, stiffened with starch. When moist, it is as mouldable as pastry and just as much fun.

Tarlatan, a starched open-weave similar to cheesecloth. Often used several layers' thick to form tips and side bands. Remember Meg in *Little Women*, who only had her outmoded, white tarlatan gown to wear to the Moffats' 'big party'? Like muslin, tarlatan was an artisan cloth that had its moment of glory as a dress fabric, but had been quietly doing its job as a millinery basic for decades.

Millinery wire, a fine, cotton-covered wire, is used to reinforce the edges. The three components are dressed in attractive fabric, then sewn together (for which you need a strong needle, stronger fingers and a good thimble).

The other traditional method of hat making is blocking.

This is the art of moulding fabric over a solid support

Wool felt hood

Damp, stiffened hood on the hat block; apply steam. Mould, pull, shape

Felt is sometimes pinned to the block.

(the 'block') using steam and heat to permanently distort the material's fibres. Once dry, the shape is set and can only be changed by re-moistening and starting again. When blocking, milliners generally begin with a hood or cone. They're usually made of fur felt or wool felt. A capeline is also an unblocked shape, generally used for wider-brimmed hats, and often made of straw or similar fibre.

Blocks come in an infinite number of shapes – infinite because if you want a hat in, say, the shape of the Sphinx and can get a craftsman to carve a block for you, you can have it. However, standard blocks are shaped like recognisable hat forms (see next page).

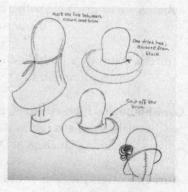

Mark the line between crown and brim

One dried hat, removed from block.

Snip off the brim

Popular hat shapes, a guide

Pillbox – originally men's military wear, resembling a box for medicinal pills. Popular through the latter part of the 19th century and in the 20th, made iconic by Coco Chanel and Jackie Kennedy Onassis.

Picture – big-brimmed, face-framing hat.

Pixie – popular in the 1930s because the fashionable, slim outline needed something brimless and simple.

Tam o'Shanter – beret with a headband, sometimes in plaid or tweed, with a rosette or pompom.

Trilby – soft blocked felt, dented crown, smallish brim.

Toque – strictly a chef's hat, but for women, a brimless cylinder.

Breton – a woman's hat with a rounded crown, brim turned up all round.

Biretta – strictly, a Catholic clergyman's hat. Flat and four-cornered, similar to a teacher's mortar board.

Gainsborough – high-crowned, big-brimmed, feathers and fal-lals, worn at a rakish slant; think Georgiana, Duchess of Devonshire.

Turban – originally Sikh or Muslim male attire, feminised by fashionable milliners. Sometimes called a *cache-misère*, meaning 'hide the shame' as it covered up bad hair days.